# WHEN

# LEGENDS

# RISE

*When Legends Rise* is an intense sci-fi thriller merged with sweet romance in a poignant redemption story. Fans of *Star Wars* or *Halo* will love this engaging story, and romance lovers will find a familiar dynamic in a new genre.

**JAKE TYSON**, author of *Vigilante's Light* and *Freedom's Fight*

*When Legends Rise* is a fantastic sci-fi thriller by Daphne Self. Combining elements of dystopia with assassins, interplanetary travel and themes of faith, it's a great read for the adult Christian sci-fi fan. The main character is a man running from an uncertain past into an even more uncertain future . . . and we're along for the ride. The minor characters are all interesting and greatly add to the story, which features jaunts to Mars and other galactic locales. Ms. Self keeps you guessing with every page, leading to an epic and unexpected conclusion well worth the read!

**C.E. STONE**, author of *Starganauts* and *Starganauts: Retribution*

Daphne Self's book *When Legends Rise* is a stellar blend of science fiction and Christianity. The story comes alive with personable, relatable characters, stunning descriptions, and gorgeous science fiction settings that will leave you excited to turn the page, but it also hits at the heart with a slow-burn romance, difficult decisions, and redemption for even those who have committed the worst of sins. For anyone who enjoys deep and realistic characterization, Christian themes without the preachiness that comes with so much of today's Christian fiction, and riveting science-fiction action sequences, *When Legends Rise* is a must-read.

**ARIEL PAIEMENT**, author of the *Legends of Alcardia* stand-alone series and the *Children of Chaos* duology

# WHEN LEGENDS RISE

## DAPHNE SELF
LEGENDS OF LIGHT | BOOK ONE

## Ambassador International
GREENVILLE, SOUTH CAROLINA & BELFAST, NORTHERN IRELAND

www.ambassador-international.com

# When Legends Rise

ISBN: 978-1-64960-348-7
eISBN: 978-1-64960-365-4
Library of Congress Control Number: 2022936236

Cover design by Hannah Linder Designs
Interior typesetting by Dentelle Design
Edited by Katie Cruice Smith

AMBASSADOR INTERNATIONAL
Emerald House
411 University Ridge, Suite B14
Greenville, SC 29601
United States
www.ambassador-international.com

AMBASSADOR BOOKS
The Mount
2 Woodstock Link
Belfast, BT6 8DD
Northern Ireland, United Kingdom
www.ambassadormedia.co.uk

*The colophon is a trademark of Ambassador, a Christian publishing company.*

*Thank you to my Lord and Savior, Jesus Christ. Without His guidance, strength, and gift, this book would never have been born. May what I write always bring glory to His Name.*

*Thank you to my family. You put up with a lot from this weirdo and nerd.*

*Thank you to my Ambassador International family. I know what it takes to release a book into the world. You have been by my side through each project.*

*Thank you to Realm Makers Consortium and The Phoenix Quill. Through you, I was able to flesh-out scenes, bounce ideas, and brainstorm.*

*Thank you to Jake and Jessica Tyson for one of the strangest things needed for a book. You two were the same height as my characters, and that helped me visualize the scenes with them.*

*Thank you to Juan-Elias Riesco and Michael Duncan. You didn't know it, but your passion for preaching the Truth birthed many of the scenes within.*

# Chapter One
# AMBUSH

Juliet 7-A stepped quietly in the soggy field. Overgrown sage grass tangled against his legs. The explosions and flares overhead cast an eerie blue and orange glow to the air. The glare of their light interfered with his headset's display. He pushed the goggles up and rested them on his head. His own senses would have to determine what threats were out there.

Juliet 7-A squinted against the night. The area ahead seemed deserted. Scrub brush offered no cover—a vast wasteland before the outer fence of the city which lay ahead.

He knelt and motioned for the man behind him to approach. "That seems to be a likely place for an ambush. Radio the lieutenant into formation. Stay alert!"

"Yes, sir, Captain!" The soldier backed away and spoke into his radio unit.

Juliet 7-A stood, slightly stooped, and advanced, senses on hyper-alert for any sound, any movement that would foretell of the enemy's position. He catalogued his surroundings. Balmy night air stuck to his skin. The pungent mix of grass and mud invaded his nose.

The insects' chirping abruptly stopped. The muffled sounds of the firefight exploded in the distance.

He sensed his quarry somewhere ahead. He held up his hand. His men behind him stopped.

Tonight, the hunter would turn into the hunted.

He sliced his hand down. A tidal wave of soft clicks rippled as weapons were made ready. He slowly scanned the area around him. Nothing hinted at the presence of those he sought.

He took a step, and his foot sank deeper into the soft earth. No. That wasn't right. The earth was too soft and the grass too sparse. He slowed his footsteps even more. His muscles tensed.

A sound didn't belong. He whirled to shout the warning. A great and heavy weight slammed into his chest. Streaks of pain and heat burned into his face.

The ground drove the air from his lungs when he fell. Mud and muck sucked at him. All around Juliet 7-A, the bodies of his team hit the ground with sickening thuds. Screams faded into the distance, and the gunfire became muffled. Then . . . nothing.

$$\Sigma$$

Pain drove into his skull. Juliet 7-A forced his eyes open, but they opened into narrow slits. Even that took more strength than he possessed. His gaze fell onto a small pool of water that glinted back at him as it reflected the sparkling array of light from the sky and then on a dark, smudged face.

Somewhere to his right, a shot pierced the air, and his body gave an indiscernible jerk at the sound.

"Check each body. Whatever moves, breathes, or otherwise shows any sign of life, shoot it. One shot." The voice spoke from his right, remarkably close by.

Another voice, farther away, replied, "All clear, sir." Another voice reported all clear after a few single shots.

The face loomed larger in the pool of water, and Juliet 7-A itched to grasp his gun, raise it, and fire it. These were the ones he had been hunting. Instead of the hunter, he had become the hunted, the prey.

"Sir, can't tell if he is alive or not."

A booted foot kicked his head, knocking his gaze skyward. The leader leaned over and peered down at him. The man's eyes gleamed, and a cold smile pulled at his lips. The barrel of the gun leveled at Juliet 7-A's head before the man's head whipped around to look over his shoulder.

Then . . . nothing.

$$\Sigma$$

A minute later? Several minutes later? He opened his eyes to a separate set of voices. Familiar voices. But he couldn't place them . . . there on the edge of his mind, too infinitesimal to grasp. He wanted to move, to reach out, to make his presence known, but nothing obeyed him. Pain surged throughout his body, one wave after another. All his nerves cried out in agony.

He forced a strangled sound from his lips and focused his mind on the pain in his body. Oblivion beckoned him. Surrender was not an option, not yet. He needed only to move just one limb—an arm, a hand. Anything to signal that he was here, bloodied, probably dying . . . but for the moment, here.

Slowly, he raised an arm.

It shone just beyond his reach, there at the edge of his fingertips. Its light was so beautiful. What was it? He needed to touch it, to bask in its warmth that had to be there. Then it dispersed, replaced by a friendly face.

"Captain?" The dark face hovered over him. Concern flooded those equally dark eyes. "Jules? Can you hear me, man?"

Callused fingers felt his wrist, and then his neck.

A hazy curtain fell between him and the man. His heartbeat thumped heavily within him. He counted the seconds between the beat of the drum.

One, two, three.

Beat.

A voice ricocheted in the dark. "Tang! Radio back to base! One survivor. Need a medvac unit immediately!"

Tang? Yeah, he was the radio operator for Juliet 7-J.

JJ!

JJ found him.

"It won't take long, my friend. I'll have you back at base soon, and we'll get you all patched up in no time. Just hang in there, man, okay? Just hang in there."

Hands tugged at his uniform and tore it open. Pain melted into numbness. Coarse gauze covered his upper chest. His friend's hands roamed over him, applying pressure along his stomach and neck. JJ's voice faded away. His face blurred and shrank into the darkness. Jules floated along in his dark and peaceful void as he claimed his sweet oblivion.

# Chapter Two
## ALONE

His peace deserted him, and in its wake, a dull pain radiated from no certain point. Wave after wave encompassed his body.

Darkness covered him; but a whisper of sound reached his ears. The medicinal fluid dripped into his IV. Shoes scuffed farther beyond. The starched sheets that covered him rustled. The machines surrounding him incessantly beeped their cadence.

Voices. He strained to understand what was being said. Why was it so hard to hear them?

"No coverage . . . not enough men to counterattack . . . wonder that he survived . . . large investment . . . " The voices faded, and darkness whirled.

"Jules?" A small nudge moved against his shoulder. "Jules? Wake up, man. There's not much time." Again, a small nudge, this time a little more forceful.

Jules moaned. No pain—just dull throbbing echoed throughout his head. He fumbled his arm out from under the sheets and clumsily lifted his hand to his head. Thick gauze surrounded his eyes and head. He grunted.

No wonder he couldn't see a thing.

Again, a deep voice whispered next to him. "Good to see you awake finally."

He knew that voice. Wasn't it there that night—how long ago was that?—he was ambushed. He forced words past a dry tongue. "JJ? What are you doing here? Where am I?"

"At the hospital in Washington. You received major injuries, and the government invested too many credits into you to let you die." The bed gave way. JJ seemed closer now. "I can't stay here long. But since you have been in here, things have been happening. Many of us have been decommissioned, and some of us . . . well, let's just say, some of us have had a change of heart. I know where your loyalties lie, Jules, so I can't—won't—tell you much. Just when you get out, I won't be here. You can find me at the Deep Blue. Remember that."

"Wait! JJ?" Jules reached out and found only emptiness. Panic—an odd sensation—set in. JJ's weight had left the bed, but Jules heard no footsteps. "Wait!"

Hard hands grasped his. "Hey. I'm here. Not gone yet."

Jules fell back amongst the pillows. "How long?"

"Six weeks in Intech Medlab. Two weeks here in this room. You're recovering." A shoe scuffled outside in the corridor. JJ tensed.

"Juliet?"

JJ's hand squeezed his. "Juliet 2-Z has been given command until you are cleared for missions." A door down the corridor opened and closed. "I have to go. Take care, my brother. So long."

JJ left, and with him Jules' only contact with reality and a friend. A cold chill followed.

His world was gone. His life was in limbo. He was alone.

Only the drip of his IV, the beep of the monitor by his head, the muted intercom system outside the room, the asthmatic whir of the ventilation overhead, and his own labored breathing kept him company.

## Chapter Three
# THE BEGINNING

"Attack!"

Jules blocked with his right forearm, twisted to the left, and rammed his other elbow into his opponent's neck. The man staggered back. Juliet followed. His foot swept his opponent's out from under him. Two strikes with his fist, cartilage crunching beneath his knuckles, and the man was unconscious.

Another came at him.

Jules ducked, turned, and struck. A solid punch on the bridge of the nose. Another turn. His crossed wrists blocked another opponent's strike.

Grab. Toss. Turn. Block.

Jules brought his knee into the midsection of one and sent him flying across the mat, and the heel of his hand met the throat of the other.

Turn. Block. Strike. Block. Toss.

Somewhere in the back of his mind, a voice commanded him to halt.

He wouldn't stop until the enemy was vanquished. The world around him faded to a dull gray. Only his enemies stayed in focus. Block. Strike.

His leg swept through the air and connected with a chest, and his hand met another in the face. He bounced once on the balls of his feet and leaped at his opponent. His arm encircled the neck to choke the life from his enemy. Fingers futilely fought against his hold. Around him, the groans of men gasping for breath barely registered.

A bright, glaring pain broke through his vision, and then darkness claimed him.

$$\Sigma$$

Jules stood on the open promenade. His plan had been to walk its length, but he had paused on the zenith of the promenade to soak up the sight of the landscape. He glanced at his wrist monitor. Thirty minutes of thinking and replaying the past weeks of training.

Somewhere along the line, he had lost his ability to focus. He needed to concentrate on the training required at the Japanese Academy. Understatement of the century calling this training complex for assassins the Japanese Academy. The academy was ruled and controlled by two universally recognized and highly lethal sensei masters, and he was lucky his rehabilitation hadn't killed him.

Jules scowled. Rehabilitation. Something was amiss in this whole situation. They were testing him more than training him. He shook his head. Maybe it had something to do with the injuries he had sustained. He had never truly recovered from them. Maybe it had something to do with Juliet 7-J's desertion and betrayal to his government. Or maybe it had something to do with something else entirely.

The memory of that phantom white light floated through his mind. A warm light, yet cool. The peacefulness of what he had seen was stamped in his memory.

Whatever it was, it left him befuddled, dangerously reckless, and angry. He frowned at his self-assessment and glanced at the bruises along his knuckles. Those two students would have been in the morgue instead of the infirmary if not for Sensei Yokomati's intervention. The master had him out of commission on the marbled floor.

Jules reached behind him and massaged the tender spot on his neck. At least it wasn't Sensei Kim, or he would have been in the infirmary, too.

The air chilled as Jules watched the sun sink until the sky became the violet dusk of evening. A damp cold seeped through the thin fabric of his uniform. He turned and stopped.

A sound that didn't belong to the night's symphony reached his ears. He cocked his head.

Hard-soled shoes clicked softly against the marbled floor of the entranceway that was two hundred yards from his place of solace.

He moved with the grace and ease of a stalking panther and headed for the source of the sound. His heart skipped a beat as he reached the entrance and peered into the darkened atrium of the sanctuary. A small contingent of men in black uniforms with red piping on the trousers stood at attention. The leader—a slender man with black hair that peeked out from under his military issue cap—spoke with Sensei Kim.

A coldness flooded through him.

The elite assassin squad of the Global Federated Territories. Juliet squad. His squad. Juliet 2-Z. They had sent Zeetoo, his second-in-command.

He narrowed his eyes. They entered the hallowed walls of the academy in full gear. No assassin could enter the sanctuary armed. To do so invited death, but . . .

What were they saying? The transmitters on the ceiling that emitted a low-level buzz prevented him from hearing. And they were turned in such a way, he couldn't read their lips.

Why were they here?

Jules pressed a fingertip against his temple. Pain flared through his head.

Stop. He didn't need to hear their conversation. They were here for him. They finally decided he was beyond retribution, beyond saving. He was a liability. His decommission day had come.

Even though he knew this day was possible, it was always a chance that it wouldn't come. Jules exhaled softly.

Never trust anyone but himself.

He hurried back to the promenade, ripping off his wrist monitor, and vaulted the shallow wall. His feet hit the narrow ledge seven feet below. Wind battered against him and caught the monitor as he flicked it into the empty air. Slowly, he inched his way down the winding stone ledge to the small depression.

He pulled the small bag from its resting spot. His cache of false papers with new background information, an untraceable account with enough credits for a ship and some to last at least a year, and the coordinates of a man who could help him disappear forever.

# Chapter Four

## HACKER

"No. No. No!" Abigail du Soleil's voice echoed through the darkened room. "Argh! That's it. If I can't access the program this way, I will find the back door. Or create one."

She pushed her dark auburn hair behind her ear. Talking to an empty room defied normality. She snorted at her thought. Her normality had meandering borders, a lot like this dratted program. She thumped her fist against the panel on the computer-lined wall. She needed another access point. Abigail surveyed the room again.

An array of wireless access machines stood in the center of the room. Risky. Less secured. But she had no other choice. She sat at its chair. This one would have to do. Should be easy.

Her jack port accessed the information. She frowned. A highly encrypted program scrolled down the screen. That was a good one. It had to contain the information on the Coalition. She quickly browsed the code that streamed across the display. Nope. Not Coalition information. But if she could download a copy of it, she could find a buyer, and that would give her enough for her passage home. But that was a mighty strong *if*. With the crackdown lately on those they deemed undesirable—hackers included—finding a buyer would be difficult.

Maybe the outlying colonies would have a buyer. She tapped her front tooth with a fingernail. That's a possibility. A buyer on one of the colonies—maybe Lunar Tarsus One—then to Jupiter Station to collect her data, and then back to Earth. Sounded simple. Abigail fought back a sneer. Couldn't let the monitors pick up on a heightened sense of agitation just because she knew that nothing in this world was ever simple. Well, maybe one thing in life was simple, but no one would believe her on that. And if she even talked about it, she would be captured and sent to the camps.

She hit a few more keys, muttered under her breath, and adjusted her earpiece. A warning ping sounded from the computer, and she froze.

"Unbelievable. I am in!"

She inserted another small, transportable jack into the computer port and watched her handheld computer. The screen scrolled sequenced numbers in a blur. Coalition data. The download actually worked this time in. Batch—her main contact for those in the territories—sure had a way with his programming.

Her handheld quickly absorbed the information. She typed on the control panel, purged the Coalition from the database, and erased her tracks and any trace of the download. It would take a serious-minded and well-schooled programmer to find any abnormality within the system. She smiled. And those types of people were not hired by the government. Those people were hunted by the government. She huffed. People like her.

She reached to unplug her handheld and paused. A high security and well-defined program flashed on her screen.

A ghost.

"Hello, hello. What are you doing there?" She tapped a few keys on her handheld. Whatever the program was, it wasn't accessible through the main programming. She watched as her handheld purged and separated the ghost program from her newly acquired information.

"Now that is interesting. New encryption system and definitely a new programming language, I think."

She inserted a data disk into the handheld and copied the two programs. Then transferred the ghost program onto another data disk. She slid her "insurance policy" into an inside slit of her jacket. Perfect for those just in case moments.

With a push, the chair rolled back into its original position. She looked around. Everything was back where it belonged. No trace.

Abigail adjusted the uniform jacket she wore and left as quietly as she came—right out the front door.

# Chapter Five
# JULIUS WILLIAMS

Abigail took a deep breath. No turning back. No matter how daunting the man who stood at the ramp of the ship looked. She needed the transportation. It had to be the one at Floridian Port that Batch was about to mention before the transmission was cut short.

The last three ships she had tried wanted too much or more than she was willing to give up. This one would be the last. Literally, as this was the last ship on the dock. Not that it was a bad-looking ship.

It gleamed in the sunlight. A well taken care of piece of machinery. This wasn't a slap-together, held-together-with-spit-and-barbwire, bypassed-and-spliced ship. It was old but not derelict. This ship was bland. An unassuming piece of hardware that did not stick in anyone's memory. This ship was perfect.

She took the last few shaky steps toward the ramp and faltered as the man's eyes zeroed in on her. Those green eyes sliced into her heart. Fear ate at her soul. He would know. He would see what she had planned. Three more steps led her to the edge of the ramp alongside an older man with white hair covered by a small headcap and white tailored outfit that contrasted sharply with his dark skin. A bishop from the nearby sanctuary.

She stood off to the side as the older man introduced himself to the green-eyed man.

"Captain Williams, I presume?"

"I am. And you are Bishop Thomas, yes? I have been waiting for you. I have the quarters to your specifications."

The bishop held his handshake with the captain a little longer than necessary and then bent his head in a small acknowledgment. "I look forward to the trip and the tour of your ship, Captain."

The captain's smile didn't reach his eyes. "I look forward to showing you. Will you honor me with your presence tonight in my office for dinner?"

The bishop stooped and collected his travel bags. "I would be delighted. Is there anyone to show me to my quarters?"

Captain Williams motioned toward the shadows of the ship. A man emerged. Abigail compared the difference between him and the captain. Deep and glinting, brown eyes peered from beneath a head of curly, dark hair. His slight build vibrated the ramp as he bounded down to greet the bishop.

"Bishop, this is Huey. If there is anything you need once settled, ask Huey, and he'll attend to your needs."

"And if we ain't got it, I can get it for ya." Huey flashed a white, toothed smile and hustled the bishop into the ship.

Abigail watched for a few moments. She bit at the inside of her cheek. Should she try and risk this ship? Risk this path she was taking? Yes, she had to risk it. Her people were waiting on her, expecting her. She was already two months late for the rendezvous.

She jerked her attention back to the captain. What a complete fool she was. He had repeated himself three times.

"Miss? Are you in need of transportation?"

Her soul seemed bared to this man as he waited for her answer. She opened her dry mouth and croaked, "Yes. But I need to know your price. You're the fourth ship I've tried today. I need a transport to the outlying colonies."

Captain Williams stood for a moment and studied her as she waited for an answer. Sweat beaded along her brow, and a drop trickled down the side of her face. There were even beads of sweat collecting along the captain's close-cropped hair. A couple trailed down his jaw over a light scar on his cheek and disappeared into his short beard.

*Come on! Hurry up.* She glanced around her, making sure she didn't move her head. Her breath caught as a troop of the local enforcers strode past. *Please don't let them see.*

"I charge only seventy-five party credits. Food is included. Leave the ship at any of the layovers at your own risk. I will not wait past the departure time. Engine room, bridge, and lower cargo areas are off-limits to passengers."

That was a steep price, but she could sell a couple of programs at the next stop to make up for the loss. She took a tentative step onto the ramp and held her hand out to the captain.

"I'm Abigail du Soleil."

The captain accepted her handshake. "Captain Julius Williams."

He motioned for the other man. "This is Huey. He will give you the tour and explain in more detail the rules of the ship. Payment shall be paid by departure time. Huey will collect."

"Thank you." She cast one last look at the contingent of enforcers and then hurried after Huey.

$$\Sigma$$

Jules watched as Huey led the small, red-haired woman into the ship. There was something about her, swimming under the surface. She wasn't someone who was running, not quite. But she was someone who wanted to stay unnoticed.

He turned back to the crowd and scanned it for a familiar face. Hopefully, his taking on the little woman as a passenger would not be a bad move. He needed the passengers for credibility, but they added a liability factor. It may not be worth the price. He needed to reach the outlying colonies without being detected.

The crowd began to thin somewhat. No indication of any other travelers interested in partaking of his ship's transportation. At least one more passenger would have been nice. Maybe there would be one at the next stop, the last one before the colonies.

He turned, walked up the ramp, and entered the main cargo area of the ship. He slapped the control panel beside the entrance. Huey walked across the gangway above as the outer door hissed closed.

"Cap, we got the passengers settled. The woman will be in the main dining around six. The bishop is ready whenever you are. Oh, and the manifest shows only one layover."

Jules climbed the steps and met Huey halfway. "You got the IDs covered?"

"Covered and falsified. Cost more this time. Timms is definitely playing both sides. I suggest going with Batch next time." Huey leaned against the railing and peered through his lashes. "Batch will be discreet. I am willing to trust him more than Timms."

Jules propped himself against the opposite railing. "I trust your insight, Huey, but make sure our change isn't premature. This is a run that has me worried. There were extra security throughout the dock this time." He pulled the small note that the bishop had given him from his pocket and read it as Huey spoke.

"Maybe it has nothing to do with our last job or picking up the bishop, but I will run a few checks. Got people owing me a few." Huey grinned and then asked, "What about the little redhead? I got a feeling about her as I showed the cabin."

He grunted and stuffed the note back into his pocket. The code the bishop had written was burned into his memory. "I'm not sure." Jules started walking the length of the gangway, heading to the main corridor. He motioned Huey to follow. "Maybe she is not running from something but definitely wanting to stay hid. I'm . . . uneasy about this, to say the least."

Jules whirled around. Huey almost collided into him.

"I want you to ask your contacts about an Abigail du Soleil. Find out what you can. We need passengers but not at the expense of blowing our cover and losing this ship. We cannot afford any close scrutiny."

Huey nodded and started to walk off but turned around. "Are you going to do your own checking?"

Jules nodded. "In good time, I will. But right now, I have to get us out of the dock and on the way. If you see Anya down there, send her up."

"Will do."

Huey sauntered down the corridor and disappeared around the corner that led to the lift shaft. Jules heaved a long sigh and headed the opposite direction to the bridge. It was time to get this ship moving and start the job. Maybe this time around, he would find JJ.

He bounded up the short flight of steps. The passenger quarters lined the small passageway. His boots thudded against the metal plating of the floor as he made his way down the short corridor. A hiss sounded to his right. Jules looked over and nodded to the bishop.

"Captain, if you can get your man Huey to collect a few more towels for me? I seem to have spilled a nice bottle of wine."

Jules paused at the opened door and peered in. A dark stain marred the red circular rug on the floor. He lifted an eyebrow. "I have him otherwise occupied. The storage bin at the end of this corridor stows the extra linen. Help yourself and deposit the soiled cloths in the chute next to it."

Bishop Thomas glanced down the corridor and nodded. "Certainly, Captain."

Jules gave him one last look and stepped away from the doorway. Next to them, a door hissed open. The redhead glanced their way, paused before she nodded once, and closed the door.

Apparently not sociable. But that brief encounter gave him a look inside her quarters. Huey had put her in the blue room. The dark blue square rug on the floor had been pushed to the side; her bunk was covered in tablets and pads with a myriad of cords linking them; and the small table set against the curvature of the wall and allowing for the passenger to see out the tiny viewport was littered with clothing.

He pushed her out of his mind and reached up to climb the small ladder that led to the front of the ship. Bright light poured from the medical bay to his left. He glanced in. No Anya. She must still be down below.

Jules ran his hand over the door's control panel and made sure it was locked and then proceeded to the end of the short hall. Up one more small flight of steps and he keyed open the door. Lighted panels, flickering monitors, and holographic projections met him as he entered his cramped bridge.

He shut down the navigation projections. The table before him still displayed the open files on Floridian Port. This port was a bust. Other than picking up the bishop for their trade. He closed down the files and pulled up the Southern Continent Port Cape files. Typographical, commerce routes, and city layout maps blossomed to life. He activated the space lane schedules. They would change over in eight hours.

Jules opened the comm. "Huey, check the chute in about ten minutes. Bring it to me when you have it."

"Will do. Anya is heading up, and I have the equipment stored."

The comm closed. Jules turned from the table and settled into the pilot's seat on the right side of the bridge. Worn and frayed cloth molded against his frame as it conformed to his body. Well, all except that one spot under his left thigh. The memory gel held a permanent knot in it. He reached forward, removed Huey's toy robot from the top of his unit and back to the co-pilot console, and then keyed open the NavComm. "Floridian Port, this is *Nightingale* asking for clearance to depart."

"*Nightingale*, please state destination and give your request code."

"Destination, layover at Port Cape. Destination, Lunar Tarsus One. Request code, zero-alpha-nine-two-beta."

"*Nightingale*, you are clear for departure. Please remain at one half impulse on thrusters until you are clear of the outer buoys."

"Confirm, Floridian Port."

Jules retracted the docking ports. A quiet bang reverberated against the hull. With quick movements, he pulled the ship away from the dock. The *Nightingale's* thrusters kicked in and pushed them further from the metal platform. Gravity brought the ship down with a small dip before it compensated and climbed into the clouds.

He entered the coordinates for the fueling station and sat back. Autopilot would keep it at quarter impulse until they reached midway to their layover.

The door hissed open.

"Why quarter impulse?"

Jules turned and regarded his medtech with a quick glance. Her white hair was pulled into a tight bun at the nape of her neck today. The white, sleeveless bodysuit accentuated her red-stained lips and paled her skin even more. She smiled at him as her ice blue eyes followed his movements across the navboard.

"We are in no hurry. The scheduled stop at Port Cape isn't until midday tomorrow. We'll be in Port for at least eight hours."

She closed the door behind her and slipped further into the room. Her citrusy scent followed her and tickled his nose. He frowned. She had a different smell about her today, though.

He sniffed. A dark, warm smell. Something earthy. "What have you been doing in hydroponics?"

"What says I was in hydro today? I've been in lower storage checking on the med supplies. We are down to dangerous levels on some of the units, especially the serum."

Jules reached out, captured her hands, and brought them to his nose. "Earth. And something darker." He smiled. "Coffee. You were harvesting the coffee beans."

She laughed and leaned against the wall. "I did. Have enough to roast and brew for the morning's offer in a couple of days." Anya surveyed her hand. "I thought I washed them well enough. So, I guess the serum is working?"

Jules shook his head. "I haven't noticed a change in awareness, other than decreased hearing."

Anya shook her head. "Your hearing is still two hundred percent above normal humans. Let me look at your eyes, Julius."

He waved her away. "Not now, Anya. Later. I'll come for a medcheck later."

"No, now." She grabbed his jaw and turned him to face her. "You've been standing all day in the sun without the shades. No telling the damage done to your retinas."

"I'll heal."

"But not as fast as you healed before. And I don't know the effects of this new serum. It may not be strong enough to keep you at your levels."

"Does it matter?" He allowed her to shine her vital pen into his eyes. The soft light soothed him. He didn't realize the effect of the harsh sunlight until now. No wonder everything seemed to have a soft haze to it.

"Yes, it does. You know it doesn't work the way you want it. The serum is the only thing keeping you alive. GFT knew what they were doing by using Serum Seventy-four on you. I can only replicate a slight variation of it. And that is what keeps your heart beating and your abilities heightened."

He pulled away. "I don't care about the abilities, Anya. Just keep me alive. That's all I ask of you."

She sighed and pursed her red lips in disgust at him. "Just alive. What else? There's more to life than a beating heart, Julius."

He was spared a retort when the door hissed. Huey stepped in. "Whew, I really should see about extending this bridge a little. Tight fit for three, you know."

Jules held out his hand. Huey dropped a small data disk into it. "It was designed for pilot and co-pilot only."

Anya grabbed Huey's arm and pulled him completely inside. "Take my place, Huey. I need to head back to Medlab. And, Julius, you stop by. It's almost time for your next dose."

The door hissed closed behind her.

"Aye, aye, madam." Huey chuckled and slid down in the copilot seat. "She sure is bossy at times. Makes me wonder if she thinks she's the captain."

Jules inserted the disk into the small slot by the NavComm and entered the newly remembered code. The display before them lit with a series of numbers and equations, followed by pages and pages of text.

"Looks like Bishop Thomas got his hands on quite a bit of info. What is his asking price?"

Jules scrolled back a few pages and tapped the screen. "That."

"Oh, man, you've got to be kidding me. There is no way that we can get that for him."

"Have faith, friend. I believe I can get some either at Lunar or Mars. Banned texts are still available if you know where to look. Bishop Thomas held up his end of the bargain. I have five places to search, and each one has been verified that he's been there. What is a little fantasyland worth? If he wants to get to the Mars Outbound Colony, then fine. We take him. If he wants us to wait there for three days and help search for this fairytale group, then fine."

Huey leaned back in his seat. "Fine. But I'm staying on the ship. I hate Mars."

"Better than Jupiter Station."

"Yeah. You have a nice scar on that shoulder to prove it."

Jules huffed at the memory.

The console pinged. "Looks like we hit the quarter-way mark. Set the engines on one-point-four impulse and fly her on, Huey. I'm heading to the medlab." Jules stood and opened the door.

"You got it. Oh . . . " Huey grinned up at him. "I uploaded the scans results to your console. They are pretty interesting."

Jules nodded and then stepped out onto the gangway. Huey's idea of interesting never amounted to much in his book, but it was worth checking out to see what had the security forces doubled at the Floridian Port.

He descended the steps. Anya already had her medical instruments laid out on the tray when he walked into the medlab.

She barely spared him a glance. "Up on the table."

Jules sighed and hopped up on the cushioned examining table. She was still miffed.

"Jacket and shirt off."

He glared at her but complied. It was just a prick on his bicep. But he had learned long ago, when she wanted to do a full examination, he had better let her. He didn't want a repeat performance of ending up on his quarters' floor, curled into a fetal ball.

Her fingers pressed against his breastbone and the scar—the biggest he sported. The rest of his body was a hack-job of scars and burns.

She picked up a small, metal stylus and poked and scraped at various places on his chest. "You still don't feel anything?"

Jules shook his head. "Never do. I told you—" Pain exploded against his chest.

Anya smiled. "That's a good sign."

He looked down at the red streak of irritated skin and probed it. Amazing. There was feeling there again. "What did you do?"

"Nothing. I told you, Julius, the serum is different. Your nerves that were severed have been repaired. I've noticed an improvement from the last time I examined you." She tapped her medpad, entering his reaction, no doubt. Always needing to know his reactions, needing to know every little change within him. He was beginning to feel as though he was one of her petri dish specimens.

Jules reached over and picked up the small vial of bluish liquid. "This isn't a variation of Serum Seventy-four?"

"Yes and no. It's something I've been working on. It's made great improvement with your eyesight. And with your olfactory nerves. And what happened just then proves that it is repairing damaged nerves inside." Anya leaned forward and placed her hands on his shoulders, squeezing. "Don't you realize what this means?"

Jules nodded. "I'll be whole again."

"Not just that, Julius. You will be able to recover from everything that was done to you."

He shook his head. "I don't know what that was, Anya. None of us do. Our memories are just the academy, the training, the missions."

She rubbed her thumbs over his shoulders, caressing his skin. Cool fingers. She leaned over and touched between his shoulder blades. "You should let me erase this."

His tattoo. His brand. J7A.

Jules shook his head. "No. Not yet."

She gave a slight huff. "I wish you would understand that if this can repair the damaged nerves, then it may repair the memories."

He had his doubts, but if she believed it, then it was worth a try. At least he had feeling back along his chest. Her hands smoothed across the red line on his chest. "What are you doing?"

She sighed. "No feelings?"

"Just your touch." He frowned. "What am I supposed to feel?"

Her lips settled into a tight line as she moved away. "Nothing?"

He raised his eyebrows. This game of hers was becoming tiresome. "I'm aware of human relations, but if that is what you are asking about, then no. Nothing. We were all chemically castrated, Anya."

Her face settled into silent outrage as she picked up the vial and inserted it into the injection gun. "I have a lot of work to do until I can make you whole again, Julius."

"And you are determined that it has to be physical interactions."

"No!" She rammed the gun against his left shoulder and pulled the trigger. A quick prick into his skin and muscle and then she dropped it onto the tray. "But you are like a robot—no feelings, no emotions, other than the standard. You are more than chemically castrated, Julius. You have been purged. I am trying to open those neural pathways. You have to feel in order to understand."

"I feel. I understand."

"No, you don't. You have friendships with me and Huey, but you look at people like they are clouds in the sky or rocks on the ground. Worth a glance, but of no consequence. I'm here because you need access to the serum, and I wanted the ability to research without GFT's involvement. Huey is here because you need a copilot and

operations man and he wanted to escape from the clutches of GFT."
She paused in her tirade and regarded him. "I doubled your dose."

"What?" Jules jumped off the table and grabbed her, squeezing her
arm until she cried out in pain. But he still wouldn't relent. "You can't
mess with the dosage! Not now! I have a meeting in two hours. What
if there are side effects? I'm in the middle of a shipment run, Anya!"

"Jules!" Tears pooled in her eyes. "You're hurting me. Stop!"

He looked down at his hand, wrapped around her, cutting off
blood supply. Jules dropped her arm and backed away. She held her
free hand over the bruised area of her bicep. He hadn't meant to hurt
her. Not his Anya. He took a step toward her and held out his hand. "I
don't know why I did that."

She accepted his hand and stepped toward him, encircling his
waist in a quick embrace. "I do. The serum is working. You will feel
angry at times, even furious, but you must learn to control it. Okay?"
She shook her head. "I didn't think it would take effect so quickly. If
I did, I would have warned you."

She smiled up at him and gave him a hard squeeze. "Soon, you
should feel a difference in how you feel about things. Try something
different. Different drinks. Different foods. No more protein and
nutrient packs. Each time you do something different, it will activate
a different part of your brain and allow the serum to work even faster."

"Okay." He hugged her back—briefly—because that was what
she wanted. "But will it really work? I'll keep my enhancements and
become human?"

Anya pushed him away with a laugh. "Julius, you are human. Just
indoctrinated and chemically altered. Get dressed. Go rest."

Jules donned his shirt. Now that she mentioned it . . . "I am tired."

"You will be, for a while. Go rest. Set your alarm for an hour. Send me the results of how you feel when you wake up. Even if it seems inconsequential. Okay?"

"You're the medtech." He dropped a small kiss on her cheek, because that was what she expected, and left her to her vials, concoctions, and instruments.

His quarters were only down the ladder and to the right. The corridor wobbled slightly in his vision. He keyed his door open and entered his room. Cool air greeted him. The small water tank in the corner bubbled. He approached it and felt the slightly gelatinous fluid. It was almost at optimum temperature. Probably another two hours and then it would be ready. He paused by his console set into the wall and reached up to bring up the stocks and trade reports. Yes, medical gel was at a premium on Tarsus One. That was good.

He closed down the report and pulled up the alarm, setting it for one hour from now. The black rug on the floor caught his shoe, and he stumbled. He frowned at his clumsiness. It had to be the serum Anya gave him. He wouldn't be taking that one again. Jules dropped his jacket onto the plush chair in the corner and then fell onto his bunk.

Anya wasn't joking about being tired. Exhaustion pulled at him, and he couldn't fight it. He turned his head and gazed across the room. Blurred vision impaired him, but it looked like a white-clothed figure stood in the far corner watching him. Then darkness claimed his thoughts.

## Chapter Six
# NIGHTINGALE

The *Nightingale*. Abigail frowned at the name. It was an unusual name for a ship.

She pulled up the GFT public mainframe. There had to be some kind of history on that name somewhere. It seemed too familiar.

Abigail opened a file about a long-ago nurse named Florence Nightingale. She read through the text. Strange to read about a war that had happened many, many centuries ago. Seemed as though war was a pivotal plot in human life. *Nurse?* She located that word. Archaic term for medstudy, a person with medical knowledge who served as assistant to a medtech.

There was lots of history on that woman. A pioneer in her field, it seemed. One devoted to helping another. But that didn't seem a reason the ship was named after her.

She entered the keyword "nightingale." Not many references. A town in the Italian Islands with that name. A list of GFT civilians with the name. She ran a quick check between them and the ship. No connections found. The biological files held an extensive file on the types of birds with that name.

Abigail expanded her search into the literary files. There.

She accessed a poem by a man named John Keats and read it. Strange words seemed to evoke some kind of imagery, but she couldn't grasp the meaning behind it.

Her personal pad lay on the bunk. She reached over, unhooked it from the jack port that was connected to the ship, and slid the datapad's access tab into the ship's console to download the poem. She'd decipher what those words meant later.

The download complete, she reattached the pad to the jack port, and let it finish downloading the schematics and navigational files. It would soon be time to try and patch into the communications to send an update to her people.

Abigail rose from her chair and keyed the door to open just a couple of inches so she could peer out.

A bang on the ladder at the end that led to the bridge echoed back to her. She pushed the door open a bit wider and glanced out.

Captain Williams staggered slightly toward his cabin. An angry, red line ran up his neck and into his hairline. He leaned against the door and swiped at his keypad. It opened, and the captain almost fell through the opening but righted himself in time.

The door slid to a close. Abigail waited a few seconds and then opened her door completely. No one seemed about. She sprinted down the corridor in her socked feet, reached up under the ladder, and attached a small monitoring device to the bottom.

She bolted back to her room and pulled up the display. The door to the captain's cabin was in perfect view, as well as the top two rungs of the ladder. It'd give her enough warning time if anyone came up or approached her room.

Abigail dug through the clothes on the table. Under the fur-lined parka was her BOD-suit. She stripped her traveling clothes away and squeezed into the tight-fitting suit. A quick twist of her hair and two pins had the thick tresses flat against her scalp so that the suit's cap would fit over her head. She reached over and pulled a face veil from the pile and attached it over her face and neck. Its clingy material nestled against her skin.

She used her personal pad to scan her body temperature. No readings other than her bare hands. She slipped the BOD-gloves over them, slid the pad into the chest pocket of the suit, grabbed some tie-lines from the pile of equipment, and climbed on top of the bunk. The top panel of the ceiling folded upward.

Abigail grabbed the sides of the opening and hoisted herself up into the narrow space between her ceiling and the flooring of the upper deck. According to the schematics, it housed Medlab, a secondary storage bay, and the observation deck. She squirmed her way forward.

She pulled out the pad. Its dim light lit the darkened space. According to the readouts, there would be a slight slope leading up, and then it would level out until a steep bump brought her to the bridge and right alongside the communication junction.

Tubing and wires caught at her and halted her progress numerous times. She had to pause each time and use one of her lines to tie them back. The slope was easy to slide over, yet it was the steep bump that offered resistance. She wouldn't fit in that narrow gap nor be able to contort her body to fit.

Abigail turned her pale light and ran it along the wall of the tight enclosure. If she could patch in through the main line, the GHOST should work well enough for her to send a message. It would have to be text only. There was no port available to access video feed.

She smiled at the thin, red line. Her fingers deftly plucked it out from behind the nav lines. It didn't take long to strip a small section off, hook her trip-mod to it, and then plug in its lead to her pad.

The lack of air circulation created a sweltering atmosphere. The gurgle of coolant underneath her could be heard as it struggled to reduce the heat. She activated the GHOST and waited. It took only three seconds to connect with the main communications. And it was enough to show her that she wouldn't be able to send a live transmission. A firewall protocol prevented her access, and the line she was connected to didn't have the parameters needed to circumvent it.

Well, at least she could compose her message, and it would be sent the next time they activated communications. She quickly typed out her message: *On way. Landing @ Lunar 1st. Be @ Mars. Advise: Jupiter? WLA.*

She accessed the GHOST and the message zipped away into a holding pattern. Her monitoring pad beeped. Someone had tripped the monitor on the ladder. Abigail pushed the wire back into place, leaving the trip-mod on it for the next time.

With a lot of squirming, she pushed her way back to her quarters and dropped down onto the bunk. The panel folded back into place. Abigail ripped her veil off and heaved a cool breath of fresher air than what she had been breathing for the last twenty minutes.

She stripped her BOD-suit off and walked to the sonic shower. What she wouldn't give for a real shower. Sonics were good, but it never left her feeling clean enough. As she allowed the shower to strip the soil and sweat from her body, her thoughts ran to the captain's quarters. She was fairly sure he had a real shower in there. And his quarters were probably a lot bigger than her little ten-by-ten.

$$\Sigma$$

An incessant beeping brought him out of a fitful sleep.

Jules sighed and propped his hands behind his head as he stared at the ceiling panels. And waited. She would call him soon.

"Jules?" Anya's voice drifted from the comm unit. "Update?"

He heaved himself off the bunk and strode to the comm. His finger jabbed the button, almost breaking its casing. "Irritated. Agitated. And quite nauseated." He let go but then pressed the button again. "You have your update. Now I have things to do, and you need to head down to the cargo bay and get a container. The gel is about ready. Time to move it to the medlab to finish the process."

He keyed open his door and strode through. She knew better than to reply. His boots clanged on the rungs as he climbed the ladder. He shifted his gaze to Medlab as he passed by. Anya was busy collecting what was needed to store the gel. She glanced up at him and shook her head.

Jules turned away. Anya could stay angry at him. He didn't care. The small nap hadn't helped dispel his exhaustion nor the irritability that seemed to be growing with each step. Huey looked up from the communications console as he entered.

"We arrived at Port Cape ahead of schedule. When we set down, we will have at least a few hours downtime before our initial load of fuel is delivered."

He fell into the chair, grimaced at the knot under his thigh, and keyed open the report the bishop compiled. "We may have some downtime right now, but when we land on Taurus One Platform, I expect to be at Bistro for a while. Did we have the payments organized?"

"Yes. I have them on this . . ." Huey reached under the console and pulled out a small datapad, which he passed to Jules. "It will allow a quick and untraceable transfer."

"Good." Jules set the datapad on the console surface to his right as Huey called in their destination and request code.

"*Nightingale*, you are scheduled for refuel. Shipment One will arrive within four hours. Shipment Two has been delayed. Please standby for further details."

"Acknowledged, Port Cape." Huey closed the connection and frowned.

Jules looked up from reading. "Notice something?"

"It was a small blip, right before I closed communications. Probably nothing."

"Once you land, run a diagnostic, anyway. Are we expecting a CME?"

Huey shrugged. "According to WeatherNet, no coronal mass ejections. Not until a day or two."

"Then maybe it's a malfunction. One of many, it seems." Jules returned to his console. "Let me know what you find or don't find."

"Did you look at the scan results?"

Jules shook his head and continued reading, vaguely aware of Huey working at the communications. His console issued a ping. He opened the new communication file and gave a small sigh. "I get it, friend. You want me to read it."

"I told you there was some interesting things on there. As in, more interesting than usual." Huey smiled and returned to piloting the ship to the tarmac.

While the thrusters sent a slight shudder through the hull as Huey maneuvered the ship into the dock, Jules opened the scan results. He sat up straighter and watched as the feed showed groups of security forces form at each of the exits.

He flipped to the next file. High-profile reports of a stolen program. He flipped to the next one. A type of encryption program apparently, a ghost program that allowed anyone to hijack navigation and communications in any system or database without leaving a trace.

Jules opened the last file. It was the security feed from The Nest Protocol, the GFT company that housed the encryption program. Body after body filed in and out of the building as they went about their daily business. His gaze fell on one figure. Red locks had fallen from the pin used to keep her hair off her neck and under her cap. And it was a "her." He could tell from her walk and the way she composed herself.

Her gray jacket was pristine and crisp. Her matching pants perfectly creased. Gloves with the NP insignia hid her hands. Yet the boots were not regulation. Close, but slight variations in color and sole gave them away. She didn't pause as she left the building, blending within the crowd of NP workers.

"Timms find this?"

Huey entered the commands for lockdown as he replied. "No. I asked Batch to do this. He had more contacts." He leaned back in his seat and stared at Jules, his fingers playing with the toy robot.

Jules paused the vid and selected the section of glass as she opened the door. Huey smiled knowingly as Jules zoomed in. She was looking to her left, yet the glass reflected her face. The same face that stared at him from the bottom of the ramp just two hours ago.

"What do we do?"

Jules shook his head. "Nothing much at the moment. After you run the diagnostic, check to see if there is even a hint of any access anywhere on the ship." He closed out the files and pulled up the security program. With a few codes, he had the security schematics on his screen. There was never a reason to waste precious power output monitoring the guest quarters . . . until now. He grabbed the stylus from the rack at the top of the console and tapped the relays he needed to activate.

Huey leaned over. "Tap that one. It's the conduit that leads to the starboard side of the bridge. She might be skinny enough to fit in there. I never thought the access hatch would be used by anyone—if she is actually doing anything, that is."

Jules activated the security for that section and closed the program. "Now we wait."

Huey nodded in agreement. "Now we wait. For fuel and for her."

Abigail entered the observation lounge. She had seen bigger ones before where couches littered the plating and small, cushioned stools were placed sporadically around the room. Yet those were on the bigger, luxury ships—the ones people traveled when they didn't care about being seen.

This ship contained no luxurious amenities. Just the basics in an area roughly twenty by fifteen. One couch sat by the long, narrow viewport. No scenic view tonight. Just the bustle and hurried movements of the docking bay at the fueling station. Nothing but gray and blues, metal and crates, fueling drivers and cargo loads.

By the couch, on either end, were tables bolted to the floor. To her left, the food stations. To her right, a table that could host an accompaniment of six. And right now, it hosted only two. She remembered Huey from her initial boarding. Yet the other person, a woman, seemed exotic in nature. Slender form, white hair that gleamed, pale skin, and ice blue eyes that watched her, calculating.

Huey rose and met her at the still-opened door. "Abigail, right?"

"Abigail du Soleil. And you are Huey."

His smile was contagious as he swept his arm around the room in a welcoming gesture. "Yes. Huey Marktov. And this is Anya Bastion, our medtech. Welcome to the Observation Room-slash-galley. Let me show you the food receptacles and how they work."

Abigail followed him to the wall where the machines were banked against a good portion of it. "These are FoodPrep Xulon Threes?"

Huey turned a surprised gaze to her and smiled even bigger. "Yes. We traded for them about four months ago. We have a larger selection than ever now." He ran a hand over the first machine. "We have chicken enchilada, chicken picado, beef tacos, cheeseburger—my favorite—vegetable soup, creamy corn chowder, and penne rosa. This is dubbed 'healthfreak.' You can select yogurt, which is hard to keep in stock, and various vegetable sticks. There's the avocado salad, which is also hard to keep stocked because of its high demand. And then there's blueberry or strawberry smoothie and various fruit slices, depending on what's in stock and available." He turned to the last machine, and his grin grew even bigger. "And this is our 'Huey's Caffeine Café.' Basically, it holds our drinks from Cap's nutrient shakes to my double shot, triple shot espresso mocha. We even have a few carbonated beverages, at Anya's request."

She glanced over the machines, surprised to find the top line on a ship like this. She wondered what was traded to gain a Xulon Three—especially three of them. "I'm impressed. The only Xulon Threes I've seen were on the *Mandolin Transport*. The design is amazing. The separation of cooling and refrigeration compares to nothing on the market. The Elon Fours were the only comparable machines, and yet they fell far short."

"You know your food preps?"

"I know machinery." She stepped up to the first machine and selected chicken picado. It had been a long time since she'd had real food—well, real food compared to what she was normally getting. True food would have been Mimi's cooking. And Miriam's. Her heart lurched at the thought of her grandmother. But she'd see her soon. First to Lunar and then to Mars. Hopefully, she would know by then if she was to return to Earth or head out to Jupiter.

The machine whirled as it rehydrated her meal. Huey leaned against the corner of the machine and watched.

"So, you're heading to Lunar? Have family there?"

"No. I'm supposed to meet a friend there; but I may be late, and he may have moved on to Mars. If so, then hopefully, I can purchase passage to Mars."

"Well, that's our second layover after Lunar, so I'm sure Cap will accept payment for an extended trip." He waited for her to collect her food and utensils and then followed as she moved down to the beverage machine. "Try the flavored spritz. It's been my favorite for a while."

She selected the strawberry-flavored drink and waited as it filled the container in the slot. Once it beeped, Huey reached in, grabbed it, and handed it to her.

"Take a sip."

And she did. The slightly effervescent feel tickled her tongue as the flavor seemed to melt across it. She gave him a nod. "I like it."

"I thought you would. Come on." He led her to the table and motioned to the bolted-to-the-floor bench.

As she sat, Anya's gaze followed her. Once Abigail was seated on the bench and started to eat, Anya returned to her food. The woman was quiet, taking in almost everything around her. Huey, on the other hand, kept up a litany of sentences as he ate. Abigail glanced at him, trying to catch up on the tale he was regaling her with.

"So, it was about three years ago when I signed my release and traveled aimlessly until about a year ago when I signed onto the *Nightingale*. And I've been with the captain ever since. What about you?"

Abigail chewed her food and swallowed before answering. "I've been on my own for about a year. My father moves around a lot, and I lost touch with him. Last I heard, he was either on Mars or Jupiter base. I'm hoping that my friend on Lunar will know how I can get in touch with him."

Anya picked at her food. "Your father moves around a lot?"

Abigail nodded. If they only knew. "He is with an excavation crew. Their contracts take them wherever they are needed." She smiled inwardly at her statement. She guessed "excavation crew" would be the truth. They did excavate the land whenever they found a new place to hide. Building underground tunnels and compounds was hard work. But it meant that her people were kept alive and safe.

Huey nodded and continued digging into his food, which had consisted of a cheeseburger and a now-empty bowl of what looked to have been corn chowder. He was currently downing a flavored yogurt. At his side was a large mug of his mocha. No wonder the man stayed hyped.

Anya took a sip of her drink. "Have you been to Lunar before?"

"Once, long ago. This would be my first time in many years. And I really don't like the idea of a layer of fused pane glass separating us from the harsh vacuum. So, I plan to stay within the walls of the hub."

Huey exchanged a quick glance with Anya. "The hubs were redesigned last year. The only closed-in areas are the personnel quarters and admin stations. All else is open to the promenade." He reached to his side and pulled a datapad off the table. "Look."

He activated the pad and pulled up the information on Lunar Tarsus One. "You may have been thinking of Tarsus Two, which is on the dark side and much smaller. It's not open to the public, though." He pushed the datapad to her.

Anya reached over and tapped the screen. It changed to the hotels and stores. "That's the part that they like to advertise. See how they make it look enclosed? It's just an illusion. All the floors and buildings open to the center area—that's called the promenade." She clicked each building in turn. "There's Hotel Reign. Hotel Rivera. There are a few restaurants: Bistro, Café Ole, and The Hot Pub. Two stores for clothing: Mamie's and GFT Subsidiaries. Then the one electronic store, D&Y. The rest are just small vendors. Since Lunar One is the main mining and exploration launch port, their revenue is determined by visitors at these places. And the visitors demanded a scenic place instead of a closed-in, metal-walled compound."

Abigail swiped at the datapad, viewing each building and noting the dark space above their "sky." She swallowed. The cold, black vacuum. Her one, true fear.

Anya gave her a gentle smile. "If you do decide to disembark at Lunar, I would suggest sticking close to the Bistro. It has the least amount of open space and uses awnings to block most of the view of space. A lot of visitors find the closeness of space to be disconcerting. Yet, credits talk, and corporations with the most credits decided on the redesign of Lunar One."

Abigail took a swallow of her drink to push back the dryness that threatened to close her throat. "Thank you. I can hopefully contact my friend and tell him I will be at the Bistro." She looked up at the woman. A warm smile greeted her.

"You're welcome. I know how a first foray onto Lunar can be."

Huey guffawed into his yogurt. "You would know!"

Abigail returned to her food and smiled as they began a light banter about who could handle Lunar Tarsus One the best.

Jules leaned back in his chair and sipped at the nutrient drink as Bishop Thomas finished his report.

" . . . it wasn't until I found the file on 7-J that was buried in the archives that I realized where he had disappeared to. Jules, you have to understand that I may be able to contact them, but I can't approach them. We bishops keep our distance in order to protect them. Our sanctuaries and our order give us immunity to GFT's law against religious orders. Because we are a benevolent society, issuing aid when needed and wherever needed and never preaching our beliefs, we are allowed to move and travel freely. The Christian Coalition and others like them, on the other hand, are an outlawed society. To expose themselves would be condemning thousands to death."

Jules regarded the older man. A half-empty plate sat before him, along with a drained mug of coffee. Between them lay a data disk that contained the latest information on JJ. JJ, who was last seen with the Coalition. As what? Bodyguard? Security? Infiltrator? Why would he join with those they had hunted?

"You said this was the latest? But it's over six months old. JJ could have moved on by then."

"It's possible. The Coalition moves around. Yet there is a permanent base. I don't know where it is. And to reach it, you must have the exact coordinates via a code, and that is given only by an elder, unless you find someone within the community. Yet they hardly ever leave."

"What about supplies? They have to gain supplies somehow."

"They are self-sufficient in many ways. What they can't produce, a select few of them are able to obtain through trades. These are usually the high-ranking members who have connections. You would be hard-pressed to find a member of the Coalition out on their own." The bishop folded his hands across his stomach and sighed. "Though it isn't unknown that there are a few who are out there, scouting out information or hacking systems to cover the Coalition's tracks."

Jules reached out and picked up the data disk, turning it over and over between his fingers. "And for this information, and what you provided earlier, you want only the books?"

"Those 'books' are the center of our faith, Julius. When you came to me two years ago for new papers and a credit line for a new ship, I told you that you were bound for something great. That's the reason you didn't die on that field. The reason you were able to escape. You told me about that light you saw. And if it's what I think it was, then these books will provide the answer you seek. And these books are needed for Mars."

"Those books can get you killed."

"Such is life. But I do not fear death, my boy." Bishop Thomas smiled. He leaned forward, propped his elbows on the table, and steepled his fingers, pressing them against his lips. "I know the risk it will take for retrieving these books. But that's the payment for what I have provided you. And once the payment is delivered, I will give you the code to access the data disk."

"It won't be a problem to gain the books, Bishop." Jules slipped the disk into his vest pocket. "I have a meeting on Lunar Tarsus. And this meeting may be able to provide at least two of them. There's also one place on Mars that I can go. It may take some time, though." Jules paused and narrowed his eyes at the older man before him. "Are you planning to leave the ship when we arrive?"

Bishop Thomas shook his head. "Oh, no. Lunar does not look too kindly upon someone from the Bishop of the Faith. I'll stay here in my quarters or in the observation lounge."

Jules nodded. "Then I will see you later, Bishop. Don't worry about the dishes. I will take care of them for you."

Taking his cue, Bishop Thomas rose and collected his coat from the back of the chair. "I'll pray for you, son."

Jules stood with him and began collecting the dishes. "Prayer is your thing, Bishop. Your God listens to you, but you need not pray for me. He does not know me."

"You'll be surprised. Nevertheless, I am praying for you."

Jules followed him to the door of his small office that was attached to his quarters. As it slid open and the bishop stepped out, a red flash caught his eye. Down the hall, the redheaded woman disappeared into her quarters. The bishop gave him one last nod, crossed the corridor, and then slipped inside his own quarters.

With the dishes balanced in one hand, Jules scaled the ladder and turned right down the narrow gangway that led to the observation deck. He bumped into Anya when the door opened.

"Julius!" She smiled and stepped back, allowing him entry. "You didn't come to dinner tonight."

"Had a private dinner with the bishop." He padded across the gleaming floor of the deck, noticing a mar on one of the plating, and deposited the dishes into the automatic cleaner.

"The bishop?" An eyebrow quirked up in surprise. "Why?"

"Why?" He paused by the beverage machine. "If I'm going to carry a member of The Faith on my ship, I need to ensure that he will cause no problems for us. Don't want the GFT breathing up our thrusters."

He reached to press the selection for another nutrient drink, but she slapped his hand away and selected one for him. "I told you to try something besides the norm. Try this."

When the machine indicated with a loud beep that the drink was ready, she reached in and pulled out a frosty glass of clear liquid. He took it from her and frowned.

"What is this?" He sniffed it. A pungent scent of alcohol invaded his nose.

"A cocktail containing vodka and carbonated tonic with a bit of flavoring." She pushed the drink back at him when he tried to hand it off to her. "No. I need to see how this Serum Seventy-four derivative handles alcohol in your system."

Jules sighed. Always with the experimenting. Yet he had time before fuel was delivered and they left for Lunar. He followed her to the couch and settled back against the soft cushions. Outside, loaders ran from one side to the other, delivering to the many ships docked at the fueling station.

He lifted the glass and took a tentative sip. The alcohol heated his throat, and it did have a pleasant burst of flavor. The taste faded, and he took another sip, longer this time. Her eyes followed his every move. Jules shrugged as the heat and taste faded again.

"It's different. I like the way the taste bursts." He leaned back. "Did you meet with the woman passenger tonight?"

"I did. She's pleasant. She and Huey got along great. Apparently, she's a technical worker of some sort. Their conversation centered more around the new Xulon Threes and then on Lunar One. She wasn't aware of the reconstruction on the colony, so we showed her where the best places would be for her to go."

"Did she say why she wanted to go there?" He pulled another long draught from the glass.

"Meeting a friend." Anya pursed her lips. "She wasn't too forthcoming about a lot, so I didn't press."

Jules nodded and then drained his glass. A slow warmth flooded his system, leeching into his bones and muscles. And just as suddenly, it left him. A bright flash hit his eyes, and he batted Anya's vital pen away.

"Stop."

"There's no reaction to the alcohol that I can see. Your eyes should have dilated by now."

"Good. But let's not use this derivative again. The reaction I had was not pleasant."

She sighed. "I already adjusted it." Anya lifted his wrist and felt his pulse. "Nothing. The serum is breaking down the alcohol too quickly for it to have an effect on you."

"So, that means I can do what I must to get what I need on Lunar. They always require drinks before a trade."

"And what is that?"

Jules barely smiled and cut his gaze over at her. "Something that doesn't concern you. Did you line up the sale for the med gel?"

Anya glared at him. "I did." She thumped his knee and rose. "I'm heading to my quarters. Get some rest, Jules. You don't get enough."

Jules shook his head. "I'm fine. I'll be on the bridge with Huey. The refueling trucks should be here soon enough."

She nodded. "Then I'll see you later. It's been a long day, and tomorrow will be longer." She stood. "Food, Jules. No nutrient packs. What's the point of the Xulons if you don't use them?"

With a kiss on the top of his head, she turned and strode to the door. It hissed open and then closed, leaving Jules alone on the deck as he watched the activity outside. He reached into his vest and pulled out the data disk. The blue metal gleamed in the harsh lights of the observation room. Jules traced the outside edges with his finger.

Just one job away from finding his friend . . .

Huey's voice from the comm unit attached to his collar broke through his thought. "Cap, found the message. You want to read it?"

He keyed open the comm. "I'll be right there."

With one last glance outside, noting the red truck heading their direction, Jules reached above the glass panel and keyed the shielding. A loud clank issued from the side, and reinforced plating slid over the viewport, cutting off the outside.

Jules dropped his empty glass in the receptacle and strode out of the observation deck. Time to see what the hijacked message said and what they may be dealing with.

# Chapter Seven
## OF THE SUN

Abigail waited. The captain never came back down the ladder. She pulled up the schematics of the ship again. Medlab to the front. Observation lounge to the right side. Storage units to the left and back. So, it was either to the observation lounge, the medlab, or to the bridge he went.

She shut down the datapad and hopped off her bunk. Time to see if there had been a reply. With quick movements, she stripped down and then donned her BOD-suit. The panel folded back easily, and with a grunt, she hoisted herself back into the narrow access.

It didn't take as long this time since most of the wires had now been tied back and out of her way. A red light on the trip-mod blinked rapidly. A message awaited.

Her fingers caught on a web of wires as she tried to fish out the lead to her trip-mod. With a grimace, she picked and pulled at them, checking and rechecking the connections to make sure they had not become disconnected with the ports. Satisfied, she gently pulled the wire to her and plugged it into her pad.

The message downloaded. An encryption program ran down the lines, dissolving the cryptic message line by line. She smiled at her father's message: *Head to 1st. Skip Jup. M timeline? MYLY. GBWY. WLF.*

A tear escaped her eye and rolled down her cheek before being absorbed by her face veil. Mars? She didn't have the credits for that. And that was the only way she was going to get the coordinates to the base.

She leaned her head against the heated metal of the access tube. It was a mistake when she had left with Liam and Fiona. Their betrayal left her stranded in the territories. And now her mistake may cost her more than she could afford.

Her thoughts ran to the program she had purged. No. It was too dangerous to sell. Maybe she could copy a few lines of code and create a weaker decryption program. It would not be like her GHOST, able to hijack nav and comms, but she could make it so that it could access weaker points of communications.

With a nod, she picked up her datapad and entered her reply: *1st. M = $. 2d/3d? Rnng Scd. Will transm after 1st. IMYLY. IAS. WLA.*

She sent the message and verified that it was in its holding pattern. There was nothing else to do but wait now. Abigail unplugged the lead, slid it against the panel but away from the wires, and then started her long, slow squirm out of the tube, her thoughts on her own longing to be back home.

$$\Sigma$$

Jules held the copy of the transmission in his hand while Huey talked with the fueling station. The second load was finally ahead of schedule and was on its way. What delayed it at first was apparently no more of an obstacle. The console pinged as Huey shut it down.

"Was that another one?" He checked the security feeds. Nothing showed on the scans. No one had accessed the tubes.

"Yes. It was in a holding pattern. Attached itself to the transmission right as I shut it down." Huey tapped a few commands and then motioned to the datapad in Jules' hand. "Should be on your pad right now. The last one slipped through when I connected with the fueling station. This one just zipped off as I shut down comms."

Jules swiped the incoming message to the top of the datapad and then pulled up the latest. He frowned at the message and then pulled up the first message that they had found. Huey had run a decryption program against them, and although it translated some, the letters made no sense in some of the message.

"Where did you get the decryption program? Timms?"

"Not this time. I used Banks. Knew him back in the day. Highly recommended by Batch. But it cost a pretty credit. Such as a lot of credits."

Jules flipped the datapad around and tapped the string of letters. "It didn't decrypt these."

Huey glanced at the screen. "Those are acronyms. It translated properly. It's a type of code. Each letter stands for a word. The smaller the transmission size, the easier it is to send and keep it hidden."

Jules frowned. "Without a reference point I can't decipher the two lines: MYLY, GBWY. And this one? Do you know it? WLF?"

"'With love father.' My parents used to sign off their transmissions to me with WLF or WLM. The other one: 'God be with you.'" Huey looked over at Jules again. "I told you my belief, Cap. Please don't let anyone know. But that is what it means. It's a saying that the Christian Coalition uses."

"Your parents were a part of that, yes?"

"Yes. Until they were killed." Huey returned his gaze back to the activity beyond the viewport. The last fuel truck pulled under their ship. Only the end of the truck stuck out. "I know you didn't kill them, Cap. I saw the men who did, and they are dead. I made sure of that. But I know you used to kill the Coalition. That's why I stayed away. So I could never reveal anything about them. Can't tell anything if I don't know anything."

Jules leaned back in his chair, pushing down at the lump of hardened memory gel with his thigh. "And I haven't pressed you on that. But I have to find them, Huey." He looked over at the younger man. He sat hunched over the console, his slender shoulders tense. The riot of curls on his head glistened under the harsh lighting of the bridge. "I need you to search for the coordinates of their base."

Huey shook his head. "Not without a promise from you. I don't care if you kill me, but unless I have your promise you aren't going to kill them, I won't help you."

Jules rose and pushed Huey's chair around until the man faced him. Huey didn't understand. Maybe he should have been angry at the insolence and stubbornness. Once, he would have forced the information from someone. But not now. That he was different now didn't escape him.

"I am not going to ever kill you, Huey. And I don't plan to kill any of the Coalition. I left that behind. I need to find JJ, and that's where he is. With them."

Huey looked up from under his brows, his brown eyes glaring at Jules, and regarded him.

"I promise you, Huey. I will not kill a single member of the Coalition. I want only to find JJ."

Tense moments passed before Huey nodded. "I will see if I can trace the transmission's destination." He turned to the console but paused with his fingers poised above the surface. "MYLY. It means 'miss you, love you.'" With a quick clearing of his throat, Huey bent down over the console. From his posture, the conversation was over.

Jules patted Huey's shoulder once and then left the bridge. So, the sender of the message had a father and apparently was part of the Coalition. He descended the ladder and paused. He needed to think.

With quick strides, he crossed to the small ladder that led to the quarter deck and then followed it down to the lift shaft in the back. He didn't have a small ship, yet it wasn't that large either. Right now, though, it seemed too small. The lower decks would ensure privacy and no interruptions.

He hit the button for the lowest cargo hold. The one that held hydroponics and his cache of weapons. When the doors opened, the odor of wet earth caressed his senses. That and the acrid smell of raw beans. He peeked into hydroponics. Looked like some vegetables were starting to sprout.

Jules turned away and entered his code on the small storage unit. It barely opened. He squeezed in, grimacing at another malfunction on a ship with too many. The lights blossomed into a dim, gray hue.

He ran a hand over the rack that held three pulse rifles, a long-range sniper—the latest model—and four titanium-ballistic sub-rifles. On the back wall, his collection of swords and knives hung on the pegs. On a small table against the right wall lay his latest project: PrecisionAim Pulse Gun. Took three months to collect the parts in order to build it. And it was almost finished.

Jules set the datapad on the console by the rifles and then sat on an upturned crate. He began building his gun. It would be needed when they arrived on Lunar Tarsus One.

As he clicked parts into place, screwed power packs into their positions, and assembled the hardware, his mind ran through each of the transmissions.

Huey knew the acronyms. He had known about Huey's background, yet the man didn't know what he knew. Huey didn't know that Jules had the information on his incarceration in the Siberian Prison. Huey had served seven out of his ten years for killing GFT soldiers. He valued Huey's experience and knowledge. That was the reason he kept him around.

The only background he didn't know fully was Anya's. Yet she was a means to an end. He needed her research and Serum Seventy-four.

Anya didn't have a father—that much he knew—and she wouldn't have risked sending a transmission. Or would she? Her tactics with him were becoming tiresome and a burden he didn't need. Yet he was finding her friendship something to explore.

The bishop would have just told him if he needed to send a transmission. His thoughts landed on the redhead, Abigail du Soleil. He paused over the meaning of her last name—"of the sun." She was the only viable person to do this, yet the *how* remained to be seen. His communication systems were top of the line. Firewalls protected them. And the main system was separate from the ship's network. She had to have used the stolen Nest Protocol program. Her face reflected on the door's glass replayed in his mind.

Those messages were sent to the Coalition. And she was his key to finding them. Yet even she didn't know where they were.

He pushed the last part of the grip into place and hit the side button. The scanner on the grip read his palm, and the light on the side turned green. He held it up and aimed at the reinforced target by the door. Quad-steel and bioPAKS lined the inside of the target and should prevent the pulse from penetrating. He snapped off a shot. A bolt of super-heated plasma hit the target, and a hole the size of his fist dissolved the target's center.

He stood and peered inside the target. The last bioPAK had melted, yet the back of the target stood undamaged. Jules raised his eyebrow and glanced at the gun in his hand. Nice weapon. Worked better than he thought possible.

He grabbed the holster from the floor by the table and strapped it on his waist. The gun slid in easily. Tendons in his neck popped as he stretched tension from his shoulders.

Now he felt complete. He had been too long without something by his side.

His comm beeped. Jules activated it. "Huey?"

"Cap. We are refueled. Do we want a layover, or should we head for Lunar?"

Jules glanced at his watch. It was late, yet Lunar was at least a day away with the permitted speed of his craft. "Ask for clearance now. See if we can shave off some of our time by speeding up."

"I will have to ask for clearance for the extra speed. Your permit allows for only stage one and stage two burns."

Jules sighed. "Ask for a stage two, plus half. If they require credits, use our surplus."

"I'll see what I can do, Cap." Huey closed the comm.

Jules hit the lights and left his storage unit. The sooner they arrived at Lunar, the sooner he would find those books for the bishop and the sooner he could find JJ.

$$\Sigma$$

Abigail set her jack port to the side. The weaker program was completed and downloaded onto a small data disk. She slid it into a small, metal case and leaned back against her pillow. Lunar Tarsus One.

The ship had given a small shudder as it lifted from the tarmac and entered the space lane. A rumble that had happened a few minutes ago throughout the ship's body indicated it had reached stage two burn.

She needed the rest. Yet the thought of being on Lunar sent waves of terror through her, causing her stomach to clench. Maybe a small tonic would help lull her to sleep. Then she could sleep through most of the journey. Wake up on Lunar. Do what she needed to do and pay her way to Mars.

Abigail shoved away from her bunk and donned her light poncho. The thin fabric settled over her white undershirt, cutting off the coolness of the ship's air—they were in space, now. Which meant the ship's coolant systems would be diverted to the main engines, allowing the tubes to generate the heat needed for the ship. Still, it would never be enough.

The door to her quarters slid open, and quiet darkness greeted her. The running lights at the top of the corridor cast a dim, bluish glow onto the grating. She padded in her socked feet to the ladder and climbed it to the observation deck.

Those Xulons had a wide variety of drinks. She didn't much care for the carbonated one that Huey had given her. It was good. Just not something she would want to drink again anytime soon. Yet he was the host. Better to sip a less-appealing drink than make a fuss and draw attention.

The lounge was bathed in darkness when she entered.

"Lights, one-eighth." Dim illumination blossomed from overhead.

She approached Huey's Caffeine Café and browsed the drinks. So many—

"If you can't sleep, try the Nutrient Three option."

She whirled around at his voice. He stood at the far corner of the viewport with his shoulder propped against the edge and his arms folded across his chest. Shadows bathed his body in darkness, yet the lights from above the couch highlighted the angles of his face.

"I didn't notice you there."

"I imagine not. You seemed lost in thought when you came in."

Abigail turned back to the machine and selected Nutrient Three. As it filled the glass, she peeked over her shoulder at the captain. He hadn't moved. His gaze stayed fixed upon her. When the beep broke the silence, she pulled the drink from the receptacle and tried a small sip.

A vanilla essence rolled over her tongue, followed by a soft heat that seemed to melt her bones. "Alcoholic?"

"No. It's alcosynth."

Alcosynth. The feeling of alcohol without its inebriating qualities.

She turned from the machine and approached the viewport. The urge to lean against the side pulled at her, but she didn't want him to think she was mimicking him. Outside the window, the Earth slowly revolved away. "Are we at stage two burn? That would put us at Lunar when?"

His gaze bored into her. "Stage two, plus half. We should arrive by tomorrow afternoon. Late afternoon. The lanes shifted. If we had left sooner, we may have had a shorter route."

Abigail nodded. Space lanes were so complex. Her thoughts fell back to the time when crashes and accidents between ships happened when they were allowed to fly whichever way suited them. Now, they had designated space lanes. Deviation was not allowed by any means.

"Are you in a hurry to arrive?"

She glanced at him while taking a sip. Mostly to hide her nervousness around him. He was dangerous. It lurked there under the surface. His green eyes, always hard and calculating, seemed to peer past each layer and defense she tried to erect.

With a mental shake, she cast off those errant thoughts. It was only her imagination.

"Not in a hurry. Not looking forward to it, either." She took a longer drink before continuing. "I am not a fan of Lunar. There's not much separating someone from the vacuum of space. A faulty connection and the fused panes can fall apart. One small asteroid and a hole can be blasted into the dome."

What sounded like a small chuckle came from his direction. "There's an electrical field that keeps those away. And there are too many redundancies to allow for failed connections."

Abigail shrugged.

He pushed off the side and took a step toward her. It wasn't a large step, yet the distance seemed to shorten by miles. She fought the urge to take a step back and put distance back between them. With hands in his pockets, he stared outside the viewport and at the blackness of space beyond.

They were on the far side of the space lane, which meant all other traffic was on the port side. She would have preferred the distraction of the other spacecrafts to the black nothingness that faced her now.

"It's the darkness, isn't it? The darkness of space?"

She frowned at him. How did he know?

"Yes." She touched the viewport. Cold, fused panes met her. It was mere inches that kept her safe. Kept her from being sucked out into the void. The clank from the sides of the viewport almost made her jump.

Abigail whipped her head around at the captain. He dropped his arm from the controls above. From the sides, metal shielding closed over the viewport until the black of space was seen no more. With another flick of switches, a narrow band around ten inches formed barely above her eyes as the top shielding partition pulled away.

She smiled. The reinforced shielding in place of a huge, glass viewport between her and space did alleviate a lot of her tension.

"You do that for my benefit?"

"I did."

He was a man of few words. Abigail pressed her hand against the glass. The coldness had lessened. And the blackness seemed more like a door barely opened, giving her a glimpse into a darkened room. A big, vast room.

"Are you meeting someone on Lunar?"

She turned back to him and drained her drink. The beverage was quite delicious. "I am. But I may have to purchase passage to Mars, too."

"Well, you asked for outlying colonies. I assumed you meant Mars and Jupiter."

"So, your price had included that?"

He cocked his head in confusion, his brows knitted together for a brief moment. "It did."

"Oh. I was afraid I would have to—" She couldn't tell him about selling a program. "Deplete my savings. The last of what I have."

He didn't seem to notice her hesitation. Or did he? His eyes traveled over her face, and a slow heat started spreading across her cheeks. "Anya said you didn't know much about Lunar." He returned his attention back to space.

"It has been a long time since I've been there. Actually, it's been since I was a child. When the construction had just been finished the prior year."

"That's a long time ago. Much has changed."

"What about you? You go there often?"

He cocked his head at her again, gauging her words apparently. "A fair bit. I run a cargo ship for trade. Some of my clients are on Lunar."

"Do you like it there?" She watched him closely. A pulse beat at the base of his neck. His hands tensed a bit, knotting his pockets. And his jaw flexed slightly.

Whatever was running through his head wasn't pleasant.

"Not really. Mars is preferable to Lunar. And Lunar preferable to Jupiter. Yet I like to try and keep the majority of my runs on Earth. Where humans belong." He turned from the viewport and gave her a nod. "Good night, Miss du Soleil. If you need anything, let us know."

She nodded. "Thank you, Captain."

He paused as if he was going to say something but strode to the door instead. The door hissed open, and his body blocked the light from the corridor for a moment. He was larger than she first thought. His shoulders brushed at the sides of the hatch. He had to duck slightly to miss the header. Then he disappeared, leaving her alone in the lounge and with her thoughts.

It felt like he was probing for information, yet he never asked anything. Just cordial conversation. Small talk. His eyes didn't miss anything that she was aware of as he spoke with her. He was wanting something, and she had the nagging suspicion that she had revealed to him what he wanted. But what? She had said nothing that would have given her away . . . or had she?

# Chapter Eight

# COALITION

MYLY.

WLF.

GBWY. It was that group of letters that Jules mulled over. *God be with you.* The bishop said his answers were in the banned book. Maybe he should try and get his hands on an extra copy if he could.

He shook his head. No. Let Bishop Thomas have them. Let the danger be at his feet. Jules had a hard enough time staying under the GFT's radar. With a grunt, he dropped his feet from the console, closed down the file with the hijacked messages in it, and stood. He propped his hands on the read-out board above him and leaned against his arms.

It was early still. Yet there was no measurement of time in space. During the night, the autopilot had switched into the mid-lane. This one would lead them to Lunar One Docking, Port Five. And that would put him over ten minutes away from Bistro. Which meant another adjustment to his timeline. This run was nothing but adjustments lately.

The console to his left pinged. A message.

Jules sat in Huey's seat and pulled up communications. And frowned. There was no message. Incoming nor outgoing. Yet that ping meant something came through. Or went through.

He pressed the comm. "Huey."

A few moments passed before the man's groggy voice answered. "Cap?"

"Need you to work your magic on the comm."

"Be right there." The comm closed.

Jules moved to his seat and waited. Huey never asked why or questioned. Unlike Anya. Always asking, always probing and prodding. Always there, wanting something from him that he couldn't give and had no idea how to give.

With Huey, it was as though he could anticipate Jules' movements or decisions. Knowing intuitively what to do or when to respond.

The door opened. Huey, his hair a mess of tangles, lumbered onto the bridge. At least this time, the man had put on pants and shoes. Amusement at the memory of when the younger man arrived on the bridge in nothing but underpants during a high-profile deal . . . That was something that no one forgot.

"What's up?" Huey dropped into his seat and spun around to the console.

"Message. But nothing is showing."

A yawn escaped Huey. Fingers danced across the board. Then a frown creased his forehead. After a few more seconds, the frown deepened. "That's odd."

Jules leaned forward.

"It shows an outgoing. Piggybacked on the autoreply to the space lane checkpoints. It's different from the other ones."

"How so?"

"The other ones—the ones we think the redhead is sending—they have the holding pattern tag. This one was sitting in the mainframe."

He tapped his finger against his lips before nodding. "Hold on. Let me check something."

A knot formed in Jules' stomach.

"That's what I thought. This wasn't the only message. There's been four over the past six months."

Not the du Soleil woman sending this one. From Huey's confused look, it was obvious that he wasn't sending the messages. So, Anya, then. But why? Medical updates? Transmissions to contacts? Those could have used the regular channels. Not be hidden deep within communications.

"Can you read them?"

Huey shook his head. "They erased as soon as they were sent. I can see the timestamp of the message but not the message itself. But . . . I can run a program that may piece some of the data together. Nothing is ever truly completely erased."

Jules nodded. "Do it." When Huey yawned again, he jerked his head toward the door. "Go back to sleep. You can do it later."

"Nah, Cap. Let me get this program going, and then I will." He bent over his console, tapping the icons and keys. Another yawn almost split his face, but Huey kept going.

"How long?"

"It'll be a while."

Jules leaned back and propped his head against the back of his seat. He should have ventured back to his room after leaving the observation deck. Yet he couldn't rest. Instead, he had been camping out in the bridge, watching the slow dance of ships in the lanes. Listening to the pops and creaks of the ship as coolant ran through the tubes and heat expanded the plating. Small bangs against the hull. Micro rocks dinging against the *Nightingale*.

His eyes drifted closed. His breathing slowed. Muscles relaxed.

Jules let the sounds around him whirl into nothing. Tremors and vibrations ran through the ship and into him.

Coalition.

Small light.

God be with you.

Father.

Answers were on Mars. Lunar held the key. Follow the woman to Bistro. That was what he needed to do. She, not Lunar, was the key. *God be with you.* The Coalition's code? Or just a salutation?

Huey puffed out a deep breath.

Jules opened his eyes. An hour had passed.

"Got something?"

"No." He pushed back from the console. "I'll let it run for a while. Our memory banks are vast, and it may take a while to consolidate the information. The code may be scattered." Huey stood and stretched. "Were you asleep?"

"Meditation."

"Man, you were deep in it. I thought you fell asleep." He paused at the door. "Cap, you aren't going to ask me to disembark at Lunar, are you?"

"No." Jules looked back out the viewport. "I want you to stay onboard, monitor communications. And when she gets off the ship, I want you to do a courtesy examination of her quarters."

"She? The redhead?"

Jules clamped his jaw before replying. "And Anya. I'm tired of her—she is pushing me too far on certain topics. And unless it's you, which I don't think it would be, then she's sending the messages. I want to know why."

"She's been with us for a long time, Jules."

He looked up at Huey's use of his name. The man's brown eyes, eyebrows furrowed, stared at him, questioning him. "I know. But she used a different derivative and double-dosed me without letting me know. That was unusual. She's pushing me to try things and—"

"I think you are reading too much into it." Huey smiled. "You mean a lot to her." He waved away Jules' reply, stopping it before it left his lips. "I know you don't and can't return what she feels for you. So, what you are sensing is probably frustration on her part." Huey gave the frame a thump with his fist. "But I'll glance through and see if there's something out of place. These messages could just be an automatic reply to something she's working on. Or maybe even a request. We've used silent channels to send messages before."

Then he left.

Jules returned to his vigil. Huey never let him down. No questions asked. And he wasn't afraid to voice his opinions. A good man, Huey. He stretched his neck to either side and settled back against his seat again. And hoped that Huey was right. Anya was just sending a request but using the silent channels to keep from arousing suspicion.

His breathing slowed . . .

$$\Sigma$$

Abigail stood at the entry port, awaiting her turn. Her line moved slower than Arctic ice compared to the Express Lane—guess that was why it was called the Express. Her gaze traveled over the line that moved three times faster than her own. Captain Williams and Medtech Anya had already reached the scanners.

The captain passed over a card and unholstered his weapon. It was checked and placed on a conveyor, and then he was waved through the portal, where he collected his weapon and card from the conveyor belt. Anya was treated the same, sans weapon.

Her line stepped forward again. Abigail followed and glanced around her. The entry ports were closed in by thick walls. Behind her was the long tunnel from the docking area. Nothing but an endless hue of gray metal. The only indication of space outside were the windows located high above them.

The line moved, and the man in front of her handed his travel card to the guard, who ran through a litany of questions. Then it was her turn.

Abigail handed over her blue card.

"Business or pleasure?"

"Pleasure."

"Your card states you are a level three IT worker."

"Yes. With Nest Protocol."

The guard entered her information, and the wait was excruciating as it cycled through her records. It beeped once; then a green light lit the console. He smiled and handed her card back to her.

"Enjoy your stay, Miss Devroe."

Abigail gave him a small smile in return as she accepted her card back and slid it into her bag, which was slung across her shoulder. "Thank you."

She placed her bag on the conveyor, passed through the scanner, and gazed around the esplanade. People jostled each other. The noise level reverberated against the metal walls, threatening to split her head open. She collected her bag, tightened her grip on it, and then zeroed in on the directory in the middle of the busyness.

Color-coded icons indicated restaurants, stores, quarters, and admin areas. Large sections were blackened and bordered with red. Mining and exploration companies. Off limits to visitors. She tapped a fingernail against the red dot for Bistro. A screen opened, showing her the most direct route to the restaurant.

Abigail closed down the information and moved away, allowing the next person to access the directory. As she headed for the far, left-side corridor, she searched for the captain or Anya. She didn't need them, yet she wanted to keep an eye on them or at least make sure they weren't keeping an eye on her.

It seemed clear.

She ducked through the throng of people and walked the corridor, swallowing against the sight of the moon's surface outside the long viewport that ran the length of the corridor. No matter what the captain said about an electrical field or the redundancies, no technology was infallible. And all it took was just one small rock, one small misconnection.

With a harsh shake of her head, she dispelled those fears. She needed a terminal. Her friend was waiting. She needed to call him.

Terminals lined the wall at the end of the corridor. Each in use. She watched and waited. People bumped into her, so she stepped closer to the last terminal to avoid them. When the older man closed down his connection, he turned and saw her.

"Here you go, young lady. Thank you for being patient." He handed her the headset.

"Not a problem. And thank you." She slid the headset on her head and set her bag on the small lip of the console. Partitions separated each terminal, giving the callers the privacy needed.

Yet when she glanced up through her lashes, security cams were aimed down at them.

With a deep breath, she eased her GHOST program from the slit in her jacket, keeping it hidden under her card. As she slid her card into the slot to pay for the connection, she used the small jack port on the side for her GHOST. To the cams, it would look like she was propping her hand on the terminal.

Abigail entered Geoffrey's code and waited. No reply. She spoke and left an audio for him. "Hey, I'm here. I'll be at Bistro. Dad says hi."

The terminal beeped, indicating that the message was received. Her card lit with a red light. She suppressed a sigh at the warning of low funds. The data disk slid out easily, and she removed her card. The headset clanked against the back of the booth as she hung it from its peg. All smooth movements.

She turned and stuffed her card back into her bag and the data disk into the small slit of her jacket. Couldn't lose that.

A wave of dizziness overtook her as soon as she stepped out of the corridor and onto the promenade's balcony. Above her, the darkness of space loomed. Barely on the horizon, a sliver of Earth was seen. She pressed a hand over her heart and tried to slow her breathing.

Anya said there were awnings. But on this side, only three awnings stood over the promenade, and those were only half-opened. Abigail cast a look around, trying to locate Bistro. And of course, it would be on the far side!

Her heart hammered wildly as she walked down the flight of metal stairs. People hurried to and fro. Laughing. Smiling. Some arguing. Vendors stood in the center of the promenade hawking their wares.

Did they not worry about what was looming overhead?

She sped across the center of the complex. Dodging people and barely missing some. The darkness loomed closer and closer until it was finally hidden by the awning.

"I told you the awnings help."

Abigail yelped and whirled around. Anya sat at a table, holding a menu. She waved to the empty seat in front of her. "Have a seat and relax."

Abigail slid onto the chair, placed her bag at her feet, and tried to calm her heart. "I didn't think I would react so badly." She peeked from under the awning and then quickly sat back. Her heart hammered in her chest again.

Anya laughed. "First time visitors have a hard time relaxing. It's tough to adjust. Sometimes, even I get a bit anxious from seeing nothing but space above me."

"Well, at least I don't feel too much a fool, then." Abigail forced a small laugh and picked up the menu. "What is good here?"

"Just about anything. They have a massive hydroponics on Lunar, and most all their produce is fresh. So, anything fresh tastes better than rehydrated." Anya pulled the top of Abigail's menu down and pointed to the range of salads. "I would suggest the butter lettuce salad or the cucumber salad. Light on the stomach. Until you adjust to Lunar's visage, I would suggest nothing heavy on your stomach."

The idea of something fresh and green and not meal packs or nutrient bars set her mouth to watering.

"I'll order that, then." She closed the menu and opened the order screen on the table. With a few taps and the last swipe of her card, her order was put through.

"Did you contact your friend?" Anya sat back as a waiterBOT arrived with her order—some kind of white, frothy drink.

"I did. Had to leave a message, but he should get it. I'm not sure of his work hours, so it's possible he's still working."

"What does he do?"

"Mining on the dark side, last I heard." Abigail moved out of the way as another waiterBOT brought her cucumber salad and water. "What about you? Are you visiting someone on Lunar?"

Anya shook her head and picked up her datapad from the table. "No. I had to meet with a few colleagues at Lunar Medical Center. Got a few updates, ordered some supplies, and arranged a sale of some medical gel we have on board." She smiled. Her red-stained lips brightened her face. "It's always business, business, business. After this, though, I plan to stroll the promenade and see if there's anything worth splurging on."

Abigail swallowed her bite. "You are braver than me!"

Anya laughed. "No. I just learned to not look up." She pushed at the controls on the table. "You don't mind if I activate the HoloNews, do you?"

"No, please. It's been a while since I watched. I don't mind catching up on what's happening in the system."

The HoloNews projected above their table, slowly revolving. Anya selected local, and they watched as they finished their drink and food.

"Medlab Four initiated a lockdown yesterday when the alarms were activated. Fear of an unknown contagion swept through until it was revealed to be a faulty lead in the security. Medlab Properties assured residents that there were no danger and that the fault is being repaired.

"Governor Lantis set a new precedent for Lunar Tarsus Two. With mining contracts falling by major points, the new precedent will allow for additional contracts to expand the mining area into Mare Cognitum and Grimaldi.

"In other local news, Lunar Tarsus One experienced a devastating blow. In three years, homicides have been seventy-five percent below Milky Way system levels, averaging one every two years. This changed with last night's double homicide. Geoffrey Timbers and Martha Goddard were found outside Observation Platform Six. Their bodies were in a depressurized airlock. Governor Lantis and Security Chief Doman have no leads as of this broadcast and have asked for any information on these deaths."

Dread pooled into the pit of Abigail's stomach. Geoffrey dead?

"It is believed that the two were members of the Christian Coalition . . . "

Anya looked up from the hologram. "That's sad. Horrific way to die."

Abigail nodded, hoping her face didn't reveal her horror.

"You look pale."

She shook her head and pushed the remnants of her salad away. "The idea of dying in an airlock like that. That's just too much to imagine." With a shudder, she stood. "Excuse me, though. I'm going to try and contact my friend again."

Abigail looked around. "Um . . . is there a terminal close by? I really do not want to walk through the promenade again."

Anya gave her a lopsided grin and pointed to the corridor behind them. "There is a small bank of them that way. Right around the bend and outside of personnel quarters."

"Thanks." Abigail grabbed her bag and turned away. Anya had already returned her attention to the HoloNews, absorbed in the next story being displayed.

She hurried past the tables and into the brightly lit corridor. She needed to get some kind of direction on where to go now that Geoffrey was dead. She would use the GHOST again to contact her father from the ship. But she would need funds for Mars. Geoffrey was supposed to supply that. There was only one way to gain what she needed.

The bank of terminals was empty. So was the corridor.

As she lifted the headset off the peg and slipped it on, she glanced up. No security cams above her. She peeked over her shoulder. But there were some on the other side of the corridor, aimed at the terminals. Easy enough to hide her movements.

She slipped a red card from her bag. It was the last one that she had gained from Batch. She had used it at Nest Protocol. And this would be the last time she could use it, since there was only one more anti-trace program on it.

Abigail slid it into the slot and entered the comm code. In moments, a voice answered. "What's the product?"

"Nav and Comm hack chip. Allows undetected transmissions."

"Length?"

"Fifteen max."

"Amount?"

"Seventy party credits."

"Sixty and it's a deal."

"Deal."

"Ten minutes. Promenade. Saks Vendor Three. Pick up the red book. Look inside. Replace it."

The communication closed. Abigail pulled the card out and snapped it in two before dumping the pieces into her bag. The headset pulled at her hair as she tugged it off. Movement out of the corner of her eye caught her attention. She glanced at the end of the corridor. No one. Just people walking by, doing their thing.

As she ventured from the corridor, she dug into her bag one more time to pull out the metal case containing her weakened program. Anya wasn't at the table. And their dishes had been cleared. A quick look around her and still no Anya. That was good.

Abigail blew out a quick breath and stepped out onto the promenade. Anya said don't look up. And that was what she would do. Keep her eyes focused on those around her and the vendors she was heading to. No looking up at the blackness above.

Her heart raced, nevertheless.

$$\Sigma$$

"Pleasure doing business, Captain." The man beside him murmured the statement as he bent to retrieve his bag from the floor.

Jules nodded and waited until his contact stepped away from the railing of the second-floor balcony overlooking Bistro and the promenade. Once he was alone, he reached above him and stretched, then covered a fake yawn. Without a glance, he scooped up the satchel beside him. From the weight of it, there may have been three books in there. A good return. Bishop Thomas would be happy with this. He slung it across his shoulder and down his side, looking like every other man out enjoying the sights and stores.

He turned left and strolled along the edge, letting his hand glide across the railing. A flash of red out of the corner of his eye caught his attention. He paused and watched as Anya and the du Soleil woman chatted at a table and watched the HoloNews. He could make out the headline: "Two murders in Platform Six."

Color drained from the redhead's face, and her hands shook slightly. She stood and said something to Anya, who pointed to the corridor beyond the Bistro. With a nod, du Soleil left Anya sitting there.

For a few seconds, Anya watched the woman as she left, then returned to her HoloNews. Jules walked to the stairs, keeping Anya in his field of vision. She looked down at her datapad, frowned, and rose from the table and disappeared into the crowded promenade.

Odd. What did she receive on that pad?

But he was more concerned with what the other woman was doing. He descended the steps and followed her at a distance. She rounded the slight corner, and soon, he did, too.

The personnel terminals.

Jules stepped around to the side of the corridor and propped against the wall. Rustling sounds reached him. She was digging in her bag. He pulled a small datapad out of his pocket and pretended to be reading it as he listened to her.

Nav and comm? So, she was selling her stolen program? Not a good idea.

Seventy credits. Okay, she needed money? But why? He told her the price of traveling to Mars was included. Maybe there was more to Mars than just her trip.

He pushed off the wall and strode past the corridor. A small area of small vendors crowded around the edge of the promenade. Jules paused at their stands and browsed the products, keeping a wary eye out for her.

She stood at the edge, glanced up once, and then squared her shoulders before practically diving into the crowd. Jules replaced the collection of gaming cards, nodded to the vendor, and moved away, keeping at least three people or more between him and her.

At the middle vendor, one that was selling books and clothing, she pretended to browse through the items. Her hands traveled lightly over colorful tunics and shawls, over a box of antique books, and then she selected a blue one. She picked it up, flipped through the pages, and replaced it. A red one stood next to it. She grabbed it and opened it. For several minutes, she flipped and read through the book before sighing and replacing it on the rack. With a small nod to the seller, she moved on, toward the directory in the middle of the promenade.

Jules hurried to the vendor and picked up the book before another lady could. "Pardon me, ma'am."

She gave a small huff, but he ignored her. The pages rustled as he opened it and browsed the words. It was a book of poems. Someone named Frost. Many of the pages were torn, and there were notations in the margins.

All seemed to be explanations of what the words meant . . . except for the one on page seventy-six. Two words: "bottom gangway."

He glanced at the directory as he put the red book back and picked up the blue. She still stood there, engrossed in the information.

The blue book was one by a man named Keats. His mind played back to the scrap of paper he had found when he bought his ship. Tucked away, stuck to the inside of a panel, were just a few lines of a poem. The title of said poem was at the top. Only a partial. Most of the paper was discolored and torn. But it read: "Ode to a Nightingale."

And now he could have the complete poem. He handed the vendor his card and let him swipe it for the required credits.

"Thank you, sir. Hope you enjoy."

Jules nodded and dumped his newly acquired book into his satchel and slid his card into his pocket. She had already moved away from the directory and was heading to the lower deck.

He took a right and headed for the corridor nearest him. The directory would take her through two corridors—one to the left, then one level down—at the seventy-six intersection, and then a sharp right to the gangway. His direction would lead him to a maintenance tunnel that paralleled the gangway. There was an access panel that would allow him to view the area without anyone knowing. So many times, he had used that tunnel.

Jules slid on his BOD-gloves as he entered the corridor, hurried down the steps to his left, and paused outside the tunnel. He retrieved the wallet that held his cards and flipped them until he found the black one. It was good for only one swipe.

He ran it through the slot and pushed open the door. It closed behind him. Red, dim light bathed him, and eerie silence descended upon him. The access panel was twenty meters away.

His boots rang against the metal grating, breaking the silence of the soundproof area. When he reached the panel, he eased it open barely half an inch. Just enough to hear what was being said.

"This is Nest Protocol programming?"

"It is." There was no waver in her voice. Which meant she was experienced in selling contraband.

"There is a high-profile alert for the hacker who stole this."

This time, there was a slight waver. "I'm not the hacker. I bought it at Floridian Port. Need to sell it for funds."

"Floridian? Let me see it work."

He moved so he could peer out. She had accepted a datapad from a slender man dressed in a worker's uniform, plugged something into the side port, and then turned it around to show him as she tapped the screen. His pockmarked face lit up as she showed him the results.

"See. You can access any terminal, directory, or mining shaft vehicle with this. As long as what you are accessing is plugged into the mainframe you are using, you can download any and all programs. Upload communications to piggyback on transmissions."

"Undetectable?"

"Completely if using this code." She tapped once and pointed at the screen.

The man nodded and glanced at his companion, a large, burly man with a bulging stomach pushing against his vest.

She removed the data disk and handed the datapad back to him. While she slipped the disk into a small, metal casing, the man conferred with his colleague. Within moments, he returned and handed her a blue card.

"Sixty party credits as we agreed."

She swiped his card into her datapad, transferring the funds to her pad and then did the same with her own to collect the credits onto her card. Jules kept his eye on the second man, who stood away from the duo. He spoke quietly into his wrist comm. Some of the words filtered over to him.

"Found . . . red hair, five-five, five-six . . . Nest Protocol . . ."

She nodded, handed the blue card back to the first man, and dropped the metal case into his hand. "Thank you." Then she turned and left. She was definitely not a newbie to this side of life.

The men watched for a moment.

"Did you call it in? What's the bounty?" The first man turned to his partner.

"Two thousand party credits." He gazed down the corridor. "When should we grab her?"

"They didn't say who we were looking for?"

"No. Only that we should look for anyone selling a Nav-Comm hack program. One thousand for the program. Another for proof of death of the seller."

"Then we will follow her and take her out before she leaves Lunar. Merc Associates will be happy with this one. Leave her body in the airlock and give them the program."

Jules snarled. Mercenaries. He did not need that headache following them. He opened the panel on silent hinges and stepped out. They stood, facing away from him, still watching in the direction she had left.

"Come on. We will head her off at the six-eight junction." They took a half step back, turned, and stumbled to a stop when they saw Jules.

"Where did you come from?" The burly man took a step forward with his hand already reaching for him.

Jules lashed out and rammed his hand against the man's face. Bones crunched, and he dropped to the floor, unconscious. The other man brought his hand down to his waist for his weapon but stopped as Jules whipped his pulse gun up and pressed it against the merc's chest.

"Don't do anything stupid. Hand me the disk."

Hate glared from the man's eyes as he fished it out of his pocket.

"Take it out of the casing."

He opened the casing, plucked the small disk from the foam interior, and held it out to Jules. He squared his shoulders. His eyes calculated his moves. His face broadcasted his thoughts. "You aren't going to get away with this. This is Merc territory."

Jules slid the data disk into his pants pocket. "You planned to kill her."

"Leave no witnesses."

Jules pulled the trigger.

The plasma bolt shot through the man's chest. Eyes bulged. Air gurgled from melted lungs. Then he landed on the gangway with a thud.

Jules grabbed the man's legs and hauled him toward the tunnel. After dumping him through the door, he returned to the burly man. A transmission card was found after a quick pat-down. Jules removed it and broke it in half. He'd throw it in a trash bin later. No need for the authorities to discover the transmission to the underground mercenary ring. Or they would be able to trace down the du Soleil woman. And eventually his ship.

He propped the man up, wrapped his arm around the thick neck, and hesitated. The man's pulse beat under his arm, thumping heavily against him. His raspy breathing filled the silent void around them.

Jules blinked and shook away the hesitation. With a quick jerk, tendons popped. Vertebrae shattered. Jules deposited his body next to the other and closed the panel. He had about eight or ten hours before the bodies were found. That would give him enough time to have the security feeds wiped.

Jules left the gangway the same direction she did. Within moments, he was at the end of the second corridor. He paused outside the entrance and dumped the broken transmission card into the trash bin. This wasn't how he planned his Lunar trip.

He keyed open his comm at his collar. "Huey."

"Cap?"

"Radio Anya. Call her back to the ship. Start the preflight."

"Trouble?"

"There will be if we don't leave soon. Access the mainframe. Send a rabbit into the security feeds on the lower gangway, the six-four junction, and surrounding areas." He climbed the short flight back to the main corridors and took the long way around, heading to their docking port. "Send me a ping when the du Soleil woman arrives."

"Will do." The comm closed.

Jules glanced around as he weaved in and out of the crowd. What did that woman think she was doing? The danger of selling a hacking program immediately after stealing it? He didn't think she was that foolish. Or maybe that desperate?

He strolled down the Port Five corridor. Hopefully, Anya was on her way. And hopefully, she had sold that gel in time.

## Chapter Nine
# T≡MP≡ST

Abigail looked up from the terminal. Same wall as the first time, yet three down from the one she had used. It was still crowded around her. And she couldn't risk the GHOST this time. Too many people bumping into her and the security cams were scanning back and forth along the people.

She keyed in the call codes for public transmissions her people used. It pinged once, and a woman's voice came through.

"Hey, girl. I see that you were able to call."

Abigail didn't recognize this voice. That meant there was a new group on Mars. "I was held up. Calling to ask if Dad has the reception set up."

"He does, and we are eagerly waiting on you. Jeff is coming, yes?"

"No. He has been permanently detained. Something dealing with work on an airlock." She sighed and leaned closer to the terminal. "He wasn't able to gain the credits for boarding. But I have what I need."

"Oh, dear. We will miss him." The woman's voice faded away for a bit and then came back online. "We'll be waiting on you. It's been a long time."

"Yes. It has. Be there soon."

She disconnected the transmission and hung up the headset. A couple was eagerly waiting for her to finish. They smiled at her as she squeezed past them. The right side of the corridor was less congested, and she weaved her way through the endless throng of people and hugged the wall as she headed back to the ship.

With each step, it seemed as though eyes followed, and space loomed above her. Well, space did loom above her. But the feeling of being watched? She paused and glanced around, trying to see above the heads of the people. Her short stature made that almost impossible.

No one seemed to be paying her any attention. She looked behind her. No one that she saw. With a shrug, she turned and hurried out of the corridor and onto the esplanade and through the exit portals. The ship gleamed in the harsh lights of the tarmac as she exited the long corridor. Its ramp was still lowered, and the airlock opened. So that meant the captain and Anya were still in the complex. Good.

Abigail hurried up the ramp. Huey stood by a terminal on the left side of the main cargo bay. He looked up and smiled.

"Have a good visit?"

She shook her head. "Not really. It was okay, but I feel much better back on the ship and not in an area open to space."

He gave a snort and turned back to his task. Which was what?

Abigail glanced at it as she breezed by. Communications? No. The codes looked wrong. But she couldn't gain a clear view. He shifted his weight to his right and leaned against the console. His body hid the rest of the screen.

She turned from him and climbed the stairs. She needed to get a message sent to her father as soon as she could. The door to her quarters slid open. Abigail stepped in and stopped.

Something wasn't right.

She crossed the carpet to her bunk and laid her bag down on it. The carpet.

She glanced at it. It wasn't pushed up against the table like she'd had it. It had been spread neatly across the floor. She checked her stack of clothing. All were in the same place. Her BOD-suit was hidden within her parka.

Her door pinged. When she opened it, Huey stood there.

"I replaced the linen in your shower. I didn't see any cleansers in there, so I restocked it for you. Afterward, I realized you may have had the carpet pushed to the side for a reason. If the carpet bothers you, I can remove it."

Abigail looked back at it. "No. It can stay. And thank you for the clean linens."

Huey nodded. He gave her one more smile and then headed for the ladder leading to the bridge.

Okay. So that was what was different. Huey had been in here. She opened the shower stall. Clean towels had been stowed away in the linen compartment, and a small bottle of body cleanser was attached to the wall.

His story checked out. But still . . . an uneasy feeling flooded through her.

Couldn't worry about it now. She had a transmission to send.

She stripped from her clothing and pulled on the BOD-suit. It would need a cleaning soon, but she didn't have the professional ability to do that without damaging the inner workings. The panel folded back easily, yet she paused before hauling herself into the space.

If Huey came in while she was gone, would they also come in while she was here? She wasn't taking any chances. There wouldn't be enough time to get back into the room if her monitor was activated. She grabbed a panel lock off her bunk and walked over to the door. The lock slid easily over the control panel. It clicked and sealed itself against it. With a push of the green button, the panel lock froze the controls, effectively locking her in her room and everyone else out.

With a grunt, already tired from her anxiety-inducing trip to Lunar, Abigail wiggled her way into the access tube. When she approached the trip-mod, a red light blinked rapidly at her.

She fished out the lead and plugged it in. Her father's message scrolled across the screen: *Meet @ Mars Comp 2. Deep Blue. Elder there. BSA. GBWY.*

That was it.

She leaned her head against the heated incline and closed her eyes. Why couldn't returning home be simple? Her penalty for leaving home when she shouldn't have.

Yet she would be there soon enough. Mars would be her last stop. An elder would find her. And she would be given the coordinates or assigned to a contingent heading home.

Abigail sighed and unplugged her lead, pushing it back against the wires. The slow squirm back seemed even longer as weariness flowed through her muscles and bones. The weariness increased as her alarm on the ladder started beeping.

$$\Sigma$$

Jules stepped into the cargo bay. Darkness greeted him. He paused by the control panel and closed the airlock, leaving the ramp down. Anya could use her code to open it when she came back on board.

His boots clanged against the cargo hold plating and gangway as he made his way to the stairs. Quiet met him as he stepped out into the main corridor. He knocked on the bishop's quarters.

The door slid open a few seconds later, and Jules slipped inside.

"Have the Bibles for you, Bishop." Jules walked to the table near the viewport and pulled out the stack of books. His blue Keats was on top, so he removed it and was about to stick it back in when the bishop stopped him.

"What's that?"

"A book I found. When I bought this ship, there was a slip of paper that said, 'Ode to a Nightingale.' I was always intrigued by what little words were legible on the paper. Found this book that has the words."

Bishop Thomas smiled. "You named the ship after a poem?"

"Seemed fitting." Jules stuffed it back into his satchel. His gaze fell onto the black cover of the Bible. A golden-embossed cross decorated it. He picked it up and flipped through the thin pages. "So, this is a dangerous book?"

The bishop sat down and folded his hands, propping them on the table. "Dangerous to a few. People in power do not like books that contain ideas contrary to their own beliefs or their narrative. Especially books that teach freewill and grace."

Jules paused at a page. *Gospel of John.* He flipped over a few pages and read aloud the passage at his fingertips. "'Greater love hath no man than this, that a man lay down his life for his friends.'"

Something stirred in his heart at those words. The memory of people he and JJ had hunted. The men and women who would step in front of them, allowing the others to try and escape. Then the memory faded.

He closed the book and replaced it on the stack. "These words have a strange syntax, Bishop."

"That is one of our oldest surviving translations." Bishop Thomas watched him. His eyes seemed to see deeper into Jules than he liked. "You can keep that one, son."

"No." Jules picked up his satchel and held out his hand. "Codes?"

It wasn't disappointment on the bishop's face. Not exactly. It seemed more like sadness . . . a deep sadness. Why would the man be saddened because he refused to read words that meant nothing to him?

Bishop Thomas reached into the breast pocket of his tunic and pulled out a small disk. He laid it in Jules' outstretched hand. "That's what you need."

"Thank you, Bishop." Jules strode to the door but paused before opening it. "I will still uphold my end. There may be a chance to gain two or more of the books on Mars. If my contacts are still alive, that is."

Bishop Thomas nodded and pulled one of the Bibles to him. "We will still be there three days?"

"That's the plan." Jules palmed open the door. It closed with a hiss, but not before he saw the bishop pull on a headset and bow his head over the book. His hands steepled in prayer. Why? They were just words. Just a jumble of letters written down because of some man's imagination.

Or . . .

He shook his head. It was time for his dose. That's why his thoughts were running astray. When he topped the ladder, the medlab lights were on. Huey stood at the production unit, reading whatever was on the screen. He looked up as Jules entered.

"Hey, Cap. Anya messaged me. Said to check on the serum since it was time for your dose."

"I was heading in here for that." He stepped up to the machine. The serum vials stood in a row. Only three, though.

"You don't have enough, Cap." Huey read the display. "And there aren't enough ingredients to make more. I thought she was getting supplies on Tarsus One."

Jules selected a vial, picked up the injection gun, and inserted his serum into it. "She was. Might have to see about getting some on Mars."

"How long can you go without it?"

Jules raised the hem of his shirt. His arm was still sore from the last injection. Better do the abdomen today. Finding a spot that was void of scars was tough, but there were a few still there. He placed the end against his side. "Probably a week, tops. Then my body will start shutting down." When he pulled the trigger, the gun's needle pierced his skin. Heat flowed through him as the serum entered his bloodstream.

Huey closed the lid on the machine. "I didn't find anything in their quarters, by the way."

Jules laid the injection gun on the counter and followed the younger man out of Medlab. "What about the transmissions?"

"It was Anya's. Requesting an updated medical file. She was using a GFT researcher's clearance." Huey palmed open the door to the bridge.

"What was in it?"

"Couldn't tell. The message was too corrupted, even after the compilation. What I could see of it, though, it seemed as though she was trying to gain alternate ingredients to Serum Seventy-four for you. Substance Eighty-three isn't readily available, you know."

Jules fell into the pilot seat. "It'll have to be black market. I'll see what I can find on Mars."

"For your sake, Cap, we better hope we can find it." He opened the comm unit. "And other bad news. Lunar Tarsus One wouldn't give clearance for departure until oh-eight-hundred Lunar Time. There's a CME heading this way, and all ship travel has been reefed."

Jules handed Huey the data disk he'd received from the bishop. "Here. Let's see what it says."

Huey slid it into the port and pulled it up on the holographic overhead. Lines of code ran across until it dissolved into a bulleted report.

- Mars, three months, Compound Two and Habitat One
- Geoffrey is contact. Middleman for travel
- Code word: ** Blue, first half unknown
- Elder Jake, Blue District, Mars Compound Two

Huey cocked his head and looked at Jules. "Does that mean he was at Mars for three months, or he will be at Mars for three months?"

"I don't know. But this . . . " Jules tapped the word "blue" on the holoscreen. "When I was in the hospital, JJ said I could find him at the Deep Blue. So, that's a code word, it seems. Maybe say it to this Elder Jake."

Huey closed down the report and handed the disk back to him. Then he was dancing his finger across the console again. "Could be. This is the closest you have come to finding him."

Jules leaned back against his seat. He opened his mouth, but a ping from the console sounded. "Another one?"

Huey's hands flew across the surface, pushing and swiping. "I was getting an update from WeatherNet, downloading Mars forecast. This came in as soon as I activated the upload." Huey pointed to Jules' datapad. "It's on your pad for you. And tell me if this isn't odd. First Bishop Thomas' report and now this message containing the same thing."

Jules opened his datapad and read: *Meet @ Mars Comp 2. Deep Blue. Elder there. BSA. GBWY.*

That GBWY again. And more. Deep Blue. JJ!

Jules jumped up from the console, throwing his datapad down onto its surface. He hit the panel with such force, the outer casing cracked. As he ran down the shortened hall, jumping from the top of the ladder and landing on the level below, he was dimly aware of Huey yelling for him to stop.

Abigail du Soleil. She would give him the answers he needed. He hit her door's panel. It wouldn't open. Growling, he punched in his override code. Still nothing.

Panel lock. She had a panel lock on it. Only explanation.

He slid his gun from the holster and aimed at the wall near the hatch's frame in the approximate location of where the inside panel would be. Huey barreled into him, barely altering his aim. The pulse bolt hit. The acrid stench of molten metal and burned electronics filled the corridor.

The door opened slightly. Huey still shouted at him.

"Captain!" Huey pulled at his arm. "Jules! You can't!"

He shoved the younger man aside, sending him staggering across the hall, and pushed his way inside her quarters. With a grunt, using all his strength, he pushed the door closed and turned to find her standing on her bunk under an opened hatch.

Fear and shock paled her face. His gaze traveled her body. A BOD-suit. The face veil hung to one side.

Jules approached her. She leapt off the bunk and pressed herself against the wall. Tremors shook her body, and her lips trembled. Her pupils had dilated to the point hardly any of the blue could be seen.

He didn't stop until he was practically pinning her against the wall. Little space stood between them as he looked down at her. Tears trickled from her eyes.

"The transmissions."

She shook her head. "You . . . you found them?"

He slammed his hands on either side of her head causing her to flinch. She turned her head away from him. Jules leaned further toward her, bringing his head down to her level, glaring at her. "What does it mean?"

Her voice squeaked. "I don't know what you want. What does what mean?"

Anger coursed through him. She would tell him. And she would tell him now.

"Deep blue. Is that a code?"

She whipped her head around at him. Confusion and fear shot through her eyes. Her trembling increased. Tears began to flow in earnest. She shook her head.

His hands itched to wrap themselves around her throat, but he shoved that urge away. He wouldn't—couldn't—harm her. Why? Because of his promise to Huey? No. Even now, being threatened, probably fearing for her life, she was showing more strength than most.

He grabbed her wrists and slammed them against the wall, holding her in place. The thought of her trying to fight back never occurred to him, but she did. Her left knee rose, striking him high on his inner thigh with enough force to cause him to grunt at the slight pain. She pushed against his hands and tried to bite him.

He angled away from her and whirled her around, violently shoving her against the wall until her face was pressed against the cold metal and her right wrist bent behind her.

Jules spoke into her ear. "I'm not going to kill you. But you *will* give me my answer. Deep blue. Is it code? Code for blue district?"

She bucked against him, trying to throw him off. He pressed harder against her, holding her still. She was limber; he had to give her that. Even with her hand twisted up between her shoulder blades, she didn't cry out. He evaluated her stance. She was relaxed, not tense. Scared and trembling, but not rigid in fear.

Her breath came out in ragged gasps.

Huey's shouts filtered through the plasma bolt hole, and Jules turned his head and glared at him. "You promised, Jules! You promised me you wouldn't kill one of the Coalition!"

Jules turned back to her. Her breathing had calmed. She peered at him from the corner of her eye.

"You know I'm part of the Coalition?"

"I do now."

"Then kill me." The words hissed from her. "Because I won't tell you anything. And I won't betray my people."

There was bravery in her. He could torture the information from her. Not even the strongest man had ever withstood him. Hurt her but not kill her.

But he wasn't that man anymore. He didn't want to *be* that man anymore.

He released her and stepped back. She turned but kept her back against the wall, watching him warily. Huey's shouts became yells. Jules strode to the door, pushed it open enough to reach through, and grabbed Huey's shirtfront.

"I promised you! So shut up!" He flung Huey to the floor, causing the leads he was using to hack the panel to disconnect. Jules grabbed the leads and yanked them out. Then he reached in and ripped the wires from the panel, severing them from the door.

His muscles strained as he slid the door closed again.

When he faced her, she stood plastered against the wall in the same position. Arms crossed against her chest, hugging herself, her shoulders hunched. Fear still colored her face. Yet there was defiance there, too.

Jules pulled a chair from the side table and sat it in the middle of the room. He straddled it, stared at her, and then glanced at his hand—the hand that still held his gun. He had been holding on to it the whole time. No wonder she was still terrified.

He shoved it back into its holster. A bit of tension left her. Jules motioned to the bunk. "Sit down."

She sat on the edge.

"I said I won't kill you."

"Could have fooled me." Now that he wasn't near her and the gun was put away, a bit of bravado apparently entered her.

Jules clasped his hands together and hung them over the chair back. Maybe he shouldn't have come in so hot, but how else was he supposed to get his information? She knew how to reach JJ. Did she know him?

"Do you know a JJ?"

She looked over at him then. The blues were starting to return, yet her eyes still held a lot of fear. "JJ? No. No one by that name."

"He's an assassin. Has any come into the Coalition recently?"

"Assassin?" She paused. A calculating look came over her, and she slid down to the foot of her bunk, bringing herself a bit closer to him. "Is that what you are?"

"Were."

"Were." She nodded. Her hand absently rubbed at her right wrist. "Hmm. If he did, then it was after I was gone."

He stood. Her breath caught, and terror danced in her eyes again. Jules sat down beside her on the bunk. "Your transmission from whomever on Mars said Deep Blue. JJ said those words to me the day he left."

"You left, too?" She angled away from him, setting herself as far away as she could.

"I did. I was scheduled for decommission."

"You mean, to be killed."

Jules nodded. Her hand still rubbed at her wrist. He reached out and grasped her right hand. Rigidness shot through her. He ignored her fear and wrapped his hand around her wrist and squeezed. Small bones, the carpals, popped back into place. She gave a quick gasp at the sudden pain and then relaxed as he let go.

"I would say I'm sorry—"

"But you aren't."

He stared at her. If he wanted her to talk, he needed to be honest. "It isn't that I'm not. It's that I don't know how to be."

She glanced at her wrist and then back at him. "I think you already said you're sorry."

Time to deviate from that line of conversation. "You used the BOD-suit to stay undetected?"

She nodded and pointed to the access tube. "I have a trip-mod up there."

He glanced up at the opened panel. The trip-mod would have to be removed, but that could wait. "Huey intercepted a security feed from the Nest Protocol. Although you left unnoticed, we saw you in a reflection. You stole the program."

Color drained from her face.

"I'm not asking for it. Only want to know what it is." He pulled the disk from the mercenary from his pocket. "I saw you sell this today. Took it back."

She plucked it from his fingers and frowned. "Took it back?" She regarded him for a moment, her unspoken question apparently already answered. "This isn't the whole program. Only a weakened version. I would never sell the GHOST."

"Ghost?"

"That's what I call it. It allows someone to hijack or hack into navigation and comms. I've been going over it each night, and I see the potential to hack into any system. And it never leaves a trace, nor is it detectable. No one can ping it for a location."

Jules frowned. "That's a dangerous program."

"It is. But it will be useful for the Coalition." She paused at that word and swallowed hard. "You aren't going to kill me?"

He shook his head and leaned onto his elbows that he propped on his knees. Once an assassin, always an assassin. He was almost at that point where he would have forced the information from her. But what stopped him?

Something made him stop. Maybe when he saw her defiance? When she looked at him in fear, yet not bending?

She waited for a reply. He looked at her . . . truly looked at her. Her freckles stood out against the pale skin. There, on her cheek, was a pattern that reminded him of the Seven Sisters constellation. Dark red lashes outlined bright blue eyes. A small lump formed in his throat when he answered.

"A year ago, I would have. I've killed many, Coalition and those not of the Coalition. But not now."

She ran a hand under her nose and sniffed. "Deep Blue is a code. I have to use it when I enter the Blue District. An elder will meet with me and give me the coordinates home or have me assigned with a group who will take me home."

"You want to go home?" It was an odd concept. Home. His home, if he could call it that, was the *Nightingale.*

"More than anything. I never should have left."

"Don't you know where home is?" It seemed ridiculous that she didn't know where they lived.

A deep frown marred her face as she glared at him. "Of course, I do. But to get inside, you will need exact coordinates. I don't own a ship, and I have never left the compound before. So, I never knew the exact coordinates."

Jules ran his hand through his hair. This was a frustrating conversation. "Why?"

"The entrance is . . . " She pressed her lips together and gazed to the side. "Hmm . . . let's just say it's deep underwater and hidden."

He nodded. There were a few Elite Squad bases like that. "Can we make a deal?"

"What? A deal, as in my life in exchange for the coordinates? No way." She stood and started to back away.

Jules rose faster than she could react and captured both of her hands. She struggled at first, but he brought her up against him, wrapping his arms around her and pinning her in place. When she calmed down, he stepped away, yet held her around her elbows, keeping her facing him. "No. Not that kind of deal. I will take you home. I will keep you safe and protected. In exchange, I want you to introduce me to the Coalition."

Her gaze searched his face, flowing from one side to the other before settling somewhere below his chin. "You plan to kill them. That's what GFT assassins do."

Jules shook his head and let go of her. This was getting nowhere fast. Time to retreat and come back at another angle.

"You won't kill them?" Her voice was soft, wondering.

He paused at the door and turned back around. "No. No, I won't. And never will. I'm not a GFT assassin anymore."

She took a step toward him. "You won't hurt me?"

He cast a look at her wrist. No. He wouldn't hurt her again. The thought surprised him. He might still have those assassin reactions, yet with her . . . She pulled the BOD-suit cap off, and strands of red hair fell across her face. Her eyes watched him those few seconds as he stood at the door.

"No. I won't ever hurt you again." Jules stepped forward. "I'll protect you. Take you to Mars. You introduce me to the Coalition, and I will take you home. Miss du—"

"Abigail. Or Abby. Most people call me Abby."

He stood there, watching her for a moment. Abby. Something knotted in his chest. He nodded. "Abby. You can call me Jules."

Huey's voice filtered through the damaged panel. "If we're through making friends, Cap, do you think you can open this door, give Abby—if she will let me call her that—new quarters, and pick up on this conversation in a better setting because I am sure she would like to take that BOD-suit off. You're being inconsiderate, Cap. Again."

Jules gave her a little smirk. When she held her hand out to him, he hesitated before gripping it. "I'll prepare new quarters for you. And—"

"You don't have to say it. I know."

He blinked at her. Gave her a nod before turning to the door and forcing it completely open. She knew he was . . . sorry? Was that what he was feeling? Huey gave him a sidelong look as he opened the quarters next to his cabin.

"You did the right thing, Cap." Huey went inside to prepare it for Abby so she could change into her clothes.

Jules looked back at the destroyed panel and the opened room beyond where she was collecting her things and stuffing them into her travel bag. It felt like the right thing to do. And at the same time, he felt uncertain. As if he had just stepped onto an untraveled road with no directions or guide.

# Chapter Ten
## JUMPGATE

Abigail set her duffel on the bunk. A small, yellow, oval rug rested in the middle of the room, which was the same size as her former quarters. But no viewport. That was a definite plus.

She walked over to the wall console and activated the HoloNews. If he had killed the buyers . . .

She selected text only and read the updates. It was the third story. Two bodies in a maintenance tunnel. No leads. No evidence. Security in a three-block radius was down. Abigail closed her eyes and leaned her forehead against the cool console surface.

If he could murder that easily, would he do that to them? She breathed out a prayer. "Please show me that I'm doing the right thing."

She hooked her datapad into the console and downloaded the report. When it finished, she retreated to her bunk. The small, metal case gleamed where it lay on the cover. She eyed it as she stripped off her BOD-suit and dressed in a pair of loose cargos and her white undershirt. Parameters would need to be set before she introduced him to an elder.

She thought back to Michael and Peter. She was never around them, but she had read their bios. They were like him, yet they had agreed to the rules. They had confessed that they had killed without prejudice and would just as soon drop a man with a sword than not. But when it came to surrendering their weapons, they did it. They followed every edict and rule, listened and learned, until one night they knelt during service and surrendered to the Lord.

Could he do that, too?

Abigail scooped up the case and slid it into her pocket. She pulled the GHOST from the datapad and dropped it beside the case. She would have to keep both with her from now on.

She keyed open her door and headed for the ladder, pausing at the camera. This deal was going to require trust. On both their parts. She pried it from under the rung and then clambered up to the next level. The bridge was straight ahead and up a small flight of steps.

The hatch was open, washing the small corridor in a soft blue light. Abigail climbed the steps but paused at the opening. Captain Williams—no, Jules—sat in the pilot's chair, a book balanced on his knee.

"You planning on hovering there?"

She jumped. "I . . . "

He swiveled his chair to look at her. His finger held his place as he closed the book. "I heard you leave your quarters."

Abigail frowned. "How?"

Jules pushed the co-pilot chair around with his foot. "Sit."

She eased inside and perched on the edge of the seat. He watched her for a moment before completely closing the book and setting it on the navboard in front of them. Her gaze fell on the title. *Complete Works of John Keats.* Same author as that poem on her datapad—the one she hadn't read yet.

"You have a lot of questions, and so do I." He pointed to her hand. "What's that?"

Abigail opened her palm and produced the camera. "I had it on the underside of the ladder to alert me if anyone came too close to my quarters." She bit her lip. It didn't let her know in time that he was at her quarters. Did he already know about it?

His eyes narrowed as he stared at the camera. "You're wondering why it didn't alert you earlier than it did?"

"How do you know what I'm thinking?" She shook her head. Reading thoughts was impossible.

"Logical deduction. You seemed too surprised when I forced myself in. The camera didn't perform its function." He plucked the camera from her hand and crushed it in his fist. A bit of anger flowed across his face before it smoothed out. He dumped the broken item on the holographic table to his left. "I jumped down, bypassing the ladder."

She swallowed the lump in her throat. It was just one squeeze. And the casing of the camera was a thin titanium alloy. It shouldn't have been that easy to break. His green gaze still bored into her, waiting. He knew she had more to show him. She took a trembling breath and held out her datapad.

"The HoloNews has already reported the bodies."

He didn't read the article. Only took the datapad, glanced at the screen, and then set it to the side by his book. "I assumed as much by now. But all traces of us were erased."

"I don't care about that. I . . . " She faltered. How was she going to be able to dictate rules to someone like him? He would never understand the reasoning behind the rules. And frankly, he still frightened her.

His eyes narrowed. "I told you I wouldn't harm you again." He stood and collected her datapad and his book. "Follow me."

It was a demand more than a request. He slipped through the opening, apparently expecting her to obey him. She grimaced and rose from her seat. He waited at the end of the steps. Abigail fell into step beside him but paused when Anya climbed up the ladder.

"Jules, what happened to the du Soleil quarters?" She noticed Abigail standing next to him. "Oh, Miss du Soleil."

Abigail nodded back as Jules took her arm and propelled her to the observation deck as he answered Anya. "The door had a faulty connection and had locked her inside. Had to blast the panel."

"Oh." Anya narrowed her eyes at them. "Where are you heading?"

Jules paused, pulling Abigail to a stop with him. "Observation lounge. I have a business deal to discuss with Miss du Soleil." He turned from the medtech.

Abigail glanced at the woman as she was pushed along toward the lounge.

Anya stared after them for a bit before she turned toward the medlab, speaking over her shoulder. "Well, I hope the newer quarters are better. Jules, I have the components. Enough for about seven vials." She gave them one more glance before slipping into the examination room. Yet Abigail still caught the cold look in her ice blue eyes.

He palmed open the door and pointed to the table. "Have a seat."

She crossed the room and sat on the corner of the bench. "Why did you tell her a different story than what happened?"

"Because she doesn't need to know everything that I do." His knee bumped against hers as he sat at the end. The datapad clicked on the hard surface as he dropped it in front of her. He held his book in his hand, his thumb caressing the edge of the worn hardback cover.

Her gaze followed the movement. It was an odd motion from someone like him. Assassins had no feelings. No desires. No compassion or compulsions. Not unless they were weaned off Serum Seventy-four.

"Are you still taking the serum?" The question blurted out before she could stop it. His thumb stilled. His gaze darkened.

"You're not the only one with questions." His stare hardened even more. "One question, one answer. Then I will do the same. If we are to trust each other, we will have to be honest."

So, he was thinking the same as her? Abigail shook her head. "How would I know if you are being truthful? Assassins are trained to govern their emotions and can lie easily. You want me to trust you and take you to my people. But I have to protect my people. You murder without thought."

A slight frown creased his eyebrows. Abigail paused. Remorse? Or even guilt? She watched his face, but no other emotion betrayed him. With a nod, she straightened in her seat and placed her arms on the table. "Okay. Answer for answer."

He leaned back. Another fleeting look crossed his face. The man was an enigma. "Yes. I am still taking the serum. A derivative, actually. We don't have the exact formula, so Anya does her best. I can't live without it. Why do you ask?"

"Other assassins have come into our fold. Yet they are weaned off the serum and do not need to rely upon it. Why is it different for you?"

He shrugged. "Don't know. That would be one thing I would like to know about myself." Jules cocked his head to the side. "Why did you sell the program? I said travel to Mars was included."

"Because I was going to book a stay on Mars until I was given a way home." She picked up her datapad and twirled it around in her hands. "But since you offered to take me home, I may not need it. Yet the Coalition may not allow you to do that. There will be strict concessions you will have to make before an elder will allow you to travel to my home."

"Which is the main base."

Abigail nodded. "Yes." She leaned forward. "You have to stop the killing. Or the Coalition won't accept you. Won't even consider talking to you."

Jules shook his head. "I killed them because they planned to kill you."

Argh. This was going to be hard to explain. She pinched the bridge of her nose. "I understand. But you must curb the impulse. Some things you will have to let slide. Self-defense is justifiable. But you murdered. You didn't have to kill them."

"I—"

"The others who found us agreed. They handed over their weapons and ships. They allowed the Coalition to help them overcome the indoctrination. They took that step of placing their lives in our hands." He scowled at her, and she rushed into the next part of her sentence. "We won't lie to you. We won't harm you or kill you. That isn't our way."

His thumb started rubbing the book's spine. He glanced down at his hand, and the thumb stilled. "You said the Coalition helped them."

"Yes."

A long silence hung between them before he looked back up at her. It wasn't a softness in his gaze. Yet the hardness was gone. Was it hope she saw in him?

"The serum allows me to see further, hear further, smell more than most. I heard your door open and knew you were heading to find me. The serum also enhances my strength and speed. If the Coalition helped the others, maybe they can help me."

He wanted help? She pursed her lips in puzzlement. "You don't want your enhancements?"

"I want to be free." He leaned onto his elbows. "I don't feel like other people. I told you earlier I don't know how to be sorry. And I don't. It's foreign to me. We were stripped of our emotions. Of feelings." He paused and then shook his head. "No. Not feelings. We learned to hate, learned anger, and how to . . . does it make sense if I say 'purged'? We were purged of any emotion that made us weak."

His eyes implored her. He was being honest. Of that she was sure. There was something within him that was compelling him to trust her. "When did it happen?"

"What? When did what happen?"

"The change you are feeling." Abigail turned on the bench and propped against the edge of the table, leaning on her arm. "Something had to happen for you to feel like this."

He sighed and shook his head. "Long story. Suffice it to say I was injured, and something strange happened. Something I can't explain. Then I was decommissioned, and I ran. Been looking for my friend who defected long before me."

"JJ."

"Yes."

The door behind them opened. Bishop Thomas entered, and his gaze fell on them. "Evening." He paused before the Xulons and selected a beverage. "You don't have to stop talking on my account."

Jules stood and waved the bishop over. "Bishop, I need your assistance."

The older man collected his beverage before walking to the table and settling down at the other end. "How may I help?"

Jules crossed his arms across his chest and nodded toward Abigail. "She's part of the Coalition—"

Abigail jumped up. She'd trusted him, and now he had told someone. Fear flooded through her. She turned to escape, but Jules captured her and wrapped his arms around her, pinning her back against him. The muscles in his arms clamped tighter and pulled her closer to his hard chest.

"He knows the Coalition." His breath stirred the strands of her hair.

His words barely registered, but the bishop's voice filtered through her fear. "Jules, let her go. It would have been better if you had introduced us without dropping that she's Coalition. Miss du Soleil, do you know of Michael and Peter?"

Abigail stopped struggling. Jules let her go and stepped back. The heat of his body left her, and the coolness of the room flowed back around her. She glanced over at Jules. He was looking at his arms in confusion before he sat back down at the table.

She settled back onto the bench and kept a wary eye on him. "Yes. They were Zulu. Came to us about five months before I left."

"Zulu?" Jules' gaze bounced from her to the bishop and back again. "Zulu went to the Coalition?"

"Only two. They had to 'dispatch,' as they said, the others." A strange look passed over his face. That was puzzling. "They agreed to our terms, by the way."

He shook his head. "Zulu?"

"Yes."

Bishop Thomas laughed. "Yes, Zulu, Jules. Michael and Peter found the Bishops of the Faith. I was assigned to them and helped them reach the Coalition. They are now a part of them."

Jules stood and retreated to the viewport. "That's hard to believe. Zulu is even deadlier than Juliet."

Juliet? That must have been him. And probably JJ? "Is that you? Juliet?"

He didn't turn to her to answer. "My squad. I was leader."

Bishop Thomas sipped his drink. "Miss du Soleil . . . your father is Jedidiah?"

She nodded. "You know him?"

"Of him. I mainly meet with Elder Carson." He raised his hand when she started to ask him another question. "I help many assassins find the Coalition."

Abigail gave a half laugh. "How do you know they aren't spies? Trying to find us to kill us?"

The bishop looked at Jules as he spoke. "There's a look about them. An action about each assassin. I can tell there's more at work within them than what the government made them to be." He turned his focus back to Abigail. "Just as I see it in Jules."

Jules turned at that and let his gaze travel over them both. He didn't deny what the bishop said. Maybe he was feeling that, too?

Abigail turned back to Bishop Thomas. "And you saw that in Michael and Peter? Even in Mandy and Dan?"

The furrow in Jules' brow deepened even more. "Who are Mandy and Dan? More assassins?"

Bishop Thomas smiled. "Yes. Mandy and Dan. Echo 3-M and Echo 5-D. They searched out the Coalition about a year ago."

Jules shook his head as if he couldn't believe what he was hearing. "Zulu and Echo. Were there more, Bishop?"

"Just a few from Sierra."

A dark look crossed Jules' face at the mention of Sierra; then it fled as he pointed at Abigail. "She said there had to be parameters set. She said no killing, only in self-defense."

"That's true. He killed on Lunar." She activated the report on her datapad and slid it across the table to Bishop Thomas, who picked it up and started reading.

Jules huffed and stuffed his hands in his back pockets before turning back to watch the moon activity. "They were planning on killing her. I had to do it."

She shook her head. "It was murder."

He whirled around. His eyebrows were drawn down so low that they cast shadows over his eyes. "Why the revulsion? You steal programs from GFT. If that's a sin, as you people like to call it, and is wrong, then why the revulsion at what I had to do? Those were mercs. Mercs who would have chased you down and would have killed you."

His gaze narrowed. His green eyes flashed in anger and hardened as he watched her.

What could she say? It was different what she did. Right?

"I stole that program because of what it would have done to us. They would have found us and killed us. Taking that program protected my people. That was the only thing I did. Normally, I'm just erasing our tracks and any information about us. To protect us. And this time, I removed a dangerous program from the hands of GFT."

He snarled. "And that's what I did! I removed a danger the mercs possessed. And you are asking me to give up, to relinquish what makes me who I am in order to talk to the Coalition. In order to find JJ."

Bishop Thomas rose from the table and walked behind Abigail. His hand fell onto her shoulder and gave it a slight squeeze. "You both will have to start trusting one another if you want to call a truce. Jules, Miss du Soleil is right. You will have to curb the urge to kill. The Coalition will not accept you if you do not. And you will have to give up your weapons and ship. You will eventually gain it back, but you will find something even better than a pulse gun or ship." He looked down at Abigail. "And you, I need you to understand one thing."

She allowed him to pull her to her feet. He held her hands in his and brought them to his chest. His amber eyes looked into hers. "I understand these men and women more than most. I've been with them and have talked to them. I want *you* to understand that, just like the others, Jules has to travel his own road to Damascus."

Road to Damascus. His own path to the truth. If she wasn't called to rescue him, then what should she do? She glanced over at the man who stood at the viewport. His arms were crossed across his chest. Dull, red scars covered his hands. There was one long scar that ran down the right side of his neck and disappeared beneath the cowl of his shirt. The light reflected off a white scar near his lips that were drawn into a frown.

Jules watched them, a shadow playing across his face, highlighting the deep lines and angles. His gaze met hers. And she saw a small light inside the green. It was definitely hope she saw there. Hope in what? Rescue? Acceptance? To understand?

That was what she would have to be for him. Just a guide. Someone to help him not only find the way but to understand.

She turned back to the bishop and nodded. "We all have a different path to follow."

Bishop Thomas smiled and patted her hands in a soft, fatherly gesture.

Confusion passed over Jules' face for a moment. He glanced outside the viewport for a spell before nodding. Whatever reluctance he had felt earlier no longer showed. "I'll do it. No killing unless necessary, such as protecting you or others. I'll hand over my weapons and ship. I'll even allow a medscan in order to understand what they did to me." He faced them and swallowed. A desperation had entered his eyes and voice. "I don't want to be like this. They made me, and I want to unmake me."

$$\Sigma$$

Jules sat on the exam table and waited as Anya refilled the injection gun. For two days, she had been giving him the silent treatment. Not that he minded, but her harsh, narrow gazes were wearing thin. She turned to him and frowned.

"Remove your shirt."

"You don't need to do a full examine. Just give me the dose in my arm." He started pushing up his sleeve.

"Not this time, Julius." She stood before him, her hip brushing against his knee. "This serum is the closest I've been able to come to the formula. I have very little Eighty-three to use. And the Versikton supply is extremely low. I need Substance Eighty-three, Paxolin, and Versikton. But instead, I have to work with what I got. So far, the serum seems to work without the Paxolin. Yet it's not at the strength I need to make it. That said, this needs to be administered to the abdomen for quicker absorption."

Jules reached behind him, gripped the neck of his shirt, and pulled it over his head. Anya's breath caught slightly. It was so slight that even she didn't notice she did it. But he saw the brief intake of breath and the microsecond pause. And this was why he hated doing this. The woman wanted more from him than he could give. She pushed him down onto the table.

The cold, conforming mesh sent a shiver down his spine. "You have the temperature turned down."

"I do. When did you notice it?" Her fingers ran across his stomach, over the raised scars that covered his body.

"When I walked in but didn't pay attention until I laid back on the table." His stomach muscles contracted as she pressed against a clear area near his navel. She wiped with an antiseptic cleaner and then placed the gun against him. A quick prick and her latest concoction burned into him.

"Is it supposed to burn?"

"It can. If it bothers you, I can add a numbing agent to it next time." She retreated to her counter.

Jules sat up and pulled his shirt back on. "No. Doesn't matter to me. Only a comment on the difference from last time."

She smiled and typed on her datapad. "I'll record that then. It's probably because I strengthened this dose. So, you won't need another until three days from now."

Jules nodded. He donned his vest and jacket. Anya placed a hand on his arm to stop him before he slipped off the table.

"Jules, we do need to talk. Soon." Her ice-blues watched him, staring at him just as hard as he was staring at her. "If not tonight, then at least tomorrow."

There was more to her voice. The timbre seemed more on edge. And her pulse had quickened. Her palm on his right wrist turned cooler, almost clammy. A nervous look fleeted across her face.

She was keeping something from him. Something important. He reached over and removed her hand. "I'll swing by your quarters later. We'll talk."

At her nod, he slid off the table and left the medlab, feeling her gaze still on him. As he climbed the short steps, he picked up her steady gaze in his peripheral. Ever since leaving Lunar Tarsus One two days ago, she had been acting strangely. Sometimes on the verge of speaking to him and then sometimes ignoring him completely. Whatever happened with her on Lunar, hopefully she would tell him tonight. Since his talk with Abby, Anya had avoided him as much as possible. Showing up only to dose him or give him an update on hydroponics or some medical file she found.

He closed down the navigational table when he entered the bridge. The holograph for the jumpgate faded. Jules removed Huey's toy robot from his console—again—and set it on the holographic table before settling down into his chair and spinning it around to face the console.

Huey entered and fell heavily into his own chair. "Jumpgate arrival in ten."

"Did you speak to Bishop Thomas and Abby about what to expect?"

Huey nodded and tapped his console. "I did. Bishop Thomas was prepared. Abby had no idea what to expect, so the bishop had her sit with him. I told her it could get rough for first-timers."

Jules scoffed. He reached under the console and pulled out a medbag. "Yeah. Here."

Red flooded across Huey's face as he accepted the bag. "Well, I didn't tell her that even the most seasoned of us still gets sick from it." He laughed and started strapping his restraints around him.

Jules keyed open his comm. "Anya, are you situated?"

It took a couple of seconds for her to answer. "I'm set."

He rose and closed the bridge. Flipped the switches, activating the mag-locks on all the doors. Then opened the viewscreen on the security console. Lower level. He scanned through the images. All were secured. "Huey, double check the lower bay."

Huey's fingers danced across the console. "Secure."

Jules switched to main cargo. All seemed secure and locked. "Check outer airlock."

"Clear."

The screen flipped through the feeds. Corridor, Medlab, lounge. All clear. He keyed open the comm to the bishop's quarters. "Bishop Thomas, we are two out from the jumpgate. Are you secured?"

His answer came back faster than Anya's. "We are secured, Captain."

Jules closed the screen and buckled himself into his chair. Huey smiled at him as Jules pulled his own medbag from the small storage under the console.

Ahead, the massive form of the jumpgate loomed. A transport approached the gate, slipping between the buoy markers of the jump-lane, and then disappeared into swirling, hypnotic mass of light.

Huey looked over at him. "It wouldn't be so bad if we weren't in solar conjunction right now."

"I know. This is going to be a rough ride." He opened the comms again. "Gateway Jump One, this is *Nightingale*, requesting access."

"*Nightingale*, please wait for IF confirmation." Seconds passed by as their ship fell into a holding pattern, circling the designated lane. "*Nightingale*, Gateway Jump One, permission granted. Sending coordinates to you now. Reminder: keep all comms closed while in jump."

The link closed. Jules sent the coordinates to Huey's console and shut down all the comms. Once received, Huey maneuvered the *Nightingale* into the lane. The red lights on the buoys turned green. "Ready?"

His finger poised over the console. Jules took a fortifying breath and nodded. "Go."

"Thrusters one and two, now." The ship gave a small lurch toward the gate. "Shutting down . . . now." The rumble from the engines died, and the *Nightingale* entered Gateway Jump One.

A riot of energy sparked across the console and viewport. The octagon-shaped ring pulsed with energy. Then the center swarmed into a pulsing, purple mass that fell into a black nothingness, pulling his ship along with it.

An invisible grip grabbed at his stomach and pulled, stretching Jules. His body was in the chair, yet a part of him was pulled and twisted about as the ship slid into an inky black sea. The bridge pulsed and throbbed around him. Pushing out and then breathing in. Heat flowed around him. Then they were out.

His body slammed back into him. Nausea gripped him. Beside him, Huey gagged into the bag in his hands. Tears flowed from his eyes when he looked up at Jules, a strand of saliva hanging from his lips.

"That was rougher than usual." He spat one last time into the bag before sealing it and wiping at his mouth with his sleeve.

Jules nodded. He unbuckled and started to turn his chair when the full force of the jumpsickness hit him. The nutrient drink he had earlier flowed into the bag. He heaved once more, ignoring Huey's laughter. With a shudder, he sealed his own bag.

"For laughing, you get to dispose of the sick bags."

That sobered Huey. He grimaced, rose from his chair, and collected the bag from Jules. "Fine." He motioned at his console with the bags. "I have her on autopilot. We are in the dark for about twelve hours. Then we will be in range of Mars."

"I'll finish up here."

Huey left the bridge, grumbling. Jules rose from his chair and sat in the co-pilot seat. A quick glance through the readouts showed no damage to the ship with this jump. Unlike his last Jupiter run. That cost him two gravity metrics, a medlab panel, and seals on his airlock.

The comm pinged. Huey's voice filled the bridge. "Cap? Abby needs a dose of sedative."

He rose and closed down the console. Then locked the bridge behind him. He glanced into Medlab. No Anya. He entered and searched the cabinet above her workstation. There. A small collection of hypo-injectors that was stored for jumpsickness.

Jules grabbed a hypo-injector and glanced at the amount. Only ten cc's. With Abby's small stature, it should be enough.

He left Medlab and clambered down the ladder. Anya was entering from the corridor from the cargo area. "Where were you?"

"Checking lower cargo." She motioned at his hand. "Who's that for?"

"Miss du Soleil." He waved her away when she reached for it. "I got it. We are in comm dark for at least twelve hours."

"Okay. When you finish with her, find me, okay?"

Jules gave her a short nod and turned away, palming open Bishop Thomas' door. The bishop and Huey huddled over Abby by the viewport. She was on her knees, bent over with an arm clenched around her stomach. Huey held her hair back, and Bishop Thomas helped her hold a medbag to her mouth.

Her small shoulders heaved, yet nothing was expelled. Tears streamed from her eyes, which looked up at him as he approached.

"Bishop, get a cool cloth." He knelt beside her. "It'll be okay. First time jumps are the worst. This will help you."

She nodded, and then her body spasmed once more as a wave of sickness engulfed her. Bishop Thomas returned, removed the medbag, and wiped at her face and lips. Jules pulled the hem of her shirt up.

At her startled expression, he dropped it. "It has to be administered via the abdomen. Won't hurt, I promise."

She gave a quick nod and allowed him to roll her over onto her back, yet her eyes jumped from the bishop to Huey, and embarrassment colored her face. Bishop Thomas looked at Huey as Jules raised her shirt.

"Huey, how about you and I retreat to the lounge? Give her some privacy."

Huey gave her knee a gentle pat before he rose to leave. "You'll start feeling better soon."

A spasm shot through her body, and she rolled to her side; her face pulled back into a painful grimace. The dry heaving slowed. Jules took her by the shoulder and gently pushed her back against the floor. Abigail closed her eyes as he set the hypo-injector against her pale skin, noticing the small collection of freckles that dotted her stomach. When her stomach convulsed, he spread his hand against her and held her still as he pushed the plunger. It would take about two seconds for the medicine to empty into her.

The ripple of muscles slowly eased under her smooth skin. And her skin *was* smooth. And soft. The hypo-injector clicked. Jules removed it and lowered her shirt. The red on her face started fading.

"Thank you." The words fell thickly from her lips. Her eyes blinked slowly. "Was that Medolin?"

Jules nodded. "Only ten cc's."

She gave him a small smile. "I'm not allergic to it, only overly sensitive. If I had known, I would have tried to get to a bunk . . . " Her eyes fluttered before she forced them open. "Think you can help me to my quarters?"

Jules slid the hypo-injector into his back pocket and helped her sit up. "Can you stand?"

She nodded. He helped her to her feet, only to catch her as she went limp.

He slid his arm under her knees and lifted her into his arms. Her head fell against his chest, and an arm dangled behind him, hitting against his waist. He rolled her body toward him until she was nestled tightly against his body, allowing him to key open the door.

Her red hair flowed around him. The scent of her met his nose. Distant memories pulled at him. Spices, sweet and sharp. Like vanilla. It was a hazy memory, one that wanted to force its way to the surface.

Jules shook his head at it and angled her in his arms so he could palm open her door. It slid open, and he stepped inside, noting the litter of datapads and wires on the table at the end of her bunk. The floor held her duffel, where clothes poured out of it. Yet she hadn't pushed the rug to the side in these quarters.

The door slid closed as he crossed the room. As he gently laid her on the bunk, her eyes opened slightly. Only inches separated them. Her bright eyes stared at him before slowly closing in sleep.

He eased the cover out from under her body and pulled it up, smoothing it along her shoulders. His fingers brushed against her hair. Like a soft cloud. Curls captured his fingers.

When she had stared at him, there was trust in there. As if she saw something within him that allowed her to trust—something that apparently even he wasn't aware of. Jules stood and gazed down at her sleeping form.

He had to admit that there was something about this redheaded woman. He fisted a hand over his breastbone. Whatever he was feeling, it was unfamiliar. And every time he looked at her, it was there.

The need to protect? His mind fell back to the dark-eyed girl during his training. He'd had the chance to protect her, to speak up. But he hadn't. He couldn't risk the lives of his squad over her. When she was carried away, he'd vowed to protect his squad no matter the cost.

Back then, he had the GFT to fear. Not now, though. And the need to protect—it was stronger than ever with Abby. He felt that toward her, but that wasn't the feeling that clenched his heart, catching him unawares.

He stepped away from her and eased out the door. He could revisit that feeling later. After he dealt with the Mars mission.

After. Not before then.

He paused at the ladder and glanced back at Anya's quarters at the far end of the corridor near the chutes. Whatever she wanted to see him about needed to be attended to before they landed at Mars.

The automatic timer dimmed the overheads as he strode down the walkway. A red light blinked on the panel. She had it locked.

Jules knocked on the door. "Anya."

After a few seconds, the door pinged and then opened. Anya leaned against the hatch frame. "I thought you would show up later. Didn't think you would actually come after tending to her." She waved him in. "How is the du Soleil woman?"

"Sleeping. She was sensitive to the meds."

"To be expected. It usually causes drowsiness." She perched on the chair at the table and brought her foot up onto the seat, wrapping her arm around her knee as she perused a datapad.

"You wanted to speak to me?" He leaned back against the support beam at the end of her bunk and attached to the curvature of the bulkhead.

"Only about what you are doing with the du Soleil woman." She glanced up at him. Her eyes flashed briefly. "You said you had a business proposition?"

"A deal, yes. I plan to employ her services on Mars. She is talented with programs and communications."

Anya brushed her short, white strands behind an ear. "You have Huey for that."

"He doesn't plan to leave the ship." There was more. She was holding back. A bit of anger flared within him. "What is bothering you? I've used passengers before. In exchange for passage."

"Passage? She plans on staying with us a bit more?" Anya placed her datapad on the table. The screen faded, but he caught the logo of GFT Medicals.

"Maybe. She hasn't said yet. She'll know once we reach Mars." He pushed off the wall and picked up her datapad. Her eyes narrowed as he opened the screen. Medical journals and updates. A small icon was at the bottom, but when he pressed it, a passcode was needed. He replaced the pad in front of her. "Medical data?"

"Checking to see if there are any updates. Paxolin is in short supply, it seems. The med gel we sold on Lunar was used to buy more medical supplies and a dose of Versikton, except not at the amount I needed. I'm trying to find where I can buy more." She pushed the datapad to the side and regarded him for a bit. "You don't normally spend this much time with passengers, yet you've spent the last three days with the bishop and the woman. I want to know why. Are you attracted to her?"

He glared at her. The gall of the woman. He leaned his shoulder against the bulkhead. "You know I don't have those abilities, those emotions. Attraction to another is not a viable option for me. Are you jealous?"

Anya stood and approached him. "Yes. In a way. Normally you come to me. Yet you have avoided me. And not just these last three days, but this has been happening over the last few weeks. You are acting out of the ordinary."

Jules shook off her hand when she reached for him. He pushed away from the wall and stalked to the door. "You're overstepping your bounds, Anya. You are here to provide me the serum and have a place to do your research. You are not to meddle in my affairs."

"Jules!"

He jabbed at the control panel and was about to pass through when her hand grabbed his elbow. Reflex took over. He whirled around. His hand slammed into her chest, gripping her shirt, and pressed her into the wall next to the door.

It wasn't fear in her eyes. It was defiance and smugness. A smirk pulled at her lips. "I rest my case."

Jules let go of her and stepped back. She toed that line that he had set from day one. Toed it one too many times. What he did with his passengers was no business of hers. The time was coming when she would have to leave if she continued. "You will drop this conversation."

He stepped through the opened door and headed for the bridge. He could still feel her gaze on him, even as he climbed the ladder. If she had a clear view of him on this level, he was sure her gaze would have still burned into him.

Huey was in the cockpit, twirling the toy robot in his hands as he watched the readouts on his console. He tapped the corner of his screen. "Are you sending a message, Cap?"

"No." The hard lump in his chair pushed at his thigh when he sat down. Anger still coursed through him.

"There's one in a holding pattern. Not the same as the others, though." Huey turned to his left and flipped a couple of toggles on the communications backup. "Hmm. I can't access it, but it's there. Hidden within the automatics. And once we are out of dark comm, an automatic message will be sent to Mars for our landing coordinates."

Jules leaned his head back. "How long do we have?"

"We still have about eight hours until then."

"Then go get some sleep. Before we come out of the dark, I'll contact Abby. She has a program that will help us."

Huey turned a startled gaze to him. "Really? The Nest Protocol?"

Jules nodded and propped his feet on the console between them. He picked up his book that sat nestled in the space between his console and the bulkhead. "Go get some sleep. Lock the bridge as you leave."

The man didn't argue or question. He gave Jules a small shake of his head, let out a big yawn, and stretched his shoulders. "Then I leave you to your book, Captain. See you in eight."

Silence descended as he opened his book. "Ode to a Nightingale."

*My heart aches, and a drowsy numbness pains my senses . . .*

Jules paused at the start of the poem. That was how he felt. Ache and numbness, a contradiction of terms. Outside, the blackness of space covered them. Inside, he felt that same darkness pushing at him.

He closed the book and set it aside. The sounds of the ship silently sliding through space entered his mind as he let himself drift away. Pings of the consoles. Groans of the metal plating and engines. Pops from the bulkhead.

He opened his eyes and set the alarm on his console for five hours, then allowed himself to drift away again. Casting thoughts of Anya and Abby away. Darkness flowed through him, and he welcomed the respite.

## Chapter Eleven

# MARS, BLUE DISTRICT

Abigail pushed the blanket off and brought her feet around to the side of the bed. She sat up and waited. The nausea had dissipated. That was good. First time through a jumpgate and she'd hurled all over the bishop's quarters.

At least Jules had brought the meds to calm it down. The memory of his hand on her abdomen pushed its way through the haze of sleepiness. Even as he had administered the Medolin, a frown had traveled across his brow. His fingers had tightened on her as those dark brows pulled down even more in confusion. Then that same look as he placed her in her bunk.

Through the hazy veil of sleep, she saw that confusion and a bit of wonderment in his green eyes. More than that, she saw in him someone who was truthful, whom she could trust. She couldn't name what she saw. Yet the thought that Bishop Thomas was right—that there was a light working within him—flooded her thoughts as she rose and went to the refreshing unit by the sonic shower.

After a few moments in the refresher, she plucked a cleansing wipe from the wall and ran it around her face and neck. The Medolin dried her mouth and tongue. She would need a drink from the lounge to keep the oncoming headache at bay.

Her console pinged. She cast a startled glance at it. No one had ever pinged her before.

She depressed the button. "Yes?"

Jules' voice filtered through. "Would you bring your program to the bridge, please?"

Abigail looked over her shoulder at her datapad that laid on her table. Trust, right? He wasn't going to take it from her. He had said that earlier—that he didn't want her program. "I'll be right there."

She closed the comm and collected her datapad from the table, then donned her light shawl. A quick glance at her wrist monitor told her it was only five hours after jump. They had a long time to go before they made it to Mars.

The door slid closed behind her as she stepped out into the dimly blue-lit corridor. She climbed the ladder and started for the lounge to get her nutrient drink first, but Jules stepped out of the bridge, holding a frosted container with a straw.

"No need." He held it out to her. "Nutrient One. Great to dispel the negative effects of a sedative and jumpsickness."

To say she was startled would be an understatement. She paused at the steps for a moment. His face was devoid of any emotion. A blank slate, carved in marble.

He backed up, waving her in.

Abigail followed and sat in the co-pilot chair he motioned her toward. He held out the drink again. This time, she accepted it and took a small sip. The flavor burst against her tongue. Vanilla again.

"How did you know I was awake?" She swallowed another sip. "And thank you for this."

He nodded as he sat down in his chair, twirling it around to face her. His hand reached under his left thigh and pushed at the cushion underneath him before he leaned back. "I heard you. And the refresher. The units on the port side pull more energy. I saw the drop in power."

"That much? Can't you fix that?" She pulled another large gulp from the straw, almost sighing against the relief it was bringing to her head.

"It's negligible. It isn't much of a drop, but I can see it."

"Like how you can hear me?"

"Yes."

Abigail shook her head. "Is that part of what Serum Seventy-four did to you?"

He nodded, folding his hands across his flat stomach. She looked around the bridge. It was cooler up here, yet he wore only a thin, black shirt with the sleeves pushed up to his elbows. The material clung to him. The V-neck highlighted the scars on his neck and collarbone. She glanced away before speaking again.

"The others didn't retain all their abilities. They were weaned off the serum, and their abilities seemed to dull, almost to normal levels. Is that what you want?"

"Yes." His reply was so immediate, she whipped her gaze to him. He gave her a small smile. "To me, it's a curse. I hear everything. From the pops of the bulkheads to the creak in the tubes. I hear you when you swallow the drink. I can faintly hear your heartbeat inside you. I can see your pulse in your neck and along your temple." He leaned forward and touched the side of her face. His finger trailed the vein at her temple; then his hand fell away. "I don't care what I lose, as long as I can undo what they did to me."

With a huff, he straightened back into his chair. "But I called you up here for another reason. Not to talk about my abilities."

She set her drink on the holographic table behind them. "You need my GHOST?"

"In front of you is Huey's console. There's a message in there in a holding pattern wrapped into the automatics. Will your . . . program be able to find the message?"

Abigail turned to the console and activated the screen. She pulled up the communication hub. Opened the main files and glanced through them. Two lines were embedded in the code. Wouldn't be easy, but it was doable.

She plugged the GHOST into her datapad, pulled the cord from the back, and inserted the end into the top slot of the console.

"Do you always use your datapad? We have more processing power than your pad."

She tapped her screen, digging deeper into the codes that scrolled across the screen. "My pad has the program I designed to quickly isolate which vectors I need. And if I need to switch, I can do it without having to close down one and then open another and then repeat the same countless times." She flicked the lines to the side, closing them down.

There it was. The trail. She bent over her datapad and activated code after code, falling deeper into the automatic reply program. Jules faded to the background. Even his gaze fell away as she concentrated on the lines in front of her.

There! She isolated the two lines, highlighting them in red, and pulled them into the GHOST. A quantum message. She frowned. They weren't messages. These were files. It was going to take a while, even with the GHOST.

"This is a quantum message. It will take the GHOST a while to decipher them."

"I have a quantum message in my system?"

"No." She unplugged the datapad from the console and looked up at him. "You have a dozen quantum messages. All on top of the other. Because they are existing as one and in the same location, it will take the GHOST program a while to isolate each one. And you're right, I need more processing power. I also put the quantum in a holding pattern. It won't transmit unless I give the code."

Jules stood. His hand hit the panel to lock the door. "Sit in my chair. To the right is an empty console with all the processing you need."

"You locked the door?"

He moved aside as she switched chairs. When she sat down, she grimaced. So that was why he pushed at the chair under his leg. A hard knot poked at her thigh and pressed into her muscle.

"I'm willing to trust you. Your messages have not been like this, and I am sure that if you needed to send a message, you would have told me. I want to continue trusting Huey and Anya, but tell me, these messages . . . they would have to be sent here from the bridge?"

"Yes and no." She plugged her datapad into the console near the bulkhead. It was a small console but one of the newest, which sported a more condensed processor. Giving her three times the power than the standards. Abigail glanced over her shoulder at him. "Yes, it is normally conducted on a bridge and on the communication console.

You would need a direct line. But if there is a line ran from another console somewhere on the ship, then it can be doable. It would take more time to condense a quantum in order to send it through normal channels such as this."

"How long?" He picked up a toy robot and played with it. His fingers bent and turned the appendages of the robot as he sat in Huey's chair, his right foot crossed over his left knee.

"Maybe three or four days depending on the processor of the console. If they used the bridge, then an hour, tops." She held up her hand over her shoulder to stop his next question. "I know what you want to know, and yes, I can eventually locate if there is a line connecting a console to the bridge. But that will take time, and I will need to use the holographic table to view the schematics." She keyed the GHOST to run its isolating program and then twirled the chair around to face him. "It will take a few hours to run. Even the GHOST can't do everything in seconds."

His hands stilled. "Your program can hack that quickly?"

"Hack. Access. Open. Lock. You name it. Usually from either three seconds to about a minute. I don't know what Nest Protocol did. I'm still working on learning the language, but it acts as a superkey. This program supersedes all programming, becoming the ultimate code."

Jules set the robot on Huey's console. "I understand now why you stole it. If GFT had that program, they would have been able to find your people . . . " He looked up at her. A deep emotion, one she couldn't place, flooded his eyes. "And they would kill them. Eradicate them."

She swallowed against the lump in her throat. "Yes. They would have. And I will do anything to protect them."

He dropped his foot to the floor and leaned forward, bringing himself closer to her. His green eyes stared hard into her own. He cocked his head to the side. His brow furrowed. "I want you to understand this, Abby. I will protect your people. JJ is now a part of them. And I will do whatever it takes to protect my brother."

It was not a hardness that deepened the green in his eyes. It was a deep resolve, a determination.

She leaned toward him, her shawl falling around her knees as she propped on them and matched his gaze with her own. "And now you understand."

$$\Sigma$$

The ship had pinged, announcing that they were out of dark comm, and silence had reigned in the bridge for the remaining hours as they approached Mars.

The lights blossomed to life. Morning had come. Jules checked the chronometer. Eight o'clock GMT X-ray. That meant it would be two o'clock Coordinated Mars Time. That would leave him enough time to escort the bishop to his contact and hopefully gain a few more of those books.

Behind him, her fingernail tapped the console in irritation.

Jules turned from the console and, for a moment, regarded Abigail, who was propped against her forearms on the holographic table. Her long hair fanned around her hands as they swiped, tapped, and moved across the surface. "Find something?"

She flipped the thick strands over her shoulder and turned to him. "There are two possible places for remote access to the bridge's communication console."

"One is in the main cargo bay. Huey uses it."

"Yes. And the other . . . " She turned back to the table. With a tap, the schematic of his ship floated above the surface. Abigail reached into the holo-projection and enlarged the center. The crew quarters. She spanned her hands across the wall between Huey and Anya's quarters. Her hands rotated the schematics around until the edge of the wall faced them. Jules rose and stood beside her as she zoomed in even more, highlighting the connections that led to the consoles in each of their rooms. "The other is one of these. I can't isolate which because they share the main line."

Jules touched the blueprints in front of him and zoomed onto the control access panels to their consoles. "It would take about, what, three days to compile a quantum message?"

"For one. For a dozen? You do the math."

And he did. Before she even finished her sentence. Approximately one month and six days. And that was being generous. He swiped the projection to the side and brought up the main ship schematics. There was one more. Maybe. He zeroed onto his personal storage unit. "Would this console do the job?"

She pulled up the coding. As lines of numbers, symbols, and letters flew across the screen, her hands would pause some and swipe at others. The lines slowed, and then the holographic table was shut down.

When she turned to him, the top of her head barely reaching his nose, there was a questioning gaze on her face. "That's your console."

"Yes."

Her eyes narrowed. "You have only one passcode that you use? When was the last time you used that particular console?"

"One passcode. And about three weeks ago." He leaned his hip against the table. "It was used, wasn't it? Did you see the code?"

She retreated to his seat and pulled her datapad from its resting place. "I can't see the code used. I will need the GHOST, but with it otherwise occupied, I would have to hack it the old-fashioned way." Her fingers danced across the datapad.

The bridge opened, and Huey stepped inside. Surprise lit across his face at the sight of Abigail in Jules' chair, yet he said nothing as he fell into his own seat.

"Coming up on Mars Sat Three." He glanced at the panel between the command consoles. "Auto updates sent. And . . . yup. We will approach Compound Two. And weather is bad. Looks like the annual dust storm. That's going to make the slaving a bit bouncy for us."

Abigail glanced up from her pad. "We have to be slaved?"

Jules nodded and crossed his ankles. "The only way Mars allows ships to enter their space. Huey, call it in."

"Aye, Captain." He keyed his comm and waited.

Abigail set her datapad back into its spot. "It's still processing. Do you want me to check out the other one?"

Jules shook his head. "Not yet. Just sit tight. I want you to contact the Coalition when we land."

She swallowed hard, glanced nervously at Huey, and turned the chair around. Her face paled a bit as she watched outside the viewport. Without anything to occupy her, the blackness of space apparently consumed her thoughts. "Abby?"

When she turned to him, he pointed to the small seat behind his chair and situated against the bulkhead. "There's a jumpseat right there. You can sit in it."

A brief smile was her reply as she hopped up and strapped into the small seat that faced away from the viewport. As she settled in the seat, her back against the wall, Jules reclaimed his chair. He picked up her datapad and passed it over his shoulder to her. Her small fingers brushed against his as she grabbed it. "Continue monitoring. Can it perform simultaneous functions?"

"I'm sure it can. Never tried it."

"Scan for any messages that may be in holding patterns. And go ahead and see if you can isolate that code for me." Anything to keep her mind off the black void beyond the hull.

Huey looked over at him. "I would ask, but I'm sure you'll let me know soon enough. If you think I'm sending clandestine messages, you are mistaken. If I need to send a message, I will let you know."

Jules looked at the younger man. His brown eyes held a raw honesty. "Call in our destination."

Huey nodded and turned back to his console. "Mars Sat Three, *Nightingale*."

"*Nightingale*, Mars Sat Three. Destination?"

"Compound Two, Habitat One."

"Confirmed. Please wait for IF confirmation." Within seconds, the disembodied voice came back. "Confirmed, *Nightingale*. Proceed to Mars Sat Two and prepare for slave to Argyre Control Tower."

"Confirmed, Mars Sat Three. Proceeding to Mars Sat Two." Huey closed the comms, set their destination, and turned to Jules. "Jules, I'm going to be honest with you."

"You weren't to begin with?" Jules ignored the glares thrown his way.

"You know what I mean." He picked up his robot and twirled it in his hands. "I won't betray you. Yet don't leave me in the dark."

"Huey, when and if I have information to tell you, I will." Jules turned his gaze back out the viewport. "Right now, there's nothing to say. Yet know this, I do trust you. But don't ever betray that trust."

In his peripheral, he saw Huey swallow hard. "I hear you, Captain."

"*Nightingale*, Mars Sat Two. Release your navigation controls to alpha-charlie-one-three."

Huey keyed the comm. "Acknowledged." He blew out a breath and released the ship to Mars Sat Two, who slaved it to Argyre Control Tower.

Jules opened his console. The path their ship would take would bring them above the Hellas Planitia. Abigail would like to see that. He paused at the thought. Why would he think that?

As Mars grew larger in their view, its rust-red hue growing brighter, Huey turned in his chair. "Abby, want to see it?"

She bumped against Jules' chair as she stood. "Is it safe?"

"It'll be a little bumpy but probably safer than manually flying in." Huey started to stand, but Jules waved him back into his seat.

"She can have mine." He stood and backed up in order for her to take his seat. She eased down into the chair, pushed at the lump under her thigh, and leaned forward. Wonderment lit her face as Mars loomed before them.

Jules leaned over her shoulder and pointed at the area before them. "Keep watching there. Hellas Planitia. As we approach closer to atmo, you can see the slight indication of the huge tower."

The ship shuddered as Argyre Control Tower brought them closer to the planet. Jules pointed to the right. Her breath caught, and a smile bloomed across her face. When compared to the visage of Earth, it wasn't much. But there, the deep, dark depression of land before them, its barren and dry formation created a crater of wondrous beauty. And in its center stood the towering Martian landmass, a sentry overlooking the Planitia. It was alien, strange.

Then they were in the atmosphere. Fire and flames lashed against their hull. Winds buffeted against them. Soon they were through, their ship flying low over the empty landscape and under the washed-out sky until before them the massive dome of Compound Two appeared.

Argyre Control Tower slaved the *Nightingale* to the docking area at the south port. As their ship drew closer, the control tower radioed. "*Nightingale*, controls have been released. Please land at LZ one-five-nine."

"Confirmed, Argyre." Huey guided the ship to their designated docking port. Thrusters kicked in, and red dust violently swarmed around the hull. The ship shuddered. "We have confirmed lock."

Jules straightened. He had been leaning against the console, over Abigail, without realizing it. She looked up at him. "Do you want your seat back?"

"No. Can you contact the Coalition? Use the GHOST so that it can't be traced."

She nodded. "Guess we will see if it can perform multiple tasks." She passed Huey the cord from her datapad. "Plug it in, please?"

As Huey slid the connection into the port, Jules locked the bridge door. The console pinged, and Abigail activated the holographic video feed. Above the console, an image of an older, dark-skinned man appeared. His color was so dark, it seemed to be carved from obsidian, until he smiled. Then his face softened until it looked like Bishop's leather books. His brown eyes brightened.

"Abigail!" White teeth flashed, and then his smile died when Jules stepped into view. "Who's this?"

"Elder Carson, this is Captain Julius Williams. I booked passage on his ship, and he has asked to meet with the Coalition." At his frown, she rushed into her next sentence. "Do you know Bishop Thomas?"

"I do, girl. Is he one of Bishop's?"

"No. He found out by other means but wishes to—"

Jules placed his hand on her shoulder, stopping her. "I'm a former assassin, sir. Bishop Thomas will vouch for me. I want only to meet with representatives of the Coalition. I know my word will mean nothing, yet I will willingly surrender my weapons and acquiesce to a medscan, if needed."

"What business do you have with the Coalition? I feel you are not asking to join."

"No, sir." Jules clasped his hands behind his back. "I'm looking for my brother. Goes by the name JJ, if he hasn't changed it. His designation was Juliet 7-J."

The elder regarded him for a moment. He turned his head and talked off screen. No sound. So, he must have silenced the audio. Then he turned back and addressed Abigail. "Abby, nine o'clock Sol. I will contact you with the exact location in Blue District." He then turned his attention to Jules. "And you, Captain. You will be allowed to meet with one elder. You will surrender your weapons. A blood sample will be taken along with a complete medscan."

"I'll be waiting, Elder Carson." Abigail smiled at the old man, who returned her affection just as warmly. "Take care. And God be with you."

"God be with you, Abby-girl."

The communication ended. GBWY. Jules balled his hands into fists. The look the old man gave Abigail. Was that how an uncle or father would look at someone? He had seen that look before on his targets on many of his missions but never considered it until now.

"Captain?"

Jules started. He had missed Huey's question, and Abigail was giving him an odd look. "Yes?"

"Should I prep for your excursion?"

"Yes. Help Bishop Thomas and meet me at the airlock." As Huey left the bridge, he turned to Abigail. "I want you to stay either here in the bridge or in your quarters. Keep at the messages and let me know when you have an answer."

"Your bridge requires a passcode. What is it?"

He gazed at her, debating. It would be easier to keep her in her quarters, yet what if she needed access to his communication console to finish the analysis? Her blue eyes watched him, the datapad hugged to her chest. He never noticed until now how red her eyelashes were. Before they looked dark, but they had been tear-laden then. Her lips parted slightly. Almost of its own accord, his hand reached for her. The urge to touch her . . .

Jules gave himself a mental shake and let his hand fall onto the back of his chair, his fingers brushing against soft strands of her wild hair. "Sierra dash seven ten."

"Sierra as in an 's' or the word?"

"The word."

She nodded and collected her datapad. "I will let you know what I find."

He almost reached for her again. Instead, he sidestepped and allowed her to leave the bridge. Then he was alone. As usual. What was wrong with him? Maybe it was the serum derivative. It was allowing something within him to . . . to what? Grow? Open? Be exposed?

That was how he felt. He felt exposed.

Jules blew out a breath and ended his self-assessment. Later. Right now, he had a mission to complete. He left the bridge and bumped into Anya. She had her dark blue jumpsuit on today.

"I was just coming to look for you, Jules." She fell into step and then followed him as he descended the ladder. "I found Eighty-six, Paxolin, and Versikton."

That caused him to pause. "Where?"

The smile didn't reach her ice-blues. "At a medlab in Habitat One. They have a few vials of each for sale."

"What's the cost?" He stuffed his hands in his back pockets.

"That's the catch. For four vials each, they are eighty party credits."

"Eighty? For the set of four or for each?"

"For the set of four of each medicine."

He kept his jaw from dropping in surprise. His frown creased his face, pulling at the scar on his left cheek. "Hold on."

He left her standing in the corridor as he entered his quarters. The door closed behind him. He needed the meds in order to have the serum. But eighty? The swindlers. Of course, he could gain what he needed without paying and without leaving a trace, but what if he picked up a tagged vial?

Jules keyed open the safe below his console and pulled out a credit chip. It didn't matter. Something told him that things were about to change. And besides, he could gain more credits on another run.

He closed the safe and rejoined Anya. She was flipping through the HoloNews on her datapad as she leaned against the wall.

When she looked up, he held out the card. "It should have enough for you to purchase not only the serum components but also to restock our Medlab with what is needed."

She stuffed the card into her pants pockets. Her hand was cool against his skin as she held onto him and rose to her tiptoes. Soft lips touched the scar on his cheek; then she was pulling away. "Be careful out there, Jules."

"You, too, Anya." He watched as she disappeared down the corridor and down the lift. It wasn't long before the hiss of the airlock opening reached him.

He turned to Bishop Thomas' quarters and knocked. When it opened, the Bishop stood there with a full duffel bag.

"Bishop?" He motioned toward the duffel.

"Captain, I have messaged my people. They need me to stay here. I've been put up in a hotel nearby, and brothers from the nearby abbey will meet with me tomorrow. If you don't mind, even though I am leaving your ship, I would still like to meet with your contact for the remainder of the books."

Jules stepped back and nodded. "As you wish, Bishop. Let's get going then. If you would like, Huey can call in a valet and have your things delivered to the hotel."

"This is all I have, Captain. After our meeting, I will depart. So, it's no trouble to carry it with me right now."

Jules motioned for him to follow while Huey waited for him at the airlock. He passed a credit chip to Jules without a word, nodded to the bishop, and then disappeared back into the shadows of the ship.

Within moments, they were out of the airlock and standing at the far end of the tarmac at a terminal waiting on a trolley to come by. Barely any traffic moved along the walk on which they stood. Jules glanced back. Only three docks were in use, one on either side of his ship. Neither were GFT ships.

A bell in the terminal announced the arrival of the trolley. When the vehicle slowed to a stop, the bishop climbed aboard, and Jules entered their destination and payment.

He sat down next to Bishop Thomas and watched the view as they went by. Above them, the dome began to darken with the approaching storm. Around him, people strolled along the walks, darting in and out of shops and buildings. Laughter, yells, the hum of machinery, and a deep, low growl of the wind outside mingled together. Groups of mine workers stepped off a westside trolley. Dust flew from their clothes as they jostled each other, some laughing, some scowling, some walking away quietly as they scanned handhelds. Crowds thickened and thinned as they rolled by. Then they were in the warehouse district.

The bell chimed. "Warehouse District Four, Site C."

He and the bishop stepped off the trolley onto the platform. As the trolley pulled away, Jules glanced around. They were the only ones around. He looked at his wrist monitor. Six Sol time. Everyone left for the workday.

"See anything?"

"Nothing." Jules turned a slow circle. "Absolutely nothing. This is the place, right?"

"Yes." The bishop walked to a bench twenty feet away and sat down. "Have a seat, Jules. You'll know they are here before they even get close."

Bishop Thomas was right. Jules sat on the edge, propped his elbows on his knees, and kept a steady scan at the buildings around him. Bishop set his duffel at his feet and activated a datapad. He quietly started reading before he looked over at Jules.

"You have something on your mind, son?"

Jules glanced at him before returning to his vigil of the area. "Yes. You told Abby I had my own road to Damascus to travel. What does that mean? I'm not going to Damascus. Was it another Coalition code?"

The bishop smiled. "No, Jules, it's not a code. It's related to the Bible. Saul of Tarsus was traveling to Damascus when he had an encounter with the Lord Jesus Christ. That encounter changed his life. So, when I said you had to travel your own road—"

"You meant that I would have to find my own way to truth."

Bishop Thomas' smile grew before returning to his datapad. "The man we are meeting . . . "

"Just left." Jules stood and gazed at the warehouse across from them. "He walked in, dropped the package, and left."

"Just now?" The older man huffed. "I didn't even get to read a full passage yet."

A laugh almost escaped Jules. He shook his head and waved the bishop back down onto the bench. "Stay there. I'll go get it."

He crossed the street, rounded the corner of the warehouse, and slipped inside the unlocked side door. Blackness greeted him, and it took a second for his eyes to adjust to the darkness. Shadowed shapes stood around him, yet none moved. He cocked his head. No sound. He was alone.

Jules kept to the wall and approached the drop. A satchel. He flipped open the flap and felt inside. Three books. Leather. Nothing more.

A small scuff of a shoe reached him. Jules pressed himself against the wall and waited as the figure approached.

He stayed in the dark, yet Jules could make out the outline of his face. Asian descent. He stepped toward the stranger, who tensed and then grew even more rigid as Jules reached into his pocket. Shoulders sagged in relief when Jules held out the credit chip.

The man stepped closer and accepted the payment, then disappeared. Jules waited. Nothing.

He exited the warehouse and walked back to the bishop and sat on the bench, crossing his ankle across a knee as he dropped the satchel between them. "Three books."

Bishop Thomas nodded and used his foot to scoot the satchel closer. "No problems?"

"None. As usual, drop the merch, leave, wait until I arrive, then come back—alone—for payment." Jules gave Bishop Thomas a small shrug. "He was a different person this time but did exactly as Batch normally does."

"Batch? You were working with Batch?" Bishop Thomas' shoulder shook in silent amusement.

Another surprising moment for him. How many more for the day? "Yes, Batch. You know him?"

Bishop Thomas laughed. And then laughed even harder. "Do I ever. Julius Williams, Batch is Coalition."

"What?" The feeling that he couldn't awake from a dream surrounded him as the Mars night descended upon them as they waited. How many more of the Coalition were going to invade his life?

"If ever there was a sign from the Lord saying you are on the right path, then this is it, my boy." Bishop Thomas turned on the bench as a trolley in the distance approached. "Batch stays in the territories, running operations. He has his hands in just about every division of government, allowing the Coalition to stay one step, if not more, ahead. When you were still running missions, did you ever wonder why some of your objectives were scrubbed? It was because Batch alerted many of them and they escaped."

The trolley grew closer. Jules counted five people onboard. Three with bulges in their jackets.

"I've never thought about it. When one was scrubbed, another took its place." He jerked his head around when the bishop's hand fell on his arm.

"That's my ride, Jules. You stay here. But remember this: trust Abigail and her people. In everything. They hold the key to every answer that you seek."

The trolley stopped. A man stepped off, placed a small box near Jules, and then stepped back onto the trolley with Bishop Thomas. As the trolley pulled away, Bishop Thomas gave him one last wave goodbye, which Jules found himself returning.

When he was alone on that dusty Mars street, Jules peeked into the box. More than he had asked for! The bishop must have requested extra payment. He pushed aside five iron ingots and picked up a canister. Half a liter of liquid chromium. He replaced it and slipped the small square out of the box. The lid slid off and nestled against the foam were three ruby-enhanced, laser-focus crystals. He breathed out a shaky breath.

This was more than he thought possible. All for six outlawed books. Were they really that important?

His thoughts bounced back to Abigail. She could explain their importance. He frowned. Why did his thoughts always return to her?

Another trolley approached. When it stopped, Jules picked up his box, entered his destination and payment, and sat on the back seat of the trolley. Only two other people accompanied him. And they were too absorbed in their handhelds to pay him any attention.

He relaxed against the cushion and watched the scenery pass him by. Dusty roads. Red, dusted buildings. Bright lights on stores and clubs. Then the marked lanes of the docking area. When the trolley pulled up to the stop, Jules stepped off the back platform and crossed the tarmac to his ship.

Still nothing around him. No eyes. No looks. No sound out of the ordinary.

He stepped onto the ramp and shrugged to himself. That was the easiest job he had ever had. And that worried him.

$$\Sigma$$

Abigail ran the results through one more time. No denying it. Every one of the files contained the information. She rose from the table in her quarters and crossed to the console. Her first comm call was to the bridge. It went unanswered.

She keyed his quarters and waited.

"Yes?" Jules' gruff voice seemed distracted.

"It's Abby. I have the results—"

"I'll be right there." The comm disconnected. Within seconds, her door hissed opened.

She narrowed her eyes at him as she stepped away from the comm. "No knock? That would have been polite."

He glanced back at the door as it closed. "Why?"

Abigail shook her head. "That's another thing you will have to learn when—if—you are allowed at my home. You can't just barge into someone's quarters. You have to knock."

He sat at the table and motioned for her to do the same. "I'll remember that, then."

She slid onto the chair and passed him her datapad. "They are your medical files. Particularly the derivatives of Serum Seventy-four that was used, your reactions to them, and how the serum's success on you is still an unknown and couldn't be isolated in your bloodwork."

His frown deepened with each scroll of the files. He paused over one report before continuing. At the end, he set the datapad down on the table and leaned back in his chair. "Where is she sending them?"

Surprise rippled through Abigail. "You know it's her?"

"Knew since your messages. Huey wouldn't betray me. Not after I learned how the Coalition behaves. Did you figure out if she accessed my personal unit?"

Abigail shook her head. "It was an older code of yours, apparently. Does she know your code for the unit?"

"Not that I'm aware of." He pushed the pad to her. "Where are they going?"

"Unified Medical. It's a—"

"GFT subsidiary."

"Exactly. I can't track down the location of which Medlab hub is receiving it, but it looked like a research branch separate from the GFT military."

She keyed open the tracking info and turned it around to show him. His eyes scanned the readouts.

"Could she be consulting?"

Again, Abigail shook her head. She hated being the bearer of bad news and, in this case, the bearer of worse news. Would they be safe to go meet her people, or would Jules have to scrub their mission here? She swiped the screen and highlighted one of the codes. With a quick key command, it deciphered the last message in the group.

He caught the datapad when she slid it to him. "Retrieval at LZ one-five-nine. Twenty hundred Sol, three, twelve, seventy-five." Jules looked up at her. An unreadable expression crossed his face. "Tomorrow." His lips compressed into a tight line before he stood and handed the datapad back to her. "Scrub the retrieval info and the bloodwork and let the quantums be sent with the next auto update."

Abigail nodded. She quickly scrubbed what he wanted and released the holding pattern.

His eyebrow arched above his left eye. "You can do that without plugging in?"

"I can now. The program still has a few kinks to be worked out, but since I already had the command codes, it was simply a matter of connecting the GHOST to the bridge. Eventually, I will have it where I can hack any mainframe via HiWaves."

"Follow me to the bridge." He rose, palmed open her door, and spoke as they walked to the ladder. "I always thought HiWaves were hack-proof."

Abigail clambered up the ladder. Exhaustion was pulling at her body with the late hour. "Not to the GHOST. Told you the program Nest Protocol designed was dangerous."

He waved her to silence and barely motioned to Medlab. Abigail glanced over at the room.

Anya was busy unpacking a box of vials and placing them into a cooling unit. They strode by without her noticing. Abigail climbed the short steps and spared one last glance at Medlab. Anya held a small vial of red liquid up to the light, looking at it. A grin spread over her face as she inserted it into the unit, turned away, and moved out of her view. Then Abigail was passing by Jules and into the bridge, where Huey was asleep in his chair, feet propped on his console and toy robot lying on his stomach.

When Jules kicked his chair, he jerked awake, his feet landing with a heavy thud on the floor.

"Wake up. Got a job for you."

Huey rubbed at his eyes. "Job? I'm not getting off on Mars. You know that."

Jules ignored him and locked the door. "Have a seat, Abby. I need you to help him with this." He leaned against the holographic table and crossed his ankles. "Anya is sending quantum messages. About me. Which means she is either using this bridge or her own console."

"Anya? The bridge would allow her to compile them faster . . . oh, no, Cap." Huey scrunched his eyes shut. "I'm so sorry. I thought I was making life a bit easier. I didn't think."

"What?" Jules cocked his head at Huey.

Abigail pushed at the lump under her thigh and turned the chair around to face both men as Huey explained.

"I hardlined the console in the bay to the bridge. It helped me when you needed me to scrub security and I was in the cargo bay. Saved time instead of having to run all the way to the bridge. It is possible she used that console. Instead of days, it would cost her only an hour at most."

Jules frowned. "How long ago did you do that?"

"Since the Jupiter fiasco." Huey turned to her. "I'll tell you about that someday. Cap got a huge scar right here"—he cupped his hand over the front of his left shoulder—"from what happened on that station."

"Focus." Jules chided him. "You didn't know she would betray us. Neither did I."

Abigail looked up at him. "So, what do you want me to help Huey with?"

"The GHOST can search the ship for unauthorized accesses?" At her nod, he continued. "Then search the ship. Use what you need. And Huey, change all passcodes on the bridge, my quarters, and all major networking. I'll take care of my storage unit."

"Gotcha, Cap." Huey turned to his console.

"Huey?" When he looked up, Abigail passed him the cord. "Plug it in. I haven't finished the tweaks, and I still need to have a hardline for some operations."

"I can help you with the programming later, if you would like." He slipped the end into the jackport on the console. "Cap, want me to filter, too?"

"Yes. Every message. Abby, use the GHOST to filter for any other quantum messages that may be there, too."

She nodded. Silence reigned for several moments as she and Huey worked. Huey's fingers flew across his console. His robot had fallen to the floor and was ignored. Jules picked it up and started manipulating the arms and legs. Just as he had done before.

She set the GHOST into search mode. Ever since discovering it could perform multiple functions, she had been experimenting. Not only could it search multiple parameters, but it could also access countless ports and mainframes, not to mention running background programs.

Abigail paused and straightened in the chair. She hadn't written a program like that in ages, but with the GHOST now connected to the whole ship . . .

When she looked up, Jules was watching her. His gaze flowed over her before settling on her own eyes. The green in his eyes darkened.

"You have an idea."

It was a statement. Not a question. She nodded. "I do. I want to link a spyware into the medlab programs. This would automatically store every file and command in medlab. Just in case she is prepping most of the messages in there. And we can monitor what she is doing with the serum."

He stood quiet for so long, pondering her statement, that she began to fear he would say no. It was a good idea. It would keep him—them—safe. She couldn't place it, but something told her to not let any of Jules' medical data leave the ship.

Jules pushed off the table, propped his arm on the overhead, and leaned against it. He nodded. "Do it."

She twirled the chair back around and started her programming. It would take a few hours creating it, but once it was in the system and being backed by the GHOST, it would be quite powerful. Probably the most powerful program she had ever written. "Huey, would you mind looking over my codes once I finish?"

He nodded absently, still working at his station.

She didn't glance up at Jules, yet she could feel his presence even closer than before as he stared out the viewport lost in his thoughts. He spared her barely a glance when she spoke. "Once the program is activated, nothing will leave the ship without us knowing."

Jules ran the trimmer over his jaw, wincing as it hit a scar on his chin. He angled his head one way, then the other, checking to see if there were any errant hairs that escaped the blades.

He ran a thumb over the raised scar on his cheek. The serum should have healed it. He dropped his hand and hung the trimmer back on its rack, noticing in the mirror that his hair had grown longer. It would need another trim.

No. That was GFT regulation. He ran his hand through the strands. He needed to cast off those impulses to adhere to GFT regs, or he would never be free.

Jules turned his back to the mirror and strode to his bunk, where he had laid out his clothes earlier before he took a sonic. He had just slipped on his pants and was buckling his belt when the door pinged.

He grabbed his shirt before crossing to his door and was slipping it over his head as he keyed his door open.

Abigail stood there, dressed in brown pants that hung loosely on her hips and a pale yellow, long sleeve shirt that flowed around her hands. Her gaze briefly ran over his chest, her eyebrow rising slightly, before she held up her datapad.

"Message from Elder Carson came in."

He waved her in. "It's early."

She stepped forward and turned slowly in the center of his quarters, scanning it. "I thought your quarters would be larger."

"Why? Because it's my ship?" He sat on his bunk and pulled on his boots.

"Well, yeah. You know, captains get perks." She walked over to the viewport and glanced out. "You have a bigger viewport."

"And a side room." He pointed to the door at the corner by his refresher unit. "I use it at times. More like an office. Sometimes I eat in there."

"Solitude?" She paused at the entrance to his refresher. "Huh. I also thought you would have an actual shower in here."

Jules almost laughed. He fastened the last buckle on his boots, stood, and crossed to the table where a variety of his items lay— credit chips, ID, voucher for the trolleys, penlight, and two pulse gun charges. "A shower uses too much water, and my reclamation units aren't designed to handle that much pull on the resources."

She gave a slight nod and walked back over to him. Her small tour over, she held out her datapad. "Blue District, warehouse zero-four-one. Code is Deep Blue Tango."

He read the message. His finger traced the letters: GBWY. Always that. Why?

It stated to be there at ten o'clock. They had an hour and a half to get there. No problem if the trolleys weren't packed. He slipped the credit chips into his back pocket and the rest into the various pockets of his pants. Then he strapped his pulse gun around his waist. "Go collect what you need. If we want to get there on time, we will need to leave now."

She nodded. "I need to grab only my jacket. And a nutrient bar." She paused before opening the door. "May I ask a question?"

He looked up at her while rifling through his satchel for one of his favorite bars. "You may, but I may not answer."

She bit at her lip for a moment. Then shook her head. "Never mind. It isn't important."

Then she left. Leaving him bewildered. And wondering what she was about to ask. He really needed to find a book on women and why they acted like they did. Those in his squad and in the other squads never acted like Abby and Anya.

Jules stuffed two bars into his side pocket and locked his door as he passed through. The metal under his boots rang with hollow thuds as he made his way to the lift and then down to his unit. He glanced into hydroponics. The plants were even taller. And green fruit were beginning to bud on the tomatoes. Huey would like that.

The door stuck again as it opened. Jules grimaced and squeezed past it. He stood before his collection of swords. The katana would be too bulky to carry with him. The short blade would do in case they ran into trouble. Alarms would pick up on his pulse gun if he fired it in a building. Unlike Lunar, Mars monitored heat signatures too closely.

He pushed the memories of his many missions on Mars out of his mind as he pulled the blade off the rack and slid it into his belt, pulling his jacket over it. His memories were filtering to the forefront of his thoughts lately. Too much, lately.

Jules pushed his unit's door closed, keyed in his new passcode, and took the lift back to the cargo bay. Anya stood at the console near the airlock as Abigail, wearing a tight, canvas jacket, crossed the gangway. He recognized the design. Perfect for missions. He had one of his own in his quarters.

Anya glanced up at her and then at him. She met him halfway. "Where are you going?"

"A job." He adjusted the blade's sheath and slid it further back on his belt. "I need you to stay on board. We won't be long."

"We?" She sent a hard glare at Abigail who waited at the airlock, her bag hugged against her chest. "What's going on?"

"Abby found a contact for a shipment run. We're going to meet him now."

"Abby? First name basis? Since when did Miss du Soleil start working for you?"

Jules glared at her, grabbed her by the forearm, and pulled her to the side. "Since now. Drop this convo. And stay on the ship."

Her eyes flashed in anger, but she kept her mouth shut. He let go of her and left her standing there, fuming. Jules ushered Abigail out the airlock and across the tarmac.

Three other ships had arrived during the night. Jules scanned them. None were GFT that could be seen. He touched Abigail's elbow.

"When we get back, would you be able to tell if any of the ships around us are GFT?"

She didn't glance around her but nodded in reply. "With the GHOST I can."

"Speaking of which, did you bring it?"

She patted her satchel. "I don't let the datapad out of my sight."

They stopped on the platform and waited for a trolley. He tugged her around to face him, shielding his hands between their bodies as he opened her satchel. "Keep this on your person, not in a bag." He pulled her datapad out and started to slip it into her jacket, but she stopped him, her face reddening.

"I got it." She slid the pad into an inside pocket of her jacket.

He stepped away from her, confused over her reaction. There wasn't any reason to become so flustered. Or was there? The bell of the trolley reached him. Within moments, it arrived, and Jules entered their destination and payment. Then they climbed aboard.

It was crowded. Bodies jostled each other as they either settled down on seats or stood using the bars for support. Jules escorted Abigail to the back of the vehicle and reached up for the bar overhead. She stood next to him but at a distance, until another man bumped into her and almost sent her sprawling against the bottom of the trolley.

Jules pulled her to him and slipped his free arm around her shoulder and across her chest. He dipped his head and whispered to her when she tensed. "Need to pretend we are familiar with each other. Look like a couple. They will keep their space from us, and you won't be knocked down."

Her hair tickled his chin. She relaxed against him, almost melting into him as she leaned back against his chest. Her heart thudded against him, and her chest rose with each breath, pushing against his hand.

That strange knot formed in his chest again, gripping him and twisting. He swallowed against the strangeness of that feeling and concentrated on the faces around him. Men and women going about their day. One woman held a bald baby in her lap, cooing at it. A gurgling giggle sounded from the little thing as it grinned a toothless smile. How could one tell if the child was male or female? A man coughed into his hand and then snapped shut his datapad book. Jules studied each face. Nothing stood out. Just normal people doing normal people things.

Outside, the buildings rolled past. Stop after stop emptied the trolley until he and Abigail were keeping company with three other men dressed in uniforms. Once most of the people filed off, Abigail had pulled away from him, and they sat down on a recently vacated bench.

The trolley driver announced the next stop. "Blue District. Stop thirty-five."

He and Abigail stepped off. Five other people boarded the trolley, and then it pulled away, puttering down the track and away from the warehouse district.

Jules scanned the busy walkway. Nothing out of the ordinary. His gaze traveled over the buildings as they started strolling toward the directory. Nothing. Looked like they were in the clear for now.

"Would you stop that?" She didn't glance at him as she read the directory. "No one knows we are here. And there isn't any danger." She turned to him and slipped her hand into his. "Have to pretend, right?"

Jules gripped her hand. "Habit, by the way. Never know."

Abigail raised her chin and nodded down the walkway. "We head straight for two blocks, then take a left."

They fell silent as they strolled down the walkway, dodging the crowd and pausing at times to consult a sign on a building. They looked like two people browsing the warehouse district and the myriad business options each provided.

He pointed to the left. A narrow alleyway led to their destination. Shadows fell over them as they entered the alley. The sounds of the busy avenue diminished. Jules read the locator signs as they passed each building. There. Just ahead.

Abigail let go of his hand as they approached Warehouse Zero-Four-One. A man stood near the entrance, reading the holographic projection of the HoloNews.

He looked up at them when they stopped in front of him.

"Deep Blue Tango." Her voice was a slight whisper.

The man nodded and keyed open the door. They passed through it and into the darkened interior of the building. Jules' eyes quickly adjusted, and he scanned the massive room. No one and nothing. An empty cavern of a warehouse. Small storage units lined the back wall. To the left, one exit. Behind them, the entrance. Above them, windows spaced five feet apart dotted the ceiling, yet the sunscreen was activated, keeping the warehouse dark.

The man held up a hand to stop them and pointed to the floor. "Wait here." Then he was heading for the side exit.

Abigail slipped her hands into her pockets and turned to him. "I take it you already checked out the place."

"Yes. Nothing stood out."

She gave a small shake of her head. "There's no reason to be suspicious about us. The Coalition isn't some enemy. We are far from that."

Jules wasn't sure about that. But then, JJ wouldn't have left him for the enemy. What if the true enemy was GFT? They were going to kill him. Even sent Zeetoo to do the job. His own squad.

He shook his head and decided to change the trajectory of his thoughts. Jules faced Abigail. She looked up at him expectantly. "Why did you leave the Coalition if they are everything you say they are?"

She shrugged. "I was stupid. Followed my friend and his girlfriend. I wanted to see what was outside our borders." A heavy sigh escaped her. "I was an idiot for doing so. Never thought about the consequences of what I was doing. When they abandoned me, I realized that I was in grave danger. If anyone found out I was Coalition, I would be dead or sent to reeducation."

There wasn't anything to say to that. He had hunted those who were discovered. Killed them. Tortured them. Sent them to the gulags that the GFT called "reeducation camps." He swallowed a hard lump that formed in his throat. If he had not left, if they had not slated him for decommission, would she have been his objective for a mission? Chances were high that she would have been.

She placed a hand on his arm. "It was a year ago. And I do thank God that it was you I found that day. Batch told me only which dock. His transmission was cut short before telling me what ship. So, I had to guess. All the others never felt right, until I saw you and Bishop Thomas. Even though you were the last ship, I knew that you had to be the one that Batch was telling me about."

He found his own hand covering hers, giving it a slight squeeze. "I didn't realize Batch was Coalition until Bishop Thomas told me. Huey uses him at times." His thumb rubbed across her knuckles. "If I was still with GFT . . . how did you escape GFT scrutiny?"

"God." She dropped her hand from his arm. "What we call Divine intervention. I prayed. And He answered."

Jules shook his head. That was too foreign of a concept for him. Time to change the subject. "Would the Coalition be willing to take me in?"

"If you do as they say. We are not strangers to taking in assassins. But there are strict rules, and you will be watched, day in, day out. Every move will be monitored."

She watched him as he stared across the expanse of the warehouse, contemplating her words. JJ did it. He would do it, too. "I understand."

"What will you do with Anya?" She grimaced at her sudden question. "Sorry. None of my business."

"Other than throwing her out an airlock?" At her startled gaze, he shrugged. "I don't know yet. Probably leave her here on Mars. She doesn't know our plans, but she does know our IF."

"Hmm. I can use the GHOST and give you a new IF signal if you want to throw her out an airlock while we leave Mars."

Surely, the woman wasn't being serious. She just said the Coalition didn't operate like that. She gave him a huge smile when he looked down at her.

"It's called a joke, Jules."

"Maybe. But the idea does have merit." He stuffed his hands in his back pockets and waited. Silence reigned again.

The door at the back creaked. The lights above blossomed to life. A man entered, followed by a small group of guards, who broke away as the man approached them. Gray hair peppered his brown hair but dominated his beard. Olive-toned skin contrasted with the black suit he wore. His brown eyes scanned Jules before lighting up when he saw Abigail.

"Abby!"

She ran to him and threw her arms around his neck. The man returned her hug just as enthusiastically. He kissed the top of her head before holding her at arm's length. "You look intact and unharmed. Word on Liam and Fiona?"

Tears glistened in her eyes. She shook her head. "I don't know. I even used the hacking program I have to find them, but nothing."

The elder sighed. "God will show us the way. We will just pray for their safe return, if it's His will." He crossed to Jules and studied him for a moment. The man's eyes seemed to miss nothing. His gaze fell on the slight bulge in Jules' jacket.

Abigail touched Jules' arm. "Elder Jake, this is Jules. Captain Julius Williams. He's the one who talked to Elder Carson."

Elder Jake stepped forward and held out his hand. "Jules."

Jules hesitated. Not sure what the man wanted. He slowly extended his own hand and grasped the older man's. Elder Jake smiled, patted their clasped hands with his free one, and then let go. "So, tell me, Jules. Why do you seek the Coalition?"

What could he say? Bishop Thomas said they held the key to the answer to his questions, and he had a lot of questions. The man waited patiently.

Maybe he should tell them a condensed version from the beginning. "It's a more complicated issue, so I will give a condensed report. If that is acceptable."

Elder Jake indicated for him to proceed with a wave of his hand.

"It started two years, six months ago. I was ambushed. Thought I was dying, but there was this . . . this light above me. Seemed to keep me awake and alive until my second squad arrived. Ever since then, I haven't been the same. While I was in the hospital, my friend and brother, Juliet 7-J left me. Then I was scheduled for decommission when they slotted me as unsalvageable. That's when I ran. And have been searching for JJ—that's Juliet 7-J—since then. He told me to remember Deep Blue. I didn't know it was the Coalition until I discovered Abby's messages with the same." He paused and then asked, "Do you know JJ? He may have changed his name."

Elder Jake smiled. "If you don't mind, go ahead and strip your weapons off, Captain Williams."

Jules noted the shadows against the wall, pulse rifles aimed his way. They weren't naïve. That was promising. He pulled his blade from his belt and handed it to the elder. Then reached into his jacket and pulled the pulse gun out by its barrel. The rifles in the shadows lowered as Elder Jake accepted it.

He waved a man over and gave him the weapons in exchange of a portable scanner and syringe. The man dropped an empty case at Elder Jake's feet before retreating into the shadows. The older man spoke as he prepped the scanner. "Remove your jacket and shirt, please."

Jules let his jacket, followed by his tactical vest, slide to the floor and then pulled his shirt over his head. Abigail's gaze fell onto his chest, following the long, red scar along his sternum and then over the hatch-work of scars that covered him. It wasn't desire in her eyes. Not like Anya. It was . . . sympathy. Sorrow.

Her eyes met his yet didn't look away. He handed his shirt to her. She picked up his jacket and vest and stepped back as Elder Jake ran the scanner from the top of his head down past his knees, then back to his chest. He paused over Jules' abdomen and chest.

"You have a lot of scars, young man."

"Injuries. Training. Torture."

Both of their heads shot up at that.

"Torture?"

"To prepare me for times I may be captured. Train me to accept pain and not reveal any information. We had to be broken and then rebuilt." Jules paused. He never told anyone this. There was never a need. Until now. "I received the worst because I never broke."

Elder Jake raised an eyebrow. "You are in superb health, despite it all. Now if you don't mind, I will take a blood sample." He wiped Jules' arm with antiseptic and positioned the syringe. "Are you still on Serum Seventy-four?"

"I am, sir." The needle pierced his vein. "I can't survive without it."

"Well, we can help you with that. We have two of the best doctors who specialize in the serum." He closed the syringe. Dropped the two items into a case by his feet. "You can get dressed now."

Jules accepted his clothing from Abigail and started pulling them back on as Elder Jake talked.

"There was a report that Joshua, who you know as JJ, was on a mission with three others. We do not call them assassins nor former assassins. Their old life is gone now. I'm not privy to his location, but he is well." Elder Jake closed the case and smiled at Jules. "Actually, son, he told us to expect a 'Jules' or 'Juliet 7-A' sometime in the future."

Shock rocked through Jules. "He knew I would follow?"

"Son, you will find that God can do mighty things. Joshua knew you well enough to know that you would come search for him." He turned to Abigail and held out his arms. She accepted his hug and stayed in Elder Jake's embrace for several minutes. "Stay with him, Abby. Joshua was right about him. Here."

She stepped back, and he handed her a data disk, which she stuffed inside her jacket.

Elder Jake turned to Jules. "You keep her safe. The Coalition will be expecting you." He motioned one of the men forward. "Return Captain Williams' weapons, please."

His blade and gun were handed back to him. Not deposited on the floor or set near him. And that was another surprise for him. They were not afraid nor wary around him.

A beep came from the elder's pocket. He pulled out his comm unit and frowned. "I have to take my leave. Abby, be safe. Come closer." Elder Jake waved them forward.

Jules stepped toward him. Abigail's arm bumped against his. Elder Jake placed a hand on their shoulders and bowed his head. Abigail followed suit.

It was a strange ritual. Bishop Thomas did it. He caught Huey doing it once. But to have someone pray over him?

A quiet amen ended it, and then Elder Jake left with the men following. He couldn't explain the feeling. It wasn't embarrassment. It wasn't . . . hesitancy or disbelief. It felt like that light he had seen had returned. A curious feeling . . .

Abigail sniffled and looked to him. "Ready to head back to the ship?"

Not trusting his voice, Jules only nodded. They turned to the entrance and took a step—

The whistle reached him milliseconds before the walls imploded. He yanked Abigail to him and shielded her as chunks of metal, steel, and concrete flew, battering against them.

A large beam sliced across his back and knocked them to the floor. He fell heavily over Abigail's inert frame. Jules scrabbled to his feet as debris rained down. The sound of another incoming missile rose in pitch.

Abigail's limp body lay among the rubble; blood trickled from her head. He bent and scooped her into his arms. Her satchel dangled against his legs as he held her close and scanned his surroundings. The far wall stood strong. Reinforced steel would have been used to support the storage units.

He ran to the back. Some of the units hadn't survived, but the lower ones had. Jules counted the units. If the warehouses stayed to code . . . there. He lowered Abigail to the floor and pried open the panel. An access tube between the storages.

It was a tight squeeze. He wiggled his way in, dragged her body through the opening, and struggled with the panel. The missile hit the entrance across the far side. Heat and fire flowed around them.

A high pitch indicated that there was another incoming.

Jules pulled her body closer to him, hooked his leg over hers, squeezing her even closer to him. Still wasn't enough room for two of them side by side, yet the height of the tube should be enough.

He growled a curse. Her limp body was deadweight, but she was light. Jules flipped onto his back—his blade biting into his spine—slid her on top of him, and then stretched past her. The heat of the panel burned his hand when he grabbed the inner handle and snapped the cover back into place. The walls rocked with another impact. Dust trickled down on them, but the wall stood.

He glanced around. A control box was near his head, casting an eerie, red light around them. He shifted her body on his and reached into her jacket. She would have balked at his intrusion had she been awake.

It was tough tugging the pad out from between them, and he smacked himself in the mouth with the corner as it popped free. He muttered another curse and plugged the datapad into the control box.

Code and lines ran across the screen. A language he didn't understand. He swiped the top of the screen. An icon showed basic commands and the few programs he recognized. He hit it, searching the programs for the one that every hacker had. There.

He tapped it and activated it. The hacking program ran through the control box's commands, and four clicks sounded in the confined space. They were now locked inside. He tapped one more command, and it increased the strength of the thermal dampening of the tube.

With a sigh, Jules disconnected the datapad, wrapped the cord around it, and slid the device between their bodies. He buried his hand in her hair, wrapped his other hand around her waist, and held her close, balancing her body on top of his.

Now they had to wait. Hopefully, she would wake up soon and use the GHOST to hack the security feeds, if they were still operational.

He listened to the voices that rose beyond the wall.

"Fan out."

" . . . GFT Base Three, 9-Z. Subjects have escaped."

"Affirmative . . . "

"Call it in . . . "

Jules let his head fall back against the cold floor of the tube. His body ran just as cold.

Juliet squad was here.

# Chapter Twelve
# THE BETRAYAL

The voices had faded long ago, yet there was the occasional scuffle beyond the panel, fading away and then returning. Jules counted the seconds between. Seven seconds. The assassin was patrolling the area or scouting for accesses. And their tube would soon be discovered if they remained.

He shifted Abigail. Her limp body sprawled against him was beginning to create awkward moments. Jules closed his eyes against the strange knot that had formed in his gut and refused to leave. It had to be the serum derivatives. Didn't Anya say she wasn't using the Paxolin?

Abigail groaned.

Jules yanked his hand from her back and covered her mouth with it, muffling her rising groans. Her eyes fluttered for two seconds before widening in fear.

His hand tightened on her jaw, and his lips barely grazed her ear as he whispered, "There's an assassin out there."

At her nod, he removed his hand. Imprints of his fingers were left against her skin. He rubbed a thumb across them in apology and then mouthed to her: *GFT raid. Control panel?* Jules nodded his head toward the panel above his shoulder.

She glanced at it and then frowned after realizing the datapad was between them and not in her jacket. Her eyebrow quirked at him, yet she squirmed up his body until she could reach the panel and plugged in the GHOST.

He found his mouth inches from her neck. Her pulse beat against her skin . . .

She tapped his shoulder. Jules craned his neck to see her datapad's screen. The schematics of the warehouse. Her fingernail tapped the screen, and it zoomed in on the tube they were in.

An access to a maintenance tunnel was only twenty feet ahead of them.

He nodded. She unplugged the datapad and stuffed it into her jacket. With his finger against her lips, he used his other hand and pointed to her, then to the access tube ahead, indicating for her to go first.

She placed her hands on either side of his head and started slithering forward. He grabbed her hips and lifted her clear; then her knees were past his head. Jules flipped around, catching his blade before it clacked against the side of the wall. He refastened the thong and pulled himself behind her as they slowly squirmed forward.

The scuff of a boot sounded beyond the wall. Jules lashed out and grabbed her beltloop, halting her movements. She stilled. As the bootsteps faded, he tapped the small of her back once. Abigail resumed.

Five minutes passed before she stopped. Her hand rose and motioned him forward. She grunted once as he moved over her, his weight pushing down onto her. He placed his hands on either side of her body, trying to keep most of his weight off her as he slithered forward.

Six feet ahead was the access tunnel's opening. Jules pulled himself along the cool metal. Abigail's breathing had become ragged as she followed him.

When he reached the opening, he paused for her to catch up. Within seconds, her hand tapped his boot. Jules grimaced as the cover scraped against the edges when he moved it aside. He paused and listened.

No reaction beyond the wall.

He dipped his head inside the tunnel. A little under six feet high. Two feet wide. Was going to be tight. Jules placed his hands on each side of the opening and slowly lowered himself into the tunnel, headfirst. When he reached the halfway point, he flipped his body and landed softly on his feet.

His eyes adjusted. A glance up and down the tunnel revealed nothing. He looked up at Abigail, who was peering into the opening. He reached up and helped guide her through the opening. Once she was on her feet, he slid the cover back, and they were enveloped in darkness.

Jules pulled a penlight from his pocket, just as she did. Two small beams of blue light bounced around. His light splayed around her grinning face. She pointed to his light.

He gave her a small smile in return and motioned to her datapad. Abigail pulled it from her jacket and showed him the screen. The tube could take them a block from the tarmac. He tapped the building the tunnel connected. Information on it scrolled across the screen.

An empty building. Good.

He motioned her forward. It was slow-going at first, until she caught on to the cadence of walking in such a narrow confinement. Then they began to make progress.

Once far away from the warehouse, Jules keyed open his comm. Huey's voice seemed overly loud in the tight space.

"Cap? You have no idea how relieved I am. HoloNews is reporting a blast in the warehouse district."

Jules caught Abigail when she tripped. He kept his hand at the small of her back, propelling her forward. "GFT hit the warehouse. We are making our way through a maintenance tunnel on the east side. It'll come out at an empty building one block from the tarmac. Is Anya still aboard?"

"She is."

"Keep an eye on her, but don't alert her to anything just yet. And start prepping the ship."

"I hear you, Jules." Huey disconnected.

The silence was almost deafening. It was broken only by Abigail's panting as she struggled through the tunnel. It took a full twenty minutes before they arrived at the building. He motioned for her to show him the schematics once more.

The tunnel let out behind the building. No security feeds. At his nod, she stuffed the datapad back into her jacket and waited until he had pushed the cover to the side. The dull Mars light shone down on them and burned Jules' eyes.

He grasped the edges and hauled himself out of the tunnel. She reached up before he could glance around to check their surroundings. Jules quickly pulled her from the tunnel.

As she regained her feet, boots thumping against the dirt echoed off the walls. Jules lashed out, pushed her aside, and whirled as the GFT assassin bore down upon him. Juliet 4-N.

Jules met him three paces away, slamming his body into the man before he could draw his pulse gun. They hit the dirt as 4-N's hand shot forward. Jules dodged it and rammed his own hand against the man's throat, silencing him.

The assassin drove his fist into Jules' side and aimed another fist at his face. Jules blocked it, drawing his knee up into the man's stomach. Then he was on his back, flipped over the man's head. The assassin whirled around on a knee. But Jules sliced his legs up, wrapped them around the assassin's neck, and yanked. Again, 4-N hit the ground hard. Jules knelt behind him, grabbed 4-N's hair, and bent his head back.

Jules yanked his blade from the sheath and held it across the assassin's throat. Resistance pulled at it as 4-N's hands pushed at the blade, trying to free it from his neck.

Jules leaned back, let go of 4-N's hair, and quickly punched him in the kidney. The man's hands faltered, giving Jules enough time to slice his knife across the assassin's throat. Jules held 4-N's head down onto the ground until his life left his body. Then he wiped the blade on the assassin's jacket before sliding it back onto his belt.

He stood and stared down at his former squad member. Vacant eyes stared down the alleyway. Jules dusted off his jacket and turned to Abigail. She had scooted against the wall of the building and sat huddled against some crates.

Her wide eyes held fear and . . . He frowned. Not disgust. It was something else. He approached her. Tears filled her blue eyes as he knelt before her.

"Abby? We can't stay here. We have to move." He held out a hand.

Her hand shook as she placed it in his, allowing him to pull her to her feet. Her gaze seemed glued to Juliet 4-N's body. Jules stepped between her and the dead assassin. Abigail's blue eyes met his.

It was horror. That was what he was seeing. At him or what he did?

He would handle this later. She allowed him to pull her down the alley, away from the body. They crossed between two more buildings before he led them onto the crowded walkway that led to their tarmac.

The crowd had begun to thin. Jules guided her across the expanse and paused outside the airlock. She glanced up at him, a question in her eyes.

"I need to wipe the blood off you."

At her puzzlement, Jules pulled his sleeve down and wiped at her forehead. She gasped slightly but allowed him to remove the smear of blood caused by the explosion. When he finished, she reached into her bag and pulled out a hairpin. With a couple of quick twists, she had her thick hair pinned up and off her neck. It was disheveled yet hid the blood that was caked in her strands.

"Will you be okay?"

She nodded. "I'm a bit dizzy, but it's not as bad as it probably looks."

"Good, because I need you to hack into comms using the cargo console since Huey has it hardlined now. I want to know who she talked to for Juliet to arrive. I want to know before I kill her."

She swallowed hard. Anya had threatened Abigail's life. And that was unacceptable. Now that the adrenaline from the explosion and fight had faded, he was left with anger. And his anger had a target.

She didn't question him. Her own eyes held a hardness in them. She reached into her jacket and pulled out her datapad. "Take this and plug it into the comm on the bridge." Abigail tapped the screen before handing it to him. "It'll help me find out exactly what she did and whom she contacted. She threatened my family, and I don't plan on her getting away with that."

$$\Sigma$$

Abigail followed Jules into the cargo bay. He paused and reached past her to close the airlock. The hydraulics groaned as the hatch rose and the doors closed. She stepped up to the console and activated the screen.

Jules' boots echoed against the empty bay as he climbed the stairs and crossed the gangway. She waited for the indication that he had the GHOST up and running. Within a few moments, the codes streamed across her screen, and she started the search.

She swiped one file to the side. No messages attached to that one. She pulled up another. Still no messages. The deeper she dug, the less she found.

Abigail opened the text-only comm. *Check spyware. See if any files were saved.*

It was Huey who responded with an affirmative. She leaned against the console and browsed through some programs. Many were Huey's. Programs for security. One for long-range sensors. Abigail paused and backed up a file.

It was a strange one, odd. The date was from a year and a half ago. An old manifest. She opened it. The list contained medical supplies, medical gel weight units, Elon 3XQ batteries, and . . . She narrowed her eyes. Spices? Odd cargo.

Abigail opened a pathway to the GHOST and ran it against the manifest. As she thought, it contained a sub-file hidden within it. As it purged the newly acquired data, she spotted Anya climbing up the stairs to the gangway.

Hopefully, Jules would take care of the woman soon. And before they left Mars.

She turned back to the file. Global Federated Territories Unit Squad.

So, she was sending info to GFT, but what? She needed a data disk for the file and needed to insert it into the datapad for the GHOST. Remote hacking wasn't doing the job. Which meant another night of tweaking the program. At least she had Huey's help now.

Abigail closed down the console, hurried up the stairs and onto the gangway. She glanced at each door of the quarters. All stood open except Jules'. And no Anya. Abigail climbed the ladder and peeked into medlab. No Anya.

She frowned. Where had the woman disappeared to? Maybe the lounge . . .

Jules and Huey looked up as she entered.

"I need a data disk. Looks like a file was sent to GFT Unit squad, but I can't hack it remotely. I can download it onto a data disk and then let the GHOST run through it."

"What else did you find?" Jules stood and palmed the bridge closed.

"Just that. And it was buried in an old manifest file. The GHOST should be able to determine when it was sent or when it will be sent." She placed her hand on his arm and leaned close. "She came up the gangway while I was working at the console. But she isn't in medlab."

Jules nodded and turned to Huey. "Finish prepping and get clearance for early departure. Let me know when you have it ready."

Huey swiveled his chair around and called in their request.

Jules turned back to her. "Let me check down below. She could have taken the lift."

Abigail squeezed past him and plucked a data disk from the pile near comms and then followed him out the door and down the corridor. It seemed eerily quiet as she and Jules walked the gangway and climbed down the stairs.

He motioned her to the console. "Finish up. I'll be back momentarily."

He faded into the dark shadows of the bay, heading for the small ladder at the back. Abigail returned to the console and reactivated it. The text-only comm pinged.

She opened the message. *Run a sensor on the console.*

Abigail inserted the disk and downloaded the file. As the download ran, she opened the sensor program; selected thermal, systems, and exterior; and started the sweep.

As the sensor ran, she opened up a remote communication line to Elder Jake. *In good health. Update on the party? GBWY. A.* As it zipped away, the file finished its download, and she erased it from the console.

She pulled the data disk from the slot just as a shadow detached from under the overhang of the gangway. Abigail looked up and caught a flash of silver swinging at her neck. Fear shot through her. She raised an arm to ward off the blow, but the needle plunged into her neck.

Abigail slid into darkness.

$$\Sigma$$

Jules closed his storage unit door. There was no evidence of tampering or bypassing. The logs showed no one had entered hydroponics for the last twenty-four hours. He turned toward the ladder.

Klaxons sounded. Its screech echoed through the lower bay.

Huey's voice filtered through the ship-wide comm. "Cap! We have a breach! Cargo bay! I can't disengage the slave, and we are five from liftoff!"

And they couldn't call in an emergency landing, or they would risk the ship being searched. And they would discover Abigail and the Nest Protocol program.

His raced up the ladder. Huey was already coming down the stairs and met him halfway.

Jules glanced around. No Abigail.

"Airlock, Huey!"

He and Huey rushed to the airlock. The control panel was destroyed; its wires hung from the wall, melted and twisted. Jules looked through the viewport of the airlock. The hatch was partially opened. Then his blood congealed.

Lying in the middle of the airlock was Abigail. Her red hair fanned around her face as she lay there, crumpled and unconscious.

"Get this door open!"

"Help me with the panel." Huey struggled with an access panel. Jules joined him, and together, they pried it off the wall.

The ship shuddered as the thrusters kicked in. The klaxons threatened to burst his eardrums, and the ship's automatic warning system activated. "Warning. Hull breach in section three zero one. Ten minutes until atmosphere depletion. Warning. Hull . . . "

Jules reached into the tube and yanked the system wires out, and the klaxons died. The *Nightingale* still issued her warning as Huey investigated the tube.

"The redundancies are still intact. If I can get in there, I can hack the system, but, Cap, it will take more than ten minutes."

He heard her before she started banging. A muffled scream from the airlock proceeded the frantic banging. Jules turned back to the airlock's viewport. "Huey, dump the reserves!"

Abigail, with tears streaming down her face, banged against the fused panels. Her eyes held more fear than he had ever seen as she whipped her head from the window to the opened hatch and back again. Above her, the reserve oxygen released and poured into the hold, mingling with the thinning atmosphere.

"Abby?" He yelled through the window, trying to gain her attention.

"Warning. Seven minutes until atmosphere depletion in section three zero one."

He turned back to Huey. "Get the GHOST. Use it! Get her out of there!"

Huey needed no urging. He wormed his way back out and raced away.

Abigail banged on the window even harder. Her scream was barely heard. "Jules! Please! Please!" Her eyes widened even more, and her face paled.

"I'll get you out!" He splayed his hand on the window. "Abby, calm down. You'll be okay!"

She violently shook her head and continued beating on the window, glancing back at the hatch. Ice had begun to collect on the bulkheads. Wind whipped her hair about her face, buffeted at her jacket, and swirled remnants of Mars dust about her.

Huey clanged down the stairs, raced across the floor, and practically dove into the tube. Curses flowed from his mouth as he squirmed into the narrow passage. Sparks flew from the control panel.

"Warning. Atmosphere depletion in three minutes."

The hatch behind Abigail started closing but caught inches from sealing. Terror etched itself across her face as she sank to the floor, pressing herself into the corner of the airlock door.

"Huey, forget the hatch. Open the airlock first!"

"Warning. Atmosphere depletion in two minutes."

The airlock hissed. It opened inch by inch. Wind whistled around him, buffeting against his clothes. A loose box hurled itself across the bay and smacked into his side.

Jules slipped his hand into the gap and pushed against the left door, forcing it open until there was enough room for her. The box tumbled past him and lodged against the narrow opening of the hatch.

"Abigail! Crawl through!"

But she was frozen in fear with her eyes transfixed on the hatch where air whistled through it and into the darkening sky beyond. Jules lifted his leg and propped his foot against the door, keeping it open. His thigh muscle screamed in agony. He reached down and grabbed her collar. Jules yanked at her, forcing her to crawl under his raised leg and through the gap.

As soon as she fell into the bay, he jumped out of the way, and the doors to the airlock slammed shut, catching the hem of his vest. He shrugged out of it and knelt before Abigail. Her eyes were squeezed shut. She had curled into a ball and rocked back and forth, holding her face against her knees. Moans alternated with cries.

Huey yelped. Sparks flew from the tunnel.

Jules reached for Abigail.

"Section three zero one sealed." The warning system fell silent.

He touched her shoulders, and she started screaming, batting at him, pushing at him and trying to crawl away from the airlock. He grabbed her, pinning her arms to her side, and tried to hold her still as she bucked against him.

"Abby! Listen to me. You're safe now." He wrapped his arms tighter around her and rocked with her, swaying with her. "Shh. You're safe. I got you."

With each sway, her frantic movements began to die. Yet her eyes refused to open. And her pitiful moans grew.

Jules fell back onto the cold floor, pulling her into his arms, letting his left leg overlap hers as he settled her against his chest. He forced one of her hands open, rubbed at the blood that had formed on her palms from her fingernails, and placed it against his cheek.

"Feel. I'm here. Not gone yet." He pressed her hand against him. "You're okay. You're safe."

Her free arm snaked up around his neck. Fingers touched him and caressed his skin. The hand under his cupped his jaw, rubbing against his beard. Her shaking began to still, yet Jules held on to her. Pulled her even tighter against him.

Huey dropped from the tube and leaned against the wall. "I sealed the hatch and doors. We can't use them until I can reroute power. She did a number, and I had to bypass too many redundancies. But we are safe for now." He wiped sweat from his brow and held up Abigail's datapad. "This GHOST is remarkable."

Abigail leaned back in his arms. Red-rimmed eyes enhanced the blue as she stared up at him. Her face was so close, he could see the merging of the freckles—the one that looked like the Seven Sisters constellation. "Thank you."

It was only a whisper, yet it seemed so much louder to Jules. He rubbed his chin against her hair. "Are you okay now?"

She nodded. Her arm dropped from his neck. Her hand slid out from under his. "For now." She fisted a hand over her heart. "I still hurt here. I've never been so terrified in my life. I just want to go home."

He kept rocking her in his arms for a couple of seconds. "I know. And we will be there soon." Jules disentangled himself from her, stood, and held out a hand to her. She allowed him to help her to her feet. "But first, I need to know how extensive the damage is."

Jules spotted the bruise on her neck and touched it. Abigail's hand covered his. "She dosed me. But I don't think she could get the full dose in. I'm groggy still, but not as much as I would have been if she had used the full dose."

Huey stood and plugged the GHOST into the cargo bay's console. The mag-locks clanged as they were activated.

Abigail wobbled a bit on her feet. Jules slipped a hand under her elbow. "Help me to the bridge?"

"Medlab first." Jules slid his arm around her, supporting most of her weight as they climbed the stairs. "Did you find anything?"

Abigail shook her head. "When I woke up, I noticed that my data disk was gone. I had downloaded the file onto it and erased it from the console, just in case she tried to send it. But I bet the spyware picked up on something."

Huey caught up with them and trailed behind as they headed for the top level. "I went over the sensor sweep. She's not on board. Security shows her leaving right before the inner hatch closed."

He forced the anger down and helped Abigail up the ladder. They veered toward medlab. "Where do we look?"

She pointed to the far corner console. "There. Huey, plug the GHOST into it and run Program Default. That's my spyware."

Jules helped her onto the exam table and caught her as she almost toppled off the surface. Her eyes lowered, but she forced them open.

"Here. Lean against me." He faced her, pulled her head down onto his shoulder, and encircled her back with his arm. A knot formed in his chest, but he ignored it. "Should I give you something to dispel the medicine?"

She shook her head. "No. Let it run its course. I'll be okay in an hour or so. I guess she got more into me than I thought."

Huey unplugged the datapad and handed it to Jules. "Take a look."

Jules turned it around and showed Abigail. She ran her finger down the screen. "She had a nanotracker in the serum she gave you. Your body would break it down in two days, but that was how she tracked you. Oh—" His hand tightened over the datapad. Abigail pulled it from his grasp. "Don't break it."

He looked down at it and read. "Julius Williams. IF Delta-nine-zero-foxtrot-kilo-kilo. D90FKK." His nostrils flared. If she were still on board, he would have flushed her out the airlock right then.

A ping echoed from the bridge. Huey grimaced. "I need to call in our destination, Cap."

"Do it." As Huey left the medlab, he leaned away and looked at Abigail. "Can you change the IF?"

"With Huey's help, yes. We can change to a new IF, change the records on Mars, and use new codes. The GHOST will do that." She sagged against him again. "Huey can do it. Tell him to use NP-zero-nine-five. That is the file he will need. I don't think I can stay awake."

Jules lowered her onto the table and bent over her, brushing at her tangled hair. "Then sleep. You are okay now. I promised you I would keep you safe, and I meant it."

Her finger reached up and traced his bottom lip. "Some promises cannot be kept." She gave him a soft smile. Her eyes drifted shut, and her body relaxed.

Jules held her hand. He meant what he said. And he would die keeping that promise to her. He pressed his lips against her knuckles. Why was it important to keep that promise? He didn't know the answer, but he did know that keeping her safe was the key to all his questions.

He furrowed his brow and looked down at the hand he had kissed. It was a strange reaction, yet he found in it a pleasant response. Jules brushed his lips across her skin once more. The thought of her perishing was unacceptable.

"Cap?"

Jules set her hand across her stomach and stepped away. He pressed the comm. "Go ahead."

"We are unslaved."

"I'll be right there. I have a job for you before we head back home."

He closed the connection, turned back to Abigail, and pulled a blanket from under the table. Jules slipped his hands under her shoulders and pulled her completely onto the table before extending the small cushion from the bottom. He removed her heavy boots and then covered her with the blanket.

"Lights, one quarter." The room dimmed.

Jules picked up her datapad, keyed open the door, and headed for the bridge. He pushed the memory of him kissing her hand to the farthest reaches of his mind, but it refused to stay there.

# Chapter Thirteen

## JEDIDIAH

Abigail stared at the lounge viewport. Beyond the shielding was open space—that endless vacuum. The one that haunted her every night, stealing her sleep, mocking her . . .

The doors hissed open. No sound other than that. So, it had to be Jules. For the last two days after the sickening jumpgate, he had been checking on her. Sometimes, he would sit with her in silence. Sometimes, he would talk with her, open up a bit about his life before. Jules never had much to say about it, other than the training he received. The torture that they put him through to prepare him. Never talked about his missions, except for that one evening.

Her thoughts fell back to yesterday after she had received word that Elder Jake and his crew had escaped with few injuries and would be on their way home, too. Jules had joined her on the couch, and their conversation had led to one of his missions. When she had asked him how they survived that battle in the South Continent Rainforest, he had said they had pumped themselves so full of adrenaline that it took two days for it to break down in their systems. GFT had learned then to administer the substance before their missions. That was the only time he talked about his former profession. Otherwise, he never spoke of it.

She had a fairly good deduction why he didn't.

He came into view and settled on the couch beside her. Heat from his body reached her, reminding her how cold it was in the observation lounge. How cold it was in space, relatively speaking. He shifted, and his thigh brushed against her leg.

For several minutes, silence reigned as she stared at the darkened viewport. She drew in a deep breath and turned to him. He had been watching her, with his arm hooked over the back of the couch.

"We are two hours from Earth orbit. You will need to contact the Coalition soon and enter the coordinates. How are you tonight?" His voice was softer tonight. The green of his eyes was more pronounced in the dim lighting of the room.

"Jumpsickness has passed." She rubbed at her arms. A shiver was determined to make its way throughout her body.

"I meant otherwise. You aren't sleeping."

"You can tell?"

"I can hear." He linked his hands together and relaxed against the cushions. "You get up, pace, work on your datapads, then lie back down. Then in a couple of hours, you do it again."

Abigail looked away and fought back a sigh. Tiredness leeched into her body and bones. It wasn't supposed to be this hard just to get home. "I want to be home. Where it's safe. I want to see Mimi and my dad. I can't sleep because of the nightmares." She turned back to him. He listened patiently, waiting. "Do you dream?"

He pursed his lips. "I don't. Never have—or at least, I don't remember it." He reached for her hand. His thumb rubbed across her knuckles. "What are you dreaming?"

"The sound of the air rushing out of the airlock. It won't get out of my mind." She turned toward him and scooted closer. Her fingers wrapped around his left hand. Just a bit of contact. To know that there was something solid here for her. "Do you even fear?"

He unhooked his arm from the back and leaned forward. His touch was cool on her temple, where he brushed a wayward strand of hair away from her eyes. "I do. Sometimes. But not often. We were trained to not be afraid of death."

"We aren't supposed to be afraid, either."

"We?" His brows drew down in confusion.

"Christians. We shouldn't fear death because of our eternal destination. This life is just a journey. Grander things lie in wait for us after we die. But we also know we are human. We can't help but fear death, leaving this world." She shook her head. "No. That's wrong. It's not that I fear leaving this world. I fear how I would die."

"I've never given it any thought. I have dealt death. I have met death. And I've escaped death. But never thought much about it."

She turned his hand over in hers and traced the slight scars on his palms. "I fear for you sometimes."

"Why?"

He let her open his other hand and smooth her fingers across the palm of it, too. "Because without Christ, Hell is your destination. I don't want that for you."

Jules shook his head and closed his fists. She let her hands fall back onto her lap. His gaze flowed over her. "I don't understand."

"I know. But you will in time."

His brow furrowed a bit. "Maybe. You say you shouldn't fear, but when we were in the alley and I had to dispatch 4-N, you feared then?"

Abigail sighed and nodded. "I did. It happened so fast. And before I could . . . comprehend what was happening, you were kneeling before me." She gave him a small smile. "It wasn't you I was fearing, if that was what you've been thinking. That man was the closest I've ever been to a GFT assassin, other than you."

It would be a brave move on her part. But seeing him there, sitting before her with the lights highlighting his eyes, casting a shadow over his lips, he seemed more than just a former assassin. He was Julius. Someone who was on a new path and who, for some reason, had captured her heart.

He sat still as she leaned forward. His eyes followed her as she stretched up toward him before he dipped his head down, meeting her part of the way. Her lips touched his.

It was a brief touch. Only a couple of seconds of pressure against his mouth. Long enough for her to notice that their lips fit perfectly together. And his were soft.

She pulled away and stood. "Thank you for saving me."

He twisted around as she hurried toward the door. Embarrassment heated her face, and his gaze seemed to burn through her. Whatever had compelled her to kiss him? And he allowed it.

The memory of his touch, of him cradling her and holding her, filtered through her mind. He seemed to care about her—to want to learn and hear more about her and her people. He wanted to understand.

And now she had just complicated the whole thing because . . . why? She thought him attractive? Handsome? Desirable?

Yet they were incompatible. Or were they?

Huey looked up as she entered the bridge. "Are you okay?"

Startled, Abigail jolted herself out of her musings. "Uh, yeah." She shook her head and started to sit down in Jules' chair, but she stopped when he walked into the bridge.

His eyes sought hers. A questioning gaze flitted across his face, but he waved her into the seat and leaned back against the holographic table, crossing arms over his chest and his right ankle over the left.

Abigail blew out an unsteady breath and tried to calm her nerves. Only a couple of hours left, and she would be home. Such a beautiful word. She pulled her datapad from the side compartment, activated the GHOST, and opened the communications to home.

Huey reached over and pulled up the holographic projection. The connection dissolved into her father's face. His eyes beamed, and a smile stretched across his face.

"Abby!"

"Dad! I'm on my way."

His grin grew even larger. "It's so good to see you. Are you safe?"

"I am, Dad. Elder Carson contacted you?" She bit at her fingernail.

His face dimmed a bit. "He did. And we will be waiting. Are you sure about this?"

Jules shifted a bit but kept his silence. He didn't look at her when she glanced back at him. "I am, Dad. More than anything. And Jules has agreed to the terms set forth."

"I see." Her father looked off screen before turning back to her. "You have the coordinates. And I'll be waiting on you. On all of you. Oh, I hear one of your party is a Huey Marktov."

"Yeah. Why?"

"Is he there?"

Abigail switched the viewscreen so that it would show the whole bridge. Her dad's eyes landed on Jules and then swept over to Huey.

"I'm Huey, sir." Confusion danced across Huey's face. "I'm part of the Coalition, but sorry to say, backslidden."

"You aren't the first, young man. But I have a message for you."

Huey pointed to his chest. "For me?"

"Your cousin, Alexander, said he'll be at the platform waiting. He's been looking forward to this day."

"Alex?" Huey's face brightened, and he looked over at Abigail.

Her father leaned forward. "Be careful. Captain Williams, you are responsible for bringing them both home." His gaze shot back to Abigail. "I love you, Abby. See you soon."

The transmission ended. He'd be there when she arrived . . .

Huey bounced in his seat with a grin plastered to his face. She glanced back at Jules.

His face was impassive; carved in marble. Only his eyes gave away what he felt. Worry. Anxiety. And . . . relief?

Huey flew the *Nightingale* low over the dark waters of the Southern Ocean. Jules checked radar again. No indication that they had been noticed. Even though Abigail said the coordinates would deliver them undetected to the Antarctica base, he still didn't trust it.

How could they have existed there and for so long without anyone ever noticing? Then again, the resources on that frozen wasteland had been diminished long ago. It was a no-man's land. Only wildlife lived there. And yet, there they were. Deep under the ice. Thriving.

"Cap, initiate submerge."

Jules reached above him and flipped the row of toggles. Loud clanking issued through the ship as all other viewports were closed. He switched the engines over to internal thrusters.

Huey glided the ship into the water. Darkness flowed over them as they dipped down further under the sea. Ahead of them was an archway of ice. The ship moved silently through the arch. Jules glanced through the viewport and up the side. Dark blue ice towered over his ship. What looked smooth was actually pockmarked and pitted.

Then the ship was rising up, breaking through the surface and skimming it as Huey guided it to an old, abandoned platform. Retro thrusters engaged, slowing them down. Jules initiated the landing sequence as Huey moved her into the LZ.

The ship rattled as it settled onto the metal surface. Huey reached above him and shut down the engines. He turned to Jules.

"Ready?"

Was he? He wasn't sure. But there was no going back now.

He stood, closed the shielding over the viewport, and keyed the bridge's door to remain open as he passed through it. Huey hurried to his quarters.

Jules ducked into his and grabbed his thick, military-issued coat. Abigail's father had issued strict instructions. No luggage. No weapons. And Jules had agreed to it. If JJ did it, then he would, too. He had always trusted his brother's guidance.

He pulled a lined hat over his head and met Huey as he came out of his quarters, bundled in a parka and carrying an overpacked duffel.

When he arrived in the cargo bay, Abigail stood at the airlock with her own bag and bundled in the parka he had seen in her quarters. The fur-lined hood was pulled up, and strands of her hair had escaped.

She smiled up at him. "Ready?"

He motioned toward the door with his hand.

Huey opened the airlock, and the hatch lowered. Bitter cold whipped into the bay, stealing his breath for a second. He followed the two down the ramp. Across the platform, a group of men stood at the far edge, near a hangar entrance. The two at the end of the group stepped away and leveled their rifles at them as the man in the center strode toward them.

Before they made it halfway, Abigail dropped her bag and started running toward him. Her squeal of delight echoed off the ice. She jumped into his arms, and he caught her, swinging her around once before setting her on her feet.

Her arms were locked around his chest, and his chin rested on top of her head. A deep pang ricocheted through Jules' body at the sight. A foreign feeling invaded him. Something pulled at his heart . . . something he couldn't place.

He dipped down and picked up her bag. As he and Huey approached, the man let go of Abigail and turned to them. The resemblance was remarkable. Though his hair was peppered with gray, the red was still as vibrant as Abigail's. His eyes were not as bright blue, but they held a deep knowledge and compassion. That was something he wasn't used to seeing in anyone.

Another man stepped away from the group and waved. Huey dropped his bag and raced to him. They embraced tightly, slapping each other on the shoulders and back. The man held Huey at arm's length before ruffling his hair.

"I thought I would never see you again. Come, come. Let me get you settled, cousin." He strode forward and picked up Huey's bag. "Jedidiah, I will take Huey to medlab for his scan and get him settled at my place."

"Very well, Alex. We will deal with him later." Abigail's father waved them on.

Jules was powerless now. No command. Uncertainty loomed before him.

"I'm Jedidiah du Soleil. Thank you for bringing my daughter home safely." He extended his hand toward Jules.

Jules hesitated for a second and then gripped the man's hand. When he let go, Abigail stepped closer to him and took her bag from his other hand. He touched the small of her back, nudging her closer to him. Her father's eyes followed the gesture. Jules dropped his hand away and took a half-step to the side.

"Tell me—may I call you Jules?"

"You may."

"Tell me, Jules, did you come with no weapons?"

"I did."

"Are you willing to hand over your ship to us?" du Soleil's eyes bored into him.

Jules glanced back at the *Nightingale*. It was his home for the last two years. The only thing he could claim as his own. He forced a swallow past the tightening of his throat. If he took this step, there was no going back.

But what was there for him? Staying one step ahead of the GFT? Always looking over his shoulder, afraid the day would arrive when Zeetoo would come and finish his mission?

Jules turned back around and fished the data disk from his pocket. He held it out to her father. "I am. Codes for the *Nightingale*."

The man accepted it and turned it over in his fingers. A fleeting look of surprise flowed across his face. He slid it into a pocket on his coat. "Then welcome to the Coalition base. Come on inside and let me show you around."

Jules looked from him to the men at the edge, who had lowered their rifles. "You don't plan to scan me for weapons, Mr. du Soleil?"

He smiled. Once again reminding Jules of Abigail. "My daughter has vouched for you. And you will find that we have ways of knowing what the right direction to take is." He waved them forward.

Jules reclaimed Abigail's bag from her and ushered her forward. When a younger man stepped toward them, hand outstretched for the bag, Jules relinquished it. Her father turned to the man, whose beard was so thick, it hid his mouth and chin.

"Devon, put her bag in my quarters and alert Mimi that we will be up there soon." He turned to the others. "Mark, Wickham, you two head back to reclamation. And John, if you don't mind, the desalination unit is down. Fix it will you?"

The man named John paused, his dark brown eyes glaring at Jules, before he nodded and moved away. As he disappeared around the bend to the right, he glanced back once more. Jules met his gaze. Something about him was familiar.

"Jules?" Abigail's touch brought him back around to them. "Come on." She nodded toward her father, who stood just inside the entrance.

He followed Abigail. The hangar bay door lowered as soon as he crossed the threshold. Her father smiled as he led them across the inner bay and to a corridor on the left.

"You will eventually meet everyone here, Jules. And you will find that some of them were affected by your former profession."

Jules paused and glanced back at the corridor John had disappeared down. Did he kill someone John knew? Maybe someone close to him?

"Will that cause too much of an issue, Mr. du—"

"Jed or Jedidiah."

"Jedidiah."

"And no." He led them through a door to the right and paused on the gangway that overlooked a large commons area three decks below. "We have had former assassins come to us before."

"Bishop Thomas told me. Echo. Sierra. Even Zulu. And JJ came to you."

Jedidiah arched a brow at him. "JJ?"

Abigail answered for him. "You call him Joshua, Dad."

Jedidiah nodded. "Ah, yes. Joshua. A fine man. Devout." He leaned against the railing and waited.

Jules glanced around him. There was no one about. Nor below them . . . but faint sounds reached him. Laughter. Squeals. They grew louder.

He glanced over at Abigail. She had leaned against her father's shoulder and had her hands propped on the railing. From her expression, this wasn't something new to her. And they acted like they expected something to occur.

Jules propped against the rail next to her and peered over. Doors at each point: north, south, east, west. Layout was similar to the old transport cargo ships. He followed the arch of the walls. No, the hull. It was an old transport converted into a living space with boxes and bookcases lining one wall and seats and chairs dotting the center.

He looked behind him at the corridors. Welded seams connected the corridors and larger areas. So well were they welded that if he didn't know what to look for, they never would have been seen.

Below them, the noise grew louder. Jules turned back as little bodies piled out of the east corridor. Tiny squeals and laughter of delight. Children poured across the area. Some dove into the boxes to the side, pulling out toys. Some strolled to the low bookcases, selecting books and flouncing onto the couches to read.

Little heads of every color imaginable. One dark-skinned girl with dark hair paused in her conversation with a brown-headed boy and looked up at them. Her shiny curls bounced as she ran to a tiny blonde-haired girl, who sat in a chair with a book balanced on her knee.

The dark-skinned girl touched her friend's shoulder and pointed. When the girls looked up, grins split their faces. They jumped up and down, waving. The boy looked up. His shout bounced throughout the area.

"Abby! You're back!"

Abigail's laughter seemed contagious as she waved back to them. Her father was grinning just as big.

They started to head up the stairway, but a woman stopped them. She glanced up, saw Abigail, and waved, her white smile contrasting with her dark-as-midnight skin.

"Abby!"

"Hey, Miriam! Tell them I'll find them later!"

The woman nodded. She kissed her fingers and then waved them to Abigail, who returned the gesture.

The cherub-looking girl pulled at the woman's shirt, her hands flashing in some sort of code.

"What is she doing?"

"Signing."

Jules frowned. The woman was doing the same thing; then she ruffled the girl's head before moving away to another group of children who were crowded around a box. The brown-haired boy moved to the two girls. He was turned away from Jules, but whatever was said set off the little cherub. She kicked the boy in the shin, picked up a bat nearby, and began raising it above her head. Her eyes were filled with tears. The bat was grabbed before she could bring it down onto the boy.

The woman started chiding them. Her hands moved in conjunction with her mouth. The girl crossed her arms in defiance. The woman—what did Abigail call her? Miriam? Miriam didn't give in. She brought her hands down, fists facing up and thumbs and small finger out at the sides and stopped them level with her waist. She repeated the gesture with more emphasis.

Jules cocked his head and mimicked her. What did it mean?

The girl scowled before turning to the boy. She held her fist over her chest and made a circle with it. The boy did likewise.

The two returned to their friend as if nothing had ever happened. Jules repeated the gesture. Did it mean "now"? When she made the gesture, the girl reacted immediately. But the other. Jules tried it out.

"Does it mean 'sorry'?" He turned to Abigail and found them watching him. "She can't hear, can she?"

Abigail shook her head. "No. Her family was killed when she was one. The concussion bomb damaged her ears, and she's been deaf ever since. John and Miriam took her in." She looked at his hands and smiled. "You picked up on the sign language pretty fast."

"It was easy. Your friend made the gesture, and I watched how the girl responded. Picked out the most logical reaction."

Jedidiah nodded at his statement. "You will meet them later. But I wanted you to see who else is also a part of the Coalition, Jules. We aren't just men and women, but families. Many with children. We aren't an army. We are just families. People."

He stepped away from the railing and motioned for them to follow him. They walked through another corridor and down a flight of stairs. All around them were people, moving about their business. Some paused and gave Abigail a hug. Some smiled. Others cast wary glances at Jules.

Jedidiah led them up another flight of stairs. To the left was the medlab section. Jedidiah motioned toward the first door. When Jules entered the spacious room, an older lady in a dark blue jumpsuit looked up. She was a lot older than she appeared at first. Her eyes held a watery gaze, and she walked with arthritic steps. Bony arms raised toward Abigail.

"Oh, my girl, you're home!" She brought Abigail's head to her shoulder and held her. Tears flowed down Abigail's face as she returned the embrace.

"I've missed you, Mimi! So much!"

The woman stepped back and held Abigail at arm's length. "You've lost a lot of weight. But we'll fix that." She turned her gaze to Jules. "And you must be Julius. Huey was telling me all about you. Come here, dear boy. I'm Evelyn, but you will call me Mimi."

Jules stepped further into the room.

Jedidiah spoke from the doorway. "Mom, I have a few more things to do. Abigail, you can finish showing him around the complex. But meet me in the galley in a couple of hours."

"Okay, Dad." She gave him one more hug and then stepped back to Jules' side.

Her grandmother waved Jules onto an exam table. "I hope you don't mind, but I need to do a full medscan on you."

"Didn't Elder Jake send you bloodwork and a scan?" He slid onto the surface of the table. The mesh gave way to his weight.

"He did. But portable scanners can do only so much. He said you are on still on the serum."

"I am. But had only derivatives."

Some of her white hair escaped the bun at her neck when she nodded. "Well, we have the formula here, so we can get you started back on the serum and then slowly wean you off."

Jules cocked his head at her. "I won't have to take it anymore?"

"Eventually. Quitting suddenly will send your body into shock, and it'll start shutting down. Small increments and then you will be free."

Jules mulled over that word. Free. That was what he had been wanting for so long. To be free.

Mimi waved toward the scanner that hung on an overhanging arm. "Move that scanner this way, Abby." She looked at Jules. Warmth and kindness lit her eyes. "Shall we get started?"

He nodded and pushed off his boots. They landed on the floor with a thud. He shrugged off his coat and handed it to Abigail. Then he started removing his shirt. He was no stranger to full medscans. They would take a while.

Abigail grabbed his shirt and laid it across his coat on the counter.

A knock at the door interrupted them. The man named John stood there, his eyes glued to Jules' chest and abdomen. His gaze took in the myriad scars.

"Do you need something, John?" Mimi looked at the man expectantly.

He nodded and kept staring at Jules as he talked. "Jed said that when you finish here to meet him in hydroponics."

"Okay. Is that all?" She turned from Jules and waited.

John shook his head. "No." He stepped toward Jules. It wasn't threatening. His steps were determined, focused. "Do I look familiar to you?"

Jules racked his memory. It was a distant image. Two men . . . no, three. Dark hair, dark eyes. Olive skin. Slight builds. Seven years ago. Romanian Providence. The Embassy mission. "You were at the Embassy."

"I was. And I escaped." He halted in front of Jules. "You killed my brother. Sliced his throat."

Abigail and Mimi stepped forward, but Jules stopped them. "No. Stay out of it." He slid from the table and stood before John. The man was a couple of inches taller than his own five-foot-eleven. "I know nothing I will say will help or mean anything to you. But I'm not that person anymore."

"I know." John's smile was small . . . sad. "You wouldn't be here if you weren't wanting to be free from what you were made to be. You aren't the only one who came to us. But you are the one who—" He paused and looked away with his mouth drawn in a tight line. Seconds passed before he turned back to Jules. "I hated you, for a long time. But when I saw you . . . I can't hate you any longer, Julius Williams. We are commanded to forgive. I thought if I ever saw you, I believed I would kill you."

Jules looked into his eyes. He didn't doubt the man, but he wouldn't succeed. Surely, he knew that.

John watched him. "Julius, I forgive you. You came to us, and I cannot deny you the chance to come to Christ." He stepped away and paused at the door. "That's all I have to say, Evelyn."

Jules watched the empty doorway long after John left. This wasn't how he expected things to go. He expected interrogation. He expected to be held in front of a group of elders, a tribunal of sorts. Not this. A tour. Smiles and laughter. Children. Kindness.

And forgiveness. That was a foreign word.

Abigail's touch was featherlight on his arm. "Jules?"

He turned to her. Her blue eyes searched his face as she guided him back onto the exam table. He slid onto the surface and lay back. A cold streak trailed down his cheek. Jules touched it. When he brought his hand away, his fingertip was wet.

As Mimi positioned the scanner over him, Jules rubbed his tear-marked finger against his thumb. Confusion rolled through him.

$$\Sigma$$

Jules turned the page and angled it so that the dim light of the library could fall onto the thin pages. For the last two days, he had been shunted around the base. Met the elders. Elder Jake had arrived yesterday. Him he knew. Then there were Davis, Wickham, Gerald, and Jedidiah, of course. The others were either on Mars or with JJ, who he had found out last night was at Jupiter Station retrieving Coalition members who were in danger.

He wasn't expected to be back for another few weeks. But Jedidiah had told him that an update was scheduled in three days, and when it came through, Jules could be present.

He turned the next page. Judges didn't make sense. No. It made sense. But the actions of the man Samson didn't. The door hissed open, and Mimi's scent, a mix of medicines and orchids, met him long before the sound of her feet did.

"Hello, dear boy." She stopped next to him where he was propped up against the curvature of the viewport. The dark waters outside the window flowed past them. "Have you eaten lately?"

Jules shook his head and continued reading. "I'll grab a nutrient bar if I get hungry, Mimi."

She ran her finger along his hand. When he looked up at her, she gave him a smile. "You need more than those tasteless nutrient bars. I have a nice meal set out for Jed and Abigail. Why don't you join us?"

"Hmmm. It probably isn't a good idea if I did." He thought back to the day after he had arrived. Jedidiah had pulled him to the side. Jules had a choice: remain but keep his distance from Abigail. Or leave.

Leaving wasn't an option. And though he agreed and promised to keep his distance from Abigail, it was increasingly proving difficult.

She had taken him to the classes. And laughed at his befuddlement. At first, he didn't understand why she had him there at the school. Yet as he watched and saw the interactions between the children and adults, it occurred to him that she was showing him yet another aspect of who the Coalition was.

He had watched the kids make pendants. Abigail even talked him into trying his hand at it. The little black-headed girl he had seen the first day, Evie, showed him how to place the glass beads in a design, then insert it into a small kiln. After a few moments, the glass had melted into a swirling design. Then they ran it through a cooling unit and tied them on strings. When it came his turn to string the pendant, he was torn between two ribbons. It was Evie who plucked the green ribbon from his hands, telling him it matched his eyes, and tied his pendant onto it.

He had tied the necklace on her neck instead of his. Told her thank you for showing him how to make it. Then he gave the little cherub his blue ribbon. She tied it in her hair and signed "thank you" to him. When he botched the signing for "welcome," it sent her into a fit of giggles, and she coached him on the proper way to sign. Apparently, there was a formal and informal, and he had used the formal.

Then Abigail had him tour hydroponics, where he learned Mimi spent much of her time. Her grandmother grew coffee plants under high intensity lamps, orchids of various colors, rose plants, and more herbs than he could name.

And so did John Iliescu. He supervised the growing of the vegetables. John saw them but didn't say a word and instead only turned away. He hadn't been around Jules since that day in medlab. But Miriam, his wife—she sought them out and would at times join them as Abigail showed him around the complex.

Today, though, he escaped into the library. Since the day he saw it, the silence called to him.

Mimi sat next to him and waited. In the days he had been around her, she never pressed him for conversation. She would sit beside him, much like she was now, and patiently wait.

"What did Jedidiah say?" He turned the page and finished the story on Samson.

"I gave him no option. How else will he learn about you if he doesn't talk to you?" She patted his leg. "What are you reading?"

He held up the red, leather book. "Illegal literature."

She huffed at his comment. "Silly law. Why are you reading it?"

Jules closed the cover and set it to the side. "To learn more about you and the Coalition, I need to understand what you value most. I've watched. No one seems to value things—items. Yes, they take care of it. But they don't honor it or covet it. I've seen . . . what's her name? The one with the short, brown hair; dark eyes; and the scar just here . . . " Jules touched his forehead above his left eye.

"Micah's wife, Sarah."

"I saw Sarah yank a book like this off the table when one of her children knocked over a glass. The drink spread, hit datapads and clothing. But she protected that book. I've seen Jedidiah read it late at night in the commons. Even saw John with it in hydroponics. Why? Apparently, this book is valued more than anything else. Even Bishop Thomas valued it."

Mimi smiled. "It is valuable. It is life to us. It is truth and guidance. It holds salvation." She picked up the book and set it back on the small table in the middle of the room. "This one stays here in the library, though. Not everyone has a copy, so this one is here for them to read."

When she motioned for him to follow, he obeyed. Mimi demanded respect and obedience. Never said a word, but he had seen almost all in the complex give her deference. It seemed to be an unspoken rule. Even he felt it. No matter what she said or wanted from him, he had the compulsion to do as she requested.

So, Jules unfolded from his spot and followed her out the makeshift library, which was a derelict ship's lounge. He glanced back at it. Looked like a C-56X Midline transport.

She hobbled down the stairs and crossed toward hydroponics. Jules followed at her pace, watching everyone as they passed by. Little Cherub CeeCee spotted him from across the expanse between the two gangways. She signed at him.

He furrowed his brow in concentration. It was a new word. He shrugged at her, which caused her to laugh as she followed her family to the galley. Guess she gave him a new word to learn.

He would need Abigail's datapad again. Mimi shuffled down the stairs and paused outside her quarters adjacent to hydroponics. She motioned him through the door.

Jules stepped over the threshold and scanned her room. It was small. A bunk to the side. A refresher unit at the back. And on the other side, containers of plants and seedlings lined the countertop. To the right of the door stood two chairs, their plush coverings inviting someone to sit and read from the stack of books on the table between them.

She crossed to her bunk and reached into a small box at the foot of it. When she turned around, she held out a small, thin, black book. The leather was cool and soft against his hand. He opened it, turning extremely thin pages.

*Holy Bible.* His finger traced the words. It was the same translation as the bishop's books.

"That is for you. Keep it and read it."

He looked at Mimi. "Are you sure?"

"Yes." She hooked her arm through his elbow and guided him out the door. "Now, about dinner. Let's go eat. And don't worry about Jedidiah. I know my son better than you."

And apparently, she did. The du Soleil quarters were down and across from his on the other side of the stairs. When they walked through the door, Jedidiah's face turned down into a scowl, but he said nothing as he motioned Jules to an empty chair—away from Abigail—at the small table set against the far wall.

Jules sat, placing his newly acquired Bible on the corner near his elbow. Jedidiah's gaze fell upon it and then flowed to his mother, who hummed ever so slightly to herself as she lifted the lids off the dishes in front of them.

Awkwardness didn't begin to explain the tension that surrounded the table. Abigail gave him a small smile. Her eyes traveled from his eyes to his mouth and then back to his eyes. His thoughts drifted to that one moment on the ship. It wasn't like with Anya. He had leaned toward Abigail that day, accepting what she was giving him.

And what she gave him sent a ripple of surprise and longing through him.

Jedidiah broke the silence and his thoughts. "What part are you reading?"

"Judges thirteen." Jules handed Mimi his plate when she reached for it.

"What compelled you to read our Bible?"

And this was the interrogation. Disguised in friendliness, in companionship. Jules replaced his plate, which was now heaped with some kind of pasta dish with a salad, to the side. She didn't give him much. For that he was grateful. The last meal of new food had his stomach tied in knots.

"I found a book by a someone named McGee. It broke down passages, and I became curious about what he was writing about. Your illegal book was on the table. So, I read it." Jules passed his empty glass to Mimi, well aware that Abigail's gaze was still on him. "To learn about someone, especially an enemy, one must learn about what they value most."

"So, we are your enemy?" Jedidiah's eyes narrowed.

"No, sir. That's my training talking. But it applies here." Jules sipped the drink. Tea. With a touch of sweetness. He swallowed another sip. Peach. From hydroponics. "To understand the Coalition, I need to understand what is valued. And that book is valued."

Jedidiah smiled, as if Jules had just fallen into his trap, and twirled his fork in his pasta. "No, son, it is not the book. It is the Words within. That is what is valued."

Jules mimicked the twirl in the pasta. And then took a tentative bite. Buttery and smooth. Light. He could handle this meal. His stomach issued a small growl in response, which caused Abigail to laugh softly.

She pointed her fork at him. "Eat up, Jules. Mimi and I made sure the dinner was light enough for you to handle."

He ate another bite, then one from the salad. A tangy oil covered the variety of leaves. The pleasant taste burst on his tongue, and he found himself taking another, then another.

Jedidiah had leaned back against his chair, watching him. Waiting until Jules took a drink to wash it down before issuing another question. "What have you learned from Judges? Are you understanding it?"

Jules set his fork down and picked up the book. This Bible didn't have such small print like the red one. He flipped to the book of Judges and found his reading. "It says here that before Samson was born, God marked him. How does a god know someone before he is born? And as I read more, it made no sense. If Samson's strength was not in his hair, but a blessing given to him, then why did he squander it? And why even mention his hair?"

Jedidiah propped his elbows on the table and steepled his fingers, pressing them against his chin. "You ask valid points. Tell you what, you finish dinner. And then let's take a walk."

$$\Sigma$$

Jules followed Jedidiah to the landing zone as he zipped his coat closed. Instead of the hangar doors, the man led him to a side hatch. He keyed it open and waved Jules through. They stepped out onto a narrow ledge with a waist-high railing. To his left, the *Nightingale* stood under the dome of ice.

"I have Huey prepping to take her under. There is an underwater cavern where we keep our ships. We made room for the *Nightingale*."

Jules looked over at him. "Then the elders have agreed to let me stay?"

"We have." Jedidiah stood next to him. "You have a unique set of skills that will help us. And you have shown that you want to leave your old life behind."

Jules placed his Bible on the grating at his feet and draped his hands over the railing. The gloves Jedidiah had loaned him creaked as he clasped his hands together. "I do want to leave that life behind. I don't want to kill anymore. Be what they made me to be." He let his gaze flow over the dark water before them. His breath hung in the air as he composed his thoughts. Jules now understood the dynamics between Jedidiah and Abigail. The man was patient. A lot like Mimi. "If your God knows someone before they were born, did He know me?"

"Yes, He did, Julius. Did you ever think that was why you were never killed? You survived situations that should have left you dead."

Movement from behind him indicated that Jedidiah had bent down and then stood back up. "You asked about Samson. Samson was given a great gift. He chose to use it not for God's glory but for his own. Yet in the end, Samson came back. Do you know what the moral of that story is?"

Jules thought on his reading. It wasn't hard to see what it taught the reader. "Samson squandered away his gift and had to pay the price in the end—a sacrifice. We are all given gifts. What we do with them defines us."

"Well said, Jules. You are learning." The older man leaned against the railing beside Jules as the rumble of the *Nightingale*'s engines filled the air. "You asked about Samson's hair. His hair was his badge, a symbol. His strength was the Spirit of God moving him. When his hair was cut, it symbolized his broken vow. I know many think that, like Samson and his hair, our strength comes from the ceremonies or rituals we have. But it is not. Our strength, as believers, is always in the Spirit of God."

This was foreign territory. He was a stranger in the land. His mind immediately jumped to that passage he had read the other day, but Jules shook the thought away. It wasn't hard to logically deduce where Jedidiah's conversation was going. "You are asking me to use what I was made to be. That isn't a 'God-given' gift. It was manmade through genetic manipulation."

"God will choose the weak things in this world to accomplish His purpose. In your case, it is your belief in Him that is weak. And what was done to you—it can be used for the greater good, which is for His glory. Used to protect His children." Abigail's father fell silent for a few seconds. When he spoke, his voice was gentle, like the small waves that lapped against the side of the balcony. "As it is said in Esther, Julius, 'Yet who knows whether you have come to the kingdom for *such* a time as this?'"

Jules mulled over Jedidiah's words. Not the same syntax as Bishop Thomas' book, yet the words rang the same. "I never asked for this, Jedidiah. I wanted to be free from it all." Jules tightened his hands around the rail, gloves creaking from the strain of his grip. "I never asked for this!"

"Never did the great men of history who sacrificed for God's people."

"I'm not great, nor do I wish to be. I am an assassin. A killer. Blood is on my hands."

Jedidiah sighed. "Even King David and Paul had blood on their hands."

Across the bay, the *Nightingale* slipped beneath the ocean's surface, heading for the underwater tunnel.

He was his ship. Slipping beneath the surface. Into a darkness he didn't know.

"Why save me if only to make me kill again?" His voice was not more than a whisper, more of a question to himself than to Abigail's father.

Jedidiah pushed away from the rail and touched Jules' arm. When Jules turned around, the worn, black book that he had set aside was in Jedidiah's hand. The scars and wrinkles on Jedidiah's hand contrasted sharply with the supple leather of the book as he held the Bible out to Jules.

Jules accepted the proffered gift. He flipped through the onion-thin pages.

"Start with Ecclesiastes. Then read about King David." The older man turned and walked away. Jules called out to him.

"Where do I find the story of David?"

Jedidiah glanced back as he keyed open the door. "Read and find it."

Then Jules was left alone with the ice and cold. And an old book that foretold the future through history.

"For *such* a time as this."

Him. Former assassin. Killer of God's children, now one of them. But in association only.

Jules sank down near the rail and leaned back against the cold metal. He turned to the chapter list and found Ecclesiastes.

Time to understand why he would not be allowed to leave his past behind.

## Chapter Fourteen

# ΛNTΛRCTICΛ, COΛLITION BΛSE

Abigail set the crate on the counter and lifted the lid. Yesterday, Jules had dropped the medicines from the *Nightingale* off in medlab, and Mimi had asked her to put them in the small cabinet they used for the serum components.

She thought back to Jules' behavior. He had spoken a bit to her. Asked how she was doing. If she had seen the kids again. There was a slight pause when he had taken a small step toward her, a question in his eyes; but then a wall had come down around him, and he had left.

The comm pinged. Abigail activated it. "Abby."

"Abby, could you please see to mixing the serum? About seven vials. The measurements are in the database under Jules' file. Do not use the Paxolin. His body isn't responding well to it."

"I can. Are you with him right now?" Now, why would she ask that?

"No. But he's scheduled for a dose in about thirty minutes and should be arriving soon." Static hissed across the comm for a moment. "I'll try to get there to give it to him, but I may be late. If he arrives before me, you can administer it. He knows where it needs to be injected."

"Okay, Mimi. I'll take care of it." She shut down the comm and opened the cabinet, setting the newer vials inside. It was a good thing

Jules brought what he had obtained—no, Anya did that, but it was Jules' credits. Anger at the woman rose within her. If she could just get her hands on that—

Abigail shook her head to dispel those thoughts. No need to venture down that road. She was home now. And Jules was safe with them. The drawer rattled as she pulled it open, searching for the injection gun.

Then she opened the medical console and searched Jules' file for the formula. Substance Eighty-three, thirty cc's. Versikton, twenty cc's. Medolin, replacement for Paxolin, eight cc's. Five minutes in the centrifuge.

She carefully measured out the ingredients and placed them into seven vials. Then inserted them into the centrifugal machine. As it spun, she finished stocking the cabinet.

It was the feeling of being watched that alerted her to someone else in the room. Abigail turned around. Jules leaned against the frame of the Medlab Two hatch.

"Where's Mimi?"

Abigail shrugged. "She didn't say. But had me prep your dose. Ready?"

Jules straightened and approached the table. He levered himself onto the surface and began to pull off his coat. "Did she tell you not to use the Paxolin?"

"She did." The centrifuge stopped, and Abigail plucked a vial out of the rack. She inserted it into the injection gun and waited until he had pulled his shirt over his head.

He was wearing that black long sleeve that clung to him. Abigail set the gun on the table next to him. "I need to get a wipe, so hold on."

Jules watched as she rounded the table and searched the med supplies for an antiseptic wipe. Even those supplies were becoming low. She grabbed one and tore the package. When she turned around, her gaze fell onto his back. Three ragged scars ran from his right shoulder blade to his left hip, as if a huge claw had swiped at him. And above his shoulders, tattooed in black, was *J7A*. She stepped up to him.

Without thought, her finger traced the scars. "What happened?"

"Mission in France. Our target had a three-pronged sword, more of a scythe really. Took a swipe at me." He shrugged. "It did a lot of damage that even the serum couldn't heal completely."

"And this?" She touched his tattoo.

His hand covered her fingers and caressed them briefly before letting go. "My brand. Everyone was branded with our designation."

She rounded the table. He placed his hands on either side of his legs and leaned forward. His feet hooked around her and brought her closer until she was standing between his knees, gazing up at him.

"I don't speak about my scars or brand. They aren't pleasant memories." He lifted a hand and trailed his fingers through strands of hair that escaped her hairclip. "It's time for my dose."

Abigail caught his hand and guided it back to the table. "Mimi said in her notes I'm supposed to ask you questions before I administer the serum."

His fingers dug into the table. "I prefer not this time around."

"You have no choice, Jules." She pushed at his feet, freeing herself from him, and picked up a datapad from the counter. "One—"

"One, how do I feel? I'm agitated. I am faced with conflicting emotions that I cannot identify. Two, what am I thinking presently? I'll pass on that one." His eyes hardened. "Three, did it make me nauseated at any time since the last dose? No."

Abigail pulled the wipe from the package. "You are supposed to answer all. So, back to two."

He ripped the wipe from her hand, swiped it across his abdomen with one hand, and lifted the injection gun with the other. Before she could stop him, he pulled the trigger, injecting the serum into his system. Jules looked up at her as he handed her the gun.

"I said I would pass on that one." He stood and began dressing.

Abigail placed her hand on his arm, halting him as he started slipping on his coat. "Is it that bad?"

A muscle worked in his jaw. He let his coat fall back onto the medbed. Conflict flashed across his face as his gaze bounced from her eyes to her mouth. Then it faded. His eyes darkened. He reached out and ran a finger along her jaw, stopping at her bottom lip. His thumb rubbed it as he bent forward.

She found herself leaning toward him, her hands on his waist.

The clearing of a throat sliced through the air. Jules ripped himself away from her, yanked his coat from the bed, and slid into it. Without a word, he turned from her, hurried past her father, and disappeared down the corridor.

Her father watched after Jules before stepping into the medlab. "He came for his dose?"

"Yes." She collected the used wipe and threw it away. Then she removed the vial from the injection gun and slid it into the automatic sterilizer. "You told him to keep his distance, didn't you?"

Her father leaned his hip against the table's edge and crossed his arms. "I did. He needs to adjust to life within the Coalition. His emotional state is still unstable, Abigail. He is an assassin."

"Former assassin, Dad. You told him once that we don't call them assassins or former assassins. Their old lives are no more."

"True. But the others are one of us, now. Their old lives are gone. But with Julius, he is still what they made him to be. Until he understands, I must limit his interactions with everyone."

Abigail slammed the gun on the counter. "No, Dad. What you need to do is allow him to interact with others. Learn from us. Talk to us. Be around us." She stopped. He wasn't doing that. He allowed Jules to be around others. Just not her. "You don't want him around me. That's it, right?" Her father opened his mouth, but she cut him off. "I get it. I do. But I will say this, Dad. I will not abandon him. I will talk with him, walk with him, eat with him. I will be around him."

"Abby, I am thinking only of your safety." He reached for her, but she waved him away.

"Jules will never harm me, Dad. That I know for an absolute certainty. But if it will make *you* feel better, then I will make sure we are not alone. Mimi or Sarah or Miriam will be around when I'm with Jules." She closed the cabinet and checked her wrist monitor. "Now, I have other things to do. I'll see you at dinner."

She stalked out of Medlab Two, leaving her father gazing after her. The gall of the man. They were supposed to be helping Jules. Not leaving him to travel his road alone.

Abigail stopped and sank down onto the stairs. She leaned her head against the railing. No, they weren't leaving him to travel his road alone. Her father and the elders would never do that. It was the serum. Until they knew if it would work correctly, they had to monitor him closely, evaluate his emotional and mental state.

She really needed to get the GHOST and see if she could hack his medical files.

Her father dropped down beside her and propped his clasped hands on his knees. "I'm not doing this as punishment. Just a precaution. Jules is making a lot of headway and improvement. Yet he still has a long way to go."

He wrapped an arm around her shoulders and pulled her into his side. "I know you care deeply for him. And I suspect he has feelings for you, too, but he doesn't recognize them for what they are. All I ask, Daughter, is for you to give him time. Keep a respectable distance in order to allow him to adjust." He kissed the top of her head. "We aren't giving up on him. We aren't going to abandon him. Give me the same trust that you give him."

She sighed and nodded.

$$\Sigma$$

Abigail ran the GHOST through the diagnostics. Normally what took them more than half a day was taking only minutes. She keyed open a file. "How about now, Huey?"

He flipped the switches and then ducked back into the access panel. "Nope. It wasn't that relay. If it isn't this one, then it has to be up top. Wait." He squirmed further into the opening. "There's a bit of corrosion on the wires but nothing substantial. This wouldn't have caused the malfunction."

She unplugged the datapad. "Let's try the second level console. If it's not that one, then you are correct. It'll have to be the top junction."

They climbed the ladder near the desalination unit. Huey removed the panel and wormed his way into the access tube.

"Ah, no. No corrosion that I can see."

She plugged in the GHOST and ran the diagnostic again. Nothing. "Not this one, then."

The comm opened. "Abby, have you seen Jules?"

She answered her father while scrolling through the lines of code. "No. Is it time for JJ's transmission?"

"Yes. So, bring your program up here."

She disconnected the GHOST and tapped Huey's leg with her foot. He wiggled his way out. "Find Jules and tell him to meet us in communications."

"Will do. Anything to get away from this area." He climbed to his feet and trotted up the stairs, mumbling about the freezing water, the freezing spray, and the freezing cold. She was sure she heard "and the freezing, freezing of my bum."

Working on the desalination unit was always the most hated job, but it was vital. She paused at the top of the stairs and strung the danger sign back across. Huey complained, but he was right. Sea water coated just about every surface down there and created a layer of ice on the walkway that won more times than not against their efforts to clear it.

The winding stairs that led to the next level creaked. She would let Wickham know about that. The welds could be loosening again. Abigail topped the stairs and met her father halfway down the corridor.

"Did you find the problem down there?" He ushered her through the doorway to communication with his hand at her back.

"Huey thinks it may be the top unit. So, someone will have to climb up there and check it out. The desalination unit will still run but at only an eighty percent capacity."

His hiss filled the air. "I was afraid of that. We'll get it taken care of. That GHOST of yours does a variety of jobs apparently."

Abigail sat at the console next to her father's and nodded. "Huey and I have been tweaking it. Trying to get it to the stage where we won't have to hardline it so much. And I've created a copy of it. Hope you don't mind that I already gave it to Elder Jake."

He seemed to mull over her words as she hooked the GHOST into comms and activated the program. "Do you have other copies?"

"No. Just this one and the one with Elder Jake. I do have a couple of weakened programs. Data disks for certain purposes. Mainly filtering, nav, or low-band comms." She glanced up at him. "Do you want those, too?"

"Nah." He laughed as they waited for the transmission. "You would only make another copy. I was just wondering if you were sharing your little gem."

She snorted. "I'm sharing."

Jules' voice filled the room. "Jedidiah, it's time for JJ's transmission?"

Her father turned to him with a smile. "It is. As promised, you are here."

She was sure that Jules didn't doubt them. But a look of relief and respect crossed his face as the frown disappeared. He approached them and stood behind their seats, with his hands clasped behind his back, feet apart, waiting. Not a surprise to find him closer to her chair than her dad's. If she swiveled her seat, it would have nudged his thigh.

The light on her handheld turned green. She reached forward and flipped a toggle. This derelict didn't have holographic displays, so they had to do with a staticky viewscreen.

The view dissolved into an extremely dark-skinned man with about a three-day growth of beard on his face. A scar ran down his left cheek and disappeared into the black beard. In his ears were two small earrings, little stones. His brown eyes searched each of their faces before they crinkled in delight.

"Praise the good Lord! You made it, my brother. God has answered my prayers." JJ leaned forward. "Something is wrong."

She sat back in her seat. It wasn't a question. And when she glanced back at Jules, he seemed the same as before. A little hard around the edges, a bit disgruntled today, eyes narrowed as he constantly observed everything around him.

"I'm fine, JJ. The Coalition has taken good care of me. And I've abided by their rules."

"Coalition? Rules?" A knowing light came into his eyes, and he turned to her father. "Ah, he's still learning, Jed. Give him time." Then he was speaking back to Jules. "You have always trusted me, Jules. And now is no different. Put your life in their hands, just as I would put my life in yours. That freedom you spoke about all those years? The one that you wanted for so long? It's here, with them."

Her father touched her shoulder and pointed to the door. "Let's give them privacy, Abby."

He stood, clapped Jules on the shoulder, and turned to the screen. "Joshua, I'll come in after you two talk. And don't worry about the transmission. Abby has a program that keeps this hidden and allows us to talk for as long as we need."

He nodded his head to the door as he passed her chair. Abigail rose from her seat. Jules reached out and hooked his small finger around hers. There was a light in his eyes, a burning behind the green. Then he let go and sat at the console, turning away from her.

JJ's voice faded as the door closed behind her, but she caught his words. "Oh, ho. You will tell me about that, my brother . . . "

$$\Sigma$$

"JJ, I understand what you are saying. Yet it's foreign territory to me." Jules ran a hand through his hair. The strands tangled in his fingers.

"You are already casting off those regs, Jules. Look at that shaggy hair." JJ's booming laugh filtered through the speaker. "Don't be so rigid, Brother. You said the Paxolin was taken out of the formula?"

"It was. Mimi said I wasn't responding well. That may be why the serum worked on me and why my formulation was different than yours. Serum Seventy-four didn't take with everyone."

JJ shook his head. "No. Paxolin was used on you. Reason you don't have memories like the rest of us." He sighed and leaned back in his chair. "But Mimi can help you figure that out. You avoided my question about Jed's daughter. What's going on?"

Jules shook his head. "There's so much to tell you, JJ. From Zeetoo being given my decommission orders, to meeting Bishop Thomas, learning that I was carrying Coalition on my ship and that my medtech betrayed me. And between all of that, I began changing. And I don't understand what it is."

"It's called living, Jules." JJ gave him a slight smile. "You only survived, never lived. You never laughed. You never dreamed. You never loved. You are waking up, my brother."

"Love?" Jules leaned against the console and regarded the man who had stood at his side since he was ten years old. He was the same, yet so different. JJ was always animated, but now he smiled. His eyes shone with a light that reminded Jules of that small light that visited him on the battlefield. "That's . . . "

"What you are starting to feel. Believe me, it was a surprise to me, too, when I learned about it."

Jules' eyebrows shot up. He narrowed his eyes at JJ. "You?"

"With Trisha Bonnet. She was one of the Jupiter Coalition that we are bringing home. After spending time with her all these weeks, I can't imagine not being around her." JJ turned from the viewscreen. The audio was off, but Jules read his lips as he talked and laughed with someone offscreen: *I'll tell him later we married. Hold onto your guns, Woman.* JJ returned to the screen.

"Married?"

"What?" JJ paused and then slapped the viewscreen. "You lip-reading monkey!"

Jules laughed. And something within let go. It was freeing to speak to JJ again. To banter with him. "Hurry back, JJ. I don't know if I can do this without you by my side. Ever since Washington . . . "

JJ sobered. He straightened in his seat and leaned even closer to the screen. "We are on the way. Should arrive in about a week. Trust Jed, Jules. Trust him. I know that ever since Washington, you have felt different. Listen to me, Jules." JJ paused and steepled his fingers against his mouth. "It's not going to be easy. And it will seem as though they are being . . . not strict, but untrusting. Yet it is not what you think. You are on one side, seeing from your viewpoint only. They have seen it from all angles. Even the Zulu angle."

JJ smiled again. White teeth flashed in a dark face as he waved off screen. A woman with golden-toned skin came into view, leaning in front of JJ. Small ringlets bounced around her face as she shook her head.

"Joshua, you didn't tell me your brother was so handsome." She gave Jules a smile. "He's told me a lot about you, and I'm looking forward to meeting you, Julius."

"Handsome? Woman, this scrawny, moody monkey is not handsome!" He playfully shoved her aside and turned back to Jules. "It's been great talking with you, and we'll catch up soon. But I need to get the report to Jed. Send him in?"

Jules stood, gave Trisha a nod, and then touched the screen with his palm. "Not gone yet."

JJ repeated the gesture. "Not gone yet."

Abigail wasn't there when he walked out. Which meant she was back at the desalination level. He turned to Jedidiah. "JJ is ready for you." As the older man started to pass by, Jules reached out and stopped him with a hand on his arm. Jedidiah looked back at him with a questioning gaze. He shook his head, the words not coming to him.

Jedidiah patted his hand. "Go on about your day, Jules."

And that was it. Jedidiah closed the communication door behind him, leaving Jules alone in the corridor, and Jules realized then, the man already knew. Already knew the battle within him.

Jules trailed his hand along the wall of the corridor as he followed it away from communications, above the commons, and into the far side of the complex where Abigail and Huey were working on the desalination units. Cold hung thickly in the air the closer he approached.

Abigail's and Huey's voices faintly reached him from his right, on the other side of the great expanse. He leaned over the railing.

It was more like an abyss. Far below were the dark waters with their sheen of ice. Catwalks crossed from one side to the next. Below him, John walked along a narrow walkway with another man, pointing to something on his datapad. The next level and far down the corridor, Abigail's red hair flashed as she moved to one of the control units.

And there at the bottom . . . three small bodies ventured out onto the lower level's ice-coated walkway. Blonde hair bobbed once as her body hit the ice and started sliding; then she was falling. No one would make it to her in time.

Jules sprinted to his right to the stairs leading down just as two screams rent the air.

He grabbed the rails and swung his feet up onto them. John had whirled around and was racing toward the stairs that led to the next level as Jules slid and landed on the walkway. Jules, ripping off his coat as he ran, sped past the man.

The little body of CeeCee disappeared beneath the water three levels below.

Time slowed.

Jules leaped up. His left foot hit the railing, and he pushed off, sending himself into the air above the water. Midway through the fall, he flipped around and curled. Ice drove into his spine. The freezing water stole his breath.

He twisted around in the dark, listening. Ahead of him, her heartbeat began to slow. Jules kicked his feet and pulled at the water with his hands, darting toward her. His fingers tangled in her hair, and he pulled. Her little body slammed into his chest. He wrapped an arm around her and kicked upward, only to be met with a layer of ice.

Jules rammed his fist into the ice, over and over. Blood spurted from his knuckles with each hit. With the last of the air in his lungs, he reared back and drove fist and arm through the layer of ice.

He grabbed the edge of the hole and hauled himself upward. The weight of them broke the sheet of ice and sent them splashing back into the water. Jules tightened his grip. Her heartbeat slowed even further.

When he broke through the water's surface again, muffled yells reached him.

" . . . grab the winch!"

"In front of you . . . "

A heavy metal hook on a thick chain fell in front of his blurred eyesight. He fumbled for it, wrapped it around his wrist and forearm, and struggled to climb above the ice. Corrosion from the salt enhanced the grinding sound of the gears as it slowly hauled him and CeeCee to the walkway. A cough ripped through his lungs.

As soon as his feet touched the edge of the barrier, Jules let go and fell to the side, keeping his weight off the little body he held. There was no time.

He was vaguely aware of Abigail stripping off her coat and flannel shirt as he ripped CeeCee's wet clothing off her. Then he was stripping his own clothes off with fingers that grew numb by the second.

His wet shirt and t-shirt landed with a thud and splat. The water was already freezing. He grabbed CeeCee and pulled her blue body into his arms, pressing her against his chest and wrapping his arms around her.

So cold was her body.

"Keep holding her, Jules!" Abigail grabbed one of the girl's arms and slipped it through the sleeve of her flannel shirt. When Jules tucked the arm back under his, Abigail repeated the process.

The distant sound of klaxons kept him awake as it drove spikes into his head. John's hands pulled him onto a blanket that now covered the walkway. Boots were stripped from him. Then his pants, half-frozen and the material crackling.

They were lifted and placed on a medical bed. The coarse material of a thermal blanket caused his nerves to scream in agony. It tightened around them, pushing at him.

Mimi's voice drifted through the haze. "Keep the blanket on them, John. Jules' body heat is what is keeping her alive . . . "

Then it all faded.

$$\Sigma$$

Voices filtered through his haze.

" . . . what were they doing down . . . "

"I've never seen anyone move so fast. He dove from three levels up . . . "

Jules forced his eyes open. Through the white veil in front of him, he could see John, Miriam, and Mimi standing near another medbed. Then darkness returned.

It was the light touch on his arm that brought him around again. He opened his eyes into slits. The lights of the medlab burned into him, creating a haze. They slowly lowered until the room was encompassed in dim shadows.

"Thank you, Jules. You saved her life." Miriam placed a kiss on his cheek. "Mimi said you are healing, and I am praying for you. When you wake up, I have a gift beside your bed."

John spoke by his left ear, but he didn't have the strength to move. Rough hands settled on his shoulder. "I said earlier that I had forgiven you, but I was lying to myself, Jules. You didn't have to save her. You didn't have to do anything. If you were the same man who had killed Samuel, you never would have thought about jumping into the water to save CeeCee. I realize now, you are not that man. God is creating in you something new." The hand squeezed his shoulder.

Jules forced his head to turn. It was painful, agonizing. Why wasn't his serum working? Tears flowed down John's face. Jules wanted to reach out to him, but nothing else moved.

John nodded his head once and sniffed. "Forgive me, Brother, for harboring hate against you. I'm praying for your healing."

Darkness closed back upon him.

"Jules?" It was Abigail's voice.

He pulled himself along the sticky blackness toward her voice.

"Hey, wake up." There was a gentle nudge against his shoulder.

He blinked his eyes against the soft, white light of the medlab. By the looks of it, he was in Medlab Two. He fumbled an arm out from under the covers, noting he was clad only in a flimsy gauze garment.

Jules turned his head. She sat beside him, perched on a high stool. Behind her, through the window, he saw John and Miriam with Mimi in Medlab Three. On the bed was little CeeCee, drinking from a glass. Tubes were still hooked into her.

He glanced down at his own body. No tubes. No restraining bands.

"We took them off."

"Off?" His voice cracked. She handed him a glass and straw. It coated his throat, alleviating the rawness and the slight nausea. Nutrient One. She remembered. "How long?"

"We had the bands on you to keep you still as your spine healed. And it's been only a day." She slipped an arm around him and helped him into a sitting position.

The room swam, dipping and swirling around him for a long moment. She settled the thermal blanket around his legs, and then pulled a rolling tray closer.

"CeeCee?" On the tray was a note and a covered dish. He picked up the folded paper: *You mean the world to her, Jules. Nothing can express our thanks and love for what you did for our little girl. Abigail said you like vanilla. I hope this is the first of many dishes I can cook for you. In His Name, Miriam.*

"What does 'In His Name' mean?" Jules set the letter to the side and uncovered the dish. Vanilla and spice reached out to him, caressing his senses. On the plate was a sweet dessert; meringue flowed around it, and a pale yellow cream was sandwiched between two layers of crust.

"In Christ's name. A form of amen or when we are saying that we are trusting Him in all things." She smiled as he sampled the dessert. "And CeeCee is going to be okay. She inhaled seawater, and Mimi is treating her for pneumonia, but she'll be okay. It was you we were worried about."

Jules let another bite burst onto his tongue. It was smooth. And it began erasing the dull ache in his head. "Me?" He held a forkful out to her.

She waved his offer away. "I already had some. No one can pass up Miriam's dessert. And yes, you. You fractured your spine, the T9 to L1, when you hit the ice. She doubled your serum dose and had you strapped down so you wouldn't move." She grabbed his hand and held it. "I'm sorry."

"Because I will have to start over on being weaned off the serum?" At her nod, he set his fork down and pulled her off the stool and around to face him. Weariness pulled at him, but he fought it back as he placed his hands at her waist, holding her between his knees. "Don't be. Not for my sake. If I have to begin again, then so be it."

A little blonde head caught his attention. Abigail leaned to the side to give him a better view when he tried peering past her.

In the other room, CeeCee ran two fingers in a circle around her face. Jules smiled. He had learned that sign a few days ago. He placed his hand on his chest and re-signed it to her. Then he pointed to her and brought his hand around his face, ending with closed fingers at his chin.

The most gorgeous smile spread across her cherub face. Jules pointed to her again. Then he placed his hand on his chest, brought it around his face, and ended with closed fingers at his chin. Then he touched his shoulders, moving his hands away in a wing pattern: *my beautiful angel.*

Her grin grew even bigger, and she signed again to him, holding her thumb, forefinger, and little finger up with the rest closed in a fist: *I love you.*

Miriam and John smiled and then closed the curtain between them, giving Jules privacy. But her little face, still pale, and her lips slightly bluish, stayed in his mind. *I love you.* No one had ever said those words to him before.

Abigail dropped a kiss onto his head. "Rest for a bit more, Jules."

He allowed her to push him back onto the medbed. A drowsiness was pulling at him. Normally, he would have pushed it aside, fought it, and forced himself to continue. But JJ said to trust. So, he would trust them with his sleep, with his recovery. With his life.

# Chapter Fifteen
## NANOTRACKER

Jules sat on the corner of the long table in the galley, far away from the doorway. JJ sat across from him on the other table. For the last hour, they had been reminiscing and teasing each other. It was a different feel to it now.

Under GFT scrutiny, they had to limit their interaction. But here, they were free. Trisha had left earlier with Abigail and Sarah. Something about measurements. So, he and JJ had coaxed Miriam into making another dish of her sweet dessert. They had polished it off moments ago.

"So, there we were in the last cubicle, had GFT blazing around us, and I turned to Trish and said, 'Marry me. What do you have to lose?' And you know what that woman had the gall to say to my face?"

Jules smiled and gave him a shrug. "No. But I'm sure you'll tell me."

"She said, 'I have everything to lose, you over-buff goat. And you don't order me about.'" JJ held his hands up in surrender. "I mean, this woman who had flirted with me for weeks, even stole a kiss on me—I see that look! You will tell me about that—anyway, she refused."

"And?" Jules leaned closer. JJ may try to weasel that story from him, but there was no way he was going to tell him. For the one reason that he himself still had no idea what to think about that night on the ship.

"And I told her, 'I'm saving your hide, Woman. I love you. So, marry me.'" JJ stretched his legs out and crossed his ankles.

When he didn't say anything further, Jules frowned. "And? Don't keep me hanging, JJ!"

"What? The woman agreed to marry me. Of course, after I blew two GFT guards out the airlock and escaped on the ship. By the way, Elder Jake sent that program to us, and we have been able to fly under the radar since. That gal of yours got her hands on a truly remarkable program. Now, tell me . . . when did she kiss you?"

Jules ignored his question and changed the subject. He propped his arms on his knees. "Jedidiah said last night that they have initiated contact with the GFT government. Remember my ambush?"

"How could I forget?"

"Well, it was a faction. There is a rogue group that is experimenting on the serum. When we were dispatched that night, it was them we were hunting. And that was the faction Anya worked with. Abby used the GHOST to hack that info." Jules ran his hand through his hair. Miriam, in her ever-surprising list of talents, had trimmed it for him the other night. "Abigail's program is allowing the Coalition to negotiate with GFT."

JJ raised his hands in victory, giving a whispered shout. "And there's a lesson in that for you, Jules."

"How so?"

"That night put you on the path to meet Abigail, who was looking for a way home, in which she discovered a dangerous program that could have brought about our demise yet instead is giving us a chance

232 WHEN LEGENDS RISE

at our freedom." JJ rose from his inclined position and thumped Jules' knee. "We don't know the ways of God, but He can use many to protect His children."

"Which you are, right?" Jules sighed. He clasped his hands together. "I've been reading a lot from the Bible. Trying to understand. Jedidiah has allowed me to come by each night when he does his nightly Bible reading."

"Really?" JJ's eyes crinkled. "So, you and Abigail?"

"No." Jules shook his head.

"Oh, you mean . . . " JJ smiled again. "Nah. Something happened, didn't it?"

Jules glared at him. "Do you want to talk about what you and Trisha do?"

That should have shut him up, but JJ only wiggled his brows at him. "Someday, I may tell you. You are so naïve to what is happening. Can't wait until you realize the truth. In more ways than one."

Jules was spared a retort when a small voice yelled at him from across the room. Evie with her sister. CeeCee signed her regular *I love you*, which he replied back. Today, she ended it with a "J," "U," and "L."

"What's that mean?" JJ looked at him as Jules signed a "2" and "C" to her.

"Jul. They've been calling me that lately." He was interrupted when Evie raced toward him and wrapped her arms around his waist in a hug.

"It'll be okay, Jul."

He returned the hug. "What do you mean, Evie?"

"You looked sad." She waved him down. When he bent his head, she placed a kiss on his cheek. Then turned to JJ. "Miss Trisha said I needed to give you this." She placed a kiss on his cheek, too.

"Evie!" Miriam motioned the little girl back to her side.

After Evie left them and continued walking with her mother, JJ turned to him, surprise wrinkling his face. "She does that often?"

"More than you would believe." He checked his wrist monitor. Time for his serum dose. "Are you coming with us today?"

"Nah, man. I told Jed I would take Mark and Wickham to the South Islands. We need clothes. Apparently, those kids grow fast. Not to mention, medical supplies."

Jules rose. JJ followed him as they left the galley. "I have some Elon 3XQ batteries on board the *Nightingale*. Nothing here takes them, and I'm not needing them right now on the ship. Use those for trade."

"Are you sure?" At Jules' nod, he continued. "Where are you heading today?"

"Dakota Plains. I even get my pulse gun back."

"What's in the Plains?"

"Shipment of beef!"

JJ stopped in the middle of the corridor. "How are you getting that?"

Jules smiled and continued walking. "From a payment on Mars. A ruby-enhanced, laser-focus crystal. I have three. Jedidiah is going to use two of them to buy not just beef, but seeds, shelf-stable foodstuffs, and a new desalination unit."

His brother shook his head and caught up with him. "Man, who paid you that?"

"Bishop Thomas' people."

JJ whistled. "I wish I were on that job. That was a nice payment."

The memory of the warehouse, of the airlock, and of Abigail in the lounge filtered through his mind. Just as quickly as it rose to the surface, he pushed it back down. "No. You wouldn't have wanted it. Ended up being bombed by GFT, betrayed by my medtech, and . . . "

"Kissed by Abigail."

Jules glared at him as they climbed the stairs to medlab. "I did not say that!"

"You don't have to. I know you well. I know that look." JJ glanced at him as they approached Medlab Two. "How much longer on the dose?"

"If it wasn't for what happened a couple of weeks ago, I would have been off of it. Right now, I'm at twenty-three percent; so, Mimi thinks another two weeks, and I'll be free from it."

JJ slapped his shoulder as they passed through the medlab hatch. "Praise the Lord for that! Mimi! I brought you our moody monkey! Can I shoot him today?"

$$\Sigma$$

Jules set the last crate on the bed of the snowtruck. Snow whipped around him. He thumped the cab and peered into the window. "That's the last one, Jedidiah!"

The older man nodded. "Grab Abby and Davis. Time to head back to the compound and let the storm blow over before we leave."

Jules stepped down and trudged across the ever-thickening snow drifts. Ahead, the silhouettes of Abigail and Davis grew larger. He paused for a moment. The last few hours had been hectic. And Abigail was angry with him.

He ducked his head down. Give him GFT assassins. Give him Juliet 2-Z. Anyone other than her. It was just one statement. But it was enough to set her off. Thankfully, she kept it to herself and didn't let Jedidiah know what he had said.

But what he had said was how he felt. He approached them. "Jedidiah is ready to go. Are you set?"

Davis nodded and collected his pack at his feet. Abigail glared at him, picked up a small bundle, and turned away from him.

They left him standing in the snow. Jules shook his head. He would need to ask JJ about this. He followed them. Abigail climbed into the cab. He and Davis stepped onto the running board and held onto the side.

It was a slow, freezing drive to the ship. The sky grew grayer. Cold thickened the air. They made it to the ship within an hour, and he helped Davis and Jedidiah unload the crates into the cargo bay of the ship. It was smaller than the *Nightingale.* By the time they had all the crates stored, only a small path was left from the airlock to the stairs leading to the bridge level.

Jules pulled his hat off and wiped sweat from his brow. He glanced up at Abigail. She narrowed her eyes at him and left the cargo bay. Jules yanked his hat back on and hurried after her.

She was midway to the compound by the time he caught up with her. He grabbed her by the elbow and twirled her around.

"Will it help if I say I'm sorry?"

Blue eyes burned through her snow goggles and into him. "You've said enough, Julius." She started to pull away, but he held on.

"I understand why you are mad. I do. And—" he muttered a curse. Her hands splayed against his chest covered by a thick parka when he jerked her closer. "I was angry. How do you think I was going to react to hear that GFT has a bounty on me?"

"And you thought to say what you did? Or to ask what you did?" She shook her head and pushed away. "Curse God in your own time, Jules, but not in my presence. I thought you were better than that. I thought you were understanding our ways. I'm not like you. I can't kill. And I won't use the GHOST to destroy others."

If the snow wasn't so thick, she would have stomped away. Instead, she sloughed through with her back and head ramrod straight, her pack swinging angrily around her and strands of red hair that had escaped blowing around the opening of her hood. Then she was swallowed by the snow.

He stood there for a moment. Snow drifts had already filled the path she took. Jules hunched against the bitter wind and swiped at the snow that collected on his lenses. He forced his legs to take the steps back to the compound. The snow and ice sucked at his feet, and each step became a chore.

Jules pushed his hood back, ignoring the stinging bite of the wind. A sound reached him but from what direction? The blinding glare assaulted his eyes, and all around him, the wind kicked up tufts of snow. It was almost impossible to tell where anything was in this place.

He tugged his hood back down and struggled the last few yards to the compound's door. Something pinged. Jules tried to whirl around, but his parka hampered him. That sound again.

This time, he shoved his hood back and ripped off his goggles. Snow bit him. Ice stung his eyes, freezing tears on his lashes. It was out there. He sensed it. He heard it. He knew it. But only the vast emptiness of whirling snow and ice gazed back at him.

With a gloved hand on the door's latch, Jules pushed it opened, not taking his eyes off the landscape.

A hot blast of air caressed him, and the smell of soup reached his nose. He finally turned and stepped inside, latching the door closed. The heat of the interior melted the snow off his parka and boots, forming a cold puddle by the door. Jules stripped his outerwear and hung it on the nearby hook.

Silence. Only the bubbling soup talked to him. He strode to the small oven, turned off the burner, and removed the pot. Where was everyone? Abigail must have gone to the other compound.

He reached behind him and removed his pulse gun from its holster, quickly looking about the small room. There was no indication of a struggle. He held his hand above one of the bowls on the table. It was still mildly warm. He sniffed. A tangy, metallic smell, very faint, flavored the air.

The barracks door stood ajar. He stepped lightly across the hard-packed floor. With his free hand, he pushed that door open. The bodies of Michaels and Sorenson were lashed to the bedding. Blood pooled on the floor. Jules approached the beds and checked each one. They were still alive, but barely.

Jules backed up and closed the door. He hurried to his parka and slipped inside it. It would be difficult crossing to the compound next door, especially in this weather, but he needed to sound the alarm. Get medical help for the two men.

He shoved his goggles on and yanked open the door, pulse gun at the ready. The wind had picked up even more, and the snow blew in angry swirls, obscuring all sound and sight. With his free hand, he felt along the right side of the compound. It was only a straight fifty yards from the edge to the next compound.

The sharp edge of the building punctured his glove when he found the corner. He kept the building to his right and stepped into the blinding white. The snow fought back with each step, and then there was something else. That same sound. Jules redoubled his efforts.

Blackness.

He tumbled forward, losing his gun into the piling drifts. Dazed, he pushed himself to his knees and felt another stab of pain slam into his head. He choked on the snow. He wanted to move, but instead, he slid into a black tunnel of nothing.

Abigail raced down the corridor toward communications. The last few hours were the worst she had ever lived. They had found Michaels and Sorenson. And then her father had discovered Jules' pulse gun in the snow. Using the GHOST, they alerted the base of their arrival, and she had Huey prepping the stations, searching for Jules.

Mimi passed her in the corridor. Wickham was transporting her on a hoverstand, heading toward the cargo bay for the two injured men.

"Huey!" she shouted at him as she rounded the corner.

He stuck his head out of the door. "I got your message. It's in, and I'm running it now. And I have Batch on."

She slid into the chair so fast, she had to halt its flight across the room. "Batch, what have you heard?"

His voice crackled over the system. "Not much. There's talk on the sub-hub. Looks like this faction, GFT Medical Unit, went rogue a few months back when GFT decided not to pursue the decommissioned assassins who had disappeared. They broke away from Unified Medical. Apparently, they want their bloodwork. And your Jules is the key. He's one of two that were a success with the serum. GFT had no option but to place a bounty on him."

Abigail ran the GHOST through a newer set of parameters. Huey reached over her and tapped the screen. It began to run a filter through a communique, too. "Did you find a destination?"

"No. But I'm sending you a couple of files. And when you are ready, I'll have a few rabbits ready."

Huey shook his head as he shifted through code. "Won't do any good unless—" He kicked back his chair and raced out of the room.

"I'll call you back, Batch. I think Huey found something." She set her datapad to the side and ran after Huey.

The crashes in Medlab Section alerted her to which direction he took. She rounded the corner to Medlab Two, where he was throwing vials of serum components to the floor. Mimi and her father were yelling at him, trying to make him stop.

She crossed the threshold as he threw the last vial to the floor. Blue liquid pooled with red. Anger flooded across his face. Veins stood out in his neck and along his forehead.

"Nanotrackers."

Her knees weakened. She held on to the table. "What?"

"Nanotrackers. I picked up on the signal. We thought the nanotracker was given to him through Anya. But it wasn't. It was in the components. All of them."

They stared at the liquid that merged and pooled on the floor. Nanotrackers needed an organic host. So, these were inactive. Yet Mimi had doubled his dose those weeks ago. And each day, he had more and more injected into him.

Mimi grabbed towels from the bin on the counter and started sopping up the mess. Huey knelt beside her and helped.

"I'm sorry, Evelyn. I should have thrown them in the sink. I wasn't thinking."

She looked up at him and patted his cheek. "You don't worry about this. You and Abby go find our boy, okay?"

Her father looked at her. "Nanotrackers have a signal. Can the GHOST find it?"

Abigail clenched her jaw. "Yes. And it won't take long. Huey, I need a new IF on the *Nightingale*. When's JJ coming back?"

"I've already sent the call." Her father waved them away. "We will take care of this. Go find that signal."

She and Huey ran back to communications. Now that they knew what to look for, it wouldn't take long. She handed Huey the cord, and he plugged it in. Code and files flew through. Systems after system, from GFT to Dakota Plains station, fell victim to the GHOST. Huey worked on the console before him, searching just as hard.

Abigail pulled up the screen before them and tapped it. "Here. There's the signal of the nanotracker at the Dakota Plains. Same as what has been here."

Her father spoke from the doorway. "When did it start sending the signal?"

"Looks like with the thickness of the ice, the signal didn't get through. Not until we left for the Plains. Then it began broadband broadcasting."

"There." She looked over and read the report Huey pointed to. "Same signal. Destination is filed for Compound One, Habitat Three. Looks like the RSD District."

Her father nodded. "Mars it is. Get your stuff. Abigail, make sure we have enough datapads for everyone."

$$\Sigma$$

Cold. Extreme cold. And buzzing.

Jules forced his eyes open and tried to move. His arms stretched behind him, immobilized and manacled to chains.

Where was he? Wherever he was, it was dark. He rubbed his face against the metal floor and felt nothing on his eyes or face. No blindfold.

What was that buzzing?

He strained his ears, trying to place the sound. Goosebumps ran down his body. Down his naked body. The coldness of the floor seeped into his muscles, and he fought against the uncontrollable shivers. He flexed his numb hands and tried to swallow past his parched throat.

Dull pain stabbed him behind the eyes as he struggled to his knees. The chains allowed him only a few inches, and that little amount of movement strained his shoulders.

Time had no judge in the dark. How long had he been here? Did he even have his eyes open? His breathing, along with that infernal buzzing, echoed in the stillness.

Cold dug deeper into him, covering his skin like a blanket. His heartbeat pounded in his head.

The lights flickered on.

He blinked hard a couple of times, trying to adjust to the bright light.

Anya came into view, a slinking viper. Jules narrowed his eyes. Hate gnawed at him.

"Julius." She knelt before him, and her eyes raked over his naked form.

"Anya." He looked forward, past her, past the bare wall.

"You are going to make this difficult, aren't you?" She ran a manicured fingernail across his chest. "You don't have to, you know.

I know you are familiar with this procedure. Didn't you use it on the same type of people you are with now?"

Jules refused to glance at her. Refused to let her goad him. Refused to show the betrayal he felt.

She was right, though. Strip the subject of all humanity, of all dignity. Then apply the torture and the drugs. He did that so many times. That was then. That was not him now.

Anya stood and disappeared from his view. The sound of a metal cart rolling across the metal floor reached his ears long before she returned. The cart, heavily laden with electro-discharging interrogation instruments, rattled to a stop.

"I really wish you wouldn't make me do this, Julius." She pulled a small strap off the cart. "Or maybe you can tell me which one of these you prefer the most. How about this strap? No." Anya reached over and extracted a small whip with numerous tendrils. "This one? Yeah. I think it would be a good start."

He compressed his lips, preparing for the pain to come.

Anya knelt before him again. "Now, now, sweetie. No pouting. I will start on the medium setting, yes?" She leaned forward and kissed his lips.

Every muscle in him wanted to turn away in revulsion, but he forced himself to stay still. Show no reaction. She grinned at him and stood.

Without warning, the whip lashed out. Pain shot across his body. He grunted. He would not move, not for her. He could withstand this.

The whip lashed out again, slicing across his stomach. He hunched over. When he straightened, he glared at her and gritted his teeth.

He *would* withstand this.

Anya's eyes narrowed, and she adjusted the setting. With a flick of her wrist, the whip lashed out again, striking him across the face.

Jules choked back a scream. Pain pulsed across his head, through his eyes. Before he gained his bearings, another lash of pain struck him across the back, then across the stomach. A lash struck him across his legs, and he fell over to his side. He tasted blood as he bit back a cry when the chains yanked at his shoulders.

He fought to pull himself back to his knees. The whip struck, lashing pain into him, over and over. He rode that tidal wave.

One lash blurred into the other. Pain melded from single strokes to broader strokes until it encompassed his body. Somewhere distant, he heard a cry, a scream.

Did the pain end? He tried to focus his eyes, but everything seemed surreal. Shadowy movements blurred in the red and black haze of his vision. The coldness of the floor seeped into his cheek. The lashes had stopped, but the pain inside him still pulsed as he lay on his side.

His stomach convulsed, and stomach acid spewed from his mouth. Bitterness hung onto his tongue, and Jules pushed away from the vile fluid on the floor.

He struggled, barely rising to his knees. A blur knelt in front of him. He wanted to focus but couldn't. A small touch on his face sent streaks of pain down him. Anya. She was touching him again, wiping at his face with a cool, wet cloth. Something was held to his mouth. A cup.

No. He shook his head, trying to turn away from the drink that was offered, but she grabbed his face and poured it into his mouth. Where was his strength? He couldn't resist. He swallowed the bitter-tasting drug.

A prick stabbed him in his thigh. The pain subsided, and his eyes focused.

"That's better." Anya replaced the cup and syringe on the cart.

Jules stayed hunched over, his stomach rolling and quivering inside. How many times did he issue this type of punishment? If this was his penance, then so be it. He'd gladly endure this if it meant keeping Jedidiah's people safe. If it meant keeping Abigail safe.

His blood pounded in his ears, swishing around. His eyes refused to stay focused on the wall. They kept traveling down the floor and tracing the lines of the metal tiles. Same color. Same size. A cold and evil order.

Where was his body? Jules tried to laugh at that absurd thought. He couldn't feel his body. He felt detached, floating away.

Did she turn up the heat? Wasn't it supposed to be cold?

Pain hit him.

"Focus, Julius!" Anya stood before him, handling a larger whip. She turned the dial on the handle. "I have it on eleven. The highest for this model is fifteen. So far, no one has withstood twelve."

Jules spat or tried to. He wouldn't give in.

"Make it easy, Julius. We want to know the location of their home base. And where the others are." Anya knelt before him again, her ice-blue eyes imploring. "I will keep on with this. I don't have to tell you what will eventually happen."

He fought against her hands as they grabbed his face again. The chains rattled as he thrashed, but he couldn't escape her touch. Her face floated inches before his. Beautiful Anya. Soft, white hair and red lips. His Anya. His evil Anya.

"You tell me. I want to hear it." She rubbed a thumb across his lips. "What happens afterward?"

He pressed his lips tighter. Tears sprung to his eyes as she touched the energized whip to the inside of his leg.

"Tell me." She whispered into his ear. Her perfume tickled his nostrils.

Higher the whip touched his thigh.

"Come on, sweetie. Tell me." Her voice purred even closer to his ear.

Higher the whip touched him. He fought back a whimper and croaked. "Blurred lines of pain. Then death."

Anya smiled in triumph and stepped back.

He watched as she fiddled with the whip's setting and then contorted in pain as the tips lightly contacted his chest. She had turned it up a level.

"Just tell me, Julius."

Jules hunched and compressed himself into as small a ball as possible. The pain would be worse this time, so he concentrated on the floor. Geometric order.

It began. Wave upon wave of pain. His face flamed. His chest burned. His legs boiled. Over and over. Jules didn't know what began where. He slid to the side, his arms stretched behind him, and he cried out.

"Oh, God, save me!" Spittle flew from his lips. Pain washed over him. Hell descended upon him.

"Tell me!"

Her grunts assaulted his ears. The demons licked at him. Not for his sake, but for theirs, he called out in his mind for God to protect him. To not let him reveal them to her.

Pain sang a chorus to him. The whip whistled overhead; it teased his body with its caress and slid away. But it never stayed away for long. Back it came, slapping against him, searing his flesh with white hot pain. Cold heat turned warm. He clenched his fist, fighting against the whip's lashes and the drugs, but it was too late.

*No! Please, Lord, keep me quiet! Keep me!*

$$\Sigma$$

Abigail held the datapad and watched. JJ and Huey leaned over her shoulder. With each lash of the whip, she flinched, and her heart felt ripped away. Anya's face was contorted in anger as she rained lash upon lash upon him.

His screams echoed. Yet he refused to give in. Then he collapsed, his arms held behind him at an awkward angle.

Anya stood over him, the whip hanging by her side. When his body convulsed, she just grinned and dropped the whip onto the tray. She walked away, leaving Jules shivering on the floor.

Abigail switched the feed to the hallway as Huey keyed a comm open to Batch. "We have the hallway feed now."

Batch would have the rabbits ready for each one when the time came for them to grab him. The hated woman was talking to the men outside the door in the hallway.

" . . . bring in the hose and wash him down."

"He isn't talking?"

She turned to a man in a GFT general uniform, apparently not surprised to find him there. "No. Not yet. But he is close to breaking." She glanced inside the room as the men hosed Jules down.

"Will he?"

Anya straightened. "I told you, General. He will. Juliet 7-A was one of the most battle-hardened assassins out there. He can withstand a lot. But he *does* have a breaking point. They all do."

The general turned and started walking away, shouting over his shoulder, "For your sake, you better hope he does."

JJ pointed to the man. "That's General Hayden. He used to be the head of the GFT-74 program. I think he was replaced a month before I left."

Huey looked up from his handheld. "We've got the codes. Now we just need a window."

JJ squeezed past her in the narrow tunnel. He squatted near the ladder that led up to the maintenance tunnel above and hooked a handheld into the control panel that had a direct line to the main corridor. He keyed his comm. "Jed, have the ship prep on my signal."

Her father responded, but Abigail barely heard the reply. She switched the screen back to the interrogation room. Jules had lifted his head, looking at something across the room. Her finger traced his face and body. He just needed to hold on for a moment longer.

"We're here, Jules," she whispered. JJ's hand fell onto her shoulder and stayed there as they watched the screen together.

Σ

"You are here." Jules looked at the white figure that wavered in and out of his vision. The manacles kept him from reaching out. "You're here with me. Please, take me." Spittle mixed with blood fell from his lips and landed with a splat on the freezing tiles. "I beg you. I won't tell. Oh, God, please take me now. I can't last much longer."

His stomach knotted as the figure seemed to approach. *I want to accept You, but I can't remember You.* "You seem so foreign to me." A bitter laugh shot from his mouth as darkness whirled about him. He was talking to nothing but the light in the room.

There was no one here with him, much less listening to him. He allowed his mind to drift into the dark void that called to him—away from the pain, away from his loneliness, away from life.

There he floated, in and out. His heart started slowing. He listened as the beats grew more and more distant.

Jules had barely registered the blast of water that hit him for the second time, washing away the stench and cooling his body. But it didn't matter. The sting of the water's pressure had no effect. It wasn't that kind of pain he dreaded. Sooner or later, he would not be able to outlast the torment.

"Pull him up."

The men set him roughly upon his knees. His head lolled forward. He had no energy left, no strength. Nausea threatened to consume his stomach. Hammers pounded his brain. The quick stab into his thigh seemed so distant.

"Open your eyes, Julius."

He obeyed that voice. That voice would give him his freedom. No, that voice would give him pain. That was the drugs talking. Or was it reality?

Jules gazed back at the woman before him through small slits. She revered him, didn't she? She knelt before him, didn't she? What drug did she give him this time? Were they the same that he had once used? His thoughts couldn't center on one subject. His eyes couldn't focus.

Her hands were ice smoothing across his face, touching his forehead, caressing his cheek, cool against his skin.

"Oh, Julius, look at you." Her fingers touched his lips again. Then she touched her own lips to his, pressing them against his. His gut wrenched, and he suppressed the revulsion.

A cup was held to his mouth, and bitter liquid choked him.

A prick on his leg once more and everything faded and then sharpened. She returned.

The room didn't exist. Only this. The numbness she offered . . . No—pain. He had to withstand the drug, yet deep in his memories, he knew that no one ever won against the chemicals that coursed in his bloodstream. They were too powerful. Consuming the most primal parts of the mind. Altering his perception of reality.

Her hands slid across his chest, feather-light touches. His skin prickled. He tried to concentrate on the window on the far side. Then coldness descended upon him.

He opened his eyes. She stood away. But that didn't matter. He hung his head and welcomed the pain. It coursed through him. His mind was sliding into the drug-haze as his resolve disappeared.

*Yes. I know the location. Yes.*

Pain kissed his body—stronger, more violent. Jules slid to the floor and pressed against the cold metal. He closed his eyes to the lure.

*No. I won't tell. No.*

*Yes.*

Pain caressed him.

*No.*

*I'm going crazy, Lord! I'm going crazy.*

Jules bit his tongue, and blood filled his mouth. He gritted his teeth. His jaw ached. He saw nothing but red haze and heard nothing but his own ragged breathing. He needed to fight against the drugs. But it wouldn't be his strength that would fight it. Jedidiah said He would answer whomever called upon Him.

"Lord, be with me," Jules groaned. One way out.

He rammed his head into the metal floor. Pain that was different. He welcomed that pain, too. Again, he raised his head and rammed it into the floor. Blackness swirled among the red. Again and again, over her shouted objections, he slammed his forehead against the metal floor.

He refused to tell her. Pain pulsed in his head.

He opened his eyes, blinking past the blood. Anya stood there, wielding the whip, lashing it against him, her face warped with rage. The whip slashed across his face.

He blinked again. Beyond her, a small, bright light hovered near the ceiling. His little light came back for him. Peace descended upon him, and Jules fell into the black void.

$$\Sigma$$

Abigail winced at the violence Jules dealt himself. Anya had let the whip fall from her grasp as Julius sank to the floor, unconscious. His arms were wrenched at odd angles behind him. She snarled, advanced, and delivered a kick into his side. No response.

Blood flowed from his head, down his chin, and pooled onto the metal floor, seeping into the grooves. Sweat glistened his skin; blue colored his hands and feet. She released his arms from their bonds. They dropped heavily against his body.

She collected a small syringe, knelt, and drew a vial of blood from him.

She keyed her radio. "Containment team, set up a Level Three perimeter around room twelve. Surveillance around the clock."

Abigail switched the feeds again as Anya strode from the room.

General Hayden rounded the corner and fell in step with her. "Still not talking?"

"It has to be the serum. It must be causing a counteraction that no one considered. I'm heading to the lab now. I should be able to devise a drug that will work against his own serum-laden blood."

"I shouldn't have to tell you that time is of the essence. We need that information. GFT cannot continue if the Christian Coalition succeeds. Already, the GFT top officials are ready to negotiate. If they come to terms, we lose what power we have gained."

Anya stopped and glared at the general. "I am well aware of that. Hence the urgency of going to the lab. My serum I have dosed him with should have allowed me to question him with no problems."

"Then what is the problem?"

"That is what I am going to find out." She held up the vial. "The Coalition had given him Serum Seventy-four. Reason why the nanotrackers activated. Those assassins can't live without it. And we know others have escaped into their fold. I'll examine his blood, and we'll go from there."

The general nodded and turned away. She stood there watching him and then rounded the bend to their medlab.

Abigail glanced up from the small handheld; its pale light illuminated Huey's and JJ's faces. "The access tunnel leads to this corridor." She touched the display. "It's about twenty paces to the room. Huey, you will have to do something about the vid-feed. I can't hack it from here."

Huey nodded. "Covered. Hold on." His radio crackled as he touched it. "Batch, I need a real-time loop on ports twenty to thirty, feeds twelve, fourteen, and . . ." Abigail flipped her handheld around. "And nineteen. Kill the IR in the room. Make it look like a down system."

Batch's disembodied voice seemed overly loud in the service tunnel. "Should I use a rabbit hole program?"

"That would be best. It would keep IT occupied long enough."

JJ put his hand on her shoulder. "It would be better if you followed. Give us time to clear the corridor if needed. How long will it take to open the door?"

"It'll take the GHOST just seconds." She took a deep breath. "Are we clear, yet?"

JJ glanced at the handheld, the one patched into the main corridor. "Yes. She just went into medlab. Let's go."

Abigail waited until they reached the top of the tunnel and then followed them up the rungs. Huey grunted once as he slid the heavy panel to the side. It was a tight fit as they pulled themselves out of the tunnel and onto the narrow floor. Huey slid a wall panel to the side and glanced out. Two beeps from the radio at his wrist signaled that Batch had the corridor cleared for them.

They piled out and lightly ran down the hall. She dropped to her knees before the console, inserted her portable, and ran the GHOST. Three beeps and the door slid open.

Blackness met them, over-accentuating the light coming in from the corridor. JJ ran a hand down the panel by the door, and soft light blossomed overhead, barely killing the shadows.

Abigail did a quick scan as she kept to the side of the room. Cold. Barren. One viewport high above them. A cart to the side was laden with tools and vials. And there, in the center, the naked form of Jules, curled into a fetal position. Seeing him on the viewscreen of her handheld was one thing, yet seeing him like this? She wasn't prepared for it. Angry welts crossed each other to the point it seemed as though his skin was a crosshatch of designs. Burns glistened along his legs and the back of his thighs. Blood had spread beneath him.

JJ waved her on as he pulled a thin jumpsuit from his satchel. "Huey, keep an eye on the monitors."

Huey's dark curls bobbed once as he bent over his handheld, his fingers flying across the buttons. Always staying one step ahead.

She followed JJ and knelt next to Jules as JJ pulled a lockpick from his satchel. Her fingers found a pulse at his neck, sticky with half-dried blood. Relief flooded through her. "He's alive—"

Pain lanced through her wrist as it was grabbed by Jules and squeezed. His eyes, dilated and unfocused, bore into her.

"I won't tell!" He hissed the words through blood-stained teeth before falling to the floor again. "Oh, Lord, I beg of You! I can't tell. I won't tell!" Jumbled words poured forth as his eyes followed something behind her.

She turned. There was nothing there.

JJ's touch on her shoulder brought her back around. "Here. Move and let me give him this. It should counteract what they gave him."

"You've seen this before?"

"Too many times. Assassins are hard to break, and it takes massive doses of the drugs to do it." He placed a hypospray against Jules' neck. A slight hiss and it was done. "Give it about—"

Jules reared up and projectile vomited across the floor. He heaved again and again, his stomach spewing until nothing else came up. Abigail reached behind her and pulled a towel from the cart.

"Here."

His eyes flashed once before recognition set in as she dabbed at his mouth, folded the towel in on itself, and then wiped at the blood on his head.

"Here." JJ handed Jules the jumpsuit. "Get dressed. And let's go."

Jules grabbed the clothing as JJ worked on freeing Jules' legs from the binders.

There was so much she wanted to help him with, to say to him, to ask him. But it would have to wait. As he fumbled with the jumpsuit, she rose and met Huey by the panel.

His eyes met hers. "They are close to finding the rabbit."

"Then let's go." Jules' hoarse whisper seemed to echo in the room.

JJ helped support him as he limped their way. "You ready?"

She glanced at Jules. The bruises and welts along his face had to be more painful than he was letting on. His left eye barely opened. Blood had dried along his hairline. But it was his eyes that captured her attention.

His intense stare was hard, lethal. "Go. I'll be fine. I can't see well, yet we can't linger."

Huey nodded. The door opened, and they slipped out into the corridor. JJ passed Jules off onto her, and she grunted under his weight as he leaned against her. Sweat, blood, and harsh body odor assaulted her.

"Sorry."

She smiled. Danger lurked, and he was apologizing for his smell. It wasn't his fault. "Don't worry about it. You'll get the best shower this side of Earth when we get back."

"Only after detox, right, JJ?"

His friend gave only one glance as he and Huey slid the wall panel to the side. The space was an even tighter squeeze with four of them in there. She knelt to the floor to give them more room to work. JJ slid the wall back. Huey pried open the access tunnel. Jules leaned heavily against the inner wall, his breathing labored.

"Inside we go." Huey dropped down, followed by Jules and herself. JJ paused at the top and closed the opening, keying the panel back into its locked state. A sudden ping issued from her handheld.

"Stop." Her whisper seemed too loud. "We can't move yet. They have countermeasures up in the tunnel we need." She looked at Jules. "They noticed your absence."

He shook his head, ignored her statement, and turned to JJ. "We have to leave now. It's been too long. And I can feel the drugs still in my system. How long do you think I have? Two, three tops?"

JJ gripped Jules' arm. "I would say two. I need to only get you to the ship, though."

"What are you talking about?" Abigail hissed at JJ and Jules. "We can't move yet. The sensors will pick up on us."

Huey held up his display. "Look, if we take this tunnel down to here, there's a reservoir. And here," his finger tapped the map, "is the tube that leads to the hold. From this access here," one more tap, "we can climb aboard the *Nightingale*."

"You brought my ship? Anya will recognize it."

Abigail shook her head. "No. New register. New specs. We gave it an overhaul when we started planning your rescue. It's broadcasting a new IF."

He opened his mouth but suddenly bent over, dry heaving. JJ motioned down the narrow tunnel to their left.

"Go. Follow Huey. The faster we get to the ship, the faster we get you back on your feet."

Abigail shifted Jules' arm over her shoulder and bore a bit of his weight. "Let's go. Do you need a dose to kill the pain?"

Jules shook his head; his hand over his mouth tightened, and his words were muffled. "No. I barely feel the pain. Just nausea."

His feet stumbled, and Abigail almost collapsed under the sudden weight. JJ caught them and transferred Jules from her to him. "I can give you something later once we get to the ship. Until then, let's try to keep a steady pace. Yes?"

Jules nodded, but she saw the unfocused look coming back into his eyes. She followed; but soon, Huey held up a hand, and they stopped.

"Give me a minute." He scrolled through his display and then nodded. "Okay. I just disabled the secondary alarms in this section. It won't be noticed for a long time. Come on, we are almost there."

Abigail fell into step behind Jules after he waved off JJ and straightened. With a deep breath, the man took one wobbly step after another. She had to give it to him—he never surrendered to defeat, and not being able to walk on his own was a defeat to him.

$$\Sigma$$

Jules tried to breathe in the close confines of the tunnel. A myriad of scents flooded his nose. The mustiness of the tunnel they were in. The electrical stench of Huey's handheld. The starch from the jumpsuit he was wearing. His own putrid smell. The slight sweet scent from Abby, who stood too close behind him.

She followed, her hand at times on the small of his back or gripping his arm. Her way of supporting him, not knowing what to do.

And there wasn't anything she could do. From that first look as he awoke from his drug-induced hallucination and seeing her there with JJ, he thought only of survival. Already, the drugs Anya gave him were changing something within him. His thoughts seemed muddled. His heart seemed to hurt. Not a physical hurt, yet it was some kind of pain that seemed to want to drive him to his knees. And the thin fabric of the jumpsuit did nothing to dispel a chill that threatened to overtake him. At times, he could feel the fabric pull away from the wounds where the blood had dried and caused the fabric to stick. It should have been painful. All he felt was a slight heat of a burn.

Her hand slipped into his, and he instinctively grasped it back as Huey abruptly stopped them.

"We're here."

Huey and JJ slid back the wall panel. Darkness greeted them until their eyes adjusted to the dim light. Abigail's hand gripped his even tighter as they stepped out into the cavern. A metal cavern. The smell of water greeted him. The colony's water supply. Unfiltered. The tang of bacteria met him.

The high, dome ceiling cast a dull light around the reservoir. As Jules stepped out onto the metal platform, Huey slid the access hatch back into place. He sniffed again. The smells were stronger and gaining strength with each breath he took.

"JJ."

JJ approached him, arching a brow at their clasped hands. "What it is?"

"I think she gave me a derivative of Serum Seventy-four. I shouldn't have my abilities right now—not with the drugs she gave me—but I can smell a form of bacteria in the water. Something pungent. And ozone . . . ."

Huey glanced at him. "That's the filters above."

JJ motioned him to the railing. "If you are gaining your abilities back in force and even stronger than before, then that's a good sign."

Jules swallowed against a wave of nausea that threatened to overtake him. The need to lash out overtook him. "I don't want them back. I was trying to eradicate them from me!"

His yell echoed back at him. Where did the anger come from? The revulsion?

JJ grabbed his shoulders. His face was inches from Jules', his dark eyes set in a hard gaze. "Not here. Later. Now, come on, focus. You're allowing the drugs to take over. Push it back and focus on the *now*."

Abigail's hand let go, and she stepped back as he bent over, hauling in breath after large breath. JJ said to focus. He would focus. If only the room would stop spinning.

"We have to jump, Joshua." Huey let the handheld fall to his side and swing along its strap. "The tube is about ten feet down from us. Then it's a slight swim up about twenty meters, forty down, and the third portal on the right."

JJ pulled two respirators from his pack. "I have only two. I didn't think it would be an underwater deal, so I knew if we hit a gas pocket or such, we could pair up."

Jules straightened and peered over the rail. "You and I don't need one. We can hold our breath long enough."

No one questioned him. They each climbed over the railing and perched on the small ledge. JJ handed the respirators to Huey and Abigail, and they pulled them on. With a tiny hiss, the seal activated. JJ gave a thumbs-up.

Jules breathed in . . . . and stepped into the void. Cold surrounded him. There was a slight effervescence to the water. The bubbles ran up his legs and arms, into his hair. He turned in a circle, locating each of his team.

His team.

When did he begin to think of them that way? JJ was always a part of him. But the others? He followed them as they swam down to the tube and into darkness. A pinpoint of light lit up the watery hole. It waved forward, and Jules pressed his hands against the smooth side, pushing against it and propelling himself up the shaft. Closer to air. And freedom.

The only sounds around were those of Abigail, JJ, and Huey as they made their way upward—air bubbles popped at times, fabric rustled, all enhanced by water—and there in the dark, his thoughts centered on the people he had grown to care about.

Every one of them at the compound cared about him, helped him, treated him with respect and that foreign feeling that they said was love. There were families there, children. Children who loved him.

He looked ahead at the shadowy figures in the faint light. Were they family to him? JJ was. But the others?

His thoughts rushed out of his head as he popped above the waterline, his mouth barely above it. The other two pulled their respirators off, and JJ stuffed them back into his pack. They swam further down until their feet reached the floor.

"Right down here. It's shallower. Oomph!" Huey disappeared back under the water and then righted himself. "There's a step there."

Jules followed Abigail and JJ. A distant rumble reached his ears. He cocked his head, straining to place the sound.

"Jules? What do you hear?"

He turned to JJ. "Water. Rushing water. Huey, did they release the floodgates?"

Huey checked his display and groaned. "Oh, man. It's the scheduled purge. I didn't realize I had my display set to Earth Time.

We are six hours off. This is the evening purge before the water is sent to be purified."

Purified in fire. Jules motioned them forward. "Hurry to the portal—"

His words became garbled as a rush of water descended upon them from above, whipping his legs out from under him and slamming his body into Abigail. She latched onto him, holding his jumpsuit as he struggled to find purchase. His hand banged against metal. He lashed out and gripped the rung of a metal ladder and pulled. Abigail coughed and gagged as she broke the surface.

Jules pushed her against the wall. The rush of the wave pulled at him, and he held them still, fighting the current. Her hands clutched at him, arms wrapped around his chest, squeezing. Filling him with a pang of foreign emotion. The current eased, and Jules pulled them along the rungs until they reached the fourth tube above them. JJ yelled down to them from where he and Huey clung to the third tube's rungs.

"Take that tube. We can double back for you once we reach the ship."

There was no way they could retrace their plight and reach JJ and Huey. Not with the force of the current underneath them.

Jules nodded and pushed Abigail up into the tube above them. Then he grasped the edge and, using his shaky arms, hauled himself into the access tube. His arms gave out, and he collapsed onto the floor. The drugs and that constant nausea had weakened him. All he wanted was to sleep, to rest . . .

A ping from Abigail's handheld brought his head up. "What now?"

"JJ said to head down and then take a sharp left. That will lead to an outside bay. They will be there shortly. He's already called in to Dad to have the ship ready for flight. We have a short window before the ship is slaved."

"Fly? No docking?"

"We're at Compound One."

Which meant ships landing inside instead of docking. Jules nodded and clambered to his knees, pushing his fatigue to the side. "This is going to be a tight fit." He sniffed his arm. "But at least I don't have that stench about me anymore."

"No. But you smell like a bog now."

"And I guess that isn't any better?"

Abigail laughed. "Maybe by a bit. At least you aren't gagging me."

Jules smiled at her light laugh and then stopped. What was it that he was feeling? The dim light from her display played with her freckles, making them seem like the stars in the night sky. He brought a finger up to her cheek and traced the Seven Sisters pattern. Her breath hitched as he ran his finger down her cheek and across her chin. And then there at the little dip under her lip.

"Jules?"

It was foreign. Different. But not unwelcomed. She did it to him in the lounge. He swallowed. "I—"

Without thought, Jules closed the small distance between them and crushed his mouth against hers. He allowed his lips to move across hers in a small but hard kiss. His hands buried themselves into her hair. He would have molded his body to hers if she hadn't pushed against him.

"Stop for a minute."

He broke away and fell against the opposite side. "I have no idea why I did that."

Abigail leaned toward him and captured his hand. "The drugs Anya—"

"Don't grace your lips with her name." Revulsion ate at him at the mention of the woman who betrayed him.

"The drugs *she* gave you probably accelerated Serum Seventy-four." Abigail caught herself against the side of the small tunnel as she tried to move closer to him. "You'll find that these feelings are natural."

"What is it? Lust? Love? Attraction? That stuff that is in the books, the photos? Is it what I've seen between John and Miriam?" Questions seemed to rush from him.

"Yes. Yes. Yes. Yes. And yes." She patted his chest tenderly as she looked up at him. "It all depends on what you do with it. But now isn't the time. Later, okay? I can explain it to you later."

Jules nodded, confusion coloring his words. "I . . . It . . . I acted without thought."

She paused and pulled the handheld in front of her. Her fingers danced across the display. A brief frown crossed her face, and anger lit her eyes for a second before she gave a small nod and turned the handheld around for him to see.

"You just hacked this?"

"Yes. Look, here." She tapped the small entry in *the woman's* database. "She used a drug that was similar to what she gave you on the *Nightingale*. It's the fourth derivative she made of Serum Seventy-four. And with the interrogation drugs, there is no telling what the reactions will be." She let the handheld dangle by its strap and started crawling down the tube.

Jules followed. Embarrassment was new to him and completely unwelcomed. "Guess we can assume that it's repairing more than we thought?"

"One can assume." There was a small catch in her voice as she replied.

If she grabbed that bit of information, did she—? "Did you just use the GHOST to access the medical database?"

Abigail nodded. "And downloaded it into a communication that I sent to Mimi. And I sent a command line to run a diagnostic on the labs, effectively destroying the blood sample she collected from you, since the blood on the floor would have been contaminated."

"She took my blood?"

Abigail paused and glanced back at him. "Yes. After you beat yourself into oblivion."

"You saw?"

She just grunted her answer. "GHOST."

He shouldn't marvel at the woman's ability to hack systems, yet it still took him by surprise on how fast she could download the info, enter diagnostics commands, *and* send a message to Mimi.

And Mimi would tell him once he arrived back home . . . Home . . . It was strange to think of the compound as home.

The rest of the journey down the tube was completed in silence. More thoughts flooded his mind, but none would stay long for him to think upon it. The sharp left quickly led to the outside. He pushed passed Abigail and peeked out. They would emerge behind some crates. No one was about.

He maneuvered out of the tube and stood. Abigail crawled out just as her display flashed again.

"They are almost here." She pushed to her feet. Her arm brushed against his. "You know you will be in isolation once we reach base?"

"I know." Jules glanced down at her—her eyes were unreadable— and sighed. "I didn't tell them anything, Abby. Your God must have protected that from them."

"He's your God, too, Jules."

He clenched his jaw to suppress the sudden rush of emotions that threatened to overtake him. "I know. Do me a favor."

"Yes?"

Jules turned her around to face him and brought his forehead to rest against hers. "Don't tell your father about what happened. I had sworn to him that I would keep my distance from you, yet I don't believe that is possible now."

He placed a quick kiss onto her forehead, strands of her hair tickling his lips, as his ship started lowering from the sky. The thrusters created a whirlwind around them, blowing their hair and clothes as they separated, and a violent hiss issued from the landing struts as the *Nightingale* settled down on the tarmac of the bay.

The ramp lowered, and Jedidiah stood at the entrance. Abigail jogged up the ramp, and Jules followed more slowly. Pain from his beating had caught up with him and made every step excruciating.

A muscle in Jedidiah's jaw flexed as Jules approached. "JJ's with Huey on the bridge. Take the GHOST up there and help out."

Abigail nodded and hurried up the steps and across the gangway.

Jules hit the panel and brushed past Jedidiah, but the man gently grasped his arm. He didn't face Abigail's father; instead, he stopped and waited, his eyes focused on the far wall of the bay.

Something else was building inside him, and he needed to fight against it. He couldn't tell if it was pain, rage, or sickness—maybe all three?

"I thought I told you to keep your distance."

Jules whirled to face him. His eyes fell on the view-panel, which showed the crates and, just behind it, the opening to the tube.

Jedidiah saw. He opened his mouth, but a flash interrupted what he was going to say . . . Which was what?

As Jedidiah plunged the needle into Jules' thigh, he reached out and gripped the older man's shirtfront. Was he being betrayed? What was he going to say? That he couldn't control his thoughts or emotions? Emotions? So foreign to him. How did they, normal humans, cope?

Darkness whirled around him, and the man lowered Jules to the floor. Did Abigail know? Was she a part of this?

"It's for your own good, son. Until we can isolate the drug, you are a danger to my daughter, my people, and yourself. Trust me." Jedidiah's face blurred, refocused, and then blurred again. A bright light seemed to encircle the older man's head and shoulders. That same kind of light that Jules had seen during his torture. The same as before.

"Jed . . . " His voice croaked, and his grip loosened on Jedidiah's shirt. "I . . . sorr . . . "

A sad look. An understanding look. Jules tried to focus on Jedidiah's eyes. They crinkled with compassion. "You'll be okay soon enough, son. Now, sleep."

A soft darkness overtook Jules, sweeping him along, and he had no control.

## Chapter Sixteen
# REVELATION

Abigail plugged in the GHOST. "Try now, Mimi."

For an hour, they had been trying to access the medical files. GFT had many firewalls and protocols in place, preventing anyone from hacking the files. And it wasn't just one program; it was five layers of quantum programs protecting whatever was in those files.

Her grandmother entered the codes for the program and tried once again to access the medical files. The screen flickered with rows of code, symbols, and words. Abigail reached past her grandmother and tapped the console. "Right there. That's the command line."

Mimi stepped aside and let Abigail work at isolating the line and filtering it through the GHOST. The screen shifted. Row after row of information appeared—lines of information. Abigail ran the decryption.

Jules' face appeared on the vidscreen, with a red "WARNING" underneath it.

Subject: Juliet 7-A, $\beta/\alpha$ $\Delta+\gamma$

Beta sub-alpha, delta-gamma protocols

Serum 74, success.

Abigail frowned. "This doesn't make sense to me."

Mimi ran her finger down the page, quickly reading it, and gave Abigail a condensed version. "He's a beta personality with alpha tendencies. Normally, those types of individuals are culled from the program, but apparently, his particular alpha characteristics made him ideal for the experiment. Looks like this Serum Seventy-four was a newer variation." She paused and looked at Abigail. "That would make sense. He wasn't responding well to what we had. If the formula changed, hopefully we can find it in here. This part, the delta-gamma protocols, shows where his strongest concentration is. And that, too, is strange."

"What is?"

"Most individuals operate at a theta, beta, or alpha brainwave when learning or concentrating. They will bounce back and forth between these frequencies. For example, the beta waves are broken down into three areas, and most people will find that they operate best at beta-two. With Jules, he's more proficient at a delta and gamma level. With delta, that's deep, meditative states. Usually a dreamless sleep. With him, according to this, his body restores itself more proficiently and at an astounding rate—enhanced by the serum—while in delta state. But this one . . . "

Mimi frowned as she continued reading. She shook her head and glanced over at the sedated form of Jules. "Somehow, he's able to operate in a constant gamma state."

Abigail tried to read the more technical terms as she scrolled down the file. "This seems . . . I won't say impossible. But am I reading this right, Mimi?"

"Yes. He's able to process many things all at once. Yet his mind is extremely quiet."

"A form of super focus?"

Mimi nodded and selected the next file. "It's also called the 'spiritual awakening.' This is the highest frequency of brainwaves. The delta is the lowest."

"Which explains why he gravitates to quiet areas."

"Yes. And why he can listen, read, operate, and learn simultaneously." She tapped the screen again. "And there's the missing puzzle to our find. The infra-low waves are more pronounced with him."

"Meaning?"

"That's how he's been able to keep his emotions buried. The biofeedback performed on him, according to this," she tapped the bottom of the report, "strengthened the infra-low and created within him the ability to become detached. Emotional and mental detachment. Add the Paxolin in, and his memories would be buried. They went through a lot of trouble to make sure he couldn't remember. And the report stops there. There's a lot more research, but sporadic. Oh my . . . "

Abigail frowned. She looked at her grandmother and then at the screen where Mimi was pointing. The date of that particular report was from twenty-two years ago. When Jules was ten. Her chest clenched, and she pressed her fist against her breastbone to ease the pain. The poor man. He had been conditioned, altered, and groomed to be what they wanted—the perfect killer.

And he was that for them . . . until now.

"There's a lot to digest here. And it's going to take me time, Abby." Mimi pulled up a stool and sat before the console. "I'll start on the Serum Seventy-four first. Since it is tailored to him, it should help repair a lot of his neural pathways and keep him alive."

Abigail walked to the window between Medlab Two and Medlab One. The doors to Medlab One had been mag-locked. Lights were dimmed. The machines within constantly monitored Jules. Mimi had called in Medtech Evan Taniff. He would be back from the Russian Compound to help Mimi in a couple of days. Until then, Jules laid on the medbed in a medically induced coma.

Mimi had said that until the drugs that were used on him were isolated, he was a danger. And being in an induced coma would allow his body to heal faster, too.

She pressed her hand against the thick pane. He looked peaceful. The harsh lines of his face had smoothed. His hair fell about his ears and forehead and would have given him a boyish appearance if not for the trimmed beard.

Abigail turned around at a knock on the medlab hatch. JJ stepped across the threshold.

"Come to check on my boy." He glanced her way and through the window before facing Mimi. "Have you found what they used, Evelyn?"

"Not yet. I have a sample of his blood in the spectrum analysis. It should be able to isolate it." At JJ's silence, Mimi looked up from her console. "Joshua?"

JJ swallowed. "It's possible that what was used is the same that we, as assassins, used." He leaned against the medbed. "I don't like talking about what we did, particularly what I did. There are lot of . . . " He sighed and looked away.

Abigail frowned. Their lives as assassins were not pleasant. They all knew this. And they knew they had tortured and killed. From what Anya had said during Jules' torture, what he underwent was the same that they forced upon others.

"That's your old life, JJ." She grabbed a stool and slid onto it. "We don't hold it against you. But if you have information that will help Jules, then please, share with us. We will not think less of you."

JJ steepled his fingers and held them against his mouth. "Abby, what we did . . . as elite assassins . . . " He blew out a long breath. His hands shook slightly. "We committed a lot of atrocities, all in the name of duty. Jules was the worse of us. The strongest, the fastest, the cruelest. His ability to detach himself came from something that happened long ago."

Mimi paused in her reading and turned on her stool. "Do we need to call the elders?"

JJ shook his head. "I just came back from speaking with them. They know what I'm about to tell you. It is just hard because Abby . . . " He looked over at her. "I don't want you to think bad of him. I know Jules. He's not that man anymore."

She glanced back at the man who lay upon the bed, covered in a silver thermal blanket. "I know, JJ. If this can help Jules, then please tell us."

JJ cast his eyes down. "He was ten when he was forced to make his first kill. One of our own but in Sierra squad. Because he hesitated that day, he was made to train with his friend's blood covering him. It was then they took him away. We didn't see him for a week. When he came back, he was silent. His accent was gone. There was no life in him. Some of us were able to accept the training and push a lot of what happened to the side. But with Jules, he could remember every mission, every target. What he didn't remember was the boy he killed. The five years prior. When asked, he would just look through you as if you didn't exist, and say, 'Memories are irrelevant.' I tell you this only because I want you to understand. Jules, when he was Juliet 7-A, tortured a lot of people. And he used the same drugs on them that Anya probably used on him." JJ cleared his throat. "On one particular mission, we were questioning a man, looking for codes. Jules gave him a dose of Paxolin, benzodia, quazolin, and sodium pentha."

Mimi entered the drugs into the console and then rolled her chair to the spectrum analysis. "You said Paxolin, benzodia, quazolin, and . . ."

"Sodium pentha."

She entered the drugs into the machine. "I have it looking for those in his blood. Do you know what it will do with Serum Seventy-four?"

JJ shook his head. "No. As you know, my serum was different than his. But you said he isn't taking Paxolin?"

"No. He didn't respond well."

"Strange. Do you think they did something to him in Washington or at Intech?"

Mimi shrugged. "Could be."

JJ squeezed his eyes. Grief wrinkled his brow. "I should never have left him."

Abigail stood and placed a hand on his arm. "You didn't know. And if you had stayed, then you and Jules would have been dead."

"And our eternal destination would have been Hell." He looked over at her. "I know. But I can't help but feel responsible for what is happening to him now."

"Don't." She rubbed her hand up and down his arm. "This could be a good thing. We isolate the drugs, purge them, and he will be healed."

$$\Sigma$$

Images drifted through his mind. A redheaded woman. A man with brown curly hair. A trio of children, smiling and laughing. Mission targets . . .

In the background, soft voices rose and fell. A deeper one filtered through. Then harsh light pushed through, burning into one eye, then the other.

That deep voice pushed through the haze again. "Wake up, Moody Monkey."

JJ.

Jules forced his eyes opened, but his strength was gone. A blurred image of JJ hovered in front of him; then darkness descended.

"Oh, no. You aren't getting out of this that easy." A sharp stab entered his arm. "Wake up, Julius."

Anger rushed through him. He commanded Juliet. Not 7-J. A hand struck against his face. Rage burned inside.

The hand descended again, and he lashed out, catching it on the downswing. His eyes popped open, and he glared at Juliet 7-J, who held a hypospray midair.

With a push, he had him by the throat against the wall, squeezing and pressing. He wouldn't kill him. Not today. But he would learn his place in this squad.

The man before him held a hand to the side, waving someone away. Then everything around Jules wavered. The room pulsed in and out. Coldness pushed at him.

That was strange. It was never cold at Medlab Twelve. It was stifling.

His vision cleared. JJ stood before him, patiently waiting.

Jules dropped his arm and stepped back. He was in Medlab One. In Antarctica. He surveyed his room. At the door stood Echo unit. Was there a mission? Did he miss the briefing?

"7-J?" The cold of the floor leeched into his feet. Jules glanced down. No boots. No pants. A flimsy, gauze garment draped over his body. "Mission report."

"None to report. You are in medlab."

Faster than 7-J could react, Jules grabbed him, rammed a knee into his face, and threw him to the floor. The blade at 7-J's belt was now in Jules' hand, and he held it at 7-J's throat. "What happened to me?"

Echo unit rushed in, but Jules jumped up and met them. He whipped his hand toward the throat of one, throwing him into the wall and ducked under the arm of another as he grabbed at him. His arm snaked around the neck of the man, but a slight hiss from the door reached him before he could deliver the killing blow.

Three darts hit him. He pushed Echo away and saw 7-J had the pistol aimed at him. Three more pops and the darts imbedded into his abdomen.

Jules rushed 7-J. Dark hands countered his every move. His arms became sluggish. His vision darkened. But he wouldn't go down without taking them with him.

There was a pop from the doorway. The stab of another dart between his shoulder blades brought him around. A man with gray and red hair stood there, a tranq pistol aimed at him.

Jules staggered against the counter behind him. Something was wrong. This wasn't Medlab Twelve. JJ's face swam before him. Then he was falling.

He didn't know how long he fell. Only that his body seemed to tumble through an endless black sea, at times hitting up against a black, glass wall. Jules would pound against it, but it refused to break. It was thicker than the ice that had trapped him and CeeCee.

CeeCee. Jules arched up. Something was wrong. He wasn't with GFT anymore. He was with the Coalition. Abigail's people. JJ's people.

He floated toward a current. Then he was shot upward, toward a harsh light that burned.

Jules gasped and opened his eyes. The Medlab One scanner hung over him, the light pulsing against him. A deep ache rolled through his body. He groaned and turned his head to the right. JJ stood to the side with his arms crossed.

When Jules glanced to his left, Dan, James, Devon, and Jackson from Echo unit stood far away from the bed and against the window that connected him with Medlab Two, where he spotted Mimi working at a console.

The comm in the room opened. "Joshua, you can take him now. Are you sure about this?"

JJ nodded. "What we will do will burn the rest of the drugs out of his system. We've done this many times, Evelyn."

Dan pushed the scanner out of the way. Jules cast a wary glance at him and sat up. JJ threw a pair of pants at him.

"Get dressed."

Anger coursed through him. Four tranq pistols aimed his way. Jules swung his feet around and sat on the edge of the medbed. "How long?"

JJ planted his feet apart and clasped his hands behind his back. "Three days. First was induced coma. The second was sedation. The third was the tranqs. We have to work the rest of the Paxolin and quazolin out of your system."

Jules stood, yanked the pants on, and tied the string at the waist. The memory of his torture flooded through him. Then the surreal dream of fighting JJ and Echo unit. Apparently, that wasn't a dream. "How bad?"

"Just bruises, Jules. This time." JJ smiled. "We anticipated you. Ready? We have the cargo bay at our disposal for this."

He straightened, ignoring the queasiness that rolled his stomach. When he turned toward the door, JJ took the lead, and Echo unit surrounded him. He never thought he would have to undergo this again. They marched him toward the stairs and down, down, down.

$$\Sigma$$

Abigail switched the viewscreen over to the cargo bay. They marched him in a tight formation. She glanced back at the door to her room. It was still closed.

She checked the security feeds. No one was around. JJ had told her father to make sure everyone either stayed in the galley or in their quarters. She leaned her head back against her cushions and continued watching on her handheld.

The only time those from GFT had to do this was with Zulu. She didn't witness it, but Mimi said that it was the only way to finish purging the drugs from their systems. The adrenaline and testosterone that the exercise produced bonded with the two drugs, and their bodies were able to flush it out.

After witnessing what Jules did during the first time he awoke, it was definitely needed. They entered the bay. JJ and the others cast their jackets and shirts to the side. Then they fanned out until they were spaced two arms' length from each other. Jules was kept in the middle.

JJ walked over to a box. He reached in and pulled out five-foot-long rods. Each man accepted one and then went into fighting stance—hand up in front, hand behind holding the rod at an angle, and legs bent.

When JJ resumed his position in front of Jules, he tapped his stick against the floor. As one, they moved.

It was a dance. A lethal one. The muscles on Jules' body flexed with each motion. A strike forward. A turn, the rod following. A jab, kick, block, and turn. Each movement grew in complexity. Advance, jab, swing, block, turn. Then they swung their left foot in an arc, swung down, turned, and kicked with a right foot, held it for a second, and then back down, turning their bodies and striking backward with the rod.

As one, they struck forward, brought their arms down to the side, and bowed.

Jules stayed in the middle as they broke away and surrounded him in an uneven circle. Jules had his head slightly bowed, cocked to the side, and the rod held to the side. She didn't register JJ's movement. He was there on the edge of the circle; then he was meeting Jules' weapon. They moved in a blur, counteracting each other.

JJ broke away, and Jules whirled, meeting Dan next. Then Devon stepped in. Jules kept both at bay. Dan's stick flew through the air. He ducked and stood back along the edge. Jackson and James jumped in. Devon fell away, and JJ replaced him.

Soon only JJ remained. Sweat poured down Jules as he blocked, parried, turned, ducked, and swung. Abigail glanced at her wrist monitor. An hour had passed.

Jules jabbed, then swung upward, his stick striking against JJ's and breaking it. He twisted around and held the tip of his weapon at JJ's throat. Then he stepped back, bowed at the waist, and stood before JJ.

The men stepped back into formation. Jules cast the rod he still held to the side, and they began another round of katas.

A knock startled Abigail. She jumped off her bunk and opened the door. Her father stepped through and spied her handheld.

"I assumed you would be watching them." He sank down on her bunk and picked it up and watched it for a moment. "They are amazing men, you know. The way they banded together to help Julius."

"They want him to heal just as much as we do."

"Yes, they do." He sighed and set the handheld down. "I came by to give you an update."

He patted the bunk. She sat beside him, and he wrapped his arm around her shoulders. Abigail looked up into her father's face. "It's about the serum, isn't it?"

"Yes. Mimi just informed us it can't be separated from him. Serum Seventy-four has to be administered daily to him from now on. Yet she is confident it will heal him completely. Without the Paxolin in his system, it will start to help him. Maybe even help him remember."

"I hope so, Dad. After reading his medical file, how could they do that to a child? They destroyed his life."

He pulled her into his side. "He's with us now. And we will keep praying for his healing, okay?"

The men continued the complex moves of their exercise. So many of them sported numerous scars. Fresh scars on Jules' back and arms glinted in the low light as he moved, his muscles rippling and flexing. She gazed back up at her father and hugged him.

"I love you, Dad. Thank you for helping him and believing in him."

"Anything for you, my girl." He kissed the top of her head and then picked the handheld back up. They watched as the men finished their exercise and then sank down onto the floor, legs crossed. Her dad turned up the volume.

Everyone's head was bowed, even Jules', as JJ spoke. "'Our Father which art in heaven, Hallowed be thy name. Thy kingdom come. Thy will be done in earth, as it is in heaven . . .'"

$$\Sigma$$

Jules stood at the viewport, watching and waiting. A line of air bubbles drifted upward past his window. Moments later, the dark form of an orca swam by, its graceful body arching and turning as it played in the ocean current. The massive animal disappeared toward the surface.

And he waited. Already, the animal had been up and down this side of the 'berg at least four times. Would it come again for a fifth?

He leaned closer and craned his neck, trying to see the surface. A faint, blue glow penetrated the darkness. So deceiving was the light. It seemed so close, a quick swim upward to reach air. Yet he was miles deep. The dark, frigid water cast its deception around him.

His face reflected in the glass. It startled him for a split second each time he saw his eyes. The serum began changing him, particularly his eyes. Some of the green had begun to turn white. Mimi had said it was a reaction to the pure formula of Serum Seventy-four. Although not harmful, it was strange to see.

A small scuffle of shoes sounded at the door, then the ping of the lock activating.

Jules barely glanced over his shoulder at Abby and returned to his vigil. "Come to check on me?"

She joined him at the viewport and stood on tiptoe to peer out. "No. Mimi said you were doing well with the serum." She let out a quick intake of breath, as if she were unsure if she should ask. "Are you all right with this? Being forced to retain your abilities?"

Jules tilted his head back and stuffed his hands in his back pockets. Was he all right with this? He had no choice, really. "It's over and done, Abby. Serum Seventy-four is my lifeline to this world. It can't be separated from me. Whatever they did to me at Intech Medlab made the serum a permanent part of me."

"And you can accept it?" She turned to face him.

"I have to." Air bubbles drifted past the glass. "Your father said I was born for a time such as this. I can help you and your people with what I have been given. It may be a burden, but it's a burden I'm willing to carry if it means keeping you safe."

He looked at her then. The orca cast a brief shadow across her face as it swam by. Her eyes had dilated. He cocked his head. Her heart sped up by a couple of beats. Something caused her to become anxious.

"Is there something wrong, Abby?" He took a small step toward her, and her eyes dilated even more, causing him to halt his advance.

Abby shook her head, red locks falling from the clasp at the nape of her neck. "No. Not really." She glanced around the small, frost-lined room. "Why here? Why did you come here?"

"How did you find me?"

"Tracker. I calibrated the sensor to look for any anomalies. There had been only three since you were released from iso two weeks ago.

Once at the far edge of the compound. Twice here at a storage unit that we don't use."

She had been by his side those two weeks. They worked with JJ and John on desalination. When Michael and Peter, who were once Zulu, arrived, they explored the edges of the compound with them, checking for fissures or weakened areas of the compound. Then there were the nights. Dinner at Jedidiah's. Sometimes, he kept Mimi company in hydroponics, and Abigail would arrive. Together, they would help Mimi with her plants. Then there were the nights spent in silence in the library. Abigail, JJ, Trisha, and he would read, content with each other's company. Yet they were never alone. Until now.

He returned to the viewport. "It helps me think. There's a lot to think about lately."

She stepped up to him, her shoulder barely grazing his arm. "Are you watching for the orca? She likes this side. There's an underwater current she rides about this time of day."

"I know. I can see the slight variation in the water, the way the small particles of flotsam drift." He closed his eyes to her presence. He could smell her. A sweet, almost musky smell. Like a cross between the dessert Miriam loved to make for him and those large orchids in Mimi's hydroponics bay. Was it the natural scent of her skin, or did she use something? He leaned until his arm touched hers, his small finger barely brushing against her hand.

Jules glanced down at her as she watched out the window. The vein in her neck pulsed heavily. Her breathing had increased. And her heart sped up another notch.

Was it because of him? Did his presence do this to her?

Every book he devoured learning about human behavior suggested this. He had purposely ignored her. The need to be around her grew stronger each day. Just to be around her, to hear her, to talk to her. To touch her.

The impulse to grab her was strong. He swallowed against it.

He had promised Jedidiah. But how could he keep that promise?

Especially when she looked at him, like she was doing now, and her eyes had dilated to the point that the blue could hardly be seen. His face reflected in those black pupils. And in that reflection, his own eyes with their green and white irises were dilated just as much.

"Abby?" He reached out and tentatively touch her face. It was supposed to be a touch, a small bit of contact. Instead, his hand caressed her cheek, her jaw. Bringing her closer to him until she was pressed against his abdomen, her head barely reaching the tip of his nose.

Heat flowed from her skin. He held her face in his hands, staring at her, warring with himself. This was new, but not unwelcomed. His heart told him to keep going; his mind yelled at him to stop.

She reached up and started to pull his hand away.

Whatever it was he was feeling, it unleashed within him. "No."

He claimed her mouth in a hard kiss. It was meant to be quick— something to satisfy his need and quell the raging fire within.

It didn't work. Thoughts of the outside world fled from him. Only he and Abby existed, there in the small storage room where the orca swam outside, playing.

She broke away, gasping for air and pushed at him. "Jules, we can't do this."

He leaned down for another kiss, speaking against her lips. "I know; I know."

Cold air hit his chest as she broke away and stepped back.

She opened her mouth to say something but looked away instead. He could hear her heart speed up even more, and her breathing became more ragged. Outside the viewport, air bubbles rose. Inside, there was a tension between them that rose. Something he didn't know how to deal with.

He reached out, taking a lock of her hair between his fingers. Then he stepped closer, letting his hand flow deeper into her long tresses. His fingers unlatched her hair clasp, and the red waves flowed around her face. The soft strands tangled with his fingers as he brought his hands through the curls.

The clasp clattered to the floor as he captured her face one more time and brought his head down to hers.

It should have been cold, there in the room, yet he barely registered the frosty air that hung between them as they stood there, foreheads touching, staring into each other's eyes. Jedidiah's reading from last night echoed in his head, but a pulsing drowned it out. This was dangerous. What they were doing wasn't meant for this time. He needed to pull away from her, to step away from her. He needed to keep his distance.

He didn't move.

Her hands latched onto his but didn't pull them away. Instead, she stepped closer.

All thoughts fled as they stood there in each other's embrace, as the sound of air bubbles raced up the side of the ship.

Outside, the orca's song pinged against the hull.

$$\Sigma$$

Abigail bit back a gasp at the cold air as she stuffed the blanket into an open and empty storage box. "Computer. Lights at one quarter."

The soft illumination lit the room. She turned and found Jules standing back by the viewport, staring at her, watching her, his face half-hidden in the shadows.

"I'm sorry."

Abigail shook her head. "As much my fault as yours, Jules."

Shame flooded through her as she searched for her jacket. He reached down and picked it up from the floor under the viewport. A beeping was coming from his jacket, which lay discarded by her own.

His eyes wouldn't meet hers as he passed her jacket to her and she quickly pulled it on. He squatted next to his own and dug in the pocket. Jules pulled the communicator out of the pocket just as the beeping ceased.

The freezing temperature in the storage room drove her breath from her as she sat on the hard floor and fought with her boots. Numb fingers barely fastened the clasps. She gave them one last check and struggled off the floor, burying her hands into her jacket pockets.

Jules waited for her to join him at the viewport. The vein in his neck pulsed heavily against his skin. "I think they are heading this way. I can hear boots down the corridor." Jules half-zipped his jacket when he held up a hand. His head cocked to the side before taking a deep breath. "I can hear them checking storage rooms. Let's get out of here before they find us together like this."

The evening security check. "We've been together before, Jules. Why would they consider this any different?"

It was his eyes—the white in his irises growing more pronounced each day from the serum—that were more unreadable than his face.

Could it be that he felt the shame of what had happened just as she did? She had kept herself from making that same mistake for so many years, only now to fall back into the temptation.

The cold assassin exterior was back as he regarded her before speaking.

He tapped the side of her cheek. "We are alone together. And we are in a seldom-used storage unit."

Her gaze traveled over him. There was something more to him now. She could see a war raging within him. Abigail stepped up to him and zipped his jacket all the way.

His lips turned up in a flash of a smile; his eyes flared with a small light before it died. "Come on before we end up repeating what happened. I'm so sorry about that."

She swallowed against the sudden embarrassment. It was wrong. She knew it. Oh, Lord, please forgive her for such a mistake. Her father's voice echoed in her head: *Flee sexual immorality . . . but the flesh is weak . . . flee youthful lusts; but pursue righteousness.*

As Jules opened the door, she ordered the lights off. Dark flooded the room. The emergency lights lit the passageway. Jules paused before pointing to their left.

"Head that way to the service tunnel. We will take that back to the main compound."

Abigail nodded. With hurried steps, they crossed the passage, slid open the door panel, and slipped down the narrow service tunnel. Far away, voices reached her ears before they faded as she and Jules trotted back to be with the others.

They stepped out into the main passage. Not many people were about as she and Jules crossed the promenade and hurried into the quarters section. Some people strolled about, talking with each other, heading to their rooms, or heading up to the galley.

Abigail nodded a greeting to Micah and his wife. They gave a knowing smile in return, their eyes sparkling. A warm blush crept up her neck. Could they tell what she and Jules had done?

She glanced up at the man by her side. His face was slightly flushed, his eyes darting around as if he couldn't look at anyone.

Maybe guilt was eating at him, too. It surely wasn't leaving her alone. They climbed the short flight of stairs and turned left. She keyed open the door to her and her father's quarters. Jules slipped in behind her.

"What are you doing?" She hissed at him. "You can't let my father catch you. He doesn't allow you in here unless he's here."

"I know." He touched her cheek, running a small caress over her jaw. "I'm sorry for what I did, Abby. I should have stopped it."

"You aren't the only one at fault. I told you that. I could have stopped it anytime, but I didn't. Look, we can talk about it later. It would be best if we just took a moment to ourselves and collect our thoughts." She placed a hand on his arm. "You aren't a believer, Jules. But what we just did . . . it was wrong. We are commanded to flee from sexual immorality. And I didn't do that."

His brows lowered, and his eyes filled with a deep sorrow. He straightened, inhaling through his nose, and nodded. "I understand."

He palmed open the door, took a step outside, and slammed right into her father.

"Jules." Her father's voice seemed cold and hard. His eyes narrowed as they traveled from Jules' impassive face to hers. "We've been looking for you."

"Sorry. Abby found me, and before long, we lost all sense of time." Jules' hands were behind his back, and his fingers worked at his communicator. He stepped aside to let her father pass and then reentered the room.

She caught sight of his communicator being pushed into his back pocket.

"Hey, Dad. I was about to prepare a drink. Do you want one?" She eased toward the small cooling unit in the corner.

"No." His gaze followed her before turning back to Jules. Her father's expression hardened even more. He hadn't believed a word Jules had said. "I tried to reach you on the communicator."

Jules frowned. "I didn't hear it." He pulled the comm out of his back pocket and turned it over in his hands. "It's dead. No wonder."

"I see." Her father set his mouth in a grim line before taking the comm from Jules' hands and inserting it into their charge port. "I'll charge it for you. And in the morning, I need you to meet me in the bay area. There are some things that we need to go over."

Jules nodded, his gaze sliding briefly over to her. "What time?"

"When you awake."

There was a slight pause before Jules nodded, and then he walked to the door. "Goodnight, Abby. I'll see you sometime tomorrow."

Then he was gone as if nothing had ever happened between them. She turned to the unit and pulled out a small pitcher of tea. It sloshed slightly in her shaky hands as she poured it into a small glass. Trying to dispel her shaking, she slowly replaced it and picked up her glass.

She took a sip as she turned to her father. He was examining Jules' communicator. "Are you okay, Dad?"

"Hmm?" He looked up after inserting the comm into the port. "Yes. Looks like the communicator has a faulty wiring. I'll issue a new one to him."

He followed her into their sitting area and sat in his chair, crossing an ankle over his knee. "So, would you like to tell me the truth about what you and Julius have been up to?"

She almost choked on the use of Jules' full name. "He told you. We lost track of time while we watched the orca play outside. I still think she has a mate somewhere. It's always at the same time of evening when she swims by." Abigail eased down on the small, gel-conforming chair across from her father.

"I see." He picked up one of the daily reports and perused it. "I had asked that you limit your time around him. It will take him a while to adjust to the serum that he was given. He had been too long without it."

"I know, Dad. I just stopped by to check on him is all. He seems to have accepted that he will have to have the serum for the rest of his life and that he will still retain his abilities."

"It's more than that, Abigail." Her father sighed and set the report back down. "His abilities are stronger than before. Which means the potential for aggression and rage have been increased. We haven't decided if he is a risk or not to us."

Abigail shook her head. "He's not! Give him time. He will prove to you that he cares about everyone here."

"Yes, he cares." Her father stood and rubbed at his eyes before pinching the bridge of his nose. "He cares about you. How deeply remains to be seen. Abigail, we have dealt with his kind before. If he thinks that you are a part of him, do you think he will relinquish his feelings for you if ever faced with a choice? If we told him he had to leave, do you think he will do it peacefully? Do you think he can separate himself from you or let you make your own choices? If his abilities are more heightened than before, then the same can be said for his training. He's an assassin. Designed to kill."

Anger flooded her senses. "He was designed to be a human. And God's purpose for him is stronger than what any man has done to him." She set her tea down on the table, rose from her seat, and strode to the door. "Why are you doing this? Why question his loyalty now? I'll be back later. I can't listen to you decide his fate before giving him a chance."

"I gave him a chance!" The rage in her father's voice slowed her steps.

She paused at the door and turned to him. In his hand was her hair clasp. She resisted the urge to reach back and touch her hair. Abigail swallowed.

He reached for the datapad he had laid down and held it out to her. She stared at it before taking it from her father. What she had thought were daily reports was the security feed of her and Jules leaving the storage unit with their hands clasped as they hurried to the service tunnel. They left the frame, and within moments, her dad and the security team entered the room. After a few seconds, her dad came out with her clasp in his hand—the metal glinting in the low light—and the blanket from the box.

"I told him to stay away from you. I ordered him. He had a choice— he could stay, but he had to keep his distance from you, or he could leave. He stayed around you—too close around you—and now, he will have to go. He's an assassin, Abigail. He's unpredictable."

"A choice? That wasn't a choice, Dad." She palmed the door open but paused on the threshold and slammed the device on the table by the door. "He was fine as your puppet and protection, as a bodyguard or a soldier for the cause, but he wasn't accepted as a human being? As my friend? As a man who has saved my life and those of others? He either had to stay and only do what you want him to do or leave and be free, but away from the only people who care about him and whom he cares about? That's some choice. You're acting no better than those who enslaved him."

She stepped out into the passageway and rushed down its length. Mimi would be in hydroponics, and that was where she would go.

$$\Sigma$$

Jules leaned against the wall of the service tunnel and closed his eyes. Jedidiah's words echoed in his head. *He's an assassin . . . he's unpredictable . . . designed to kill.*

A pain clutched at his heart. It was his fault. He couldn't control his desire, and now it had caused a rift between Abby and her father. Jedidiah was right. He was good only as a soldier, a killer. That fairytale he had dreamed about with Abby was just that, a fairytale. A dream for fools.

Companionship. Acceptance. Love. Those didn't belong to GFT assassins. He was nothing more than a scientist's invention. A past eradicated. A future obliterated.

He needed to collect his things and leave. It was for the best.

Jules pushed off the wall in the darkened tunnel, a pressure building in his head, and slipped down the grated walkway to his own quarters. The du Soleil door gaped open. Her father stood there on the threshold, watching down the passageway where Abby had disappeared. The man's gaze caught his and then jerked toward the service tunnel, apparently realizing where Jules had been and that he had heard them. Jedidiah's voice called out to him. He ignored it and kept walking, stumbling slightly against the railing. There was nothing else to be said.

He was nothing to them. And soon, they would be nothing to him.

Huey. He'd leave Huey behind. This was a good place for the man to start over. And JJ would forgive him for leaving.

Jules palmed open his quarters, reminding himself of one more mistrust they had of him. No keypad. He hurried inside. There were a few articles of possession in his cell. Yet everything could be left behind, except for one. Jules grabbed the Bible Mimi had given him. The only other person who seemed to truly accept him for who he was. She and Abigail.

He ran a finger along the black cover. Did Mimi ever do the same? She always ran her finger across his hand just as he was doing with the Bible. She never cast him aside. Always giving him a drink of tea when he stopped by her quarters near hydroponics. Or sat with him during his late-night dinners. Keeping him company as he read from the books. Her soft voice saying, "Goodnight, dear boy," as he would leave her with her plants echoed in his head.

Mimi. He should say goodbye to her before leaving tonight. Abby's heart would heal. But he owed Mimi more than he could ever repay.

A violent wave of dizziness overtook him. Jules reached out and grabbed at the wall. The pressure in his head threatened to burst through him. Voices rushed into him, flooding his senses. Strange dialects. Voices he didn't know and couldn't understand. They rode over each other, battering his ears, bringing torment and anguish.

He grasped the Bible and fought to stand upright. Each voice drove at him, driving him into the wall, battering his head with steel spikes, pushing and clawing at his brain.

Jules fell to his knees and clutched at his head; the cool leather of the Bible pressed against his temple. Something inside was trying to push its way out of his skull. Pain pushed at his eyes. Somewhere in his quarters, he heard a scream, a piercing sound of pain renting the air.

"You are everything to me, Seth."

"Look out, Seth. Don't worry, Bud; you'll get it next time."

"Seth, hide!"

"Run, Seth!"

Images clouded his vision. A woman. A man. Their faces blurred as they swam in front of him. Green eyes focused on him before falling back into shadow. Hands grabbed at him, pulling him over. Voices yelled at him.

He fought prying hands from removing the Bible, but it wasn't just hands, and it wasn't just his Bible. It was gloved hands, sweeping in, grabbing him, yanking him away from the couple, who knelt there screaming after him.

Then the image faded; the voices faded. In its wake was Jedidiah's face, looming over him. The man's mouth moved as Jules fell into a soft light and another face filled his vision.

"Tell me the story, Dad." He whispered the forgotten memory as he was washed away from the world.

"I just couldn't stay in the same room with him, Mimi." Abigail sat on the bench and watched as the older woman packed wet soil around the plants. Wrinkled hands reached up and adjusted the overhead lights. The heat lamps grew warmer. For the last fifteen minutes, she had been helping her grandmother plant the new bean plants. And confessing her mistake, feeling like an awkward teenage girl again.

"He's your father, Abigail. He only looks out for you, and he worries about Julius. Assassin or not, Julius is dangerous. Do I think he will hurt us? No. The man will die protecting us. But he doesn't understand his feelings. Not yet." Mimi hobbled to the washing bin and dipped her hands into the water, swishing them around to remove the dirt. "What was done to him was done at an earlier age than most of them. His memories weren't erased. They were blocked. So as the serum rebuilds his neural pathways, it will also cause him to feel things he has forgotten or never felt before."

Abigail plucked a towel from the pile next to her and held it out to her grandmother. As Mimi dried her hands, she waited for a response. Abigail tried to compose her thoughts in a way that would make sense. "I can't figure out how to ask this . . . I understand, technically. But . . . " She huffed before beginning again. "Is it like . . . an awakening? Song of Solomon?"

Mimi shrugged her shoulders. "A combination really. He wasn't allowed to feel anything. No desire. No love. No compassion. From what we have been able to glean from our previous experiences with them and from what the medical records hold is that they feel, yet they had learned to bury it deep down. They had to. They were only children; and any sign of compassion, love, or mercy was met with severe punishment and torture. So, it was only natural for him to hide that part until he forgot. Then add the drug they were given that keeps those natural feelings buried and hidden . . . " Her eyebrows drew together, and sympathy filled her gaze. "Humans are designed to seek companionship. And through marriage," Mimi cast her a pointed stare, causing heat to flow into her hairline, "a physical closeness. Julius was conditioned and chemically and genetically altered. He never felt those emotions, those desires. Think of it as a storm of hormones released into a man's body. It would be uncontrollable. He would need direction in order to do so."

"And I didn't help the situation. Oh, Mimi. I fear the damage has been done. I gave away what I shouldn't have. He took what he shouldn't have. And I never even considered the consequences of our actions. I just allowed myself to be governed by . . . " She faltered to a stop. "I don't know what to do now. As in Song of Solomon, I awakened love before its time . . . There's no stuffing it back into the box now."

Mimi shuffled to her and patted her hand. "You aren't the only one to have made such a mistake. I did. Your father did. Countless others here have, too. Everyone sins, my dear. But we do what is commanded."

"'Go and sin no more.'"

"Exactly. It will take your father time to calm down. And he won't send Julius away. All that was a veiled threat to keep Julius in line. Give them all enough time to come around to their senses."

Abigail sighed and scooted over for her grandmother to sit beside her. She leaned her head against her grandmother's shoulder. "When we rescued Jules, I thought things would change. We would be free. Jules would heal. We would be together, living our life. Instead, the only thing this has done has caused us to prepare to run again. My GHOST allows us to communicate with GFT government without being traced, but, Mimi, I feel as though this safety won't last."

Mimi hugged her and kissed her brow. "Child, things are always in motion. We live for today and let tomorrow worry for itself. We are not guaranteed safety in this world."

They looked up as Huey suddenly rushed into the bay, his breath heaving. "Evelyn, it's Jules. Something happened. Jedidiah sent me to ask you to help in medlab. Abigail, you need to come, too. They can't control him."

Abigail helped her grandmother to her feet, and they followed Huey as fast as her grandmother's legs would allow. Davis arrived outside the bay on a hoverstand.

"Here, hop on Evelyn. I'll carry you there." He looked at Abigail. "Your father said for you to hurry. It's taking six men to hold him down. And Jules is screaming for you."

Abigail ran. Ran faster than she ever had before. The whine of the hoverstand grew distant, and Huey's huffing eventually faded as she left him behind, too.

She grabbed the frame of the Medlab One door and halted her flight. In front of her, six guards struggled with a flailing Julius. His fist connected with one of them and sent him flying into the wall. Instruments scattered to the floor.

"Abby!" His voice rasped the air. His eyes searched the room, seeing only what was in his mind. "No!" Then his body became rigid, veins popped along his neck and face. The downed guard returned to his station, gripping Jules' wrist and arm. They took that opportunity to strap the restraints against him.

Her father stepped out of the room, holding a towel to his eyebrow.

"Dad? What happened?"

He glanced around. "Where's Mimi?"

"On her way. Davis has her on the hoverstand—"

Her grandmother stepped into the medlab. "Jed, move aside. Bring me the hypo. I have a dose of sedative-laden serum prepped."

"What's happening?" Abigail followed her grandmother to the door as Jules started fighting against the guards again.

Her father followed them into the room. "He started screaming in his quarters and then collapsed." He removed the towel, displaying a long cut above his eye. "He's replaying everything that has happened to him. I needed you in here with me. He will recognize your voice. He may or may not react to you, but he will start to calm as the memories flood through him. I need you to talk to him. Ask him to tell you what's happening."

Abigail looked at her father. Worry creased his brow, and his eyes held the greatest amount of sorrow she had ever seen.

He nodded toward Jules. "I'll be right here, sweetie."

Abigail stepped up to the bed. Her grandmother hobbled Jules' side. His shirt had ridden up during his thrashing, revealing the myriad of scars that traversed his body. Mimi pressed the hypo against his stomach and injected the serum into his system.

Jules slowly relaxed, but his voice cried out.

"I won't tell! Oh, God, please take me now. I can't last much longer."

With a deep breath and quick prayer, she stepped up to Jules' side, looking up at her friend. "You can let go, Sam."

The older man released Jules' shoulder and stepped back.

"Jules?" She caressed his forehead, running her hand over his head as she leaned in. "Jules? It's Abby. Tell me what's happening. Where are you? I can't help you if you don't tell me."

His vacant green eyes turned to her. "You're here. With me."

"I am—"

Mimi spoke from her side of the bed, poised with another hypospray. "Remember, it's not you he's talking to. It's whatever memory is playing out in his head."

Abigail nodded. "Yes. I'm here."

"Keep me safe. Please. I beg you. I want to accept You, but I can't remember You. You seem so foreign to me." His voice broke off, and he gritted his teeth as if in pain. His head thrashed back and forth, spittle flying from his lips. His body arched, pushing against the restraints, cutting them into his skin. Blood trickled from underneath the metal. Then, just as suddenly, he collapsed back onto the bed.

"Jules, tell me where you are?"

His gaze turned to Mimi. "Do you see them, Mom? I want to fly one. I want to fly one of those big ones." A smile drifted across his lips as he gazed at Mimi. "Someday, I will fly a transport like Dad."

He looked at the ceiling above him, and his smile faded. "No! Mom! Dad! No!" The scream was blood curdling, piercing into her ears and echoing off the walls.

She bent closer to him. "Where are you? Tell me what you see."

His gaze returned to her; his pupils were constricted so tightly that the green with its white seemed otherworldly. "They took them away. They took me away. Away from home. No! Stop! Please!"

His sobs grew louder; tears coursed down his face as he was lost in his mind. She bit her lip and tried not to cry along with him. Seeing him like this, broken, flailing about, lost to something beyond his control.

It was only when something wet hit the back of her hand that she realized she was crying, too. She sniffed and took a fortifying breath.

The door hissed, and JJ entered. His face contorted in grief as he came to stand near them.

Jules had grown quiet, silently enduring his horror. She slid her hand over his. And once again, his gaze returned to her. "Where are you?"

"The academy."

"What is happening?"

Tears pooled in his eyes. "I must sentence Sierra 7-N. Stephen."

"Tell me. What are you doing?"

Jules looked at the ceiling. "I have my blade. Stephen was found with a Bible. My Bible. He wouldn't tell them it was mine. He's looking at me, telling me that it's okay. To do it. He forgives me."

His voice broke and became a whisper. "They are holding a gun on me. If I don't, I'm dead. And then JJ will die, too." Terror poured from his eyes, and a raw sob fell from his lips. "It took only one swipe. The blood is on me. And I can't get it off . . . I can't get it off!"

JJ squeezed his eyes shut, placing his hand on Jules' booted foot.

Jules succumbed to the sedative.

Mimi nodded. "It took a while for the sedative to work." She clamped a vital clip onto his right wrist and then strapped a neural relay across his head. "We'll be able to tell when he's remembering and when he's dreaming." She pointed to the low band waves that ran across the screen. "The delta waves indicate he's in a deep sleep. We will need to watch for either theta or beta waves."

Her father brought a stool to Abigail, and she fell back onto it. Exhaustion flowed through her.

She turned to her father. "He . . . no wonder his mind blocked it all." She glanced at JJ. "He was only a child!" She pressed her fingertips against her temples. The horror Jules had to endure.

No wonder his mind blocked it all from him. He needed a way to survive. JJ's hand covered hers and squeezed. And she realized, Jules was reliving his memories. And now, so was JJ. She gripped his hand and held on. Giving him as much support as she could as he was giving the same to her.

Her dad spoke from the doorway. "We'll discuss this later. I'm calling an emergency meeting with the elders. Mom, will you make a duplicate? They need to hear what we did. Abby, bring it when it's finished."

Mimi nodded as she finished hooking monitors to Jules. Huey came into the room, set a stool down next to her, and perched on it.

She wasn't surprised that Huey wasn't going to leave Jules' side. And neither was JJ. Guess they were in it for the long haul.

She walked into the conference chamber. Her father stood near the back wall talking with Elder Jake. The younger Jake stood with his hands clasped behind his back, his expression grave. Abigail crossed the floor and held out the small data crystal.

"Mimi said some of the audio is corrupted, but most of it is there. Huey said to let you know that he rigged up a live feed so that you can watch in case he wakes up anytime soon. JJ is staying at his side, keeping an eye on him."

Her father slipped the crystal into the console. "Computer, lower lights two-thirds." The overhead dimmed, and then he looked at her. "Do you want to be in here for this?"

Abigail nodded. "I need to see what they did to him and know what he had suffered."

He took her by the arm and pulled her to an empty corner. "Abby, I'm sorry. You are a grown woman, and I treated you like a child."

She shook her head at him. "No, Dad. I understand; I do." She tried to smile at him. "I'm sorry I disappointed you. I know you know what happened."

"Oh, my girl, you haven't disappointed me. You've done no more than many of us." He pulled her into an embrace and set his chin atop her head. His beard tickled her hair as he spoke. "And I take back what I said about Julius. Knowing what I know now shows how heartless I was being. Jules needs our compassion and strength." He took her by the shoulders and gazed into her face. "When he cried out for you, I realized that it's been you that has kept him grounded and fighting to leave his past behind. He loves you. That is evident. He may not realize it right now, but he will soon. And seeing what his memories are doing to him, I can't help but think that the Lord protected him this long in order to bring him to us."

"Jedidiah, it's ready." Elder Jake's voice called out to them.

Abigail gave her father a small hug. "I know I have to see this, hear this. But I'm terrified."

Her father heaved a heavy sigh and rubbed his hands up and down her arms before leading her back to the group. "I'm here with you, my girl." He stood behind her as they crowded around the viewscreen. His hands landed heavily onto her shoulders, giving her support and offering her comfort.

The video started abruptly. Jules was brought in kicking, twisting, thrashing, and screaming. It was four men who held his legs, and the other two pulled him onto the table. Then they were holding him down, at times laying across his bucking form.

But it was the words that echoed in their conference chamber.

"Dad! No! Leave them alone!" His eyes widened before rolling back. Sobs racked his body. "My birthday cake! No! Mom! They shot him! They shot him. My mom . . . Oh, Lord, let me forget! Make them stop! No!" His arms pulled away as her father walked into the frame. A booted foot slipped free and flew toward her father's face. He backed away but not fast enough as the boot connected with his forehead before it was jerked down by Danny and Wickham.

Jules bucked again, straining against the holds on him. "My name is Seth. I'm not Juliet 7-A. I'm Seth . . . Stop! Stop! Leave her be! Yes, yes. My name is Juliet . . . Juliet 7-A. I'm Juliet 7-A." His sobs fell away, and his eyes, with a look of defeat, became lost in something as he looked past Sam, who held his arm. "Have to find Abby . . . Anya is after me . . . " A coldness filled his eyes, and his body relaxed. "Hold him down, 7-J . . . " His voice dripped with ice, and a shiver ran up Abigail's back. "What's the code?"

His eyes squeezed shut. "I have to . . . I can't release him . . . JJ, I gave him a quick death. I had to. They would have found out. Burn the books . . . Leave them be, Juliet 7-J. Let the children run this time."

*This time?* Abigail felt as though her knees would give out. If not for her father's arms, she would have fallen. He had killed children. They had made him kill children.

Jules became quiet as he turned his gaze toward the ceiling. They traveled across some hidden vision. Then fear filled his eyes and contorted his face. He started flailing again, punching the men and kicking at them. Many of his hits landed until they were able to pin him back down. Even then, they struggled to hold him still.

"Abby! Run, Abby! Get away from me!"

She turned to her father as Jules kept repeating the line. "I don't understand. He never said those things to me. What kind of memory is this?"

Her father shook his head. "It could have been his thoughts. His memory of what he was thinking at some time not too long ago."

Abigail leaned back against her father as Jules looked back at her on-screen father. "Tell me the story, Dad."

Then he was still again, his gaze pinned on her father and some unheard conversation he was apparently having with his own father. Then just as quickly, he started screaming for her again. He fought against the men as her father activated the comm.

"Huey, I need Mimi's help in medlab. Get Abby, too. Jules is screaming for her. We need to find a way to calm him."

Huey's reply wasn't heard, but within moments, Abigail saw herself on screen, taking hesitant steps toward Jules' bed.

She turned away from the scene. It was still fresh in her mind, and his screams would never leave her. Her father followed her into the corridor.

"Just hearing that much . . . How could he withstand such a life?" She paused. His real name was Seth.

Her father opened his arms, and she fell into his embrace, quietly crying for all the pain Jules had endured and was now enduring. Her heart hurt at all the agony and emotional pain that poured from the man she loved. Her soul hurt from all the death that had happened at his hands. She cried even harder as a silent plea to God to heal him, to save him, left her.

$$\Sigma$$

Jules parted the vision before him. If he reached out, he could brush memory after memory aside as if he were searching on his datapad. Abigail stood there at the bottom of the ramp; her gaze was frightened but determined. The blue of her eyes so deep, he felt he would fall into them. She jerked her head to him.

He swiped the memory away. She stood there at the window, the orca playing outside. Again, her eyes gazed at him, so trusting, so soft. He swiped that memory.

The last girl in his squad—big, round eyes with a brown that reminded him of his mother's pudding. She was screaming as they carried her away. Never did he see her again. He grabbed that memory, crushed it in his hands, and threw it aside.

Children looking at him in terror, with horror. His rifle lowered, and he waved his men down. So many eyes—black, brown, blue, and green like his. One girl, tears coursing down her face, looked up at him. Blue, like the glacier ice, begged him.

Jules crumpled that memory and hurled it away from him.

Swipe after swipe. He was looking for a particular one.

There. He remembered her face now. Green eyes that rivaled his own. Her smile was soft on full lips. She spoke something to the man next to her. He laughed and then turned around to Jules. Laughter crinkled at the edges of his eyes, but his face was blurred.

"Seth!" He whooped and reached for Jules. But it wasn't Jules who was lifted into the air, yet he was seeing them below him as though he was floating above them.

A flash caught his eye, and he looked up. In the mirror, a dark-haired boy with startlingly green eyes looked back, laughing as his father twirled him in the air. Then it was he, the adult version, reaching out from the mirror's image.

Light shattered. Pieces fell apart, and Jules fell with them. He landed heavily on a crowded sidewalk. He watched as a youthful hand in front of him opened the door to the barracks and pushed in. Feet that weren't his, yet seemed familiar, pulled him into the barren space dotted with bunks.

"Stephen! They're here." The voice sounded young and had an accent. "What are you doing?"

Smoke swirled, surrounding him, until he found himself sitting on the bunk beside Stephen, reading the small, green book. Two ten-year old boys, sharing a secret.

"I like Paul. He was Saul of Tarsus, and he killed them. But it didn't matter that he killed the Christians; Christ had plans for him. He fell before the Lord and accepted Him. Then became the best Christian teacher. His letters are my favorite. No sin shall be unforgiven if we call upon Christ."

It was his voice, yet he didn't remember having such a heavy accent. But then, the scene changed. He stood before Stephen, his sword poised inches from the bare neck of his friend, his brother-in-Christ. Stephen looked at him. "You are Saul, Jules. I am Stephen. I see Heaven. It awaits me. It's okay. The day will come when you will be Paul."

A booted foot kicked at Stephen, knocking him over. Then they lifted him back into position. The sound of guns made ready echoed in his head.

The world swirled, and he found himself standing in a void of white light. Blood stained his hands, his clothes, and the sword he held at his side. He reached up and touched his face. It was sticky. He held his weapon up and looked at his reflection on its blade. Blood covered him. He could taste it.

Jules clutched at his chest as his heart hammered against his ribcage. He had killed Stephen. Take him away from this. Let him forget.

"It's time for you to awaken."

Jules looked around him. No one stood near. He glanced at his hands. The blood was gone. All around him was nothing but a formless light, cool and soothing.

"It's time for you to awaken."

"Who are you?" Jules spun around, but there was no direction from which the voice came.

"It's time for you to awaken. Time for you to remember."

The light receded, and Jules fell. He screamed and clutched at darkness. There was nothing to stop his fall. He imagined himself climbing a ladder and found himself stuck in nothingness. Above him was the light. Slowly, he rose to it, pulling himself through the dark, sticky void. Weakness threatened to pull him back under, but he heard a voice. Then voices he knew.

Bit by bit, he pulled himself along. Bit by bit, the light grew brighter.

Jules blinked. Soft light caressed his eyes, allowing him to look around the room. He was in medlab. He tried to move, but metal bit into his skin. His gaze fell on the restraints that held him down.

He let his head fall back onto the thin cushion under his head. A pounding headache thumped behind his eyes. His eyes blurred as he let them travel the panels above him while he catalogued his memories.

His name was Seth. Seth Marcou.

His father was killed, and his mother tortured, then executed. He was made to watch. It was the day before his birthday. He was to turn six.

Stephen was his friend. The only boy there his own age.

He had to kill Stephen to protect his squad. All seventy-seven of them.

He chose to bury the memory of that day when the blood wasn't allowed to be washed off of him. Punishment for hesitating.

Every mission filtered through his mind. Every death at his hands, those who deserved it and the multitude who didn't.

The day the mortar hit him. The day JJ walked away.

The day Abigail stood at the end of the ramp.

His father, Donovan, speaking and telling him: *In the beginning was the Word, and the Word was with God, and the Word was God.*

"You're awake." Mimi's voice brought him out of his memories. She reached down and unfastened the restraints. "The serum has completed its mending."

He sat up, fighting the nausea, and hung his numb legs over the side. His voice cracked as he spoke. "Is this a dream?"

"No, my dear boy." She reached up and removed a band from his head, and the headache eased somewhat. "It shows you bouncing between beta and alpha waves. You are awake."

*It's time for you to awaken.*

The voice played around in his memory. "Mimi, I'm awake. Fully awake." He looked into her old and wizened eyes. "I remember. Remember it all."

"We know. You screamed a lot of it out. Spoke at times." She reached for him and held his hands. "Tell me, who spoke to you? You kept asking who was there."

Jules glanced around. Against the wall behind him, Abigail lay asleep on a cot, curled onto her side, and wrapped in a dark blanket. Her soft breathing stirred wisps of hair that fell across her face.

"She has been here for days. I finally gave up trying to convince her to go to her quarters. So, her father brought a cot in here for her. She didn't want to leave your side. Trisha convinced Joshua to return to their quarters. Huey left just moments ago to get a bite to eat."

"Days?"

"You've been thrashing and screaming for five days. The sedative stopped having an effect on you after the first day." She shuffled to the cooling unit on the counter and then brought him a cold drink.

The cold liquid, a medicinal protein tonic by the way it tasted, soothed his raw throat. If they had been monitoring him, then he didn't have to tell them everything. They already knew. Knew what he had done. "Mimi?"

Her soft eyes followed his movements as he drained the rest of the drink, waiting for him to speak.

"Stephen said I was to be a Paul. And the voice I heard, it said it was time to awaken." He let himself fall back onto the bed. Exhaustion pulled at him. "I know what it means. I must protect Christians instead of executing them. I must fight for them."

Mimi pulled a blanket up around him. "And you will, Jules. You are awake now. And things will change. It will be a long and hard road, but in the end, you will succeed." Her lips placed a soft kiss on his forehead. "Sleep now. Rest. Know that you are no longer alone in this world. And you are forgiven by us all."

Her words followed him into a dreamless sleep. He was forgiven by them all.

# Chapter Seventeen
# ASSASSIN NO MORE

Jules held the scanner in his hand, analyzing the readouts. He pointed to the west wall of the commons. "About eight feet that way, Michael. It's not registering as a fissure behind the hull, though."

The former Zulu assassin—no, Jedidiah said not to think of them as that—attached a thermal node to the wall. He shook his head after a moment and disconnected.

Michael and Peter didn't speak much. Since they had arrived back home and met Jules, even working with him at times, they said a total of twenty words between them. Some of that assassin training was still hard to overcome.

Jules reconfigured the scanner. "Let's try the east side." He looked at the thick mass of children in the middle of the commons area. "If we can survive the mini-horde."

That elicited a grin from Michael. As they approached the center of the room, the brown-headed friend of Evie's ran up to them.

"Can I work with you today, Jul?" His round, brown eyes implored them. He skipped alongside them as they navigated the maze of toys and little bodies. Sweat broke out along Jules' brow. Mimi had said he needed to face his memories in order to heal. But not that one. He ignored the piece of his past that was trying to capture his attention and forced it back down into the abyss.

"No. Not today, Danny. Aren't you scheduled for helping us tomorrow?" Jules glanced down at him before returning to the scanner in his hand.

"I am?" Danny stumbled to a stop. Then he raced forward to catch up with them. "What am I supposed to do?"

Jules arched an eyebrow at Michael. "What was it again?"

Michael paused and held his hand to his chin, giving a good impression of trying to remember. He held up a finger as though he remembered. "It was the daily checks. I do believe we were to take some young hopefuls on the outer bay checks."

Jules grinned and ruffled Danny's hair. "See?"

"I didn't know that." He thought for a bit and then nodded. "I can do that. So, who will I be with?"

Michael didn't hesitate. He pointed a finger at Jules and kept walking.

"With you, Jul?" His face lit into a broad grin. "Awesome! See you tomorrow!"

Then he was gone, rushing toward Evie and CeeCee, who signed her ever-constant *I love you*. Jules signed it back, causing a red blush to bloom across her face. He turned away and again pushed the memory that tried to resurface back down into the recesses of his mind.

He followed Michael up the short flight of stairs and to the center of the east wall. Out of Danny's earshot, Jules keyed open his comm. "Jedidiah?"

"Yes?" The man's voice crackled in his earpiece.

"Who's scheduled for the outer bay inspection tomorrow?" At Michael's chuckle, Jules aimed a kick at him, which the man dodged.

"We have Joshua and Devon."

"Replace them with me and Michael." The man glared at him before rolling his eyes. "I apparently had an apprentice latch onto me asking to help."

Jedidiah's chuckle was loud in his ear. "Ah ha. Young Danny. You walked through the commons, didn't you?" Tapping filtered through before Jedidiah replied again. "Okay, I have you and Michael scheduled, along with Danny. Have you discovered what the anomalies are?"

"Not yet. We are checking the east wall now. So far, nothing. We may have to take a submergible out to see if we can find it."

"I'll alert the bay. Keep me informed."

Jules ended the transmission. Michael had his thermal node against the wall, ready for Jules' scan. He ran it over the wall. And nothing.

He shook his head. When Michael dropped the thermal node down, a blip issued across his scanner. Jules frowned and aimed his scanner at the base of the wall. The blip barely registered.

Jules angled his hand down, tapping the air twice with his finger. Michael eased away and slid into the shadows. In seconds, a tap came across his earpiece. Jules moved to the ladder and climbed down, meeting Michael at the bottom. His thermal node was attached to the base of the wall, aiming down and across the complex. Jules removed the cover on the mag-lock, positioned the scanner next to the node, and activated the recording.

Together, they stepped back and waited. A blip ran across the scanner one way, then crossed back along its path. It moved slightly up, then back down, before settling into a holding pattern. It was a faint read.

Jules ended the recording. He keyed his comm. "Jedidiah, I'm sending a file to you. Have Abby run it through the GHOST."

"Signal?" Michael detached the node.

"Looks like it. Though it's erratic. Reminds me of the pattern of the service tunnels."

"Reminds me of a bit of flotsam." Michael stood. "Let me check out the lower levels."

Before Jules could reply, the man was already disappearing into the shadows of the lower levels. He gathered the scanner and retraced his steps to the commons. Miriam and JJ's wife were rounding the children, ready to take them back to their classes.

Abigail came across the comm. "Jules, it's a signal and not one of ours."

Michael's voice spoke into his ear. "Bogey inbound."

Jules snapped into action. He hurried forward and grabbed Trisha by her arm and pulled her aside. Confusion wrinkled her face, and her light brown eyes searched him. He didn't give her time to respond. "Get the children to the galley and stay there. Move."

She didn't stall. Her long legs ate up the space between them and the group. Her whispers to Miriam had the woman ushering the children up the flight of stairs. She glanced once at Jules as he hurried past them and bolted up the steps.

Then he left them behind. When he reached the upper storage units, JJ and five other former assassins flowed from the service tunnels.

Michael dropped down from the ledge above and landed next to Peter, who passed Michael's sword to him. "There was a submergible in desalination. Hidden under the lip and ice sheet. I caught the movement of someone as I entered the lower maintenance tunnel. Followed him to the upper level. Then he went back down one of the service tunnels, heading to cargo bay."

"One of ours?" Even though he asked, he knew it wouldn't be. JJ handed Jules his pulse gun.

"No. We all cast our old uniforms away."

"Squad?"

Michael looked at Jules. "Juliet."

Silence reigned for a second. Jules ran the scenarios through his head. Two outcomes would work in their favor. Only one would ensure success.

"Devon, James, west-side level. Dan, Jackson, you have this side. Michael, Peter, start with the tunnels. JJ, you and Mandy have topside. I'll take this level and below." Jules checked the plasma level on his gun.

JJ looked at him, his eyes hooded and dark. Waiting.

Jules turned from them and began his advance. "No mercy."

They fanned out. Jules keyed his comm. "Jedidiah, keep everyone in place. No one moves about. Stay off comms."

"We have it taken care of, Jules." His sigh echoed through the earpiece. "May God be with you."

Then all fell silent. Jules mulled that phrase over in his mind. Always that.

Ahead, an errant sound reached him. He slid into the darkened recesses of the hallway and waited. Two clicks sounded. Devon's voice barely whispered, "Bogey. West."

Jules grabbed the ladder next to him, placed his feet to the side of it, and slid down its length. He hit the grating and squatted, listening. Ahead. Ten meters. He slinked forward, keeping to the shadows. A click issued in his earpiece.

Devon again. "West, still. Level down."

A shadow detached itself. Michael and Peter. They moved as one. Peter angled his hand to his right. Michael broke off. Jules stayed still. Their prey was below, underneath him. Peter paused and pointed once at the walkway under Jules.

He moved to the rail and ducked as a plasma bolt shot past him. The heat singed the skin on his forehead. Jules grabbed the support beam next to him and swung over the side. He landed on the railing below him and launched forward, slamming his body into the man in the shadows. Michael and Peter had dropped down and were engaging two others.

A click sounded across his earpiece. Dan's voice was lost in the static, "Eastside of the complex."

The body under him bucked, but Jules wrapped his arm around his neck and yanked, stretching tendons and muscles. A gurgle flowed past the ever-closing throat. Jules yanked his pulse gun from the holster, jabbed it into the back of the man, and pulled the trigger.

The shortened beam of the gun shot from the chest. Then the body hit the deck with a thud.

"Clear." Jules spoke into his comm.

"Clear. Two down," Michael replied into his.

"Clear. Bogey down on three." Devon's voice filtered through.

Dan reported from his position. "We are at the desalination. The submergible has been destroyed. And I'm picking up a faint energy reading from the south."

"Regroup at the bay. JJ, prep three attack subs." Jules waved to Michael and Peter. "Let's go. I want to see what was sent."

$$\Sigma$$

Abigail zoomed in on the viewscreen. "I see what you are talking about. Looks like a Class-N sub. Can hold up to four people. I can't pick up the IF, though."

JJ responded. "We'll see if we can get closer. Michael, tighten your vector. Devon, close that gap. Let's triangulate our scans."

She plugged in the GHOST and keyed in their codes. "I'm using the GHOST to see if I can piggyback on your waves."

Jules' voice came through the comm. "Look under the code alpha-zero-seven-dash-five."

"What is that?"

"Juliet code."

She ran the clearance code through the filters. File after file flooded her screen. "Got it. I'm pulling everything onto a secured and isolated line. What are you going to do with the sub?"

On the screen, the sub imploded. The shockwave rolled through the water. A faint energy spike registered on their monitors.

She looked at her dad. "Well, I guess that answers that."

"We're heading in. We will dispose of the bodies, Jedidiah."

Her father leaned over her shoulder. "Already taken care of, son. Just you boys, get back. I'm starting the evacuation."

$$\Sigma$$

Jules stood near the bank of consoles as Abigail and Huey searched through possible places. Evacuation had already begun. He had spent the last two hours packing the library, helping JJ and John move two of the Xulons from his ship to the *Lonestar*, Jedidiah's ship. Then helping to assign quarters on John's old ship, the *Dawnbringer*.

Most all the areas had been cleared and only command rooms, such as comms and nav, remained active. Medlab would be the last to be packed away. Taniff would be assigned to the *Nightingale*. And Mimi would be with John. In a way, he had wished Mimi would be with him, yet she was part of the second wave to leave.

After Abigail's GHOST filtered through the sub's files, they found the hidden signal within their base. And it was his fault. No. It was Anya's. She had a GFT Medlab signal buried in the *Nightingale's* memory banks. It had remained silent until their trip to Mars. Then the signal had activated, though the ice had prevented the signal from going through and giving their exact coordinates. Until the last storm. There was just enough of a fissure above his ship for the signal.

Anya. Revulsion still ate at him at the thought of her name. She was gone, now, though. Somewhere deep within GFT's rogue faction. Too many quantum layers protected her from the GHOST, and the elders had scrubbed their request at finding her.

Abigail moved in her chair, breaking through his thoughts, as she leaned across Huey's console and tapped his screen. "Try now."

Huey tapped the keys in front of him. "Yup. We are ready to go." He turned to Jules. "Where do we search?"

Jules leaned forward and entered the parameters. "Try these two." His old underwater bases. Most were destroyed. Some were in the radioactive zone. There were still a few that were only abandoned.

As they scanned through the records, Jules leaned over Abigail's shoulder and tapped the screen. "This one here, Huey. The Alaskan base was an unsanctioned Juliet base. Only local squad used it. And JJ and I are the only survivors of that squad."

Huey highlighted the area and opened the file. "Cap, you sure Anya doesn't know about this place?"

"Positive." Jules leaned down and tapped in a code, one of his private GFT ones—one that even JJ didn't know about. "Use this one."

Abigail frowned and turned to him. "Is that one of your personal codes?"

He nodded as programming codes streamed across the screen before the GHOST filtered the language. Abigail turned back around and leaned forward. Her long locks fell past her shoulder and brushed the console.

With an absentminded flip, she sent it back over her shoulder to lie with the rest of her hair that flowed down her back. She shifted to the side. Hair fell again around her shoulder.

When she threw it back, most of the hair escaped her hand; yet she was too engrossed with the information on the screen to bother with it.

Jules collected her hair in his hands and brought the heavy locks back around. He pushed the thought of doing this once before from his mind. His fingers brushed against the nape of her neck. "There are only about three entrances. The last time we were there, I blasted the back entrance. The north entrance is damaged, and water flooded the lower levels. West entrance should still be standing."

Abigail straightened and looked over her shoulder at him. "Are you sure this wasn't ever on the books?"

Jules nodded. The blues of her irises deepened. Her heartbeat jumped up a notch. He stood too close to her—again. "Positive. We used it sparingly and only as a layover. GFT didn't care where we bunked as long as we stayed under the scopes and completed the mission."

She turned back around to the console, pulling her jacket tighter around her. "Then, Huey, let's see if we can access any of the mainframes there." Again, her heavy locks fell around her shoulders, yet she continued typing, isolating commands, and issuing new lines of code.

She and Huey may never be soldiers, but give them their computers and a console, and they would work for days. All he saw was gibberish. Numbers. Letters. Odd phrases and symbols. They saw a language and information to gather or manipulate. Her hand knocked aside a few curls that strayed onto the console.

Jules reached over her shoulder again and once more collected her hair. He pulled it around, running his fingers through the soft tresses. Silken strands caressed his fingertips; curls captured him, and he threaded the unruly hair through his fingers.

He parted the deep red strands, creating two thick sections, and twisted them. The two pieces laid against her back as he reached around her and pulled her hairpin from her jacket pocket. She barely glanced at him. And a soft smile flitted across her lips when her gaze fell on the hairpin.

Then she was back at the console, typing and whispering to Huey. Jules barely registered her words. "Use that one . . . there's an errant command there . . . "

He collected the two strands, gave it one twist like he had seen her do before, and clipped the hairpin in place. Loose, shorter strands curled around the clip and brushed against his scarred hands. The vibrant red of her hair complimented the red scars on his hand and contrasted with the paler unmarked skin.

Jules let his fingers run through the length of her hair that hung below the clip. A sudden pain clutched at his heart. And the urge to cradle her head against him, to hold her to him, to wrap his arms around her and never let her leave him almost undid him.

Shock rippled through him as he found his hand inches from the side of her head, ready to cup it and pull her close.

The pain clenched his heart even more, and his breath hitched. This was too new, too much. He couldn't allow a repeat of what had happened before. For her sake. Yet this was different than that desire he had felt. This was too overwhelming.

Jules took a step back. His heart raced. His chest felt as though he couldn't get enough air sucked into his lungs. He took another step back from Abigail and Huey. They still talked in undertones, not paying him any attention.

He needed to get to medlab. He couldn't operate with these . . . feelings hampering him. They couldn't be allowed to take over. His gaze flowed down her form. Every inch of her called to him. To take her into his arms and hold her, kiss her. Keep her safe. Something he said he would do, but even she knew that he couldn't promise that. Life was too uncertain.

But he needed to do it. To keep her safe. Never let GFT or the squads find her.

Jules stepped forward. There was one way to control this. He eased his hand into her left pocket. The weakened program never left her jacket. Never. He pulled out the metal case, opened it, and slipped the data disk into his own pocket before depositing the case back into her pocket.

She must have felt his movements but not known what he had committed. Abigail gave him a sidelong glance. "Jules? Are you okay?"

He nodded and backed away, the feeling to embrace her growing ever stronger. "I will be back."

Abigail straightened from the console. Worry creased her forehead. "What's wrong?"

Jules shook his head. "Nothing of consequence. Finish here with Huey. I'll be back soon." He ignored her and now Huey's questioning gaze, turned to the door, and slipped through the opening. Huey was reaching for the comm as Jules passed the window and into the service tunnel leading to medlab.

He hurried through the tunnel and then stepped out onto an abandoned platform. Medlab One stood empty. Medlab Three had Medtech Taniff with—Jules craned his neck and peered through the half-shaded window. Looked like Davis in there. The window between the two medlabs had the privacy screen down. Medlab Two was dark.

Jules silently stepped to Medlab Two and pulled Abigail's weakened program from his pocket. He slid it into the slot and waited. After several seconds, the door slid open. He entered a new code for the panel and then pulled it from the lock. After he found the medicine, he would change the code back to the original.

The door slid closed behind him.

"Lights one-quarter." Overhead, the soft illumination lit the room in a bath of blue light. Jules scanned the area. Mimi would have the Paxolin with the other potent drugs.

He padded to the back of the room. A small container stood on the counter. Substance Eighty-six, Paxolin, and Versikton. The most used substances in the serum and the only components that weaned the assassins off the serum . . . except him.

Jules opened the container and picked up one vial after another. He needed only the Paxolin. It would isolate the emotions. It would bury them again. With it, he could once again become detached from this torrent of emotions that plagued him.

There. A half vial. Mimi would notice if he used a full vial. Jules selected it and closed the container. Instruments rattled as he pulled open the drawer. He glanced through the window. Still clear.

He didn't need an injection gun, but that was the only thing available. The hypo-injectors weren't there. He opened the next drawer. Not there either. Drawer after drawer, case after case . . . no hypo. Jules glanced back at the gun. It would have to do, and he would have to aim it closer to his heart than he would like.

He picked up a syringe, pulled out twenty cc's, and then inserted it into a new vial. It clicked into the injection gun. Jules' heart raced.

His hands shook. But he couldn't stop now. The clear liquid of the Paxolin called up to him. It would erase the tidal waves of emotions that threatened to consume him. What he felt before, that was tolerable. It was distant, dim. Like the early morning sun on a distant horizon. But this . . .

Jules shook his head. This was a lightning storm, flooding his senses, distracting him from what he needed to do, driving him to something he didn't want—no. It was driving him to something he feared. And that was not acceptable.

He slipped off his jacket and pulled his thick shirt over his head. With a finger, he traced his scars until he found an area that was clear. To his left, an inch from his sternum, between his second and third rib.

Jules blew out two breaths and positioned the gun over the spot just as loud bangs issued from the door. He looked up. Mimi, Jed, Abigail, Huey, and JJ stood at the door. Abigail and Huey ducked around them. No doubt using the GHOST on the door.

They wouldn't stop him. Not this time. This time, he would have the emotions buried once again. He wouldn't feel so many urges, desires, wants, and fears.

He pulled the trigger. The door whooshed open.

Scorching heat flooded into his body. A scream tore through him, and he crumpled. His body thrashed about, slamming into the cold floor. His jaw clenched, and blood filled his mouth. Then blackness came.

Distant sensations of hands grabbing at his body swept him along his black void. Sharp stabs into his abdomen barely registered.

Soft light approached him, washing over his body until his eyes flickered open.

An irate Abigail, an incensed Mimi, and a furious Jedidiah surrounded him. Jules swallowed, fighting back a severe wave of nausea as JJ herded them out of the medlab.

As Jules lay on the medbed, his senses reeling from the overdose of Paxolin and apparently a double dose of his serum to counteract it, JJ's voice filtered in and out.

" . . . I know what he is feeling right now . . . . Leave him to me . . . Evelyn, trust me."

There was a long period of silence before someone spoke again. And even his enhanced hearing couldn't pick up on the words that were whispered. Then JJ was back in the room.

Anger colored his dark skin. Eyes narrowed. He shook his head. "Get up. Get yourself to the library."

Then he was gone. Leaving him.

Jules lay there for long moments. Humiliation was new. And according to the psychology books he read, that was what he was feeling now. He preferred the threat of death and the burying of his memories and feelings to facing the unknown of what was happening.

He was trained to kill. To fight. To show no weakness. But was it weakness? JJ allowed himself to feel love and to care for Trisha. And his brother was not weak. And didn't he sign *I love you* to CeeCee? He cared about the little girl. Was that really love?

He was willing to die to save her. That line from the Bible filtered into his mind: *"Greater love hath no man than this, that a man lay down his life for his friends."*

Jules rubbed his hands over his face, swung his feet around, and sat up. Time to face the repercussions of what he had done.

The corridor was relatively quiet when he stepped out. Medlab hissed closed behind him. Two decks below, he heard soft voices discussing the manifest for Jedidiah's ship. To his left, in the service tunnel, footsteps faded away as they moved toward the commons area. Otherwise, only the dripping of melting ice met his ears. He moved silently down the grated walkway.

JJ stood at the window, waiting for him, when he entered the library. His brother had his arms crossed over his chest and his feet spaced apart. Jules stood next to him, looking out at the dark waters beyond.

"It was stupid."

JJ huffed. "You think?"

"How do you handle them?" Jules stuffed his hands in his back pockets. "That overwhelming urge. The fear that something will happen. The—"

"It's called life, Jules." JJ turned and faced him. The anger was gone. In its place was an emotion he had never seen on JJ's face. Compassion. "Remember when they took you away?"

"I do now." He didn't want to revisit those memories. They weren't gone, weren't buried, yet he kept them locked away.

"You were . . . conditioned to feel nothing. And now, all that which you would have felt, it hit you all at once. And it is natural for us. It's a part of our healing, of our casting off our old lives."

To hear JJ say that was more than he could fathom. So, all of them, from Sierra to Zulu, had undergone the same? "You don't fear for Trisha?"

"I do." JJ returned to his vigil of the ocean. "Every day. But I know that I don't need to fear. I can't fear. The Bible commands me to not fear. And if I feel that fear, then I go to God with it."

Jules shook his head. He had read all those passages. A total of 365. It was a part of John's weekly study. Every once in a while, he sat in on it, trying to understand.

"Jules, you can't hide from what you feel. I know you love her."

"Is it really love? I say that to CeeCee, but I don't feel the same way toward CeeCee." Jules leaned against the wall, craning his neck to peer up at the faraway surface of ice.

"There are varying degrees of love." JJ turned back to him. "Do you love Mimi?"

"I would die for her."

"What about Jedidiah?"

"I would die for him, too."

"You love them. What about me?" He lifted his chin and gazed down at Jules.

"You're my brother. I would die, even kill, for you."

JJ laughed and slapped his shoulder. "No killing for me, Moody Monkey. But you get my angle. You love each of us, all in different ways. What you feel for Abigail—it is the same that I feel for Trish."

The thought of JJ and Trisha sent a warmness through him. He was happy for his brother. To have someone by his side. And the way Trisha looked at JJ, touched him . . . . Jules' mind fell back to that day in the storage unit. Then further back to when he kissed Abigail in the tunnel. Even further back to when she kissed him in the lounge on the *Nightingale*. It didn't begin like that.

It seemed to grow, to mature into something deeper. And what he felt in the comms room, it was his need to protect her, to keep her safe, because . . .

"I love her." He whispered the words.

JJ smiled. "It makes a right mess of things, doesn't it?"

Jules could only nod at the understatement.

$$\Sigma$$

Jules handed Abigail the datapad back. "I'll see them off while you help Huey. Is this the last ship?"

She glanced up at him for a moment, her irritation still apparent. "Yeah. After this, we can begin transferring the last of the command codes."

She turned and began to walk away, but Jules caught her by the elbow and pulled her into the shadowed recesses of the walkway. For the last three hours, he had been trying to calm her down, explain to her why he did it, but she refused to listen.

Jedidiah's comment when he had spoken to him about it all was, "She's a spitfire. Takes a while to put out her flame."

At first, he didn't understand it. Then John had explained, when Jules sought him out, that redheads were stereotyped as hotheads or possessing red-hot tempers. Apparently, Abigail was no exception to that.

Her blue eyes glared at him, shooting lasers. If they could have harmed, he doubted even his enhanced healing would have kept him alive.

"You talk about forgiveness. Can I not have that from you?"

Her eyes narrowed even more. Her lips thinned. He ran a thumb over them, willing her to at least smile at him.

"If you don't move your thumb, you will lose it."

He drew in a breath and straightened. It was a losing battle with this woman. He waved her away. "Go. Do what needs doing. I'll catch up with you and your father in a bit."

She whirled around and stomped off. Jules scratched at his head. JJ's chuckle from the level below reached him. His brother was enjoying seeing Jules' misery. He looked up in surprise when Abigail returned to him.

"I am not ready to completely forgive you." She grabbed his shirt, yanked him down to her level, and placed a small kiss on his lips. It was only a few seconds. A gentle pressure against his mouth, and then she broke away. "We'll talk later about all this."

Then she was gone again, and JJ was climbing the ladder nearby.

"You will learn, Brother, that women are not these delicate creatures they make themselves out to be. They have razors and barbs underneath that silk."

Jules shook his head. "I don't have time for this."

JJ laughed. "Are you going to pretend to be so moody?"

"I'm not being moody. I'm being realistic."

JJ thumped his shoulder as he walked toward the upper-level stairs. "Might as well do as I did." He gave Jules a wink before taking the steps three at a time.

As he did? Jules glared at the empty air. He was not going to visit that option.

He turned to the ladder and descended to the bottom bay area. He had work to do. But he wanted to see John off first. It would be days before he would see his friend again.

The grating clanged as he landed on it. In the center of the bay stood John's ship and Jules' own. The last two transports. Around the ramp, men and women loaded the crates. This one would transport the children to safety. The children and their mothers, the expectant mothers, Mimi . . .

That one memory that wouldn't leave, wouldn't stay locked away, grabbed at him. And it took only one look at a child. Like little Evie. Or CeeCee. The two girls darted in and out around the adults. Their peals of laughter echoing in the cold air. The innocence of being alive, being a child.

Jules fell onto the step and leaned back against the rail, his breath heaving within him. The memory of killing Stephen was horrific, but he had learned to accept it—learned to live with it. Stephen had forgiven him, knowing his death was saving seventy-eight other lives, Jules' own included. Yet he was haunted by the many-colored eyes in a sea of small faces.

He grabbed at his head and through his fingers watched the families down below him. Evie turned from the group loading crates and supplies onto one of the last ships. The girl smiled, motioned at someone passing her family, and ran to where Jules sat.

Evie, her black hair held back with a ribbon, approached him, and squeezed herself past his arms, which were propped on his knees, holding his head as if it might fall off. Her small, soft, dark hands pulled at his as she squirmed onto his lap.

"Jul? Why are you sad? Because we are leaving?"

He lifted his head, aware of a tear that escaped his eye. "Of course, little Evie. I'm going to miss your bright smile. Miss you telling me it will be okay."

She wrapped her arms around his neck. "It will be okay, Jul." Her voice was just a whisper as she spoke in his ear. "I heard Daddy talking one night when I was supposed to be asleep."

His breath stilled. Please, don't let it be that memory they talked about. "What did you hear?"

"You killed many of us. I told Danny and CeeCee." At the mention of their names, her two friends approached. CeeCee climbed onto his other knee and placed her hand on his chest. She always loved to feel the rumble as he talked. And Danny—the bravest of all little boys in the compound—sat beside him, wrapping his arms around Jules. "We know you didn't know better."

Danny nodded. He was so solemn as he spoke. "Jesus cried out to God and said to forgive them because they know not what they do." His eight-year-old eyes, wiser than they should have been, yet much more innocent than Jules was ever allowed to be, gazed up at him.

CeeCee signed to him, slowly so he could catch the words. "We forgive you, Jul. You protect us." CeeCee replaced her hand on his chest and leaned her head against his shoulder.

That was his undoing. Tears coursed down his face. The last of his defenses fell at the innocent love they were showing him. He put his arms around them all and pulled them tighter against him, kissing each of their heads in turn.

Evie wiped the tears away from his face, her fingers cool against the hot paths the tears had made. "Elder Jed said forgiveness is not earned. It's given."

He placed a kiss on Evie's head again. The silky tight curls tickled his lips when he spoke, his mouth still pressed against her. "You are wise beyond your years, Evie. Please don't grow up too fast. Promise me you'll stay a child as long as you can."

Miriam looked up, and her face softened at the sight of the children in his embrace. She waved at him, and he nodded. He looked at each child, signing in his broken way so CeeCee would understand, even though she was proficient at reading lips. "Evie. CeeCee. I need you to be safe. Pray for me. Danny, I need you to protect them. Keep them safe for me."

Danny nodded, his face serious as he took in his new task. "I will." The boy wouldn't fail him.

"It's time to go." He scooted the girls off his lap and stood, Evie's and CeeCee's hands in his, and followed Danny as he led the way back to the ship. Jules stood in front of Miriam. He opened his mouth, but she cut him off with a grand hug.

She leaned back from him, her hands gripping the sides of his face. "Keep them safe, Julius. Please."

"I will."

John approached them. "Jules," he greeted. He ruffled Evie's hair. "Come along, Kids. Time to board."

CeeCee and Danny gave him one last hug around his waist and leg, then they rushed ahead up the ramp, their eyes glistening in the harsh overhead lights. Evie started to step away, but her little body plowed back into his, her arms squeezing his waist so hard, pain shot up his back.

He squatted to her level. "I'll see you again." He lifted her hand and kissed little fingers that smelled like citrus. Then he stood as she nodded and started to walk off, Miriam guiding her.

But Evie broke away and raced back to him again. "Jul!"

She reached to her neck and removed her necklace. The one with the round, glass pendant of swirling colors. It was her favorite, the one she had made with him. He didn't understand the need for stopping at the school then. But now . . .

She pressed it into his hands and then ran away, bravely holding back her cries.

Miriam pressed a hand to her mouth, nodded at Jules, and then followed her daughter.

John waited until Jules stood before he held his hand out. "Take care of yourself, Jules. I'll see you soon, my brother."

Jules clasped his hand, his nostrils flaring out, holding back a tidal wave of emotions. John slapped his shoulder; then he was gone, up the gangplank and into the bowels of the ship.

With the necklace firmly within his grasp, Jules crossed the bay and walked out of the hangar. Away from his friends. The walkway shuddered as the ship's engines kicked in. He climbed to the higher reaches of the bay and headed for the service tunnels. A chance to avoid people. A chance to give him time to compose his thoughts, to push his emotions back down.

A fist suddenly gripped his heart before he could make it to the tunnel, and Jules fell to his knees, his forehead on the metal grating, his tears falling through the openings and into the darkness below.

He didn't deserve any of this. *"None is righteous, no, not one."*

His chest heaved with a knotted pain. *"There is none that doeth good, no, not one."*

Evie's pendant clicked against the grate as his fingers wrapped around the metal, squeezing. He gave in to the emotions that boiled within.

*"Verily, I say unto you, Except ye be converted, and become as little children, ye shall not enter into the kingdom of heaven."*

Like a child being held in his father's arms, Jules wept. Giving everything within him to the Lord. With each tear was his prayer, his sorrow, his shame, his guilt. With each tear, a newformed peace replaced the void within him. With each breath, his soul was stitched back together.

## Chapter Eighteen

# ONCE MORE UNTO THE BREACH

Jules brought Abigail closer to him and nuzzled against the side of her neck. Strands of her hair caressed his face and tickled his chin. She pulled at his arms, bringing them tighter around her and leaned against his chest.

When he had sought out Jedidiah earlier, the man had taken one look at him. Saw the tear-stained trails on his face. Then he pulled Jules into an embrace. It should have made him uncomfortable. It should have embarrassed him. But it reminded him of the hugs his father had given him as a child. Then Jedidiah broke away and patted his cheek.

"The memories won't go away, Jedidiah," he had said. The man smiled and told him it would take time to allow Christ to heal him. And when the memories started to rise, turn to the cross.

Then Abigail came into the room. Jedidiah left them alone. And the tears that glistened in her eyes, the relief, the beautiful smile she gave him—it was worth it all. Knowing that if anything happened, she would never be gone to him.

Now he leaned against a dead console with her in his arms. They were about to begin their trek to the ship and leave for Alaska. But first, Jedidiah led them in prayer.

" . . . Amen." They raised their heads. Jedidiah smiled at their embrace and then turned to Younger Jake. "Let's grab the last codes."

As they worked, JJ opened a communication to the *Dawnbringer*. Trisha came online. As they spoke, JJ giving her their flight path, Jules whispered into Abigail's ear, "Tonight. I don't want to be away from you any longer."

She craned her neck and smiled over her shoulder at him. The smile grew from her mouth to her eyes. Her lips parted—

Everything went dark. Then the complex shuddered, almost throwing everyone to the floor.

Concussion bombs.

Jules pushed Abigail down next to the inner wall. "Stay there."

He and JJ approached the doorway and peered out into the corridor. More concussion bombs hit the complex, sending layers of ice that grew at the top to crash down.

"Jedidiah, are the consoles completely dead?"

A dull light lit the room. Abigail's handheld. He turned from his surveillance. Waiting.

"They're dead, Jules. But backup comms should be working."

Abigail angled her handheld toward Huey. "There?"

He nodded and turned to Jules. "I can set charges at the south end. A distraction that will pull them away and allow Jed to use the backup. If they are monitoring the signals, then they will find the charges. Only need to give us a small window. But I have to use the console on the fourth level. It's the only one hardlined to lower-level maintenance."

Jules nodded. "Then go." He grabbed Abigail's arm as she tried to leave, too. "No, not you."

"Jules, Huey will need me to use the GHOST. He can't do it all on his own in the time needed."

Indecision warred within him. He couldn't risk her. Not now. Not ever.

Jedidiah waved them on. "Go. Hurry up and take the south ladder up to cargo bay."

Jules glared at her father. She gave his arm a squeeze before disappearing into the dark with Huey.

JJ leaned toward him. "They will be okay, Jules. Come on."

Jules gave one last glance in Abigail and Huey's direction and then led point. His pulse gun tracked the walkways, gangways, stairs, and ladders as they made their slow approach to the far end communication room. He motioned JJ toward the room with his right hand.

As JJ herded the last of the elders and Taniff into the room, Jules peered over the railing. Another concussion bomb hit, shaking the complex. He backed into the comms and hit the control panel. The door hissed closed.

Jedidiah turned to him. "We got the security feeds up. Looks like they infiltrated from the top level. Making their way through the service tunnels."

Younger Jake tapped the console in front of him. "All the codes and records are purged, Jed—"

Another bomb hit. Jules and JJ grabbed each of the elders and slung them to the floor. Sparks flew from the consoles. Monitors exploded, flinging debris and shrapnel throughout the room. A couple of the elders grunted as metal and glass hit them. A wave pummeled into Jules' back.

Another bomb hit. More consoles erupted into flames.

"Get to the cargo bay!" JJ pulled at Jedidiah's collar, yanking him to his feet.

Jules pushed at Younger Jake and Taniff. When he and JJ turned, four of Juliet appeared outside the window, tracking their rifles over them as they climbed down from the railing.

As one, he and JJ raised their guns and fired. Holes peppered the fused glass; then they were diving through. Jules slammed into two of the assassins—7-L and 3-T from his second squad. Juliet 2-Z's men.

They flipped over the railing and landed heavily on the next level. They scrambled to their feet. Jules rammed his elbow into 3-T's face, slid his knife from his belt, and swiped across 7-L's throat. He completed his turn and drove the knife into the throat of the other, ripping it out. Gore splattered against him. Then he was standing over the two fallen assassins.

JJ kicked one of his dead Juliet out of the way. "Let's get them to the—"

A hiss issued from a comm unit on 7-L. Jules scooped it off the floor by the dead man. The staticky feed barely filtered through. "Approaching two targets. Fourth level catwalk."

Jules launched himself over the railing to the level below. He raced down the corridor, heading to the desalination area. He met an assassin coming out of the service tunnel, the one that led to the top level area where Abigail was. Jules jumped, used the wall as his launching point, and slammed down on the man.

His blade buried deep into the neck and shoulder. Then he was barreling down the tunnel before the body hit the deck.

$$\Sigma$$

Abigail activated the GHOST and handed Huey the handheld. "Do it quick. We don't have much time."

Huey nodded as he plugged it in, and his fingers flew across the console. "I'm activating the charges in sequence. That will give us plenty of time to make it to the *Nightingale*."

A deep rumble shook the walls around them. Small bits of ice fell from the deck above. She glanced up, spying the small cracks that ran the length of the gangway above them. The shock charges on the surface would destroy the complex before their own charges would.

Abigail raised on her tiptoes and peered over the rail at the chasm below. Two of the lower deck catwalks collapsed and fell into the dark sea below. Only two left before it became their deck.

She glanced back at Huey as another vibration shook the deck. "Did you do that?"

Huey shook his head. "No. The lower decks are losing their integrity. Hold on . . . " His fingers hit the last button, and he disconnected the handheld. "Come on. Time to run."

They turned; their only way across the catwalk was barred by a GFT assassin. His gun tracked them as they flattened against the wall. The console bit into Abigail's back as she slid closer to Huey, and she couldn't take her eyes off the muzzle of the pulse rifle. The man approached. He started to reach for his comm—

Abigail caught movement from above. A dark figure vaulted the railing three decks up.

Jules landed on the catwalk behind the man, his knees bent just enough to absorb the shock. His hand ripped the pulse rifle out of the assassin's grip before the man could react. It was Jules' roar of anger—primitive, violent, blood-congealing—that caused Huey to grab her shoulders and force her down to the metal floor as the assassin pulled a pulse gun from his holster and shot above their heads. His aim was destroyed by Jules as he grabbed it. Then it, too, went sailing into the air. The two assassins grappled with each other.

She had known that the serum would take him back to what they had designed him to be. But she wasn't prepared for what was happening. He was more than what she had previously witnessed.

Jules' tactical vest sported several burn marks, and his face was hidden behind blood and gore, but it was his gaze. Cold. Heartless. Ruthless. His eyes—half white, half vivid green—tracked every movement, and he countered with ease.

The catwalk vibrated and shuddered as elbows, fists, knees, feet, and hands landed with sickening thuds. Jules and the assassin flashed in almost superhuman speeds. A deep grunt issued from Jules, and he doubled over. But before the assassin could land a blow on his back, Jules grabbed the man's legs, rose, and pushed. The weight of the impact caused the catwalk to sway, and the railing connecting it to the deck cracked.

A small oath poured from Huey. He let go of Abigail, pulled himself to his knees, and turned to the console, his fingers flying across the surface once again, sweat beading along his brow. When Huey held out his hand, Abigail held up the connecting cord for the GHOST. She didn't care what he was doing, only that he was doing something to help.

She pressed back against the wall, only able to watch. And pray.

The two men rolled, each trying to kill the other. Jules' hand flashed out and batted the assassin's hand, and a knife flew into the opening. His knee rammed up, and the man was flipped over Jules' head, landing with a bone-crunching crash. Jules twisted around and leaped to his feet the same time the assassin did. And again, they collided into each other. Neither gaining the upper hand.

"Jules! It's on the way!" Huey yanked the connection free.

If the statement Huey shouted ever reached him, he didn't acknowledge it.

"I know this will sound crazy, but help me cut the bolts."

Abigail glanced at him as she wrapped the cord around the handheld and stuffed it inside her jacket. "You're bringing a hoverstand, aren't you?"

Huey nodded as he passed her a torch from his toolkit at his side. Together, they rushed the railing and started heating the cold, frost-covered metal. As they worked, the weight of the men's fight and the weakening support caused the catwalk to dip lower and lower.

The assassin suddenly noticed this. He shoved Jules, turned, and made to dive toward the closer end where they worked. Jules leaped and landed on him, pinning him to the grate. He looked up just as the last bolt fell away.

The catwalk crumpled, taking a slow, swinging arc to the other side. Metal groaned. The bolts from the other side issued high, popping sounds.

It was with agonizing slowness that the catwalk started to fall away from the deck. Jules kicked once at the assassin, and then, he was leaping into the air.

Abigail's heart lodged in her throat as his fingers barely grasped the hoverstand's platform on its descent. Below them, the catwalk and the assassin fell, then disappeared. She swallowed against the scene. The man never screamed. Never yelled. He just fell away in silence.

So inhuman.

Huey rushed back to the console and activated the navigation on the hoverstand. The motors strained as it inched its way toward them, yet it was dipping down a bit at a time.

Jules looked around him. Veins stood out along his hands and arms as he strained to hold on. "Give me three more feet!"

The machine started to sputter. And Jules was too far below him to grasp the railing or for them to grasp him.

He swung his feet, back then forward. On the second swing, he let go and flew through the air to the deck below them. His grunt of pain was the only indication that he had landed his mark.

She ran the length of her level to the service hatch at the far end. The metal grate pressed through her pants as she knelt and pushed at the covering. Huey joined her. Once the plating was removed, she hit the switch above her, and the emergency ladder descended to the next level. Jules' feet found purchase on the ladder the moment the deck below them disappeared.

He popped up onto their level, grimacing. "Let's go. Not much time."

Huey pointed to the opposite end. "The service tunnel is on that end."

Jules rose to his feet. Abigail raced alongside him, struggling to keep up. At times, he reached out, grabbed her arm, and yanked her forward, creating a kind of run-run-hop to her movements.

The groans of the collapsing base followed them as they raced their way to the end and into what seemed like an endless up, up, and up. Distant explosions sounded. Huey's charges were activating.

Jules leaped from the platform by the service tunnel and landed on the grating below with a thud. A massive shudder ripped through the complex, and chunks of ice fell from the dome above. He waved up to Abigail, who had run to the edge of the broken catwalk twenty feet above him.

"Jump!"

He held up his arms. She looked once and jumped off the swaying catwalk. Her body weight slammed into him, yet he set her on her feet and tugged at her as Huey dropped from the edge and landed heavily. Huey scrambled to his feet and followed them as they raced across the lower bay floor to the *Nightingale*.

"JJ!"

His friend stuck his head outside the airlock. "It's in preflight."

"Switch it. We can't make the air."

JJ grimaced. "The ship isn't in good condition for a long haul."

The ramp rattled as they bounded up it. Jules slapped the panel and moved out of the way as the outer hatch started closing. "At least until we reach the outer Hawaiians. Then we can breach and fly the rest of the way."

He hurried up the stairs, only to be pitched back onto the cargo bay floor as his ship tipped from a large projectile hitting the hull. He collided with Abigail, and they tumbled to the floor. "Huey!"

"I'm on it, Cap!" Huey fought the pitching of the ship as he raced up the stairs and across the gangway heading to the bridge.

"JJ, we will need to close all viewports. Keep the quarters opened. The ship won't withstand the pressure this time around." Abigail latched onto his vest and pulled herself up against him as he stood. His arm snaked around her and held her steady as the ship tilted again.

JJ pushed at Jules. "Go on, man. I got her. We will take care of the viewports."

Jules let go of Abigail. Another pitch and they fell against the metal grate of the stairs. He snarled and rose. Heavy hits thudded against his ship. From the sound of it, the ice shelf was breaking apart from the concussion bombs.

The railing bit painfully into his side as he was rolled once more, yet he made it to the corridor. Behind him, the grunts of JJ reached him. But he couldn't spare the glance.

Huey's voice sounded from the overhead comm as he raced up the short ladder from the main corridor. "Jules, we're going in."

His right boot just landed on the medlab corridor when he was sent sliding into the far wall. His head slammed against the stairs, and stars exploded behind his eyes. Jules, barely rising to his feet, clambered up the stairs and fell into the bridge. Huey strained at the controls, fighting the pull of inertia as the ship fell into the black waters beneath the ice.

Jules fought for balance and flipped the toggles above the control panels. Thick plating closed over the viewport, and a holographic display rose in its place. He fell into his chair and strapped in before keying his comm.

"JJ?"

"We have everyone strapped in. Have heavy casualties. They're secured in medlab and the quarters." His voice faded before coming back. "Abby said all doors are locked opened, and we are ready. All viewports are closed."

Jules nodded to Huey. "Take us as deep as we can go."

*Nightingale's* nose dipped, and the ship dove down and down into the darkness. Chunks of ice fell with them. Creaks and groans echoed throughout. A spark flew out from the console nearest him and hit Jules across the cheek. He slapped at the burn and activated the fire protocol. The sounds of hissing and spraying reached him, some as far away as the quarters. An alarm sounded. Lower storage was breached. He reached to his right and flipped two switches, increasing cabin pressure to push out the water.

Perspiration beaded along their brows as they fought against failing systems while the pressure built on the outside and tried to keep the ship on a steady course. Jules looked at his depth gauge. They were approaching the ten thousand mark. The *Nightingale* wouldn't be able to withstand any more pressure.

"Level her out, Huey."

Pressure built in his ears and pushed against his head. Huey reached forward and touched the holo-display. "There's a substation along this route. We will have to go around it to avoid detection."

Jules nodded and plotted a course. "I'm taking her through the deepest part. It will play havoc with many systems, and we will need to run as silent as possible. But here," he tapped the lower chain of islands, "this is still radioactive. We can breach about a thousand from shore, use the radioactivity as a shield, and slip into the lanes without being detected."

"That will work, Cap." A red light blinked on his console. "Looks like hydroponics became hydrated. I'll head down there and pump it out. And check the ballasts. She still has a bit of strength left in her, Cap. She'll get us there."

Jules gave him a slight smile. "I hope so. See to lower storage unit, too. I increased cabin pressure."

Huey rose, thumped Jules' shoulder with a fist, and disappeared out the bridge. The door closed and then opened again. Abigail stepped inside. She paused and keyed the door to stay open.

He finalized the course setting and activated autopilot before turning to her. A red gash marred her forehead, and her red hair tangled about her face. He turned his chair around to face her as she sat in Huey's chair, leaning toward him with a wet cloth.

"Let me get this off you." She dabbed at his face. "You must have dealt a lot of blows for this much blood to cover you."

Jules held still as she wiped at his cheek. Her blue eyes held back from him. She had questions. Concerns. "How is everyone?"

She folded the cloth in on itself and scrubbed at his jaw. "Dad is with many of them. JJ has some in medlab, and that's where Dad and Taniff are tending to them. I told JJ to meet me in the lounge. He has deep gashes along his back, and I need to remove the glass. Same for you. What happened?"

"We took out our squad." Her eyes met his. "Zeetoo wasn't there. JJ and I took them out through the window at the same time they tried to take us out."

"And glass went flying?"

Jules shook his head. "Not exactly. JJ and I went through the window and knocked them back to the lower level."

Abigail paused. Her hand stilled on his neck. "I still have difficulty separating what you are now and what you were. With having JJ again, it seems as though you are back to what you were."

"No." Jules grabbed her hand and brought them to his chest, stopping short when he noticed the dried gore attached to him. He let go and let them fall back to her knees. "I am not what I was. But I haven't lost the abilities I was given. I used them."

Abigail smiled and touched his cheek. "It's not that, Jules. I'm just amazed at how you do this without thought of your own safety."

That gave him pause. His safety? His life was forfeit. He existed to protect them. He opened his mouth to speak, but she rose to her feet. "You may not see your worth yet, but you will. I will have your dose ready in a bit, so meet me in the lounge so I can remove the glass from you."

At his frown, she reached over his shoulder. There was a slight burn along his shoulder blade, and when she straightened, she held a jagged triangle of glass. "This is the biggest piece."

She dropped it into his hand and left the bridge.

Jules stared at the thick glass in his hand. He had never felt the shards, and even now, there was no pain from them. He reached behind him. Sharp points pricked his fingertips.

Huey reentered the bridge. His face and hair were wet, and he sported a clean shirt and vest. A food container was balanced in one hand as he maneuvered into his chair. "I can take over, Cap. Go get cleaned and rest up."

Σ

Abigail leaned over JJ's back, scraping the rest of the glass from his skin. One long, deep gash ran from his left shoulder blade and traversed down his spine. She wiped at the blood pooling and then held the cloth against the worst of the wound, staunching the flow. The tub of water at her elbow was already dark with blood and gore she had washed from him. With her free hand, she waved toward the bandage tool.

"Hand me the bandage gun, please."

JJ plucked the tool from the tray and passed it over his shoulder. "You should say yes to him."

She squeezed the trigger and allowed the liquid bandage to flow along his gash. "How do you mean?"

"He hasn't asked? I thought I heard his whisper."

"No. He asked. And before I could reply, things happened. I'm beginning to understand this burning hate he has for them." She shook her head and used a cloth to wipe away the excess bandage from his skin. "I take that back. It may be an inconvenience to me, but it can never compare to what they did to him." She slapped his shoulder. "I'm finished. The bandage will dissolve as your wound heals." A puckered scar marred JJ's dark skin between his shoulders. "Was this your brand?"

He reached behind him and touched it. "Yes. One of the first things I had them do when I arrived was burn it off. I wanted nothing to do with my former life."

"Except for Jules."

He laughed as he pulled a clean shirt over his head. "Except for Jules." JJ turned on the stool and faced her as she cleaned up the workstation she had erected in front of the couch. Used and bloody gauze littered her tray along with shards of glass and burned metal. "When did you and he get together?"

"What?" She dumped the pieces into the trash bin at her feet before looking up at him. Even sitting on the stool, the man seemed overly large. A dark mountain with a ready smile and deep, piercing eyes that seemed to know more and see more than most. "Get together? As in . . . ?" Her words faltered as heat flooded her face.

JJ stopped her with a hand on her arm. "No. Look at me. I don't mean that, but now I'm curious."

Abigail sighed and sank down on the couch. "I really hate it when you two do that. Do you have to know so much about someone?"

JJ laughed again. "We were trained to observe. And I saw how he automatically turns to you, to protect you or to touch you. And you don't leave his side unless you must. There's more, such as the distance you two stand apart, the way you look. Shall I go on?"

Her voice was a whisper. "No." She reached forward and sealed the bag in the trash bin. It stuck for a bit as she exchanged it for an empty one—keeping her hands busy as she considered JJ's question.

"I don't mean to make you uncomfortable."

"Well, you did."

JJ snorted and propped his hands on his knees. "When I left GFT, abandoning Jules in that hospital knowing that the day of his decommission was coming, it was the hardest thing I ever did. Leaving GFT? Easy. Learning about Christ? Easy. Leaving my brother? Difficult. And every day I prayed. I prayed he would find me. I prayed he would find us. I prayed he would find love. I prayed he would find Christ."

Abigail picked up the box next to her and set it on the couch. The last of Jules' serum. One week's worth until they met up with Mimi and the others. She opened it and brought out the injection gun, prepping his dose.

"See, even now, as you are avoiding my question, you are thinking of him."

She swallowed and set the dose back into the case. How could she explain this to him? "I don't know how to answer that." Well, maybe she could. With a deep sigh, she looked into JJ's eyes. "I think the day he hurt me and when I saw the revulsion of what he had done, I saw him then. The true him. The one that wanted to be free."

"He hurt you?" A bit of anger coursed through JJ's words.

Abigail waved away his concern. "It was just a sprained wrist. He didn't know how badly he hurt my wrist, and I never told him. It was when he learned I was sending hijacked messages via my GHOST through his comms. He slammed me against the wall." She held up a hand to stop him. "No. Listen to me. He, at the time, admitted he didn't know how to feel sorry. He did pop the bones back into place for me. It was then that I saw his . . . longing? His desire? He may not have known it then, but I could see something at work within him. I think that was when I saw Jules for who he is and not what he was."

JJ leaned back. "Takes a special person to see that in someone when no others can."

Abigail nodded. "True. But he proved himself, over and over. And now . . . he's a child of God." She picked up the bag and rose from the couch. JJ picked up the used tub and followed her to the receptacle. "And as for the other . . . that's private, JJ."

She turned from the unit after dumping the bag. JJ poured the dirty water out. He stood before her, looking down, his eyes soft. He reached out and touched her cheek.

"Thank you for caring for him. He needs that. More than anyone realizes."

"I realize it." Her voice barely carried in the quiet lounge.

"I know you do." He stepped back as Jules entered through the opened door. JJ pulled his friend into a hug. "Let her clean you up, Brother. Enjoy the pampering!"

Jules only shook his head. "I'm sure you did." There was no bite to his voice, just a weariness.

The thought of how much he may have overheard ran through her mind. But she cast it aside. It didn't matter what he heard. If it bothered him, he would say.

JJ winked at Abigail before turning to Jules. "I'll bring you a fresh tub of water before I head to the bridge. What do you have it at? Fifteen?"

"Ten. She won't be able to handle more than that." Jules stuffed his hands into his back pockets, leaning his head back. Vertebrae popped as he stretched his neck to the side. "And we'll breach at the outer Hawaiians."

"Deviation of the *Samson*?"

At Jules' nod, JJ turned and left.

"Deviation of the *Samson*?" Abigail followed him to the Xulons. She pressed the Nutrient Three drink for him.

"One of the maneuvers we did on a mission a few years back. Had to run silent for about three days to escape detection. Our ship, the *Samson*, was barely running and short of supplies. We breached at an island chain well off our approved path. Saved our lives. Found out later an ambush lay in wait along our sanctioned course."

The machine beeped. She pulled his drink from it, handed it to him, and motioned him to the couch area. "Sit and let me tend to your wounds."

"Why here?" He sank onto the stool and sipped at his drink.

"Medlab is full. And right now, it has the worst of us. Dad has them in various bunks after he tends to them. I put Younger Jake in your bunk. He has a broken arm, leg, and shattered ribs. Dad has him sedated."

Jules nodded. "Use whatever is available."

"I told Dad you would say that. So, I took the liberty of saying the same thing."

He smiled at her. But the light didn't reach his eyes. She motioned to his vest.

"Take it off. Let's see to your back. And I need to sterilize an area for your dose."

He set his drink on the table before he unlatched his tactical vest and groaned as it dropped from his shoulders and onto the floor. Blood had soaked through his shirt and dried. She helped him pull it over his head and grimaced at the new wounds peppering his back.

"You can talk if you need to while I work." She picked up a stylus and started scraping at the glass. Shards fell into the small tray she held against his back and under the wounds.

"I don't have anything to say."

Of course, he didn't.

The *tink, tink* of the glass landing in the metal tray seemed overly loud in the room. "Well, at least talk for my benefit?"

Jules craned his neck to look over his shoulder. "You chitchat with JJ?"

Abigail snorted. "Of course. Although he did most of the talking. Did he talk a lot when you were with GFT?"

He shrugged, causing her to miss a piece buried in his shoulder. She grabbed him and held him still. "He was the most talkative. It was as if he couldn't stand the silence."

"Whereas, you enjoy it." She pointed to the spray in her kit. "Hand me the spray. I will need to numb the area before digging for the rest."

He passed her the spray and straightened back up. As the numbing agent soaked into his skin, she leaned forward and grabbed the wet towelettes from the pack. "Here. Start scrubbing at your face and hair. The blood is starting to smell."

As he scrubbed and rubbed at his short strands—at times so hard she was sure there would be bald spots—she dug for the last shard and eased it out as he picked up another towelette and started scrubbing at his hands, face, and neck. JJ entered the lounge and set the tub of fresh water and clean towels beside them on the table. He gave Jules a thump on his shoulder and then left.

Jules started to reach for one towelette, but she stopped him.

"I need you to be still for a moment." He paused as she squeezed out a cloth and washed at his back. A couple more dips and squeezes, the water becoming a deep rust color, and she was able to administer the bandage along his gash. His wasn't as deep as JJ's, yet he sported more shallow cuts and numerous bruises.

He reached forward and snagged a clean towel as she finished up with his bandage. She pulled the cloth from his hand. "Turn around."

His eyes followed her as she dipped it in the water and wiped away the rest of the blood and sweat. His hairline lightened as dried gunk was removed. She grabbed an antiseptic wipe and ran it over the cuts and burns along his cheek and jaw. One larger spot traveled from his collarbone to his ear. She cleaned it and brought him closer, letting the cloth travel around his neck, through his hair once again, and over the other side.

His hands landed on her hips, stopping her movements. She held her breath as his arms slid around her waist and pulled her closer. His head fell against her chest as he gripped her tighter. She dropped the cloth into the water and wrapped her arms around him, pulling him against her.

Clean strands tickled her nose as she held him. "Jules?"

His voice was muffled against her shirt. "This is new to me. The fear of losing you."

She pushed at him, and when he released her, she sat on the edge of the couch. "Everyone has that fear, Jules. We all fear losing someone. But we can't let fear rule us."

He moved from the stool and sat beside her, taking her hands once again. "That is written 365 times in the Bible. Variations of us to have no fear." He kept his eyes downcast as he rubbed his thumb across her knuckles. "And normally, I have no fear. No fear of death, of pain. Yet . . . this time, I feared for you."

When he looked up, confusion danced in his gaze. Abigail slipped her hand from his and cupped his cheek. "And that's normal, Jules. We are human. We fear. Even when we try not to. Yet it's our fear that drives us to trust the Lord. And that trust in Him is what drives our fear back so that we can do what needs to be done." She leaned forward. "It's okay to fear. But please remember, if any one of us dies today or tomorrow, you will see us again. That's the promise of being a child of God."

Jules brought his mouth to hers and kissed her. It was a small touch, just a quick slide over her lips, a slight pressure, and then he pulled away. "It's time for my dose."

Which meant his emotions were getting the best of him. She picked up the injection gun and searched his bare torso for a spot. "You are fast running out of places. I need a clean area, devoid of bruises and scars."

Jules leaned back against the arm of the couch and touched the spot left of his navel. "Right there under that scar. Mimi said it was the best spot to use."

She ran her finger over the tight muscles and through the soft layer of dark hair. The spot seemed clear of knots, allowing the serum a clear trajectory into his system. She wiped at his stomach with antiseptic, noticing the tightening of his muscles under the raised scar that slashed across his abdomen and side. She glanced up at him as she positioned the injection gun over the spot. His eyes darkened, and a fire lit behind them. She pulled the trigger, and he flinched as it jabbed into his body.

She sat away from him, removed the vial, and replaced the gun back into the case. He rose from his inclined position and reached for her. With quick movements, his mouth crushed against hers. Heat flowed through them, and she was almost lost in the moment until he let go.

His forehead pressed against hers. "Tonight. Before we reach Alaska."

Abigail smiled and patted his cheek. "Let's help Dad first." She pulled a clean undershirt from the case at her feet. "Put this on."

Jules smiled and slid the shirt over his head. "There isn't a lot involved, is there?"

Abigail ran her hand through his hair, eliciting another fire from his eyes. She caressed his cheek and then ran a finger over his bottom lip. "No. The Coalition doesn't have the luxury of ceremonies like we used to have. Dad can do it, and JJ and Huey can be there as witnesses."

Jules gripped her hand and placed a kiss on her palm. "Then let me finish helping Jedidiah." He rose and helped her to her feet. "You get this cleaned up."

He started for the door, but she stopped him. "Jules?"

He paused and turned toward her, waiting.

"Use the sonic and put on clean pants before you help my dad. You reek."

It was the first smile in days that spread across his face. One that not only split his face but also reached his eyes. "Yes, ma'am."

Σ

It was simple. After settling everyone in bunks, helping Jedidiah administer the meds, splint the broken bones, and apply medical gel to the worst of the burns and wounds on a few of them, Jules had approached him.

Jedidiah's hand landed heavily on his shoulder before patting his cheek for the second time that day. It was a gesture he remembered his own father doing. Warmth flooded Jules' chest. "I'm happy to do it for you two. Let me get the Bible. I'll meet you in the lounge."

He disappeared into his quarters, peeking in at Younger Jake. He was still asleep. Jules grabbed his duffel. Using the tight enclosure of his small office, he quickly changed into his black long sleeve shirt. Abigail's eyes had shone the first time she saw him wear it. And he would wear it for her tonight. Before leaving, he grabbed his Bible that Mimi had given him.

When Jules arrived in the lounge, Abigail stood near the covered viewport. Her hair had been pulled back and pinned at the nape of her neck. Someone must have loaned her a shirt. The white material hung loosely around her. A short tunic that swung below her hips. The pants were the same loose-fitting brown ones she wore back on Mars.

Her eyes brightened when she saw him and then heated as her gaze traveled along his torso where the black material clung to him, the V pattern of the neckline allowing for Evie's pendant to show.

JJ and Huey stood to the side. Jules stopped in front of Jedidiah and handed him his Bible. "I want it to be read from my Bible."

Jedidiah paused before he set his own Bible aside and accepted Jules'.

This was foreign to him. It would be the second foreign act. When they landed in Alaska, he would be baptized. But first, he was to be married.

"Face Abigail, Jules."

Abigail looked up at him as he stepped closer to her. Her bright blues gazed up to him as she slid her hands into his.

Jedidiah opened the Bible. "As it is written in Genesis, 'God formed man of the dust of the ground, and breathed into his nostrils the breath of life.' The Lord God placed man into the Garden of Eden. 'And the LORD God said, It is not good that the man should be alone; I will make him an help meet for him . . . And the LORD God caused a deep sleep to fall upon [man] . . . and he took one of his ribs . . . And the rib, which the LORD God had taken from man, made he a woman, and brought her unto the man. And Adam said, This is now bone of my bones, and flesh of my flesh. Therefore shall a man leave his father and mother, and shall cleave unto his wife: and they shall be one flesh.' Genesis two, eighteen through twenty-four." Jedidiah flipped toward the end of the Bible. "And as one flesh, Julius Williams, 'love your wife, even as Christ also loved the church, and gave Himself for it.' Abigail Maureen du Soleil, 'submit yourself unto your own husband, as unto the Lord.' Julius, love Abigail as you would yourself. Abigail, love Julius as you would yourself. As it is written in Ephesians five, twenty-two to thirty-three.

"Julius and Abigail Williams, treat your union as the holy bond it is." Heads bowed. "Holy Father, bless this marriage. In this world of uncertainty, we rely upon Your everlasting promise. May our lives be for Your glory. Amen."

Abigail started to stretch toward him, but Jules dipped his head down, cupped her face, and captured her lips in a soft kiss. Her arms wrapped around his waist, pulling him closer until their bodies touched. He broke away. Tears overflowed from her eyes, and he kissed each one away, erasing their trails with his thumbs.

Jedidiah, JJ, and Huey quietly left. The door hissed closed behind them.

Jules smiled down at her. "A simple ceremony."

"Means more without the pomp."

"*You* mean more." He sank down on the couch and pulled her nearer. Unlike last time, this felt right. She stood between his knees, looking down at him, her fingers tracing heated trails over his eyebrows and down the scar on his face.

His fingers fumbled with her hairpin. It tangled briefly before it clattered to the floor. Then her long hair cascaded around him in a red waterfall.

Jules brought her down onto his lap, encircling her soft body with his arms. *"Bone of his bones, flesh of his flesh."* No truer words spoken. His lips sought hers.

## Chapter Nineteen
# WHEN LEGENDS RISE

All day. All day sunlight. No darkness. Just dawn, day, and dusk. Jules propped against the overhead display as Huey and JJ flew the *Nightingale* to the coordinates. It had been so long since he had seen Alaska. Back then, he had thought nothing of the landscape. Now, watching as it whipped away underneath the ship, he could appreciate the beauty. In the distance, tall, snow-covered mountains loomed over a tree-filled expanse.

They would be at the midpoint of the coast soon. Over the centuries, the land had changed. Last night, he and Abigail had used her datapad and browsed through the history of the place. While she nestled against his chest, her hair fanned all around him, covering him like a blanket, they compared the changes that man, environment, and the ever-changing climate had made to it.

The console beeped. Huey glanced down at it. "We are here."

JJ leaned forward and pointed at the blackened and scarred building in the distance. "There. Wow. It's pretty derelict. What did you do to it?"

Jules shrugged. "Mini war." And no one ventured to asked more.

Huey flew her in low. The thrusters slowed them, and then the ship shuddered violently as it landed on the hardened ground near

John and Jedidiah's ships. A console behind him sparked once before it died.

JJ shut down the navigation board. Huey closed down the comm. He looked at Jules. "Does she have it ready?"

Jules nodded. "Has it plugged into the cargo bay console. As soon as we leave, she'll run it."

They turned from the bridge. Medlab was empty, dark. As they climbed down and passed by the quarters, Jules glanced into each one. Empty, dark. Barren.

All had been moved to cargo bay and stored in crates, ready to be moved into the base. Even hydroponics had been emptied during their travel from Antarctica to the Islands and then as they flew in a congested ship lane toward Alaska.

Jules paused at the top of the gangway and leaned against the railing. JJ gave him a small glance and continued down to the bay. The hatch had been lowered, and a steady stream of people came in, grabbed crates, and carried them away. Abigail passed off smaller bags and sacks to other women and some of the older teenagers. Micah and John brought in a load driver and collected the last Xulon unit.

Within fifteen minutes, his cargo bay was empty. Abigail stood at the console waiting.

Jules let his hand travel across the rail as he descended the stairs. "Are you ready?"

She nodded. One tap. That was all it took. And the *Nightingale* began dying. All memory purged. All storage erased. Systems clicked, and lights died. Her hand sought his in the darkened interior.

Jules pulled her closer to him, passed through the airlock, and hit the control panel before walking down the ramp. The two-second delay allowed them to pass from metal ramp to hardened earth. Then it groaned as it rose.

He stopped and looked back her. She sat quietly. Her final resting place.

"I know it was your home." Abigail wrapped her arms around his, pulling him closer.

He turned his gaze to her. She was beautiful. The daylight brought her freckles out in force, flowing across her brow, her cheeks. He rubbed a thumb across her bottom lip. "You are my home now."

Jules would have kissed her then, but a little blonde head bobbed toward them. CeeCee flung her body at him, and he caught her, lifting her high in the air. Her small hands clasped his face.

He brought her down and hugged her to him, kissing her cheek. When he sat her on her feet, he grabbed her hand and held it to his lips. "I love you, my beautiful angel."

Radiant. That was how she looked as she followed his lips with her fingers. Then she grabbed his hand and brought it to her lips. *My handsome hero.*

His heart swelled. CeeCee slipped her hands into theirs. With the little cherub between them, they strolled toward the drab, metal building that sat low on the ground. The musty smell enveloped them when they entered.

The massive commons area was a hubbub of activity. The others had been here for a week. And although progress had been made, there was still a lot to do. And he was needed in the command room.

Miriam waved at them and then signed for CeeCee to come with her. Abigail ruffled the girl's hair. CeeCee gave his leg a hug and ran back to her mother.

Abigail smiled at him. "I never thought she would become so attached to you."

He shrugged. "She's an angel. I think I'm more attached to her than she is to me."

"Really?" Abigail raised a brow at him as they followed the narrow hallway toward the back where command stood. "I thought you were attached to me."

He whipped his head around. "I am. That's not what—" Her small chuckle had him shaking his head. "A joke?"

"Someday, Jules, you will understand when we are teasing you." She slid her arm around his waist. "Go help them. I need to find Mimi and help her get things sorted."

He dipped down and captured her lips in a small kiss. "I'll find you later."

They held hands until the last possible moment. Then she was gone, swallowed up in the crowd of people.

By the time he arrived at the command center, Jedidiah had the base schematics pulled up on the holographic table that was situated in the center. "Jules."

"Did you already run the GHOST for the codes?"

"We did. Almost all the files are accessible, but some are corrupted. Looks like we will have to remove a lot of the software." Jedidiah swiped the projection to the side, and the feed showing the outside appeared. "We've been scanning the perimeter. Haven't searched it yet."

"I can lead that group, since I know what to look for." Jules entered one of his old codes. "These are the rooms that need cleaning. Mainly quarters. This is the shielding. We can use the GHOST to reboot it, and it will protect against scans. But it won't reach the outer barrier walls. The quarters are limited. Until we open up the flooded areas and start building more, we will have to double up on quarters. And here . . . " Jules ran his finger down the image. "This wall runs from the pier to the highest point on the hill and wraps around the base. There's a relay here at the pier and one at the top of the hill."

Jedidiah nodded. He motioned toward Elder Jake. "We can assign duties tomorrow. Give everyone a chance to rest."

Jules gazed at the schematics. It would be hard work. But his old base, the one that almost killed him at one time, would become his new home. He smiled at that. Home.

$$\Sigma$$

SEVEN WEEKS LATER . . .

Jules tamped the dirt down around the last of the plants. He stood and allowed Danny to pour the water onto it. Abigail rolled a wheelbarrow to them.

"Here are some more. Mimi said to use a mound for these."

"What are they?" Jules picked up one of the plants with a yellow bloom.

"Squash. JJ found a trader who had these and those tomatoes you just planted."

Danny sniffed the plant. "They smell funny."

Jules flicked dirt off his fingers and at the boy, who spat and sputtered as some landed on his mouth. "Everything smells funny to you. Even girls."

That started a dirt fight with the boy. They flung handfuls of dirt at each other, Danny trying to score a direct hit at Jules' mouth. And it would have continued if Abigail had not interrupted.

"Boys. Are you through?" She laughed and held out a plant. "Let's get them in the ground. I'm getting hungry and tired."

They dug, piled dirt, and inserted plants. Up one row and then down another. As they worked, he and Abigail spoke of their plans for the greenhouse. He had never thought he had any skills other than what he used to be under GFT, but he quickly learned that he had what Mimi and John called a "green thumb."

Soon, night came. Danny was collected by his parents. He left only after Jules promised him he would take him hunting tomorrow— he was wanting to learn to hunt elk.

Jules agreed only after Danny's father gave his permission. Then he and Abigail were left by themselves. And they talked even more. She spoke of her childhood and how she tried to grow an aloe vera plant but killed it because she watered it too much. He spoke of how he had once caught Stephen freeing a kitten that had been caught in the fence at the training compound. They spent their free time that afternoon petting the creature, feeding it, and then spiriting it away. They had sneaked out that evening and released the kitten near a group of houses.

He had always wondered if someone found it and took it in. Abigail said she was sure that happened. His memories of Stephen no longer hurt him. They would make his heart tighten into a knot, but it would fade the more he spoke of his friend.

Then they fell into silence. Another hour passed as they worked side by side, content with each other's presence.

He stood and arched his back, working out a kink, and gazed around what they had built. The greenhouse was a converted munitions storage building. He had directed the crew to remove the roof and use it to patch the main building. Then he worked with them to dismantle the fused panes from the *Nightingale* and install them as the roof of his greenhouse. The hydroponics equipment were now a part of this building. Giving them a year-round crop season. He slid his gaze to the far corner. John promised to finish the installation of the *Nightingale's* high-intensity lamps so that Mimi could grow her orchids and coffee.

His ship was slowly being cannibalized. One home used to make another.

He returned his gaze back to the glass dome. The Alaskan sky shone down upon him.

It was already past ten thirty. And the sky was its dusky hue. Never night. Never will be until another month.

"What are you thinking?" Abigail came up beside him, slipping her dirt-covered arms around his waist. Her head rested against his chest.

"Thinking that I like the sky. No more darkness." He dropped a kiss on her forehead and then grimaced at the taste of dirt and sweat. "How about we get cleaned up before we head to bed?"

"How about food before bed? I'm pretty starved. It's like I've been staying hungry lately."

Jules smiled and slipped his hand into her back pocket, keeping her pulled against his side, and they left the greenhouse and entered the main compound from the side entrance.

For the first two weeks, they had shared their place with JJ and Trisha. When some of the lower quarters were repaired, JJ and Trisha moved into one of the larger ones. That afforded Jules and Abigail longer times in the small refresher unit attached to their quarters.

The plan was to quickly get cleaned. But that didn't happen. As many other nights, the water had started turning cold before they climbed from the tub. Then they walked the silent hallway to the commons, collected a small platter of food from one of the Xulon machines, and hurried back to their room.

The food grew cold as other things grabbed their attention. Then they snacked on the cold meal as they watched the HoloNews. Jules rose to his elbow and gazed down at her as she lay on her stomach, swiping through the stories. He trailed his finger down her back.

"Did your father say anything about the communication they had this morning with GFT?"

She nodded. Strands of hair fell over her bare shoulder, exposing the collection of freckles. "They are willing to negotiate. With the new administration taking office, things have been progressing quickly. And they are considering allowing us to have this land. Isn't that wonderful?"

"It is. And knowing that the GFT Elite program has been scrubbed is good news, too." He bent his head and kissed a freckle. "They don't know I'm here, do they?"

She placed the datapad by the plate of food on the small table that stood by their bed and flipped around to face him. "No. We used the GHOST to show that you perished in Antarctica."

"Strange that I have to die in order to live." He captured her hand and kissed her fingers.

"Isn't that what we do when we come to Christ?"

He shook his head. "You sound like your father."

"Is that a bad thing?"

Jules smiled. "It is when I'm thinking of other things that don't and never will involve your father."

A long time passed before they settled down to sleep. Her breathing lulled him into a drowsy state as he lay there, with his arms wrapped around her, staring out the window at the never-dark sky. Eventually, he drifted into a deep sleep, void of dreams and nightmares.

It was the loud bang on their door that had Jules on his feet, pulling on pants and hopping to the entrance. The door slid open. JJ's face said all he needed to know.

Abigail had the cover up around her, her eyes widening as he hurriedly pulled on his shirt and boots. "What is it?"

JJ spoke from the door. "We got a GFT message. And Jules," he placed a hand on Jules' arm, "we have inbound."

"Go, Jules. I'll catch up."

He rushed after JJ, yanking his jacket on as he did. Jedidiah looked up as they entered. The elders surrounded the holographic table.

"There was a mole. Jules, they know you are here. And they don't want just you, but every former assassin who has found refuge with us. They are sending Juliet." Jedidiah pulled up the message on the screen. "GFT will be here if we call them. They are willing to negotiate with us, Jules, and they are willing to help protect us from the rogue faction."

Jules leaned against the table. His knuckles whitened as he gripped the edge. "You know I don't trust them."

"We know. But trust God in this, young man. We can use the GHOST. It must be done." Elder Jake spoke from the other side. "If you and the others can—"

The building shook as a concussion bomb hit. The windows rattled. Jedidiah switched to security. "Our main relay is out."

JJ growled. "What about the pier? Can we use that one to contact GFT?"

Wickham tapped the panel in front of him. "The pier is unharmed. It doesn't have the same strength as the hilltop. Chances are it didn't register on their scans. And it won't have the boost needed to send a message."

"It will with the GHOST." Jules looked at Jedidiah. "Get the rest to a safe place. I'll get Abigail to prep the GHOST to be able to send the message."

He and JJ turned from them. They stepped into the hallway, and Abigail plowed into him. He steadied her. Her datapad almost clattered to the floor, but he caught it before it hit.

"Get Huey. Your father will explain what is going on."

"Where are you going?" Fear dilated her eyes.

"I'll catch up, JJ." He led her to the small hall to the left. She leaned against the wall. "GFT said they will help us, but before we could get a message off, our relays were hit."

"I know. I felt it." Another barrage hit their complex. The power flickered.

"You know I have to do what I can to keep you safe. JJ and I are getting the others." He trailed his finger across her cheek. "It'll be okay. I'm no stranger to this."

A tear trailed down her cheek. He wouldn't tell her about Juliet. If she knew, she would try to stop him. She nodded. "Go. Do what has to be done."

The kiss lingered on his lips long after she left him. The library was the only room in the hallway. Jules slipped inside. There in the dark, he knelt. Juliet was on the way. Zeetoo was coming. This wouldn't be a quick fight. It wouldn't be an easy fight. Not this time.

He knew Juliet. They suffered too many losses at the Coalition's hands. Now they would be coming for everyone's death. Not just his or JJ's or the others. Everyone.

The faces of all those he knew flew through his mind. From Miriam and John, laughing. From Evie, Danny, and beautiful CeeCee. From Mimi and Jedidiah. Abigail's face lodged in his mind's eye. Her blue eyes, her red hair that felt like silk, her skin against him. His wife.

The first book of the Bible he read flowed through his memory. He pressed clasped hands against his forehead. "'O LORD God, remember me, I pray thee, and strengthen me, I pray thee, only this once, O God, that I may be at once avenged . . .'" He squeezed his eyes tighter, pouring his soul into the prayer. "Give me one last bit of strength, and if it's Your will, let it be that my sacrifice may save them."

He rose. "Be with her, Lord."

Then he kept to the shadows as he headed to the medlab. His eyes quickly adjusted to the darkened interior. Third cabinet. Second drawer. He grabbed five hypoinjectors and shoved them into his side pocket.

JJ was waiting for him when he arrived at the commons.

$$\Sigma$$

Abigail stood by her father with a heart heavy within her chest. The red lights flashed overhead. Too many alerts had filtered through their systems. The old and the young hunkered down in the middle of the complex, waiting, praying . . . staying safe.

She gripped the GHOST in her hand and swallowed as Jules approached. He clipped his vest closed and slung a pulse rifle over his head and across this chest.

"Jedidiah, we have only one shot at this. At my signal, open the gates at the far end near the pier." He looked at her then. A deep anguish flooded his eyes. He reached forward and touched her chin. "When your dad opens the gate, give the GHOST to Huey."

He had kept the knowledge that it was Juliet coming from her. Her heart had twisted when her father had told her. She nodded as a tear slipped down her cheek. "You'll stay safe? Yes?"

He looked at her for a long moment. With a quick glance at her father, he stepped back from her. A wall came down between them, closing off his expression, and the light in his eyes faded, replaced with a hardness.

Abigail forced the lump back down her throat. He reached for his holster on the table. She snatched it up and handed it out to him. His fingers met hers, and in that space of time, she saw his love and his resolve; then he was walking away, buckling it around his waist.

JJ met him at the door, holding two swords. He passed one to Jules, who slid it into the scabbard on his back. Two more guns were attached to his vest, and another rifle was passed to him.

She looked around. Mandy and Dan passed by her and her dad. Echo squad. From the shadows of the far side of the center complex Michael and Peter approached. Only the pale face of Michael and the olive skin of Peter appeared through the black clothing that covered them.

Swords—one on their backs, another at their sides—were the only weapons visible. Zulu squad.

Boots echoed in unison. Behind them, Sierra and the rest of Echo squad approached. She watched as they gathered around the only two Juliet assassins. No, not assassins. They stood in rigid formation. Not a word said. Not a movement made.

They were warriors. Soldiers of the cross. Protectors of God's people.

Jules held up a hand. He closed his fist, and heads bowed. Still no words. Each silent in their own prayers. Then he turned and strode through the door. JJ was next, silently followed by the rest.

The eerie sound of nothing but boots in the great hall sent shivers down her spine. She had already seen Jules in action, but this was different. This was a level she had never seen.

As the door slid shut, she whirled and ran back to the comms room. Her father followed.

"Abby?"

"I'm not going to sit by and do nothing. They have comms on, right?"

"Yes." He followed her.

"Then I will monitor the feeds and comms." She met Huey halfway, and he spun on his heel and caught up to them. "They can't catch everything while out there, and I'm going to make sure that nothing gets past them." She sat at the line of monitors and booted the system. One flicker after another rode a wave around her as she activated all the feeds. "Hold on, Huey. I need one thing from this."

She inserted a small data disk into her handheld and copied part of the GHOST from the main program. Only the comms were needed for this. She pulled the data disk out and handed her handheld out to Huey.

He grabbed the machine and raced back to the door.

Her father sat at the comms with her. She slid the disk into the slot. It immediately started searching the communications on all channels, sending the results to the monitor next to her.

Abigail displayed the main gates and the outer gate doors at her station. Her father pulled up the displays for the pier gates. Before long, two other elders joined her, each taking a portion of the compound as their duty. Then Trisha sat down beside her and pulled on a headset, her mouth drawn in a grim line. She activated comms and started searching the signals. One less that Abigail had to do. A bit of the fear within her abated as they each worked at the stations.

On the main screen above them, their soldiers stood in the courtyard. Jules, lacking the two or three inches that most of the men carried, seemed larger, his stance strong. He raised his right hand and pointed with two fingers to his right.

She frowned. No one moved, and it took her a moment to realize that Michael and Peter were gone. Vanished. She blinked. Jules had told her Zulu were covert assassins. In and out without a trace. Moved with no noise. No one ever saw them until it was too late.

And she had just witnessed how true that was.

He held up his left fist. Half the line spread out and disappeared. Taking positions.

"Trish, did he give a command?"

She shook her head. "Comms are quiet."

Her dad looked over at her. "They know what to do, Abby. He doesn't have to give a command."

She returned her attention back to the screen. Only Jules and JJ stood in the middle of the grounds, arm's width apart, in front of the gate.

A sudden blast shattered the windows above them. The complex shook from the concussion bomb. On the screen, Jules and JJ had already skirted up the scaffolds and had their pulse rifles out and firing into the distance.

Distant screams could be heard. Another concussion bomb hit the gate, but it held for the time being. Abigail zoomed the monitor in on the far right of the gate, on top of the third hill. The so-called "catapult." An extended arm sent another volley rocketing toward them.

"Jules, third hill."

No reply came from him, yet a bright flash of a pulse fire tore through the soldier operating the machine. From that distance and that much power, he must have had the rifle at full power. She reached over and pulled up the main grounds security feed. Jules was beating his hand against his leg, putting out a fire. He ripped the destroyed glove off his hand with his teeth. He cast it aside and pulled a syringe from his pocket, jabbed his leg, and then returned to firing the rifle.

A bright explosion hit the gate, sending him and JJ crashing to the ground. They rolled with the hit and spun around to stand side by side as they threw their rifles to the ground and pulled the next one around to spray at the top of the entrance.

The low voices of the elders and her father called out positions and vectors to the other squads. Trisha relayed updates on the signals that jammed their radars to Michael and Peter.

To the side, from the top of the hill outside the gates, pulse beams hit the small army of soldiers trying to force their way in. So that was where they had gone. Abigail switched her monitor to the outside feeds. Three low-tanks made their way toward the hills.

"Three low-tanks zeroing in on the hills."

Three clicks sounded across the comms. Soon, a pulse beam hit one, and a concussion bomb hit another. The third managed to gain the hill, but the feed was lost as Abigail's monitor lost the signal.

Elder Jake was talking into his headset, giving coordinates of the third tank. Abigail returned her attention to Jules and JJ. They had taken cover behind a barrier. Jules had taken another syringe and plunged it against his leg.

She glanced at her father's feed. Trisha's voice crackled through the headsets. "Signal is down. Relay is open."

The pier was clear.

Jules' voice filtered through the din. "Huey."

On her father's screen, Huey raced toward the pier. Peter stood there with his sword out, waiting. Huey suddenly ducked and slid across the ground to the gate's control panel. Above him, soldiers dropped from the top of the wall. Peter's sword flashed, never stopping.

She glanced at her feed. Jules and JJ had advanced toward the gate. JJ's rifle fizzled, and he cast it aside. Jules fired three more shots and then threw his to the side. They never glanced in the direction of the pier.

She looked again. Huey huddled at the panel, the GHOST in his hands. Peter stood with two swords. He suddenly moved, and the dark form that had leaped from the wall met Peter's sword. The man was thrown to the ground, and Peter was back over Huey.

"Got it! Message sent."

Peter grabbed Huey and pushed him toward the compound, then jumped, grabbing the edge of the wall, and vanished.

Huey raced back. He disappeared from her father's feed and then reappeared onto hers. The inner gate exploded into shards, and the building shook.

On the ground, Huey struggled to rise before collapsing. Jules and JJ retreated to Huey's position. JJ laid down cover fire, and Jules reached down and dragged Huey's body behind a large portion of the gate that had landed to the side. Three men approached through the smoke from their left.

Abigail keyed her comm. "To your left."

As one, Jules and JJ turned. Three bodies flew back from the pulse guns. Then they were running toward the gates. Jules bent and scooped up a rifle. As he bent, JJ fired over his head. When he rose, he aimed over JJ, who had bent for his own rifle.

It was a dance with them. They moved as one, each anticipating the other. When JJ moved right, Jules was going left. Then their backs pressed against each other as they raised their rifles to their shoulders and fired.

Each shot hit their mark, sending soldier after soldier back through the destroyed gates.

"Low tanks destroyed."

"Pier gate closed."

Jules ducked and rolled as a shot narrowly missed him. JJ twirled to the right, out of the pathway of a pulse beam. It hit the complex, and half the monitors went dark.

Abigail turned to Elder Jake. "Use the backups. Reroute through stations four and six."

They hurried to the stations as she turned back to hers. Trisha acknowledged a message through her headset.

She turned to Abigail. "Peter and Michael's comms were destroyed. The rest of Juliet squad are heading this way."

Abigail caught Jules' sudden jerk. He hit the ground hard. Yet he spun to his knees and fired twice before holstering his weapon. Another syringe was pulled from his pocket and plunged against his leg.

JJ was further away, fighting a group back through the gates. She keyed the comms. "Jules, Juliet squad is moving up to the gate."

One click echoed across the comms. He heard. She leaned forward. The pathway was clear. Huey could be retrieved. "Dad, we can send a group to grab Huey. They have cleared a way."

Her dad rose from the station without a word. She waited. Before long, her dad, John, and Micah reached Huey and were dragging him back into the complex. Another concussion bomb hit, and all the monitors went silent.

"Jules. JJ. If you can hear me, we are blind."

$$\Sigma$$

Jules rolled forward and rose to a knee, driving his sword into the gut of the man before him. Without a pause, he ripped it out and spun, slicing the blade across the chest of the next one.

Blood splattered across him. Another man met his blade with his own. A parry to the right, then a feint left, and Jules' blade drove deep into the chest. The blade lodged in the bone. Jules let go and ripped a pulse rifle by his feet from the ground and another off the body in front of him.

Abigail's voice filtered through the noise. " . . . blind."

He was used to being blind on the field. No comms. No backup.

He fired as he retreated through the destroyed gate. The return fire was sporadic. JJ met him with a broken sword in hand.

"Peter radioed. Juliet 2-Z escaped them."

Jules hissed between his teeth. "Let him come this way, then."

He fired at a shadow in the smoke. The dark form fell out of sight. JJ held a rifle at the ready, scanning the area in front of him.

Jules touched his comm. "Echo squad?"

"Clear."

"Sierra?"

"Clear."

"Zulu?"

"One bogey."

Jules nodded and motioned JJ behind the barrier. "We will have to wait." He keyed his comm. "All squads, stand ready."

Three clicks signaled their response.

JJ leaned against the barrier with a groan.

Jules glanced down at his leg. The burn had cauterized the wound. His side was still bleeding, but it had slowed down. And the burn on his hand was aggravating. But the serum was handling all that.

He glanced over at JJ. "I didn't think I had enough room for any more scars."

JJ laughed. "You pick today to make a joke? Ah, man, guess better late than never."

Jules smiled. "I made a joke?"

Laughter rolled across the air as JJ shook his head; then he held up a hand.

A scrape on a rock. To his right. Left side of the grounds. In one motion, Jules and JJ rose and fired. Their pulse rifles ripped through three bodies. As they collapsed, a pulse beam shot through one of them, and the weakened shot slammed into Jules' tactical vest, sending him flying back and landing hard against the ground. Around him, plumes of dirt shot upward.

Blood spurt from his mouth. He rolled and struggled to his feet. It wasn't just a pulse rifle. Another concussion bomb had been set off. Silence filled his ears, and a wetness flowed down the side of his face. JJ stood over the last body and had turned toward him as another body stepped out of the cloud of dust.

Jules whipped his rifle up and fired. Nothing. He cast it aside, pulled a knife from his belt, and ran. His booted foot hit one of their barriers, and he launched himself through the air, slamming into the soldier. The knife sank through the soft skin of the neck, severing the artery.

Jules rolled off him, grabbing the man's rifle and bringing it to bear at the gate. But no movement, save the settling dust. He waved

JJ back. No response. He glanced back. JJ was speaking, his mouth moving. But nothing.

His ears. The concussion bomb. Jules pulled another syringe out of his pocket. The serum flowed into his blood stream. His pulse filled his head, threatening to burst his skull open. He slowly backed up, keeping the gate in his view. The last of the dust veil fell, giving him a clear look into the distance.

Burning hulks of metal stood among the hills. To his right, Zulu and half of Sierra arrived. To his left, Echo and the rest of Sierra made their way down the hillside.

A touch on his shoulder brought his gaze away. He kept the gate in his peripheral. He didn't see Zeetoo fall.

JJ mouthed at him. "It's over. No one is left."

Jules shook his head. "Zeetoo?"

JJ frowned and keyed his comm. Whatever was said had JJ bringing up his weapon. They walked backward, shoulder to shoulder, keeping the gate in their view. The rest were scanning the area. Michael had his scanner held out in front of him, sweeping it side to side.

He paused and held up one finger, slicing it to the ground.

Jules swept his rifle's sight from body to body, sending a bolt into each one. Nothing. Michael twirled his finger once in the air. Zeetoo was in the immediate area.

JJ touched his shoulder and pointed with two fingers to the left. Jules nodded and sidestepped, keeping as much of the gate as he could in his view. He reached ten feet and started his approach to the gate. Then stopped.

The hairs on his neck stood. Around him, his men systematically searched the bodies and grounds. So, what was it? Jules took half a step and then stopped as the feeling intensified. Abigail's word came back to him when she was going over some the specs she had found during one of her hacks—they have a concussion bomb that will drop more than one payload.

He slowly turned, checking each spot where the concussion bombs hit. A faint sound reached him. Too faint. The serum wasn't working fast enough! He sidestepped around the corner of the building's opening. Nothing.

Jules eased back toward JJ. When his brother looked over at him, he raised one finger to the air. JJ whipped his rifle up and spoke into his comm unit. Michael scanned the roof. Then shook his head.

Nothing.

Jules lowered his rifle and walked back to JJ's side. Maybe Zeetoo had been killed and not found yet. The thought of another decommission denied to his former second-in-command was almost a comfort.

A small shadow fell across JJ's shoulder as he turned toward Zulu and Sierra as they approached. Jules shouted, turned, and spied Zeetoo's prone position on the top of the wall, and fired. His bolt missed as the man started falling from the top of the wall, firing as he fell.

Jules catalogued it as it happened. His serum-heightened senses seemed to cause everything to slow.

A bolt shot toward JJ. Jules shoved him aside, but it grazed JJ's shoulder, knocking him to the ground.

Jules fired again before JJ could recover. His pulse hit Zeetoo, but the man kept walking toward him, dragging his leg and firing bolt after bolt. Hitting the compound, grazing JJ again, and trying to pierce Jules.

His bolt destroyed Zeetoo's aim at the rest of his team who had ducked out of the way. The man started to topple, but he fired one last bolt at the same time Jules let go of another.

The blue fire lanced through Zeetoo's body. White hot heat seared through Jules' abdomen. His legs gave out from under him. He fell to his knees, keeping his rifle on Zeetoo. But the man didn't move. Jules risked a glance at JJ. He was struggling to his feet, his hand trying to staunch the blood that poured from his shoulder.

Around him, his team rushed toward him. He tried to push up, but his body wouldn't respond. Zeetoo's eyes stared vacantly at the sky. Jules looked around. The man had made it ten feet from them and with five bolts having pierced his body.

Did they find another candidate for Serum Seventy-four? That was the only way he could have withstood so much.

Jules fell to his side, his strength leaving him. Something was wrong. His legs refused to move. White heat flooded through his body. JJ was bending over him, shouting, but it seemed so far away. Hands pulled at him, tugging him from the ground.

Abigail?

He needed to see her. Needed to make sure she was safe.

Above him, a white light floated into view.

Abigail raced through the corridors behind JJ. Jules was held in his arms, and blood dripped everywhere. They burst into the medlab. Her grandmother had the surgical table prepped, and medstudies stood nearby, ready to save her husband.

She stopped at the window. JJ pushed through the doors and deposited Jules on the table. Abigail activated the comm on the panel and listened.

"Julius?" Mimi leaned over him. Taniff and Medstudy Pitts cut away his clothes, accessing the damaging. "Jules. Can you hear me?"

Jules raised a hand, touched his ear, and shook his head. He then touched his lips, his eyes glassy and unfocused.

"Pitts, give me the serum."

The young man opened the cart's drawer, then the next and the next. Taniff pulled a battered syringe from Jules' pants. He held it in his hands and looked at Jules. "Williams, how much did you take?"

Mimi glanced at the syringe and then at the medstudy. Pitts shook his head.

She leaned over him. "You took the serum. How much?"

Jules didn't answer. His eyes closed as medstudies hooked the monitors to him. His heart slowed.

"Jules!" Mimi looked up at Abigail. "Find out how much he took!"

Abigail's heart slammed in her chest. Those times she saw him plunge a syringe in his leg. She didn't think much about it at the time, knowing that they used adrenaline at times when they fought. Wasn't that what he had said that time in the lounge when they left Mars?

She closed her eyes and thought back. She saw three. Did he take more? "How much did you have, Mimi?" Her voice cracked.

Mimi held up five fingers.

"I saw him with three syringes, Mimi." She flattened her hands against the window as her dad entered the room. He stood behind her, holding her up.

Mimi leaned over Jules. "Focus, Julius. Did you take three or four?"

Jules held four fingers in the air. He clenched his fist and rubbed it in a circle over his chest. *Sorry.* Tears flowed down Abigail's face. With that much in his system . . .

They pulled a sheet up to his waist as Mimi slid a line into his arm. The only thing they could do was make him comfortable.

"Abby?" His voice was hoarse, and the syllables barely understood.

Mimi waved her in. She needed no urging. Abigail pushed open the doors. Her father followed her in.

Jules' soft gaze followed her as she approached. She stepped around the bed and leaned over his left side. His beautiful green eyes with the white filled with tears.

He signed *sorry* again. Followed with his little finger rising, then his index, finally his thumb. *I love you.*

Tears fell from his eyes. She leaned down and kissed his lips. "I know. I love you, too, Julius. Everything will be okay. No fear, remember."

His hands lifted, barely rising above his chest. Then his fingertips touched and slowly pulled away, signing in the hybrid speech that he and CeeCee had created. *Unafraid.* She smiled.

His body arched, and the monitors beeped erratically. Abigail gripped his hand tighter. "Are you with me, Jules?"

He suddenly opened his eyes. A bright light lit behind the green, and a small smile drifted across his mouth. He pulled his hand away, touched his ear in wonderment, then reached out and pressed her abdomen. His hand settled over her navel, and a softness filled his face. Then that part of him faded. The light in his eyes dimmed, and his hand fell away from her.

Her father's arms caught her as a wail rent the air.

## Chapter Twenty

# SETH WILLIAMS

"Hey, look, Mom!"

Abigail turned from the gates. Her son bounced around on the scaffolds by the nearly completed section of the wall. She grabbed the back of her son's coat and yanked him down from the platform by the entrance.

"What have I told you about showing off? You can't let people see what you can do."

Seth sighed and scuffed the frozen ground with his boot before scampering up the ladder that stood by the newly built wall. He perched on the top and looked down at her. The white irises shone with merriment. "I just wanted to see how fast I could get up there."

Abigail shook her head. "You have the obstacle course Uncle JJ made you. Use that. But stop doing this outside where they can see you."

"Yes, ma'am." He shaded his eyes and then hopped up to stand on the top of the ladder.

Maybe she should have been like the other mothers who would almost faint at the sight of their child precariously perched on a rickety ladder. Yet Seth wasn't a normal child. And ever since he had learned to walk, nothing had kept him still.

"Do you see something, Seth?" Her father approached them. The set of elders followed.

Abigail glanced at her watch. It was approaching the time for the scheduled negotiations with GFT. Five long years—and now their freedom was about to be granted.

"Yes, sir. I see the envoy. Uncle JJ's transport is leading them. I count four . . . no, five GFT sub-transports. Why do they have different flags, Grandda?" He continued his surveying of the distance horizon. Abigail peered through the gates. She saw only a plume of dust rising in the distance.

"Representatives from the different countries. We aren't the only compound." Her father reached up and snapped his fingers. Without thought, her son leaped from the top and into his arms.

As he set Seth back on the ground, a deep rumble reached them. "You two head back inside. Keep Seth hidden." He looked at her son. "Stay inside with Mimi, okay? Remember what we talked about?"

"Yes, sir. They cannot know that I exist, or we risk our freedom." He smiled and took Abigail's hand. "I know my duty."

His grandfather reached out and ruffled his hair, causing her son to protest. "That's my boy."

Abigail hugged her father as the first envoy vehicle topped the ridge in the distance. "Do you think we will succeed this time?"

"Yes." He placed a kiss on her forehead. "The winds have been changing for years now. And everything we have fought for—we are now achieving, such as the right to live like everyone else." He gave her a small push. "Take him in."

She tugged at her son, and they left the gate. The winds had picked up, swirling the dusty snow around them. Summer was fast approaching. Days of no more darkness. She smiled inwardly at the hidden meaning of that thought.

Her steps slowed as they approached the domed buildings that gleamed in the Alaskan light. Peppered around a central, larger dome were the homes of countless Christians. Underneath ran the network of tunnels that provided the freedom of movement. The central tunnel led to their docking port deep below the water's surface. She smiled at the thought. Some habits were hard to break; they continued to keep their base underground.

As she pulled open the door to the central dome, Seth sniffed once before his face beamed. "Mimi's spice cakes!"

He let go and bolted down the corridor toward the galley. With a shake of her head, she followed her son. His dark hair bounced around his head as he bounded down the hallway. Always full of energy. Always full of laughter. Jules would have been proud of him. He would have loved him.

Her heart gave a small lurch. No. He had been proud of his son, even though he hadn't been born yet. That last touch by him on her abdomen, a soft light in his eyes before they faded. He knew what he had sacrificed. Seth was his redemption . . . and his legacy.

And her son was back by her side with a plate full of small spice cakes and two bottles of water. "Mimi said to go to the lounge."

Abigail smiled. Her grandmother always knew when Seth needed to calm down, and the lounge with its scenic view was the only thing that did it. She took the bottles from his hand before they caused the plate of cakes to tip. "Then come on."

She led Seth to the lounge on the far side of the central dome and closed the door behind them. Ahead of them, a soft couch sat before the viewport of one of the derelict ships that had been converted. It reminded her a lot of the lounge on the *Nightingale*. Of those times she stood with Jules.

The view of the life under the water was always surprising. Today, it was otters. Yesterday, a pod of orcas had swam nearby. The day before, there were seals.

Seth pressed his forehead against the fused panes, smiling at the otters as they zipped through the water.

"Come sit." She patted the cushions beside her.

He turned from the viewport, placed the plate of cakes on the table, and crawled upon her lap instead. "Tell me about Dad."

She smiled. It was always the same. Sit at the viewport. Tell him the story. And she never left anything out. He had learned about what his father was. What they made him to be. What he did. And what he had eventually become.

She brushed his hair off his forehead. "Your dad was taken at an early age and was subjected to genetic manipulation. He was designed to kill, yet God had another design for him . . . "

He nibbled at his cake while his eyes were latched onto her in rapt attention. Tears would form when he heard about what they did to his father. More tears would form when he heard about the atrocities his father committed. Even more tears would form when he learned about what his father did to escape that life. And then they would fall when she would tell him of the sacrifice his father made to keep them all safe. The sacrifice he made to keep them alive.

"He knew you were on the way. The last thing he did was touch my abdomen and smile. He would have been so proud of you, Seth."

Seth brushed at his eyes and leaned against her shoulder. "Mom, I know what Dad was made to be."

"What do you mean?" She glanced down at him. This was different. So much of Jules had passed on to Seth. It wasn't just the eyes. It was also the abilities. He saw further. Heard more. Smelled more. He healed faster. Grew faster. Learned faster. So, she wasn't surprised to know that he would have analyzed the stories from every angle.

The green borders around the white irises seemed brighter as he looked up at her. His tears didn't fall today. Instead, a new look shone on his face. A softness.

"Dad may have killed for them. But he was more when he woke up." Seth smiled. A great love filled his eyes. "God made my dad a hero."

Abigail kissed Seth's forehead. "Yes. Yes, He did. God made him a legend."

COMING SOON . . .

# WHAT

# LEGENDS

# BECOME

# Chapter One
## SΞTH

Seth stared at the dark gravestone. Age had weathered the stone, and ice had collected in the grooves of the words. No date. Never a date. A custom that began so long ago.

Yet, each year, they kept these that rested on the hill cleaned and repaired. He stooped down and brushed away the dusting of snow that had collected on the top of his father's grave.

*Julius Williams*

*Husband, Son, Brother, and Father*

*Child of God*

It was one thing to have always heard his father's story growing up. Even becoming his true namesake. Then there were the times he wished he knew the man who fought for his freedom and gave his life for his family.

The smell of fresh dirt invaded his nose, and Seth turned to the headstone next to his father's. Barely three days old. It gleamed in the soft Alaskan sunlight. Tears pricked his eyelids as he read the inscription.

*Abigail Maureen Williams Marktov*

*Wife, Daughter, Sister, and Mother*

*Child of God*

She fought a brave fight, but even with their advanced medicines not all illnesses could be conquered. So many times, throughout her illness and with his stepfather, Huey, at her side, Seth had wished he could have used his own advanced healing to save her.

When he had mentioned it to his mother, she had smiled, patted his hand, and said that when a person's time came, it came. And it was her time to go.

A shadow fell across the stones. Seth didn't look up. Today was Sunday. And that meant the shadow belonged to Michael, who came every week to visit his brother's grave.

Seth let his mind fall back onto that word: *brother*. His father had no biological brother yet had claimed Uncle JJ as his. Michael's brother, who was also not his biological sibling, was Peter, former Zulu assassin. Growing up he had heard all the tales. And the last of the Global Federated Territories assassins to arrive to the Coalition was the day they gained their freedom and land.

The day before his sixth birthday.

Seth rose to his feet and backed up from the headstones. There were no bodies here. Just stones marking the area where ashes were buried. Another custom that started when his father died. No one could take a chance that GFT would obtain his body and blood. Even now, the curse of GFT limited the movements of the assassin descendants.

"Thinking again?" Michael's soft voice drifted across the cold air.

Seth shrugged. "Always." He turned and faced the aged former assassin. Heavy lines pulled at the man's face. His gray hair sported his trademark style: shaved head with tight braids on top. Yet his blue eyes still held a lot of energy and youth and a peacefulness that Seth wasn't feeling. He returned his gaze back to the headstones.

"She found it hard to live without him until you were born."

Seth whipped around. "What?"

"Your mother." Michael walked to the far end where his brother was buried and sank, cross-legged, onto the ground. "She and Julius were in love. Julius would do anything for your mother and the weeks after arriving here, he did just that. The day he died . . . he knew he wouldn't survive. It was hard on your mother. Then you came into this world. Looking exactly like your father. And hope was rekindled in Abigail."

Rarely did Michael talk. In all of Seth's forty-seven years, he had heard Michael speak this long only a handful of times. Peter had once told him that Michael spoke only when there was something to say.

"You know a lot about love. Especially for a man who never married."

"Granted." Michael gripped his knees and rubbed at them. "But love was never in the future for Peter or me. We had too many demons."

"As a Child of God, shouldn't those demons have already been slayed?"

"For some." Michael smiled softly. "We focused what love we could give onto our families here. You are included in that."

Seth nodded and sank down beside the man. In front of them stood Peter's gravestone, its dark gray surface a shadow under the trees.

*Peter Christian*

*Brother and Child of God*

Christian. He and Michael had no surname. So, they took on the name of who they were, how they saw themselves. "Why wouldn't you let Mom find out when you and Peter were born? I've always wondered why you two refused to know more about your former lives."

The wind blew and stirred the leaves and grass around them. Overhead a cloud passed in front of the sun, sending shadows dancing around them. A small shudder ran through Seth's body.

Michael sighed. "Our lives began the day we accepted Christ. What GFT did to us in Zulu was worse than what happened to Juliet. I do not care to remember those times. And I do not care to know who I was before then. Christ made me new. And I do not look behind me to the past." He looked over at Seth. "But that is my road to follow."

Seth nodded. "It still feels surreal."

"It will for a time." He closed his eyes and fell silent.

Seth stood, gently squeezed the older man's shoulder, and left him to his prayer. The trek back to the compound was a cold one. The weather was turning again. Their days should have been warming up, but the cold fronts kept their hold on their little home at the top of the world.

The sounds of the compound reached him long before he could see it. The idle chatter of workers in the fields, at the walls, around the domes and buildings. The drone of hovercrafts and children laughing. He caught the faint laughter of his daughter, Sierra. No mistaking that lilting chuckle. He always compared her to a delicate windchime in the rain.

He ran their schedule through his mind. Today was her time with the small children, teaching them Bible lessons, or—knowing Sierra—incorporating the history into some fun activity.

She would be with the school today, teaching the children herbology. And probably a bit of geology, too. Unlike her twin brother, Stephen, she easily settled into a profession and study. His mother had said her "green thumb" had come from her grandfather.

He smiled and hurried across the well-worn pathway leading to the side medical building. Today would have been his shift in Medlab, but he had received a five-day bereavement. Still, whether he was working or not, he still needed to run scans.

Being the child of the only GFT assassin that Serum Seventy-four succeeded on meant monthly scans and bloodwork. The genetic manipulation that was done to his father had passed along to him and to his children. And while the rest of the assassins had the serum in their system for many years, its effect never took . . . until they had children of their own.

Seth pulled open the door. The pressurized air stirred his hair. The smells of medicines, electronics, and sterilized air surrounded him as his mind ran through the names of the children.

Tamara, his wife, daughter of JJ. Donald, son of Mandy and Dan. Denise, daughter of Devon. Samson and Jade, son and daughter of James. The last to be born was Peony, daughter of Jackson.

Although the effects of the serum were not as strong, a bit passed along to their children. Through his genetic research, he found the recessive genes that had been mutated by the serum. Given enough years, the gene would either weaken or be eradicated. But not so for his children and Donald's children.

For Donald, the son of two former assassins, he gained the benefit of faster healing and advanced learning. His children inherited the same, yet at a more diminished scale.

Tamara inherited from her father much of the same. Yet when they married, he never thought that the abilities he inherited from his father would bond with the genes she inherited and create a new set of genetic mutations.

While his eyes remained white with green borders, their children's eyes were a deep green with flecks of white surrounding their pupils. Their comprehension rivaled his, as did their strength, speed, and healing. While Sierra stayed levelheaded, Stephen remained reckless and full of rage.

Seth crossed the empty lab room and entered his work area. The door clicked softly behind him.

"Lights, one eighth."

Dim illumination lit the room. Being at his mother's grave gave him extra incentive to solve the genetic equation. The Coalition would never remain safe if GFT knew about them. There had to be a code somewhere within that would stop the passing along of the serum's effects.

He activated his computer and entered the parameters for his search. The computer screen scrolled through line after line of code. He ran results of scans and bloodwork. Seth pushed away from the counter and strolled to the full-body medscanner. As he stood on the platform, his door opened.

Tamara, her chestnut-toned skin shining under the harsh lights, smiled as she walked toward him, her silvery poncho swaying around her hips. Her curls had started sporting more gray hairs in them lately, giving her an ethereal look. Almost exotic. His gut clenched at the sight of her.

The scanner beeped. Seth stepped off and swept her into his arms, claiming her mouth in a kiss before she could greet him. He pulled away, twisting a curl around his finger.

She smiled up at him. "How was your trip to the Hill?"

"Michael showed up." He held her hand as he walked to the other side to draw his bloodwork.

"He misses Peter." She sat on the stool and pulled a rolling tray between them.

In silence they worked together to draw his blood and insert it into the spectrum analysis. Then to run his medscan through all the set parameters.

She read the preliminary results. "Nothing has changed."

Seth shook his head. "I keep hoping that I will find some kind of cure to this."

Tamara reached out and gripped his hand. Her deep amber eyes softened with compassion. "Seth, this isn't a disease to cure. Our genes are a part of us. Don't become like GFT and manipulate us or them."

He shook his head as he ran a thumb over her knuckles. "I don't plan to do that. But if I can dampen the effects or at least stop the genes from being inherited, then I will rest easy knowing that we are safe. As it is, we are prisoners in our own country."

She sighed but kept quiet. For the last seven years, when the urge to do this hit him, she had tried to stop him. Then tried to distract him. Finally, she decided to work alongside him. Although he knew, deep down, she was still hoping he would give up this fruitless effort. Only he didn't find it fruitless.

He computer beeped. The results on the first search were finalized. He pulled up the readout and sagged in his seat. Nothing. It would take another six hours for the second set to finish.

"Come on." Tamara tugged at his arm. "You aren't supposed to be working today. And even if you were, you are scheduled for security and ops, not Medlab."

Seth allowed her to lead him away from his workstation. "I can do both, you know."

"I know." She pushed open the door and shot a quick glance over her shoulder at him. "But you really shouldn't. Why couldn't you just settle for one job? One career? Instead, you studied medicine, botany, military ops, and literature."

"Why settle for only one when I could do it all?" He almost collided into her when she stopped suddenly and whirled around to face him.

"Really? So are you not satisfied with me? One wife? One lover?"

Seth laughed and captured her face in his hands. "Can't banter with me, wife. You know the answer to that."

She rolled her eyes at him before releasing a soft laugh. "Come on, my stubborn husband. I came to get you because Huey left something for you at our quarters."

"What?"

"He said it was something your mom and he worked on for years. He said your mom wanted you to have it when she passed. An answer to many of your questions."

With his curiosity piqued, Seth found himself walking faster toward the far side of the compound where their quarters were. If Huey and his mom worked on it, then it was important. And he had a good suspicion it dealt with his father.

"By the way, our son has been ignoring my calls for the last two days."

Seth sighed. He shook his head. "He's twenty-five, Tam. There's not much we can do at this moment. We can only pray he will come to his senses."

She huffed. "And when will that be? Dad had called him a moody monkey, and I'm beginning to believe it. He's chomping at the bit about something."

"Chomping at the bit?" Seth smiled and gently poked his wife in the ribs. "Have you been reading some of those classics lately?"

Tamara started laughing as they exited the main building and veered toward the seaside area. "The ancient books. Something that was called 'westerns.' Really strange reading something so old."

He slid his arm around her waist as she chatted about the titles and authors that were discovered in an abandoned building buried miles away. The excavation team had delivered loads and loads of books and tomes to the school and library. So far he had made it through a quarter of the books. Some were as boring as sterile dirt. Others invoked feelings and desires that left him wanting there to be more to devour.

Tamara's soft voice floated along the air, drowning out his negative emotions, burying his fears and indecisions. Only she and her voice existed as they walked home.

Stephen stood at the window. The fused glass heated the sun's rays as it shone through and hit his bare chest. He curled his toes into the plush carpet and crossed his arms.

His visits with Danica were getting old. She had begun to demand more of his time and more of his attention. Time to move on. But not just yet. She still fulfilled a need.

Guilt at his actions tried to rear its head, but he shoved it down. He was tired of feeling guilty. Of feeling shame. Of being the good man, the rule-abiding man. That man was boring. That man didn't live.

Slender arms snaked around his waist and up his chest. Danica purred into his ear. "What are you thinking? Why not come back to bed?"

He turned in her arms and leaned back against the window. His hands rested on her hips, keeping her close, yet still away from him. Her long, black hair hung in soft waves to her waist. Dark eyes regarded him. "Have you ever ventured beyond our borders? That was what I was thinking."

She frowned and leaned back with her hands clasped around him. "Beyond our borders? Once. On a supply run. We went into the Canadian Province. To Vancouver. Why?"

"What was it like?"

She shrugged. "Nothing special really. Even though Vancouver was a decent sized city, it never recouped from the last war." She pulled away from him and settled down on the chaise lounge in her living room. Her plush robe fell open as she pulled her feet upon it. "Are you thinking of signing up for a shipment run?"

"No." He sat on the edge of the chaise and leaned over her. "I'm thinking of traveling."

Danica frowned up at him. "Why? You know we aren't to leave our borders. Especially you and your kind."

"My kind?" Stephen snarled and straightened up.

She shook her head and gripped his arm. "I don't mean it that way. I just mean that you and the others are supposed to stay within our borders, to keep you safe."

Stephen regarded the older woman. She worked as his father's understudy in the medlab. At fifteen years his senior, he had found her enticing and seductive. And from the first time they were together, he discovered he could learn more about what his father was doing in Medlab. Even though he could hack just about any system out there, his father had one advantage. He used the

GHOST to protect his research. Effectively preventing any hacking into the system.

And Stephen had not been able to get his hands on his grandmother's old program. He was never a part of the security detail or privy to the elders' meetings. In fact, he was shuttered from just about any meeting unless it was the general meetings.

Danica ran a finger over his brow. "Why are you so upset?"

He shook his head. "I feel . . . stifled."

"How so? You are the top hunter and guide. You range across all of Alaska. You teach the highest self-defense class. And the school calls you in to help with the higher mathematics. You are valued here, Stephen. You can do just about anything you want. Even join your father's Medlab study."

"No. Not that. He would allow me to train in Medlab, but not be a part of his research." Stephen twisted around so that he could stretch out beside her on the chaise. "Besides, I don't want to do those things anymore."

"What do you want?"

He smiled and began to show her what he wanted. And a part of his mind was screaming at him for doing this. For using her. Because when she fell asleep, like she normally would do, he would swipe her card to Medlab. And he would have his father's research, finally. And he would discover why he was subjected to medscans and bloodwork every three months. And then he would find a way to leave this hated place. Once and for all.

For more information about
# Daphne Self
and
## *When Legends Rise*
please visit:


www.authordaphneself.blogspot.com


Ambassador International's mission is to magnify the Lord Jesus Christ
and promote His Gospel through the written word.

We believe through the publication of Christian literature, Jesus Christ and
His Word will be exalted, believers will be strengthened in their walk with
Him, and the lost will be directed to Jesus Christ as the only way of salvation.

For more information about
AMBASSADOR INTERNATIONAL
please visit:


www.ambassador-international.com


*Thank you for reading this book. Please consider leaving us a
review on your social media, favorite retailer's website,
Goodreads or Bookbub, or our website.*

# More from Ambassador International

After his rescue from guerillas in Venezuela, Gideon finds himself with super-abilities, result from genetic engineering during his capture. When he returns home, he finds his beloved city in shambles and torn apart by crime. The police are understaffed and most do not care about the poor side, The Brooks. Gideon becomes a vigilante to protect his city and uses his newfound abilities. But he learns that being a vigilante comes with a price.

Doyle is used to being on his own ever since the war devastated the land. Until he has to stop at a city for repairs and provisions. One heroic act and now he's the leader of a small band of Christians determined to spread the Gospel to the rumored neighboring cities. It's a task he's qualified for, but he didn't plan on the effect this little group would have on him as they battle their way through cannibals, militant atheists, and a mysterious super soldier.

Contestants Jeda, Spoena, and Artil are under the careful watch of the sinister Hod-ya as the duels draw ever so near. Will Jeda rise to the competition or fall short? As Bonu and Scrung set out to uncover the Swords of Vedic, they are met with numerous trials and even rescue missions. With temptations, unexpected treasures, dangerous treks, and a deadly competition in the mix, the stakes are higher than ever before. Will the trumpets of doom sound?